We presented arms as the crowd cheered. The band played the 'Gott Erhalte', and the red-white-red flag of Imperial Austria was run up the flagpole to flap languidly in the tepid breeze. The natives of Bunceville cheered lustily in that curious high-pitched ululating way of theirs – though from what I could hear of it they still seemed to think that we were Australians. Fireworks began to crackle around the field amid the cheering, the Geschutzmeister having virtually emptied the pyrotechnics locker to put on a suitable display. Signal rockets hissed into the sky as the townspeople fired off their dane-guns with bright flashes and clouds of white smoke. Flocks of parrots ascended screaming from the trees around the field as the vultures flapped heavily into the air from the hut roofs, rudely disturbed from their afternoon siesta and no doubt wondering what all the fuss was about. Mere birds, how could they know that Austria-Hungary's great colonial adventure had just begun?

John Biggins was born in what is now South London in 1949, but grew up in the Welsh border country. He was educated at University College, Swansea, and later spent four years in Poland as a research student and lecturer. He has also worked at the Ministry of Agriculture and since leaving there has earned his living as a journalist and technical author. He is married with two children and lives on the Essex coast near Colchester. He is the author of *A Sailor of Austria*, *The Emperor's Coloured Coat* and *The Two-Headed Eagle*.

*Also by John Biggins
and available in Mandarin*

A Sailor of Austria
The Emperor's Coloured Coat
The Two-Headed Eagle

Tomorrow the World

A novel by

JOHN BIGGINS

*D'ou venons-nous? Que sommes nous?
Ou allons-nous?*

Mandarin

A Mandarin Paperback
TOMORROW THE WORLD

First published in Great Britain 1994
by William Heinemann Ltd
This edition published 1995
by Mandarin Paperbacks
an imprint of Reed Consumer Books Ltd
Michelin House, 81 Fulham Road, London SW3 6RB
and Auckland, Melbourne, Singapore and Toronto

Copyright © John Biggins 1994
The author has asserted his moral rights

A CIP catalogue record for this title
is available from the British Library
ISBN 0 7493 1810 4

Printed and bound in Great Britain
by Cox & Wyman Ltd, Reading, Berks

This book is sold subject to the condition
that it shall not, by way of trade or otherwise,
be lent, resold, hired out, or otherwise circulated
without the publisher's prior consent in any form
of binding or cover other than that in which
it is published and without a similar condition
including this condition being imposed
on the subsequent purchaser.

ABBREVIATIONS

The Austro-Hungarian Empire set up by the Compromise of 1867 was a union of two near-independent states in the person of their monarch, Emperor of Austria and King of Hungary. Thus, for the fifty-one years of its existence, almost every institution and many of the personnel of this composite state had their titles prefixed with initials indicating their status.

Shared Austro-Hungarian institutions were Imperial and Royal: 'kaiserlich und königlich' or 'k.u.k.' for short. Those belonging to the Austrian part of the Monarchy (that is to say, everything that was not the Kingdom of Hungary) were designated Imperial-Royal – 'kaiserlich-königlich' or simply 'k.k.' – in respect of the monarch's status as Emperor of Austria and King of Bohemia; while purely Hungarian institutions were Royal Hungarian: 'königlich ungarisch' ('k.u.') or 'kiraly magyar' ('k.m.').

The Austro-Hungarian Navy followed contemporary Continental practice in quoting sea distances in European nautical miles (6080 feet), land distances in kilometres, battle ranges etc. in metres and gun calibres in centimetres. However, it followed pre–1914 British practice in using the twelve-hour system for times. Its vessels were designated 'Seiner Majestäts Schiff' or 'S.M.S.'.

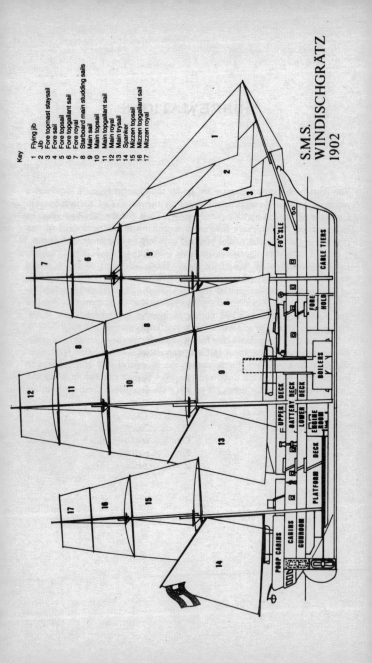

PLACE NAMES

In view of the fact that border changes resulting from the two world wars have altered many of the place-names used in this story beyond recognition, a glossary is attached giving the names and their modern equivalents.

The list merely attempts to reflect Austrian official usage at the turn of the century – though this itself was by no means consistent – and implies no recognition of any territorial claim past or present.

Abbazia	Opatija, Croatia
Cattaro	Kotor, Yugoslavia
Cherso Is.	Cres. Is., Croatia
Fiume	Rijeka, Croatia
Kremsier	Kroměříž, Czechoslovakia
Lussin Is.	Lošinj Is., Croatia
Pago Is.	Pag Is., Croatia
Pola	Pula, Croatia
Quarnerolo	Kvarner, Croatia
Sansego Is.	Susak Is., Croatia
Trautenau	Trutnov, Czechoslovakia
Troppau	Opava, Czechoslovakia
Veglia Is.	Krk Is., Croatia
Zara	Zadar, Croatia

This book is dedicated to
Charles Midgley
1947–1993
in the hope that he would have enjoyed it

1

FULL CIRCLE

> Recorded at
> SS of the Perpetual Veneration
> Plas Gaerllwydd
> Llangwynydd
> West Glamorgan
>
> February 1987

They say – whoever 'they' are – that a drowning man's entire life passes before his eyes. But as a lifelong sceptic, and also as one who has himself come near to drowning on several occasions during a long seafaring career, I must say that I find myself raising a number of queries about this confident assertion. Quite apart from the obvious one: how do they know (did they ask people who had nearly drowned and then been fished out and resuscitated?) there is also the question of whether this is a privilege granted only to people dying from an excess of water in the lungs. Do people who are in the process of being run over by a lorry experience the same phenomenon, or those who are slowly and unwittingly being asphyxiated by a leaking car exhaust? Surely, if time is an illusion, then where reviews of one's entire life are concerned it makes no difference whether one is dying a leisurely gurgling death by drowning or being summarily snuffed out by the high-speed train at Taplow Station after venturing too near the edge of the platform.

Many years ago now, about 1908, when I was a young lieutenant in the Imperial and Royal Austro-Hungarian Navy, my ship was on a visit to Toulon and I went for a day's outing to Marseilles with a lady acquaintance. Not having much else to do, since it was a public holiday, we went for a stroll and chanced upon a small museum of the police force, packed with relics of notable crimes solved by the local Gendarmarie over the years. Among the exhibits, I remember, were two mounted skeletons of convicted mass-poisoners. Each had the fifth neck vertebra painted red to show how neatly the guillotine blade had sliced through it, 'thus causing' (the display card read) 'no suffering or distress whatever to the condemned person'. Even then I found myself moved to ask: how were they so confident of that? But suppose that the entire life-passing-before-the-eyes business applied to them as well, when did it start and when did it finish? When the catch clicked to release the blade, or as it struck, or as the head tumbled into the basket? And if they did have their entire lives pass before them in that instant, was it the whole thing: every last cup of coffee and every last darned sock over forty-odd years? Or was it only selected highlights? If it was the former, how did they distinguish it from the real thing? And if it was the latter, on what basis were the significant bits selected? And did they view it as spectators or in the starring role?

No, no: the whole thing is too shot through with difficulties and unresolvable questions for people to pronounce upon it with any confidence. All I can add to the debate is to say that on the occasion when I came nearest to drowning, aboard a sinking U-boat off Corfu in 1916, I was perfectly conscious almost until the end and really felt nothing but a curious inner calm and a strong desire for it all to be over with as soon as possible. My last thought before I passed out, I remember, was that I had not settled my wardroom bill for September and that I hoped my servant back at Cattaro would find the envelope and take it to the purser's office for me.

But even if I doubt this business about drowning people being treated to a replay of their entire lives, I have to say that now my own life is drawing to a close – and about time too I might add, now that I am into my hundred and first year – I have noticed lately that long-forgotten events have been bobbing to the surface among the flotsam of the present, as if my past life was indeed passing before my eyes as a series of disconnected episodes, like pieces of film salvaged from a cutting-room wastebin. I suppose that this is not to be wondered at really: just before the Sisters moved me down here to Wales last summer my old photograph album from the First World War was retrieved from a West London junk shop and restored to me; an event which might well be expected to turn even the most hard-boiled materialist towards reverie. That started me talking with young Kevin Scully, the handyman here, about my experiences as a submarine captain, and that in its turn led me to commit other memoirs to magnetic tape, once he and Sister Elizabeth had persuaded me that it was worth recording. Then I was laid low with bronchial pneumonia over Christmas – but perversely refused to die of it. So now that the harsh weather of January has given way to a February of equally unusual mildness, I find myself once more with time on my hands, allowed now to get up and dress and even to sit out in a sheltered corner of the garden, provided that they wrap me up well beforehand and keep me under supervision.

I was out there this afternoon and really it was quite delightful: the usual westerly half-gale subsided into a calm, the sun shining and the waves rolling gently on to the sands of Pengadog Bay. With the limestone headland in the far distance at the other end of the bay, I might almost have imagined myself to be at Abbazia in late winter – minus the palm trees, of course.

No, most definitely not with palm trees: the Antarctic beeches of Tierra del Fuego would have difficulty surviving the wind out here on the far end of the peninsula, with nothing beyond for three thousand miles until one reaches the shores of Massachusetts; nothing but a heaving expanse of slate-grey waves and roaring westerlies. The trees about the Plas are no more than bushes and grow along the ground to escape the wind. All things considered the Sisters would have been hard put to it to find in the whole British Isles a spot less suited to be the last earthly abode of fifty or so aged Polish refugees of the male sex, attended by eight or nine almost equally decrepit Polish nuns.

By the looks of it Plas Gaerllwydd was built about the turn of the century by one of the Swansea copper barons, who chose this windswept headland partly (I suppose) out of late-Victorian romanticism and partly from a more practical desire to be upwind of the poisonous fumes from his own smelting works: also perhaps with an eye to defence against his own employees if things got nasty, since the house is at the end of a two-kilometre sunken lane and Llangwynydd post office would have had ample time to telephone for the mounted constabulary. Such considerations aside though, the place was clearly an ill-judged venture. A low, two-storey building in Jacobethan style – all mullioned windows and oak panelling now painted a dingy umber colour – the house is surrounded by terraces cut into the hillside above the cliffs, long since overgrown by shrubbery run wild and connected by slippery flights of rocking flagstone steps which produce such a regular crop of broken hips each winter that Swansea Hospital now keeps two beds and a Polish-speaking nurse on standby from October to April. And not only broken hips: Mr Stankiewicz went for a walk the November before last, I believe, and was picked up six weeks later on Ilfracombe beach, to be identified by his false teeth. The roof leaks, the gutters are collapsing and while I was laid up in December a gale brought two chimneys crashing through the roof, which has now been patched up with plywood and polythene sheeting.

Young Kevin does his best with the place, but the Sisters of the Perpetual Veneration are hard up, and anyway it would need a regiment of pioneers permanently based here to keep the place in order. They should really have sold it and used the money to extend the Home in Ealing. But then, who would have bought it? It was a deathbed bequest from a local Polish farmer who purchased it with a partner in 1946, then (it is said locally) killed the partner in a drunken quarrel and disposed of the body so neatly that in the end the police had to accept his explanation that the man had gone back to Poland and been liquidated by the communists. The people hereabouts regard the Plas as being haunted, Kevin tells me, and, although most of the land was sold off over the years to allow the proprietor to maintain his daily intake of vodka, no one would come near the house. I suppose when we are all dead, in about twenty years' time, the Sisters will move out and the place will finally fall into ruin or suffer a convenient fire.

Myself, having been a seafarer, I do not mind the Plas Gaerllwydd very much. But for my fellow-inmates it is a bleak place to spend their last years: a place of exile for people who are exiles already, uprooted from their own land-locked country and dumped here at the very outer edge of nowhere, left to quarrel among themselves and to dream their dreams of a world dead now for half a century. Exile to the moon could scarcely have been crueller, since one can at least see the moon from Warsaw. For them, brought up among the cabbage fields and pine forests of the Polish plains, a thousand kilometres from saltwater, it must be a very unsettling place indeed. But for me the howl of the ocean wind and the crash of the gale-driven waves on the rocks below are not at all disquieting. True, I am a Czech by birth, brought up in northern Moravia at the very centre of Central Europe. But I chose a searfaring career at a very early age, and, even if it is now many years since I felt a ship's deck roll beneath my feet, there is nothing particularly alarming for me in the faint but still perceptible shudder when a particularly large wave hits the headland below, or in the salt spray being lashed against the window panes by the winter gales.

Yesterday afternoon though, the weather was fine and calm. Dr Watkins had examined me that morning and found me to be in reasonable shape, so Sister Felicja, the large and ugly Prussian-Polish nun who acts as adjutant here, gave leave to Kevin and Sister Elisabeth to take me out for a couple of hours' drive to give me a change of scene: very welcome indeed as it was the first time I had been outside the confines of the Home since last autumn. It was not very far: only to the other end of Pengadog Bay, but it was most refreshing to be out for a while away from the miasma of incontinence and pickled-cucumber soup that hangs over the Plas like the clouds over Table Mountain. So we set off in Kevin's battered, rust-pocked Ford Cortina with a vacuum flask of lemon tea and a couple of rugs to put over my knees. Sister Felicja was even in sufficiently jolly mood to wave us goodbye from the kitchen door as we left, perhaps hoping that they would bring me back wrapped in one of the same rugs, much as the Spartans came home on their shield rather than with it.

I suppose that for someone who has already passed the century I am not really in too bad shape at all: continent, still mentally alert and capable of getting up flights of stairs without assistance. Cataract and stiffness of the joints trouble me a little and I get breathless, but apart from that I am not in bad condition. They helped me out of the car when we arrived at the bottom of the muddy lane beside the little church, but after that they merely stood near by to assist me if needed: none of this officious fussing around supporting me under the armpits and steering me by the elbow as if I would wander down the beach and into the sea unless guided around by my attendants.

They are an ill-assorted pair, this uneducated, uncultured Welsh youth and the dowdy little Austro-Polish nun in her mid-sixties with her wire-framed pebble glasses and her mouthful of stainless-steel teeth. Yet both are wonderful companions, instinctively kind and with none of this tiresome nonsense about speaking loud-ly and slow-ly to an old man whose wits are undimmed and whose hearing is still quite sharp. I suppose it was as much an outing for them as for me. Kevin is long-term unemployed apart from this job 'on the side' arranged for him by Father McCaffrey, confined otherwise to some dreary housing estate in Llanelli; while as for Sister Elisabeth – or Elżbieta as they call her here – the Order of the Perpetual Veneration has been her prison ever since she came back from Siberia in 1956. We looked at the little graveyard (the church has no congregation and is permanently locked now). There were a couple of Commonwealth War Graves tombstones, one from each world war – Merchant Navy badges, so drowned sailors washed up on the beach I suppose – and a row of nineteen creosoted wooden crosses marking the graves of Poles from the Plas. I said that they ought to run a sweepstake on who would be number twenty: me or someone else, and Sister Elisabeth laughed – without affectation

6

since I can safely make heartless jokes of that sort with her. Then we walked down to the shore.

They are fine sandy beaches here at the end of the peninsula, but too windswept and difficult of access to attract more than a handful of holidaymakers even at the height of summer. Above the sands, cast up by the storms, is a long bank of pebbles curving the length of the bay. We stumbled up the reverse side, Kevin and Sister Elisabeth supporting me, until we were on the crest and could watch the blue Atlantic waves rolling on to the beach. Then I saw it some way along the bank: the skeleton of an old wooden ship embedded in the shingle; blackened ribs of oak eroded now to spikes, some side-planking and a few rusted iron knees, a decaying stem and rudder post, and the rotting stumps of three masts still pointing forlornly at the sky. She must have been quite large, I thought; perhaps eight hundred or even a thousand tonnes. We went to examine her. A sizeable section of deck with the remains of a hatch coaming lay on the landward side of the bank, dune-grass growing up through the cracks between the crumbling planks. Sister Elisabeth and I sat down on a fallen deck beam among the ribs while Kevin leant against the stump of the mainmast and pulled a little book out of his pocket.

'There, Mr Procházka, always prepared: that's me. Brought a guide book with me I did.' He thumbed through it. 'Ah, here we are then: Pengadog Bay. "In the beach below the church, visitors can see the remains of the Swansea copper barque *Angharad Pritchard*, 830 tonnes, built 1896 and beached here in October 1928 after a collision with a steamer in fog off Lundy Island. The ship's figurehead can be seen outside the Herbert Arms public house in the village." '

I was silent for a while. Surely not?

'Excuse me, Kevin, but what was the name of this ship?'

'The *Angharad Pritchard*, Mr Procházka: built 1896 and wrecked 1928.'

Yes, it must have been her: the name and age, and the tonnage and the Chilean copper trade. It was a very curious feeling, to realise suddenly that, eighty-something years before, my own juvenile feet had trodden perhaps that very same section of silvery-bleached deck that now lay decaying there among the grass and pebbles. And that now we had met again, both washed up at the end of our days on this lonely shore at the far edge of Europe.

Kevin wandered down the beach after a while to throw pebbles into the incoming tide while Sister Elisabeth produced her mouth organ from the folds of her habit (the Sisters of the Perpetual Veneration still cling obstinately to the old long-skirted style of dress). She really plays quite well, having learnt the instrument about 1940 in a labour camp in Kamchatka, but she has little opportunity to practise up at the Plas. Émigré Polish Catholicism is intensely conservative, and harmonica-playing is still regarded as an improper pastime for a nun whatever the Second Vatican Council might have had to say on the matter. It was a sad little air, 'Czeremcha' or something of that kind, the wind sighing in the far-off Polish birch trees as we both sat absorbed in our own thoughts.

So the wheel had come full circle: eighty-four years since I had last been aboard the *Angharad Pritchard*, the day of the earthquake at Taltal. It was – let me see – February 1903 and I, Ottokar Prohaska, third-year cadet in the Imperial and Royal Naval Academy, was with the steam corvette S.M.S. *Windischgrätz*, eight months out from Pola on a scientific cruise which was now turning willy-nilly into a circumnavigation of the globe. We had been there for two days in Taltal Roads off the desert coast of Chile, anchored among twenty or so other ships: mostly sailing vessels like ourselves but with a sprinkling of steamers now that the despised 'tin kettles' were eating even into the difficult and unprofitable South American trades.

In normal circumstances Taltal was a place such as no self-respecting European warship would have deigned to visit. It was a typical West Coast South American port, like several dozen others straggling the three thousand miles up the Andean coast from Coronel to Guayaquil: just like Talcahuano and Huasco and Caldera and Iquique and Antofagasta and all the rest. There was the same bay with the masts wagging like rows of metronome pointers as the ships rolled at anchor on the oily Pacific swell. There was the same drab greyish-brown shoreline of the Atacama desert and beyond it, seeming close enough to touch in the clear, dry desert air, the same row of mauve Andean peaks capped with snow. There were the same rickety wooden loading jetties and the same miserable cluster of adobe-and-corrugated-iron shacks along the same dusty streets where sewage ran in rivulets, the flies buzzed and the trains of half-starved mules staggered in from the desert laden with sacks of nitrate and copper ore. And there was the same local populace: a dispirited collection of mestizos squatting about dozing in their ponchos or occasionally stirring themselves to do a little desultory cargo-handling when the mood took them or when they were low on pisco money. It was the stultifying indolence of the locals which allowed sailing ships to hang on in the West Coast trades. A steamer had to be moored against a wharf and loaded in a couple of days to be profitable to its owners. But here where the loading was by bags into lighters and then into the ship's hold, the sailing vessel had the edge, being perfectly able to wait here for months on end and use its own crew as stevedores.

In the normal course of events, no European warship would have bothered with Taltal. But S.M.S. *Windischgrätz* in February 1903 was in no position to be fussy. We had recently spent six weeks trying – and failing – to get around Cape Horn into the Pacific, and then a month cruising in the waters off Tierra del Fuego. Our orders now were to sail up the Chilean coast and make for Callao before turning west to cross the Pacific. But our progress up the Andean coast had been miserably slow in the light airs of summer, and the ship's wooden hull was in poor shape after eight months at sea, leaking like a basket so that the crew were now having to work at the pumps for a couple of hours in every watch. We had put into Taltal so that the ship could be heeled to allow the Carpenter to get at a particularly troublesome and persistent leak about a metre below the waterline.

Like most of the harbours along that coast, Taltal was a poor anchorage. The seabed fell away so steeply that even two hundred metres offshore the depth was seventy fathoms, and the ground so hard that throughout our stay there we were obliged to post an anchor watch to warn us if the ship was dragging. It was mid-morning now and most of the port watch was ashore on various errands. One exploration party led by the anthropologist Professor Skowronek had landed armed with picks and shovels to look for Inca cemeteries to pillage for the Professor's skull collection. Another party had set off for the mountains on hired mules to assist the expedition's geologist Dr Pürkler. As for the officers, although Taltal had not been included in our schedule for official visits our commander Korvettenkapitän Festetics and the GDO Linienschiffsleutnant Mikulić had decided to make a virtue out of necessity and had gone ashore in the gig at eight bells, cocked hats balanced on their knees, to meet the District Governor and representatives of the local German community: mostly Scandinavians and Swiss in fact but never mind. Leave ashore had been offered for those not detailed for anything else, but few men had taken up the offer. In so far as Taltal ever came alive it did so only at dusk when the sailors' bars and the delicately named 'fandango halls' opened for business.

The same could have been said of most of the Chilean coast. Bleak and arid by day, the onset of darkness would cast a magical veil over the place. The sun setting below the dark rim of the Pacific would light up the distant mountains into an unearthly blaze of ever-changing oranges and purples. Then the ultramarine velvet night lit by brilliant stars would fall over the ships rolling at anchor on the swell. Many of the ships in those waters were Welsh copper barques, like the one next to us in the row: the *Angharad Pritchard*, which had just finished loading ore for Port Talbot. I had been aboard her the previous afternoon. One of her apprentices had developed appendicitis and our surgeon Korvettenarzt Luchieni had been summoned over to operate, taking me as an interpreter since he knew very little English. While not interpreting, my duties had consisted of bringing the sterilised instruments from the galley stove to the scrubbed table beneath an awning on the poop deck where the young sailor was being operated on.

It had been a straightforward enough operation. Dr Luchieni had popped the appendix into a jar of spirit to give to the apprentice as a souvenir when he came round, then he had washed his hands, rolled down his sleeves and packed his instruments, pausing only to receive the Master's thanks at the gangway as we climbed down into the boat. The Welshman was due to sail next morning. That afternoon the last bag of copper ore had been swung up from the lighter with an apprentice standing on it waving his cap to a chorus of cheers from his shipmates. And that evening, as the carpenter finished battening down the hatches for the long journey around the Horn, the Southern Cross had been hoisted: a wooden frame with paraffin lamps hung on it in the shape of that constellation, swayed up to the masthead as the ships round about gave three cheers. The song 'Homeward Bound' rolled out across the dark waters of the bay. Then there began an impromptu concert of Welsh hymns and music-hall songs. We were all agreed that steamship men were a pretty spiritless lot, no more than paint cleaners and grease monkeys: but aboard the sailing ships everyone still sang to ease the burden of the work, and most vessels could turn out a band of some kind even if it was only a broken-down concertina and some beef-bones. The crew of the big German windjammer the *Paderborn* gave us the 'Wacht am Rhein'. Then it was our turn. Whatever the deficiencies of S.M.S. *Windischgrätz* as a sailing vessel, we were an Austrian warship, and no Austrian man-o'-war could possibly sail on an ocean voyage without taking along a Schiffskapelle of naval bandsmen. Our twenty musicians gathered on the fo'c'sle deck and did us proud over the next couple of hours with a concert of marches and waltzes such as would have done credit to the Prater on a Sunday afternoon in May: Strauss, Millöcker, Ziehrer, Suppé; the entire café-terrace repertoire. They finished, I remember, with Lehár's 'Nechledil March' which had been all the rage in Vienna the previous year. This brought so many encores that it was almost midnight before we were finally allowed to turn in.

So much for fun: the next morning had brought us work once more, shovelling our remaining coal over to port and lugging guns and stores across the ship to give us the necessary heel for the Carpenter and his assistants to strip off the copper sheathing over the leak. With the captain and the GDO ashore, the officer of the watch was my divisional commander Linienschiffsleutnant Zaleski. The pump had not been drawing well of late, so now that the ship had been heeled and the water was low in the bottom of the ship, Zaleski had determined to send someone down to see what was the matter. The choice had fallen on me. I had been obliged to undress to my underpants, a bowline had ben slung beneath my armpits, and I had found myself being lowered into a ridiculously narrow pipe leading down into the very nethermost bowels of the ship. I have never suffered much from claustrophobia, but I came as near then as I have ever done to a fit of panic, as the light diminished to a greyish dot above me and the dismal, slimy shaft echoed to the sound of my breathing. As I sank up to my knees in the bilgewater at the bottom I became painfully aware that if the ship were to come upright again for any reason the water would surge back up to its original level and I would drown – that is, if I had not already been asphyxiated by the foul air at the bottom of the well.

It was certainly far worse than I had imagined, down there in the lowest part of the ship. The *Windischgrätz* had been in service now for nearly thirty years, and all the effluvia of several hundred men crowded together into a wooden hulk over a quarter-century had accumulated here: all the off-scourings and slops and seepage from provision barrels mingling with the oozings of decaying wood to produce a liquor rather like that evil-looking greyish jelly that one finds inside the U-traps of old sink wastepipes. And here was I, shoulders pressed together and standing up to my thighs in it, waiting for further instructions. I felt sick and already rather faint. At last an electric lamp shone into the shaft and Zaleski's voice came echoing down.

'All right down there, Prohaska?'

Restraining a desperate urge to vomit I called back: 'Obediently report that yes, Herr Leutnant.'

'Good man. Now, put your hand down and find what's blocking the pump inlet filter. It's a sort of bronze box-thing with holes in it.'

'Very good, Herr Leutnant.' I clenched my teeth, and bent my knees to try to get my hand low enough under water to find the inlet. The well was too narrow to allow me to bend down. I found it at last, thickly encrusted with slime – and straightened up suddenly with a yelp of pain. Something had bitten me! Blood was already dripping from my finger. I wondered desperately whether I could climb up the well by bracing my back against it. Court martial for disobeying orders seemed infinitely preferable to another five seconds at the bottom of this sewer pipe.

'For God's sake Prohaska, what's the matter down there?'

'I obediently report . . . something bit me, Herr Leutnant.'

'Bit you? What do you mean, you young idiot?'

'There's something alive down here, Herr Leutnant, in the pump inlet.'

There was silence for a while. I knew that a debate was taking place above me. But as I waited, hoping desperately to be hauled up from this slime-pit and whatever nameless horror was lurking at the bottom of it, I became aware that something out of the ordinary was taking place. The water in the well was shaking and slopping to and fro as the ship shuddered around me. And there was a curious noise: a heavy, irregular rumbling like a train with badly worn wheels in a railway tunnel, or perhaps large empty barrels being banged about in a cellar. I called up.

'Herr Leutnant!'

The lamp shone down again, blinding me.

'What on earth is it now?'

'Herr Leutnant, I most obediently report that there's a funny noise down here.'

There was a pause.

'What sort of noise?'

'A kind of rumbling and banging, Herr Leutnant; coming from below the ship I think.'

There was silence again, broken only by shudders and more dull concussions. At last Zaleski called down.

'We're hauling you up.'

I emerged from the well like the prophet Jeremiah to find the entire ship suddenly alive with men turning out and running to quarters: feet pounding on decks and up the companionways as the starboard watch scrambled into the rigging to loose sail. Men were already at work dragging the guns on the battery deck over to starboard to rectify the list.

'But the pump, Herr Leutnant . . .?'

'Damn the pump. The pump can wait. There are more important things to worry about than the pump. Get aloft now!'

So I lay aloft with the rest to make sail. After eight months at sea I was well used to this sort of thing and would have found my way to my station blindfolded or asleep: port-yardarm man on the royal yard of the mizzen mast, which was the province of the forty cadets aboard since the sails were somewhat smaller – and thus rather lighter work – than on the other two masts and there was anyway one less of them to handle. I scrambled up the rope ladder and out on to the swaying footrope, sliding down since the ship still had a marked heel to port. My friend Max Gauss, our mess-mate Tarabochia and a fourth-year cadet called Arváy were there with me. As we loosed the gaskets holding the furled sail to the yard I began to realise that this was no random sail-drill to keep the crew alert: a sudden tremendous rattling and clouds of red dust up forward, followed by a splash, announced that we had slipped our anchor cable in our haste to put to sea. But there was no time to wonder. We let go the last gasket and the canvas tumbled down to be sheeted home as the men on deck hauled at the halyards to raise the yard. Gauss and I stayed aloft to overhaul the buntlines, as was the custom, but Zaleski's voice called up to us:

'Never mind the buntlines! Get down on deck and man the braces!'

This was clearly an emergency, so Gauss and I slid down the mizzen backstays instead of going via the shrouds in the approved manner. As we left I saw that whatever this madness was that had gripped our ship, the *Angharad Pritchard* alongside us had been seized by the same unaccountable frenzy. They had been preparing to sail anyway, but now they were raising the anchor and loosing sail as though the Devil himself was rowing out towards them from the shore. I also caught a glimpse of the seaward horizon, and noticed – although it meant nothing to me at the time – an unusual straight, dark line extending across it.

Down on deck once more, I hauled at the braces with the rest to trim the yards around to the light morning breeze. As the ship began to move through the water I noticed that the air was tainted with a faint but disturbing whiff of rotten eggs, and that the sea around us was boiling and throwing up stunned fish to float belly-upwards. Something sinister was happening. By now Taltal Bay was filled with a frightful clangour of bells and sirens and anchor chain rattling through hawse pipes as ships tried to get under way, or at least to veer enough cable to ride out whatever was coming. For the first time since this alarm began I felt frightened.

Not the least of my reasons for feeling uneasy was the fact that just as this all started the Captain had arrived back aboard from his brief visit ashore. He was now engaged in a loud argument with Linienschiffsleutnant Zaleski as the latter tried to get the ship under way.

'Zaleski, I demand to know the meaning of this. Have you finally taken leave of your senses? Why is the ship putting to sea? Why have you just abandoned an anchor and five hundred metres of cable? I swear I'll pay for it in person . . .'

'A moment if you please, Herr Kommandant, I shall explain – yes that's it you men there. Don't bother about squaring the lifts. Just let's get moving for God's sake! Yes Herr Kommandant, I know . . . A moment if you would be so kind.'

As the mizzen topsail filled with the breeze and was sheeted home I did indeed wonder whether Zaleski had gone mad: so many strange things had happened on this voyage and misfortune seemed to have dogged us ever since we left West Africa. But speculation ended at that moment as the tidal wave hit us, fine on the starboard bow. It was most dramatic: one moment the clear Pacific blue sky above the fo'c'sle rails, the next a glassy, seemingly motionless hill of dark green water looming ahead, capped by a crest of foam. That was the last I saw for several moments because, like most other people who were not holding on to something, I was thrown off my feet as we met the wave. The ship's bow rose to the surge – and rose, and kept on rising as the masts and rigging squealed and groaned in outrage above us, flung back only to be flicked forward again as the ship breasted the first wave and plunged down into the trough, burying her bowsprit before shaking herself and rising to meet the second wave rushing landwards from the epicentre of the earthquake far out to sea. Our vessel had not been too solidly built to begin with, and by the sound of it her brief but violent switchback ride at Taltal that morning was doing nothing to improve her structural soundness.

But somehow we surmounted that peril as we had surmounted so many others since we left Pola the previous summer. The only other ships unscathed by the tidal wave were the *Angharad Pritchard* and a Spanish vessel which had just arrived at Taltal and which still had sufficient steam up to be able to put to sea. Without Linienschiffsleutnant Zaleski's presence of mind we would have suffered the same fate as the rest. Loss of life had not been great, apart from a few unfortunate boat's crews and the men aboard a lighter which had been swamped. As for the townspeople, they were well used to this sort of thing and had all run to a hillock behind the town at the first rumblings of the earthquake. But the other ships anchored in Taltal Roads had suffered badly. The magnificent *Paderborn* had been struck broadside-on and rolled on to the shore, to lie there in a sorry-looking mess of broken masts and tumbled yards. Two ships had foundered, two more had been smashed against one another and an Italian barque whose anchor had held had remained afloat only at the price of having the chain cut down through the hawse-hole like a bandsaw blade and tear out most of her bow timbers.

As for the pump inlet, by the way, and the bitten finger, once we were at anchor again and the ship had been heeled I was sent back down into the well, this time with a spanner and hammer, to unbolt the inlet filter box. When we got it up on deck we found that it contained a fair-sized crab which had evidently taken up residence there while it was small and which had grown fat on the nutritious soup at the bottom of the well until it could no longer get out. It must have been there for years. Herr Lenart the biologist pickled it in alcohol for his collection.

As we lay there back in the wreckage-littered bay, with our diver down looking for the lost anchor, we were passed by the *Angharad Pritchard*, heading now for home after returning to pick up two of her men who had been ashore when the wave struck.

'Are you all right?' Zaleski shouted through the speaking trumpet.

'All right thank you, *Windischgrätz*. No damage. How are you?'

'All right also I think. But what a wave.'

'Oh, that's nothing, look you. Only a little one, about forty feet I reckon. You should have been in Valparaiso back in '73: an earthquake, then a fire, then a tidal wave there was. Lost half our crew when a dance hall slid down the mountainside we did. This one here was just a little love-tap. Anyway, thank you for operating on our apprentice. Send the bill to the owners at the address I gave you in Carmarthen.'

'Thank you. We will. And bon voyage!'

The *Angharad Pritchard* sailed on, and that was the last I saw or thought of her for eighty-six years, until I found myself sitting among her bones on the beach below Pengadog Church. The old *Windischgrätz* is long gone now, like the empire whose flag she flew. And as for the men who sailed aboard her, I was one of the very youngest and I am now nearly a hundred and one, so I imagine that the rest of the 356 have gone to their graves many a long year since. As for the ports of that coast, Taltal and Meillones and Arica and the rest, they too must have been dead for a good half-century, the loading jetties silent now as the deserted adobe houses crumble in the desert wind and the ceaseless Pacific rollers crash on the shore where the sealions bark undisturbed by human traffic. Only I am left now, come full circle at last to join the remains of this long-forgotten ship.

These thoughts on the transience of earthly things were only interrupted when a man came past us walking a dog. Clearly unused to the spectacle of mouth-organ-playing nuns and ancient mariners sitting among the timbers of wrecked ships, he bade us a rather forced 'Good-afternoon' and hurried off towards the church and the lane. It was beginning to get dark now and Sister Felicja would expect us back for tea at 5.00 p.m. sharp, so we called Kevin and the two of them helped me into the car to take me back to the Plas. As we drove past the Herbert Arms I looked for the ship's figurehead, but failed to see it. I did have the satisfaction though of seeing the man with the dog standing outside the telephone box by the pub, talking with a policeman in a patrol car and pointing him down towards the beach.

Back in my room that evening I thought on the afternoon's events, and of that ill-starred voyage when the twentieth century had scarcely begun. I have recorded most of my wartime reminiscences over the past few months – for what use they may be to anyone – and I could very well leave it at that, with two entire shoeboxes full of tape cassettes in my cupboard. But the meeting with the remains of that old sailing ship had set my mind rolling back towards my far-off youth. And I thought, Why not? I have not got far to go now: perhaps only days rather than weeks. Dr Watkins says that my heart is unimpaired by my illness, and that the Swansea area already contains two of the oldest people in the world – one of them 114, apparently – so there is no reason at all why I should not last for years longer. But inside me I know better. Once I have told you this last tale I shall be ready to leave, knowing that so far as I am concerned nothing more of any importance remains to be said. So let it be told: the story of the world scientific cruise of His Imperial, Royal and Apostolic Majesty's steam corvette *Windischgrätz*. And of the colonial empire that somehow never quite came into existence.

2

SEA-STRUCK

It is a matter of intense regret to me that my old photograph album contains no pictorial record of that first ocean voyage of mine. I was a keen photographer in those days and took an early Joule-Herriot box camera along with me aboard the *Windischgrätz*. But most of the photographs were lost when I accidentally parted company with the ship off the coast of New Guinea, and only one survived: taken not by me but by the expedition's official photographer Herr Krentz that Sunday morning in June 1902 as we prepared to sail from Pola. It stood for many years in my father's house in Hirschendorf, in a silver frame on the sideboard. It showed me, a naval cadet of sixteen, standing on the bridge of the *Windischgrätz* in my best blue jacket and white duck trousers, a notepad in my hand, the very picture of juvenile self-importance, while Linienschiffsleutnant Svoboda stood beside me checking the standard compass for deviation and my divisional officer Linienschiffsleutnant Zaleski leant nonchalantly against the engine-room telegraph, his face sombre and his eyes suspiciously half-closed as was his wont. Behind us, hands in jacket pockets, legs confidently planted astride, towered the majestic fork-bearded figure of our commander, Fregattenkapitän Maximillian Slawetz, Freiherr von Löwenhausen, head raised to scan the distant horizon even though we were still at anchor off the Scoglio del Olivi. Ah, the blind optimism of youth. If only I had known what lay ahead of me that day, what adventures and what troubles on that voyage and the ones to come. If only I had known . . . then I suppose I would still have gone on and done it just the same. As we say where I come from, there's no medicine for stupidity.

Every voyage has to have a port of departure, so by your leave I shall start mine at the very beginning, sixteen years and two months before the shutter clicked to record that Sunday-morning scene in Pola harbour. I was born on 6 April 1886 in a house on the Olmutzergasse in a small town called Hirschendorf on the northern fringe of the Austro-Hungarian Empire, in the Czech-speaking province of Moravia near where it used to border with Prussian Silesia. My father was Václav (or Wenzel) Procházka (or Prohaska), thirty-five years of age, an official of the district branch of the k.k. Ministry of Posts and Telegraphs, the Germanised Czech son of middling peasants from near Kolin in Bohemia. My mother, Agnieszka Mazeotti-Krasnodębska, twenty-eight years old, was the fourth daughter of a family of decayed Polish gentry from near Cracow. I was the second child, my brother Anton being eighteen months my senior. And since our mother was in poor health both physically and mentally – as well as being on increasingly distant terms with our father – there remained only the two of us.

As regards Hirschendorf, there is not a great deal to be said, and I suspect anyway that I may already have bored you cataleptic with reminiscing about the place. It was a dowdy little town of about eight thousand inhabitants, located in a shallow valley among that insignificant range of hills called the Silesian Beskids, straddling the River Verba about twenty kilometres upstream from its confluence with the Oder. There was the usual large baroque church with twin onion-spires, the ruins of a medieval castle, a railway station, a hotel-cum-café on one side of the town square and an ochre-painted block of government buildings on the other. There was a weekly market, and a few rural industries: brewing, beet sugar and so forth. But as was usual in the old Habsburg Monarchy, by far the largest single employer in the town was the state administration: the revenue department, the customs and excise, the postal and telegraphic service, the land registry, the veterinary department. And of course the yellow-helmeted gendarmery, and behind them – always ready in case of need – the soldiery in their red-brick quadrangle of barracks up on the Troppau road.

There it sat in those tranquil last years of the nineteenth century: a town most of whose inhabitants were born, lived their lives and died without ever travelling more than a day's journey away from the place; a little German-speaking island of gaslight and bicycles, wing collars and straw boaters set amid a sea of Czech-speaking peasantry who still wore striped breeches and embroidered waistcoats to drive their plough-oxen to the fields; who kept geese, herded swine and lived in wooden huts along muddy village streets exactly as their grandfathers had done, and their grandfathers' grandfathers before them. That was the rural world my father had escaped from into the Habsburg civil service. For most people who made that transition it remained largely a matter of outward form, of speaking official German while at work. With my father however the transformation was internal as well. It took a good few years, otherwise I imagine that I would not have been named 'Ottokar' after the medieval Bohemian king who had almost defeated the Habsburgs at the Battle of the Marchfeld. But by the time I became aware of such things my father, despite his stocky Slav appearance and his strong Czech accent, had turned himself not just into a German-speaker but into a rabid Pan-German nationalist.

This would be taken nowadays as evidence of what I believe is called 'a personal identity-crisis situation'. But believe me, in Hirschendorf in the 1890s there was nothing at all out of the ordinary in this. Like much of the Danubian Monarchy by the turn of the century, the town was in a constant state of low-level nationalist ferment: a place as totally devoted to the manufacture of personal identity crises as Montelimar is to the production of nougat or Bokhara to the manufacture of rugs. The trouble was that the town and district were disputed territory between the German majority, who called it 'Hirschendorf', and the large and rapidly growing Czech minority, who called it 'Krnava', which they said it had been until the seventeenth century when the local magnate, the Prince von und zu Regnitz, had renamed the place. To complicate matters there was also a small but vocal Polish faction who said that the town was in fact called 'Sadybsko' and ought to be part of an independent Polish state if and when such an entity could be set up.

As my brother and I grew up the factions were becoming increasingly noisy and violent, ready to turn the smallest matter – the siting of a lamppost or the name of a street – into a cause for demonstrations which had a way of turning into riots. The worst of it was the way in which the constant acrimony was forcing everyone to declare themselves for one nationality or the other for the sake of self-protection. The town in those years sprouted deformed loyalties and ingrowing nationalisms like an asparagus bed. People with German names who could barely manage a coherent sentence in Czech would suddenly turn into fiery Czech patriots, while others who had never spoken any other language would take to denying that they were Czechs with a vehemence worthy of Saint Peter as the cock crowed for the third time. When I was about ten years old the leader of the German nationalist faction on the town council was called Herr Przybyszewski, the leader of the Czech party was Herr Nutzdorfer and the Polish party was led by one Herr Marinetti.

While we were children most of this adult insanity passed us by. We were supposed to be German-speaking at home, of course. But our father was too busy with his official duties to supervise us very closely and we had relatives in Austrian Poland with whom we spent the summer holidays, so we grew up to be pretty well trilingual. Our mother had withdrawn from the scene soon after we were born, to live in her own rooms and devote herself to hypochondria and a circle of Polish women friends as vapid as herself. So my brother and I were entrusted to the care of a Czech countrywoman called Hanuška Jindrichova, the wife of the head forester on the Regnitz estates. Her cottage was in the street behind our house and was our real home for most of our boyhood.

It was really not too bad a childhood I suppose. My father had some investment income to supplement his official salary, so we lived in modest comfort; and anyway people in Central Europe in those days were content with very little: no television, cinemas or aeroplanes, but unlimited amounts of time in a world where life had still not been completely taken over by the clock and the motor car; a world where foreign travel was a rail excursion to Bohemia and where worldly sophistication was a dog-eared book of dress patterns handed to the local seamstress, or a travelling repertory company putting on the last-season-but-three's Viennese operetta in the fusty little municipal theatre on the Trautenaugasse. The townspeople anyway kept themselves pretty well amused by demonstrating and pamphleteering and occasionally brawling in the streets for or against this, that or the other. Most of it was fairly harmless I suppose. The only fatality was in 1896 or thereabouts when a riot over the naming of the railway station spread into the town square and troops were called in to fire above the heads of the crowd – in the process incidentally killing an Italian waiter who had been watching the fun from an upstairs window of the Hotel Zum Weissen Löwe. Most people in Hirschendorf hated one another only in their official, national capacity, so to speak, and were perfectly cordial towards one another when not actually rioting over something. And anyway, as children we had a temporary exemption from national allegiance.

Besides minors, the other group in Hirschendorf who stood outside nationalist politics were the Jews. But that was only because all other groups detested them more or less indiscriminately. For the life of me I could never even begin to understand why Hirschendorf's few hundred Jews should excite such universal dislike, a disdain which was all the more sinister because it was so general and so devoid of passion; rather like the vague aversion that people have for spiders or cats without having any particular personal animus against them. Of course the usual rationalisations were wheeled out in defence of this dislike: money-lending, ritual murder, deicide, involvement in white slaving and other dubious trades. But our Jews were few in number compared with a small town (say) in Galicia, where they would often make up half or three-quarters of the population. Likewise they were a world away from the wheedling hook-nosed usurers of popular legend. Our Jews were solid, worthy members of the black-coated professions, grandchildren of the Emperor Joseph's decree of emancipation a century earlier; Herr Litzmann the notary and Dr Grünbaum at the Kaiserin Elisabeth Hospital, Herr Jelinek the town photographer. And of course Herr Zinower the bookseller.

Herr Zinower had been a particular friend of mine ever since I could remember. I was a rather precocious child as regards literacy. By the time I was six I could read both Czech and German quite fluently, and was fast catching up in Polish. Not that there was a great deal for children to read, though, in any language in northern Moravia in those days: only the *Tales of the Brothers Grimm* and *Struwwelpeter* in German, a few insipid collections of fairy stories in Czech – and of course the Imperial-Royal Ministry of Education's 'Approved Reading Texts for Use in Junior Schools'; an achingly dull collection of politically sound and morally improving tales about charitable archduchesses working in fever hospitals and gallant young Fähnrichs dying in defence of the regimental flag on the field of Solferino. It was really the English who invented children's literature, I think, about the end of the last century, and with it the idea of childhood as an idyllic and innocent state. Where I grew up it was still sensibly regarded as a condition rather like measles: inevitable and necessary, but one to be got over with as soon as possible and certainly not one to be looked back upon with any regret. We Mitteleuropeans are generally a pretty nasty lot: embittered, vindictive and sodden with self-pity. But at least you very rarely hear us in our adult years maundering on about trainsets and tea in the nursery.

But this lack of interest in the childhood state, though admirable in many ways, did have the drawback that until the late 1890s there was very little children's literature around; not until Robert Louis Stevenson, Jules Verne and G. A. Henty started to appear in German translation and local writers like Karl May got to work producing adventure stories. So for the time being my own reading had to be of a more factual nature, and in this Herr Zinower was of the greatest possible help to me.

The town bookshop was in fact largely concerned with the sale of paper and writing materials: a major item of commerce in

Habsburg Austria, where the simplest transaction with a government department could drag on for years and generate enough correspondence to fill an entire suite of filing cabinets. Besides the sale of stationery, Herr Zinower also ran a book bindery, a card-printing business and a small bookshop for new and second-hand literature – chiefly school textbooks and women's lending-library novelettes. One Saturday morning in 1895 or thereabouts I wandered in to purchase a pencil and eraser. Herr Zinower greeted me as the doorbell rang: a tubby, balding, bespectacled little man in his late forties.

'Grüss Gott, Herr Ottokar,' he said, rubbing his hands and emerging from behind the counter as though I were a valued trade client with pockets full of gulden instead of a small boy with a few kreuzers clutched in his grubby palm. 'And in what may I perhaps be of service to you this fine morning?'

'Good-morning, Herr Zinower. I would like a pencil if you please, and an india-rubber eraser.'

'Of course, of course: hard lead, soft lead, medium-soft lead, compressed carbon, medium lead with eraser at the end, bonded lead guaranteed shock-proof from Staedtler of Cassel – very fine, the latest thing, we've only just received them ... Ah yes, but I forgot: I have something else that may perhaps be of interest to an intelligent young man like yourself. Tell me, young sir, do you have an atlas of your own?'

'Please, Herr Zinower, what is an atlas?'

'A book containing maps of all the lands of the earth. Here, see: these have just arrived ...' He reached behind the counter and produced a large, gleaming volume bound in dark-blue oil-board embossed with gold leaf: '*Mollweide's Concise Atlas of the Known World (Amended to Include the Latest African Explorations)* Berlin 1895'. Curious, I turned the freshly cut pages: Europe (Political), Europe (Physical), the Atlantic Ocean, the Pacific; North Africa, India, Oceania – the lands of the entire earth cascaded before me in a torrent of brown and green and pale blue. Mysteriously numbered spider's webs of lines radiated from the poles; puddles of azure ocean lapped the shores of the continents; straggling white icefields decorated the intricate ridges of the Himalayas and the Andes. Surely when Satan took Our Lord up to the top of the temple and showed him all the kingdoms of the earth it must have looked very like this.

Until now the only map with which I was at all familiar had been the oilcoth map of 'The Lands and Ethnic Groups of the Imperial and Royal Monarchy' which hung at the front of my school classroom, below the crucifix and the portrait of the Emperor Franz Joseph in his white tunic and side-whiskers, his piercing blue eyes fixed upon us to detect any misbehaviour. Yet, compared with this multicoloured feast of cartography spread before me now, that classroom map was a dingy affair indeed: our venerable Monarchy a shapeless lump of territory stuck squarely in the middle of Europe with nothing around it to give any reference to anything outside itself apart from a small patch of discoloured blue down in the bottom left-hand corner where Austria-Hungary touched the Adriatic – and even this was obscured by an officious block with the title: 'Länder und Völker der K. & K. Monarchie' and a key to shadings. Cursory reference was made around the periphery to 'Preussen', 'Italien', 'Russland', 'Serbien' and other such regions; but otherwise the Danubian Monarchy was the very centre of the earth, a European version of the Chinese Middle Kingdom.

Yet when I looked at it now on a map of the countries of the world the Austro-Hungarian Empire seemed a pretty unimpressive affair, even if it was the second largest state in Europe after the Russian Empire (though still only slightly larger than France). It suddenly occurred to me, standing there in Herr Zinower's shop, that there was so very much more to the world than the lands of the Habsburg Monarchy: regions vastly more exotic and interesting. And suddenly, I have no idea from where, a desire came upon me to visit these places of whose existence I had never dreamt until now: Honduras and Sumatra and the Sea of Okhotsk; to prove for myself that Cape Town and the Marquesas Islands lay on the same circle of longitude as Hirschendorf, and Seattle and Vladivostok on the same parallel of latitude. I simply had to possess that atlas; to bear it away with me and make the entire habitable globe my own. Herr Zinower was accommodating as usual: said that the atlas was slightly shop-soiled – although I am perfectly sure that it was not. So pocket money was mortgaged into the distant future and treasured possessions sold to schoolmates to fund the purchase. I bore the volume home with me the following Saturday and my career as a seafarer began.

In so far as my father and my schoolteachers were aware of this sudden passion for geography, they regarded it as a mild but probably harmless aberration. Old Austria was a profoundly incurious sort of society: mentally land-locked and too preoccupied with its own tribal disputes to take much interest in the rest of the world. It would have been an interesting exercise, I think, to have drawn up a mental map of the world as seen by the average Viennese about 1900. To the north lay the 'Teutschern': German-speaking but utterly alien in spirit and temperament. To southward, beyond the Alps, lay the Wellischen; untrustworthy and rapacious. And to the east, down the Danube towards Pressburg, lay a vast, vague expanse populated by Slavs, Magyars, Turks and other exotic and cruel peoples of the east wind; savage tribes who, when they were not fighting one another, would erupt into Lower Austria to besiege Vienna either with cannon and earthworks or (in latter days) by hawking boot brushes and wooden ladles on the streets around the Neumarkt. Beyond them lay Russia, where wolves howled on the permanently frozen steppes, and then India, China and other such fabulous kingdoms. Africa was 'Negerland', where people ate one another in the steaming jungles, and America was peopled by cowboys, gauchos, Red Indians and so forth. But really, when all was said and done, no one either knew or cared much about what happened beyond the tramlines of the Gürtel. And that was Vienna, the metropolis. So imagine for yourselves if you will what must have been the world-picture of the burghers of Hirschendorf, for whom a rail excursion to Prague was a lifetime's adventure.

Thus I grew up and passed from childhood into early adolescence. Yet my childish desire to explore and to see remained with me, and grew rather than diminished with the years. I read *Treasure Island* in German translation, and all the adventure stories and books of travels that I and Herr Zinower could lay our hands on. He was delighted to foster my interest. I can scarcely think that he made any money out of me, so perhaps it was because he himself had wanted to travel when he was young. He confessed to me one day that when he was nineteen or thereabouts he had booked a ticket from Hamburg to New York, invited by relatives. But at the last moment his father had died and he had stayed behind to take over the family business. He was philosophical about it.

'Who knows, young Herr Ottokar? Who can say what might have been? Perhaps they have riots and break shop windows there in America as well: there are hooligans in every country. No, it could have been worse. Here we are poor and have to work hard for our bread. But the Germans are civilised and law-abiding people and a Jew can get on as well here in Austria as in any country on earth. I shall never be a millionaire, but at least I can sleep safe in my bed here at night without any fear of buffaloes breaking in and smashing up my stock, or Red Indians scalping Frau Zinower.'

Sympathetic as he was, Herr Zinower could offer no useful advice on the steps to be taken to start a seafaring career, an idea which increasingly grew upon me as a practical proposition from about the age of twelve. But then, nor could anyone else in Hirschendorf. Certainly my relatives were no help whatever. When I put the matter one summer in Poland to my mother's eldest sister, Aunt Aleksia – the only one of my Polish relatives for whose intelligence I had the slightest respect – she sucked her teeth and promised to ask around among family and acquaintances. In the end, though, all that she could come up with was that a distant cousin, one Józef Korzeniowski, had gone abroad years before and was reported to have become a sea-captain in the British merchant service. However, nothing had been heard from him for years past so it was assumed that he had drowned; probably no bad thing (my aunts agreed), since he had always been rather odd and frankly something of a ne'er-do-well.

The only person among my acquaintance who had ever sailed upon saltwater was – oddly enough – my nursemaid Hanuška.

She had been in domestic service in Germany before she married and, being a bright and personable young woman, had become a lady's maid with the Puttfarken family, one of the old Hamburg shipping dynasties. She had once sailed with them on a summer voyage to Oslo – or Christiana as it was called in those days – and as a result her opinion of seafaring was highly unfavourable.

'Really, young Ottokar,' she would say to me as we sat by the cottage stove (we always spoke Czech when my father was not around), 'really I can't recommend it at all. The ship goes up and down, u-u-up and d-o-o-wn all the time, and you keep thinking that it's going to roll over and sink. But soon you feel so ill that you wish it would. And everything's damp and you can't dry anything out. And there's nowhere to wash – but it doesn't matter anyway, since there's no water for washing. And as for space, honestly you'd have more room to lie down in a coffin. And after a couple of days the food tastes funny, but you can't smell it because everything reeks of tar. Really if you ask me you'd be better off in Olmutz jail than aboard a ship: at least the floor of your cell would stay still under your feet.'

But such is the perversity of youth that this highly negative opinion served merely to increase my desire to go to sea. So, being of a practical cast of mind, I set about turning this desire into reality. Not that I could expect much help in that direction from the adults around me: not in northern Moravia in the closing years of the nineteenth century. The Dual Monarchy had a coastline of sorts: about four hundred kilometres of it, extending down the eastern shore of the Adriatic from Trieste to just south of the Gulf of Cattaro. But this littoral was a remote, stony, poverty-stricken region which fronted nowhere in particular except the endless, arid mountain ranges of the Balkans. Austria had acquired it only a century earlier after pocketing the Venetian Republic, and once Venice itself had been lost in 1866 what remained was of little consequence to anyone; not much more than a cut-price Riviera in summer and a tuberculosis sanatorium in winter. Very few ordinary Austrians had ever visited it or ever wanted to. We had a medium-sized navy of course, and a substantial merchant fleet, but few of the Emperor's fifty million subjects had ever set eyes on either or knew anyone connected with them. Even in Vienna naval officers were liable to be accosted in the street in English under the impression that they must be United States military attaché. As for the folk of Hirschendorf, no one could remember even having so much as seen a sailor visiting on leave.

All that Herr Zinower could suggest in the end was writing around. So I penned several polite letters in my best school-copybook hand and sent them off to the shipping lines – Austro-Lloyd and the Hamburg-Amerika and the rest – asking how I might become an apprentice. Only Norddeutscher-Lloyd bothered to reply, telling me that I had to be at least sixteen years of age, of sound health and good moral character, and have a substantial bond put up by my father. Unfortunately I also had to be a German subject, so that was the end of that. Even with an Austrian shipping line I would have to wait another five years, so I determined to fill in the time with self-instruction in the basics of seamanship and navigation.

Hirschendorf was not well provided for in this respect. The River Verba which ran through the town was barely twenty metres wide, and murky with the effluent from the coal mines and steelworks further up the valley towards Karvina. No boat had ever been seen on it. The best that Anton and I could do was to beg a number of cabbage barrels, waterproof them with tar and canvas and nail them together to make a raft. We launched this one morning above the castle weir and managed to sail at least fifty metres before we were caught in the mill sluice and nearly swept to our deaths. The gendarmery fished us out – neither of us could swim – and then arrested us for conduct likely to cause a breach of the peace since they could think of no other charge. Our father was called from his office to collect us from the gendarmery barracks. We were soundly thrashed with a leather belt and confined to our rooms for a week. But later experiments followed this disaster, conducted in greater privacy on a country fishpond with an old duck-punt which I had bought for five kronen and repaired myself with glazier's putty and beaten-out tin cans. It was quite good training in its way, since apart from size there is no great difference in basic principles between navigating a punt and a sixteen-thousand-tonne battleship.

Self-tuition also proceeded at a more theoretical level. After canvassing relatives in Vienna and Trieste Herr Zinower had managed to procure me a copy of the Austrian naval seamanship manual: Admiral von Sterneck's *Handbuch des Bootswesens, Takelage und Ankerkunde* (1894 edition), with its wealth of beautifully detailed copper engravings. I sat down with this, and within a month had learnt by heart all the parts of a fully rigged sailing ship from truck to keel and from jib boom to taffrail. I had also acquired an English chart of the same thing, so I learnt the names of the parts in both languages. The German-speaking nations had come late to deep-water seafaring, so German marine terminology had been hastily put together from a variety of sources – some Dutch, some Scandinavian, some English – and thus to my non-German ear always had a faintly made-up ring about it. For this reason, by the way, I shall stick to the English terms throughout this tale. I know them quite as well as the German, and it will only cause you annoyance (I imagine) to hear me banging on about the Grossoberbramraa and the Aussenklüverniederholer when I mean the main royal yard and the outer flying jib down-haul.

Theoretical seamanship was easy enough, then, but what about navigation? Having always had a fair aptitude for mathematics, I set to work to teach myself the basics of marine navigation. A magnetic compass was no great problem: officers of the k. u. k. Armee used them as an aid to getting lost, and if one looked in the pawn-shop windows one might come across a specimen which some needy Oberleutnant had popped mid-month for drinking money and not redeemed. Latitude and longitude were more troublesome though. In the end I built myself a crude wooden sextant with a plumb-bob to give the horizon and set this up on Castle Hill on the morning of 21 September 1897 to take my first midday observation. Imagine my delight when, after having half-blinded myself sighting the sun at its zenith, I did the calculations and found that Hirschendorf was indeed 49° 57' north of the Equator as stated in the gazetteer of my atlas. I felt like Magellan after he had spent three years proving that the world was indeed round. My self-satisfaction was only deflated a few minutes later when a gendarmery corporal arrested me on suspicion of espionage. The result was another summons for my father to come to the barracks and collect me, and another serious thrashing. But afterwards I felt at least that, like Galileo, I had suffered in the cause of science.

I studied maps and I learnt the names of a ship's sails and spars. But I was still frustratingly aware that I had never seen the sea or been afloat in anything larger than a punt on a pond. The best that I could do was to make pledges against the future, like Sir Francis Drake climbing a tree on the Isthmus of Panama in a story that I had read and swearing that one day, by God's leave, he would sail the distant Pacific Ocean. About ten kilometres south of Hirschendorf there lay an insignificant hill called the St Walpurgisberg, totally unremarkable except for the fact that from its sides there issued three springs which turned into three brooks. One of these flowed into the Verba, which flowed into the Oder, which flowed into the Baltic. Another found its way into a tributary of the Elbe, which flowed into the North Sea. And the third flowed into the March, which joined the Danube below Vienna to make its way to the Black Sea and the Mediterranean. Anton and I would go there sometimes on our bicycles in spring or autumn when the water was flowing strongly and cut three little wooden-chip boats with my penknife, then place one of them in each stream to scurry away with the current. I suppose that they lodged in the sedges a few hundred metres lower down, but still it pleased my childish imagination to think that perhaps, months from now, my little craft might bob past the Golden Horn or the castle of Elsinore, or round the north of Scotland and into the Atlantic. For me it was a personal covenant, like the Doge of Venice wedding the sea by flinging his ring into the waves.

To cut a long story short, by the time I was twelve I had contrived to persuade my father to let me follow a career at sea. He was reluctant at first; in a large measure because he had never seen saltwater or a ship in his life and was simply unable to conceive what a seafaring career might involve. But in the end he had grudgingly consented – largely as a result of reading an article in a Pan-German nationalist journal which had confidently predicted that the great war for Germany's mastery of the world would take place on the oceans, first with Britain and then with the United States. My petition to be allowed to become a sailor was also greatly assisted in the summer of 1897 by a stroke of luck. My father's shares had done unexpectedly well, and so we all set off for a family holiday – our first and last – in the fashionable Adriatic seaside resort of Abbazia. We were carried in a fiacre from the railway station and left our bags at the hotel. Then I rushed out of the foyer and across the promenade and lo, there it lay before me, the element which I had dreamt of and yearned to embrace these three years past: flat and shining, deep-blue beyond the lemon trees and the ornamental limestone balustrade of the seafront. To the holidaymakers strolling by in their straw boaters and crinolines it was just the sea in a sheltered bay at the head of the Quarnerolo Gulf; a body of salt water so tame and domesticated as to be little more than a lake. But to me that sheet of ultramarine rippling gently under the midday sun, dotted with the sails of pleasure boats, was something far more than a tasteful adjunct to a holiday resort. To me, standing there enthralled on the promenade, it was the start of the ocean: the world's great highway, leading away into the far blue towards whatever adventures and marvels a boy's heart might imagine. The passing crowds saw only boats and swimmers and the twin, misty humps of Cherso and Veglia Islands almost blocking the horizon to southward. But in my sight it was all there: the flying fish of the tropical seas, spouting whales, palm-fringed atolls and the fever-ridden mouths of the African rivers, the teeming wharves of Canton and the Arctic pack-ice and the howling wilderness of the Southern Ocean. I had only to scramble across the railings and down on to the narrow rocky shore to touch her and make her mine, my life's mistress lying there now so demure and seductive, but potentially so cruel and dangerous; ever-capricious and totally indifferent to frontiers and conflicting national historical claims. No one, I felt sure, was ever going to produce a map entitled 'Provincial Boundaries and Ethnic Groups of the Atlantic Ocean'.

Considered as a family holiday, the fortnight in Abbazia was an unmitigated disaster. My father fumed while my mother sulked and suffered from alternate fainting fits and bouts of hysterics, eventually being admitted to hospital in Fiume with suspected rabies. But as far as my own career development went it all passed off in a most satisfactory manner. I went for my first sea voyage, on a passenger steamer to Cherso – and was disgustingly seasick, since even in summer the upper Adriatic can become quite rough when the sirocco has been blowing a few days. It was on this outing that my father (who had also been extremely unwell) went below into the saloon once the weather had calmed down and fell to talking with a young naval lieutnant called Heinrich Fritsch. Since, like all good Pan-Germans, my father regarded Habsburg Austria as a tumbledown medieval slum standing in the way of a Greater German Reich, it followed that he had not been at all keen on the idea of my applying to be an officer in the Imperial and Royal Fleet. Approaches had already been made to the Marine Ministry in Berlin to see whether I might be granted a derogation to serve in the Imperial German Navy. However, once my father had got talking with Linienschiffsleutnant Fritsch, who was with the torpedo-boat flotilla at Lussin, he started to come round to the view that the Austro-Hungarian fleet might not be quite such a bad idea after all. Like my father, Fritsch was an ardent German nationalist – he later became a prominent Austrian Nazi. But he assured my father that once the old Emperor was dead and Franz Ferdinand took the throne, Germany and Austria would swiftly be merged into a unitary state – whereupon the erstwhile k. u. k. Kriegsmarine in which he was serving would become the Mediterranean division of the German High Seas Fleet: a navy which would soon be powerful enough to challenge Britain and the United States together. Such a navy, he said, might be well worth belonging to. This chance conversation bore fruit the following year when my petition to become one of Kaiser Wilhelm's naval cadets was rejected out of hand. The result was an application for me to take the 1900 examinations to enter the Imperial and Royal Marine Academy in Fiume.

By this time my brother and I were pupils at the Kronprinz Erzherzog Rudolfs Gymnasium in Hirschendorf. It was a dismal place. Even the name was like a funeral bell, commemorating as it did the Emperor's poor half-mad son who had shot his girl-friend and then himself in the hunting lodge at Mayerling. His requiem mass in the parish church of St Johann Nepomuk had been the very first public occasion that I could recall. I was not quite three years old at the time, but my father was a prominent civil servant so we had to attend, along with all the other local dignitaries and their families. I can still remember the candles and the incense and the tolling of the bells – but not (since I was too young to understand) the impact on those within earshot of our nursemaid Hanuška's loud whisper to her own children to sit up and pay attention because it wasn't every day that you saw the church putting on full canonicals to honour a murderer and suicide.

If the Kronprinz Rudolfs Gymnasium was as uninviting a place as its name suggested, the programme of studies offered in this drab, cold, prison-like building was unquestionably thorough, both in concept and in application. My performance in mathematics and the sciences was judged to be more than adequate to get me through the Marine Academy entrance examinations, even though these were said to be formidably tough. The only thing likely to give me any trouble was English: a compulsory subject for all aspiring cadets and one that, sadly, was not taught to a high standard at the Kronprinz Rudolf or anywhere else in northern Moravia. In the end my father solved the problem by engaging for my brother and me the services of a resident tutor in English: a Miss Kathleen Docherty from County Cork, an itinerant Irish piano tutor and femme fatale who had recently been cast off – though naturally we boys were told nothing of this – as the Prince von und zu Regnitz's mistress. She was a woman of powerful character, with a violent and unpredictable temper which I now suspect may have been a symptom of latent syphilis.

But whatever her mental instability she was an extraordinarily effective teacher of English. When I finally sat the hour-long oral examination in English in Vienna in the early summer of 1900 I passed out with the highest marks in my year. One of the examining board was a real, live, tweed-clad Englishman, the first I had ever met. He said very little, but smiled a good deal and seemed to be enjoying some private joke. It was only later that I learnt that this was the legendary Rear-Admiral Lord Charles Beresford, C-in-C Mediterranean Fleet, whose ship was visiting Fiume and who was in Vienna for a few days' leave. The Admiral – himself an Irish Protestant – had many friends in the Austrian fleet and had kindly accepted an invitation to sit on the examining board. I was told later that his remarks upon me included the comment: 'Although an exceptionally able candidate as regards fluency and grasp of English idiom, this young man is the unfortunate possessor of an Irish accent so thick that a spoon might well be stood up in it. He must take urgent steps to rid himself of it, and should also be made aware that the use of music-hall Irish expressions like "sure and it's . . ." to begin sentences and ". . . at all" to conclude them will assuredly make him a laughing stock in every wardroom in the fleet.'

At last the letter arrived to inform me that I was among the forty candidates – out of several hundred – to have been selected for admission to the k. u. k. Marine Akademie with the rank of Zögling: something rather above a mere pupil but something slightly less than a cadet. My course would last from September 1900 to June 1904 and upon successful completion I would be able to enter the Imperial and Royal Austro-Hungarian Navy as a Seekadett: about the same status as one of your midshipmen. My life as a seafarer was about to begin. The necessary items of clothing were bought or made for me, the necessary textbooks were ordered from Herr Zinower, my trunk was packed and a railway ticket was booked for Fiume: a two-day journey which would include an overnight stay with my Aunt Aleksia in Vienna. I was about to embark upon the eighty-six-year voyage which brought me through two world wars to die here alone in exile on the outer rim of Europe. All I can say is that on balance I think it was worth it. After all, I could have achieved exactly the same outcome by being a local veterinary inspector and not had nearly so much diversion on the way.

3

MARINE ACADEMY

As I first saw it that September morning, arriving by fiacre from Fiume railway station, the Imperial and Royal Marine Academy was something of a disappointment. Perhaps I had expected it to be encrusted with a riot of stone tritons blowing conch-shells; dolphins and voluptuous mermaids writhing amid a petrified tangle of anchors and cordage like that gloriously improbable piece of statuary 'Austria Ruling the Sea' which I had seen the previous evening on the Michaelerplatz in Vienna. In the event though, what confronted me at the top of the steep driveway, above the laurel bushes, was a large, plain, rather blank-looking building constructed in an economy version of that nondescript style -- known I believe as 'neo-Moorish' -- which the Habsburg Monarchy favoured for barracks and military academies. Apart from size, the only difference from our barracks in Hirschendorf was that, since this was the Mediterranean, the brickwork was covered in stucco and the windows had slatted wooden sunblinds. Likewise the only outward token of its naval purpose, apart from the red-white-red ensign flying above it and the bluejackets standing sentry at the gate, was an inscription over the door: K.U.K. MARINE AKADEMIE: CS. ÉS KIR. TENGERÉSZETI AKADEMIA; and the fact that the imperial coat of arms was supported on each side by the winged lions of St Mark, since when the Academy was set up in 1857 Venice had still been an Austrian city.

My trunk was collected by a surly naval pensioner with a barrow, and I shuffled nervously into the doorway. A man in uniform stood there with a clipboard.

'Name?' he barked.

In my confusion I saluted disjointedly with my left hand and stammered, 'Er, Prohaska, Herr Kapitän.'

He looked down the list of names. 'You're late. Get in there with the rest now. Oh, and don't keep saluting me; I'm a civilian official.'

I entered the dark, echoing entrance hall to find myself among thirty or so other embarrassed-looking youths. All things considered, we had a good deal to be embarrassed about that first morning, because we had been instructed to arrive wearing not our walking-out uniform, which looked quite tolerable – peaked cap with double-breasted blue jacket and white duck trousers in summer – but the everyday working dress prescribed for cadets of the Marine Academy. And this simply had to be seen to be believed. In later years, as I came to understand the characteristic k.u.k. way of doing things, it dawned upon me that our Tagesanzug was the outcome of two official committees being unable to agree on a design. As it was, the result was quite preposterous even to those who had spent their entire lives in a country that swarmed with fanciful uniforms. The headgear was the standard naval rating's peakless cap, with a gilt-and-lacquer rosette bearing the FJI monogram and a cap ribbon with the words K.U.K. MARINE ACADEMIE embroidered in gold thread. So far so good: it was lower down that the trouble began. The rest of the outfit consisted of a seaman's jersey with square-rig collar and lanyard, blue serge trousers (white duck from April to October) – and inside the jersey – perhaps as a token of our future officer status – a stiff white shirtfront and black bow-tie. The over-all effect was quite ludicrous: rather as if someone had been asked to a party, was unsure whether the invitation specified fancy costume or evening dress, and had decided to play safe by wearing both. I wore that outfit for a large portion of the next four years, but at the end it looked no less absurd to me than it had done at the beginning. I believe that just before the First World War a Bosnian Muslim cadet was admitted to the Marine Academy and out of respect for his religious traditions was permitted to wear the fez with his uniform instead of the sailor's cap.

I never saw it myself, but I imagine that the result must have been worth travelling far and paying a great deal to see.

We shuffled nervously about the main hall, waiting for the welcoming address from the commanding officer. Most of my fellow-entrants ignored me, but as I was queuing up to collect some forms from a desk I was jostled by another lad. He was a large, sturdy, hearty-looking youth with black curly hair and a dark complexion. He had a breezy, cheerful air about him; but I knew from experience that such people often turned out to be the class bully. I had never suffered much from the oppression of my fellows while at the Kronprinz Rudolfs Gymnasium, despite having a Czech name and appearance in a largely German-speaking school. But there I had my elder brother to give moral and physical support. Here in Fiume I was a very long way from home and completely on my own. A sudden pang of fear gripped me. Was this such a good idea after all? The stranger surveyed me for some time – then extended a hand. He spoke with what I could now recognise as a rather well-bred Viennese accent.

'My name's Max Gauss. What's yours?'

And thus began a friendship which, though it was suddenly cut short seven years later by a duellist's pistol bullet, remains one of the most enduring of my life. Gauss, it turned out, was almost the same age as myself, all but a few days, and was the third son of a wealthy Viennese Jewish advocate. Jews had always been depicted to me as a pallid, hypochondriacal tribe of flat-footed shirkers, an indoor people even by Austrian standards. But Gauss was quite unrecognisable in that mould: more Spanish or Italian than anything else in appearance, and an active, robust, enterprising sort of lad with a relish for reckless adventures; a predilection which, sad to say, would be his undoing when transferred from the upper rigging of sailing ships to the boudoirs of married women. I learnt later that this was a family trait. His elder brothers were both doctors, and while at medical school in Vienna in the late 1890s had become very tired of being jostled and insulted by aristocratic louts from the Pan-German drinking and duelling clubs, the Burschenschaften, who used to make a habit of forcing unpopular fellow-students into duels and then killing them. They had both applied themselves to the study of fencing, and after six months or so had made themselves such lethal swordsmen that in less than a fortnight they had accounted between them for five or six Burschen. In the end the student clubs had been able to stop the carnage only by issuing a hasty decree that, since Jews were creatures beneath contempt and incapable of honour, no duels must in future be fought with them.

We shook hands, and I introduced myself as Otto Prohaska: I had already found it advisable to contract the Czech-sounding 'Ottokar' into something more Germanic. Then Gauss announced: 'Here, Prohaska, there's someone else you ought to meet. Sandro!' He turned, and hailed a lanky, thin, rather leptic-looking boy gazing absent-mindedly out of the window. He turned towards us and regarded us vaguely for some moments, rather as if he had wandered into this gathering by mistake and now realised that he ought to be somewhere else. This was Alessandro Ubaldini, Freiherr von Topolizza, a native of Ragusa – or Dubrovnik as I think they call it nowadays – and heir to one of the most ancient of the Dalmatian seafaring dynasties. His grandfather had served with the Archduke Friedrich at the storming of St Jean d'Acre in 1840, and his father – now dead – had won the Order of Leopold for conspicuous gallantry at Lissa in 1866, when the old wooden battleship *Kaiser* had survived an exchange of broadsides with one Italian ironclad and then sailed on to ram another. Though with a lineage like that Ubaldini should have had every reason to set himself above the rest of his fellow-cadets, he was in fact the very soul of modesty, and only used his air of patrician vagueness in order to irritate our instructors. From that day on, Gauss, Ubaldini and I always went around together, knowing that pure joy of comradely irresponsibility at the only time when one can truly experience it: in youth, before the accummulation of gold braid and the cares that go with it start to drag us down towards our graves.

The mob of cadets was called to order by a shout from a warrant officer. We formed up into an irregular, untidy square and tried to stand to attention as a short, peppery-looking man strode into the hall and stumped up on to the platform, the end of his trailing sword banging the steps on the way. He took off his cap and placed it on the table, then stood with his hands behind his back for a minute or so, surveying his new charges with no very evident satisfaction. I saw that he had a slight nervous tic in one side of his face. This was the Jahrgangsoffizier who would supervise our education over the next four years: Linienschiffsleutnant Ernst Ljubić.

'Cadets of the 1900 intake,' he said at last, 'when I look at you assembled here I realise that it is indeed the year of Our Lord one thousand nine hundred; that we are now only a century away from the millennium, and that mankind is fast falling into that state of degeneracy foretold in the Book of Revelation, the prophecies of Daniel and other such parts of Holy Scripture. But there: I shall not live to see the end of the world, and in the mean time it is my sworn duty as a sea-officer of the Noble House of Austria to make the best possible approximations to sea-officers that I can manage even out of such a miserable rabble as yourselves. And sea-officers you will become, or die in the attempt! Always remember, cadets of the 1900 year, that our philosophy of training is a simple one: it must be so arduous that, if and when hostilities should come, you will look upon war as a pleasant relaxation!'

Linien-schiffsleutnant Ljubić and the k.u.k. Marine Akademie were as good as their word. It was intensely rigorous training, and none of it worse than that first term, as the dark winter mornings and early winter evenings set in. The Austro-Hungarian Navy was always too short of money to train enough officers even for its own not very great needs, so it had long since decided that what the sea-officer corps lacked in numbers it would make up for by its high quality, even if this meant cramming us with knowledge like Strassburg geese and training us from before dawn until long after dusk each day, until we were wobbling at the knees and our eyeballs dropping out from sheer exhaustion. We started out with forty cadets in my intake, and by Christmas the number had dropped to thirty-four. Three had simply left, unable to stand the pace; one had been thrown out as useless; one had been transferred to continue his studies in the local lunatic asylum; and one had gone feet-first to the cemetery above the city, victim of a brain inflammation. For the survivors it was Auspurren at 5.00 a.m., twenty minutes for breakfast, then study and exercises until the dinner hour, then more study and exercises until supper at 7.00 p.m., then more study until lights-out at 9.30 p.m. There were examinations in all subjects at the end of each term, and anyone failing to reach the pass mark in any one of them would be summarily thrown out: none of the endless repeat-years which were – and I imagine still are – the bane of Central European schooling.

Our programme of studies comprised mathematics, chemistry, physics, German language and literature (since for most of us it was not our mother tongue), English, Serbo-Croat, one other of the Monarchy's languages – I chose Italian – geography, meteorology, naval history, strategy and tactics, naval architecture, ballistics and navigational astronomy; classes in the last subject being conducted usually at about 3.00 a.m. on freezing winter mornings in the Academy's observatory, peering bleary-eyed through the breath-fogged telescope trying to catch Arcturus and Aldebaran as they appeared briefly over the horizon. Practical instruction consisted of seamanship; bends, hitches and splices; signalling; boatwork; coastal navigation; and, in addition to all the foregoing, infantry drill and tactics. Dear God, how did we stand it all? It makes me feel faint to recite it even now, eighty-odd years later.

That was just the formal study programme though: there was also the instruction in social skills to be reckoned with, for we were destined not just to command ships and lead men but also to be officers of the House of Habsburg, sworn servants of Europe's most august ruling family; worthy representatives of our ancient dynasty and tireless upholders of the honour of the Monarchy and its officer corps. This meant that we had to be turned into gentlemen by means of instruction in fencing (at which I was quite good), riding (at which I was rather poor) and above all in social etiquette, since it was still assumed that, if left to their own devices, middle-class boys like myself without an 'Edler' or

'Ritter' in front of their names would infallibly break wind in company or blow their nose on the tablecloth.

The only remotely enjoyable part of all this was the weekly dancing lesson in the main hall, under the needle-sharp eye of Herr Letzenmayer the dancing tutor. Partners were provided for us: girls marched along for the afternoon in crocodile from a nearby convent school. I soon perceived though that the girls did not look forward to the afternoon quite as much as we did, that from their point of view the chance of rubbing themselves up against members of the male sex was largely offset by the fact that we were gauche, hard-up and as generally pushed-around and put-upon as themselves. In those days nice middle-class girls of fifteen or sixteen were within a year or so of marriage and babies, so their beautiful liquid black eyes – most of them were ethnic Italians – were fixed on beaux a good deal more dashing and eligible than a lot of pimply naval cadets in silly uniforms with clumsy provincial accents. All the same I became greatly attached for a while to one girl called (if I remember rightly) Erszi Kethely, the daughter of a Hungarian railway official. She was much less offhand than the rest, and vivacious, mischievous and delightfully pretty into the bargain. To my surprise Erszi quite seemed to like me. I was even guilty of verse, for the first and last time in my life. It was only after six weeks or so of surreptitious squeezes that I overheard two fourth-year cadets talking:

'I hear that la Kethely's getting engaged.'

'Lucky fellow. I hope he doesn't catch anything. Poor old Sarkotić had to place himself in the hands of the surgeon for a month I believe. When that girl gets married half the pox clinics in Fiume are going to go out of business.'

'Did you ever manage it with her?'

'No, worse luck. She charges too much.'

But we were not at the Imperial and Royal Marine Academy in order to perfect our dancing. The serious stuff of our business was to learn to be fighting sailors, and we began this process where seafaring itself began: on a rowing bench, lugging at an oar. Our first vessel was an ancient, massively built twelve-metre barge salvaged from an old ironclad. We would board this uninspiring vessel down at the Molo Valeria below the Academy, and then spend exhausting hours pulling it up and down, up and down the harbour inside the breakwater, among the flotsam and the oil slicks from the refinery. It was heartbreaking toil, designed (I am sure) to crush our spirits so that we could be rebuilt as proper Habsburg naval officers. The barge was a ponderous old tub with benches for twenty rowers – half the year at a time. It weighed four or five tonnes, and the oars themselves were the size of small telegraph poles, so heavy that we adolescents could barely lift them into the rowlocks – which were not pivoting iron crutches but simple square notches cut into the massive gunwales. All things considered, rowing that damned barge around Fiume harbour was a pastime about as pleasurable and satisfying as cutting down an oak tree with a blunt breadknife. The only difference that I could see between us and the galley slaves of past centuries was that we were not actually chained to the benches. No doubt the idea had been considered. But if we had been then it would have given our instructors the bother of unlocking us all after a two-hour stint of rowing so that we could go ashore and limber up with a couple of hours of arms drill on the parade ground. However, just in case any faint element of pleasure should have crept into our rowing – for example when we were coming back to the Molo Valeria with a brisk north-easterly breeze behind us – the ferocious old petty officer who coxswained the boat would normally trail a couple of buckets over the stern to act as drogues.

Once we were judged to be competent oarsmen, we moved on to proper ships: spent eight or nine weeks memorising the spars, rigging and sails of a miniature three-master made from an old ship's boat fitted with wheels so that it could be trundled into the lecture hall for our instruction. That process concluded, it was the real thing at last: learning to work aloft.

I suppose that there were only a few of us who were not trembling inside as we marched down to the Molo Valeria that grey December morning, to where the Academy's sailing tender, the brig S.M.S. *Galatea* was fitting out for the coming season. This was to be it at last, the moment we were most of us dreading however diligently we had practised climbing ropes and bars in the gymnasium. We were now to turn ourselves into circus acrobats in the rigging of a real, full-sized ship. We saw that safety nets had been rigged for us, but even so the *Galatea*'s two masts looked terrifyingly high as we halted below them on the quayside. She was only a little ship with a great deal of canvas to carry, so the whole towering, intricate edifice of wood and cordage seemed much higher than it would have looked aboard a three-master, to a point where the topgallant masts appeared to be touching the low winter clouds. Many of us would have turned and run if naval discipline and the fear of being thought cowards had not kept us in place. In the event however our first harbour drills aloft, though rigorous, were not conducted with homicidal indifference to life and limb: we experienced nothing, at any rate, of the horrors with which the older cadets had sought to terrify us; of bodies being scraped up off the deck planking into a bucket or of some poor trembling young wretch who had never ascended anything more dangerous than a step-ladder in an orchard being called at random from the ranks and told to climb up to the mainmast truck and stand on it gripping the lightning conductor between his knees. We had been expensive to recruit, questions might be asked in the Reichsrat, and in any case the Imperial and Royal Ministry of Finances would soon object to having to fork out for our burial if too many of us fell from aloft. So we started by climbing to the tops, then in the afternoon began to edge gingerly on to the footropes of the lower yards. Next day we went up as far as the cross-trees, and finally we were sent up in parties of four to the royal yards, the ship's uppermost spars, forty metres above the deck and (it seemed) about the thickness of broomhandles. We had a petty officer below us in the top to urge us on in case of any reluctance as we shuffled along the wire footropes, hanging on for dear life and trying not to look down. 'One hand for the Emperor and one for yourself' was the rule urged upon us. We knew perfectly well that at sea, while handling sail, we would need both hands for the job and would have to balance ourselves across the yards as best we could, hanging on by luck and our eyebrows. Even so there was some sense in the maxim. The one indispensable rule for work aloft in a sailing ship was never to let go of one handhold before grasping the next. If one remembered that, then there was no great danger in working among the rigging, however alarming it may have looked from below. The really hazardous place to be aboard a sailing ship in heavy weather was down on deck. For every man killed by falling from aloft a score must have been washed overboard by waves sweeping the deck before they could leap for safety in the shrouds.

It was certainly alarming at first, to perch up there on that slender, shuddering wooden pole the height of a church spire above the deck, the ship below us shrunk to the dimensions of a toy boat in a bathtub. But it was surprising how quickly one got used to it, and how confidence and agility grew to a point where, after three or four days of this, I would obey an order to shin up to the main mast truck with no more trepidation than I would climb an attic ladder at home. Not that all of us were in equal need of such confidence-building though. There were two cadets in our year for whom I did not greatly care, both Croats from the island of Lussin: Ante Tarabochia and Blasius Cattarinić by name. Like my friend Ubaldini, they both came from ancient seafaring families. Their ancestors had been admirals in the galley-fleets of Venice while the Habsburgs were still hard-up squires somewhere in the Rhineland. All their family for generations past had been captains and shipowners, and they themselves had both been born at sea, Cattarinić in a Lussin barque off the coast of Tasmania. They viewed the rest of us with amused contempt as a pack of landsmen pretending to be sailors. Quite early on Tarabochia had dared to correct an instructor on a point of seamanship – and had been vindicated after an appeal to the course tutor. On our first day aloft, out on the main yard, while the rest of us were clutching the jackstay with our knuckles white and trying not to look at the waters of the dock below, Cattarinić, who had been chosen to be earring-man – the one who works at the very tip of the yardarm – had nonchalantly swung his legs up swung his legs up and turned a double somersault around the end of the spar. The result had been an immediate bellow of rage through a speaking trumpet from down on deck.

'That cadet there! Stop playing the fool, damn you, and get back down here on deck this instant, do you hear me?'

Cattarinić glanced below. 'Jawohl, Herr Leutnant.'

And with that, before our horrified gaze, he swung his feet up from the rope on to the yard, stood up and walked along it with his hands in his pockets, odiously confident as a cat on a garden fence, bidding us a casual farewell before swinging himself into the rigging with one hand and sliding down the topmast backstay. The result was two days in the cells for insubordination, but he left us in no doubt afterwards that he considered his little display of prowess to have been well worth the trouble.

What with our copious programme of studies, and our practical instruction, and our tuition in the social graces, it seems scarcely believable that we had any time to ourselves at all. Yet we did get occasional free afternoons during the week, and public holidays, and – usually – Sunday afternoons after mass. One of the most peculiar features of the Marine Academy was that our spare time was completely unsupervised. Discipline was ferociously strict when we were on duty; but when we were not, then within the limitations of military and civil law our guardians cared not a fig or a bone button how we amused ourselves. Dr Arnold of Rugby had never got as far as the Austro-Hungarian Empire, so team games were completely unheard-of – swimming was the only compulsory sport – while as for our moral welfare a thoroughly ancien-régime code of conduct still prevailed. Our main obligation outside the gates of the Academy was to uphold the dignity of the House of Habsburg and its officer corps. We were as yet no more than embryo officers, but each of us wore an implement called the 'Zöglingssäbel' as part of our walking-out dress: a weapon considerably too short to be a sword but still rather too long for a dagger. It was not just for ornament either: we were left in no doubt that we would be expected to use it to avenge any serious insult to the dynasty or the Offizierstand.

Quite how serious would be left to our own judgement and the civil courts to work out: if we failed to punish an affront we could end up in front of a court of honour and be cashiered in disgrace – as happened to a fellow-midshipman in Trieste some years later after a drunkard on a late-night tram had laid hold of his sword. But if we got it wrong then we might find ourselves before a civil court on a charge of murder.

Code of honour aside though, the attitude of our superiors towards our off-duty amusements was – to modern ways of thinking – one of quite hair-raising laxity. Things were not quite as laissez-faire as they had been at the Maria-Theresa Military Academy in Wiener Neustadt about 1850, where one of the regulations had been 'All cadets shall be sober at least one day in each month'. But I well remember that our list of standing instructions pasted up in the entrance hall contained the following items:

§ Cadets are reminded that attentions paid to ladies may not always be reciprocated, but none the less may still lead to complications with husbands and fiancés.

§ Cadets will be liable for the full costs of treatment of diseases contracted while visiting non-approved places of entertainment.

Some of the third- and fourth-year cadets, seventeen- and eighteen-year olds, were very knowledgeable about such non-approved places of entertainment – and also the approved ones. Fiume in those days was a busy city and had plenty of diversions of one sort or another. Quite apart from being the Dual Monarchy's second seaport, with a crowded and dramatically filthy harbour (there was almost no tide this far up the Adriatic), it had the distinction of being the entire coastline of the Kingdom of Hungary: four kilometres of it in all. The city's population was exclusively Italian and Croat, but under the Austro-Hungarian Compromise of 1867 the place had been assigned to Budapest as a 'corpus separatum' of the lands of the Crown of St Stephen, even though the nearest Hungarian territory was several hundred kilometres away by rail across Croatia and Slavonia. The place had been built to look as much like Budapest as possible, and, although in 1900 it contained no Hungarians apart from the Governor and a few hundred officials, the Magyars had already set about Magyarising the city in their own inimitable way: that is to say, gradually making life so difficult for non-Magyars that they would either get fed up and leave, or give in and learn that graceful but fiendishly difficult tongue. Already the city partook of the vibrant, bustling, near-oriental atmosphere that one associated with Budapest: something between Munich and a bazaar in Cairo.

And well it might bustle, because in those days Fiume was a remarkably busy and prosperous port, handling almost the entire sea-borne trade of the Kingdom of Hungary, which ran its own tariff system and which had pumped money into the place for decades past to make it a rival to Trieste. Each year, from about the end of July, the rail wagons would arrive at the quayside and the golden stream of wheat would start to pour into the holds of the waiting ships, flowing out from the vast landed estates of the Hungarian puszta. By August the harbour would be so jam-packed with shipping that one could cross it without getting one's feet wet. This is no idle figure of speech: we tried it once, at Max Gauss's instigation, and did it in under five minutes even if it did mean scrambling perilously along bowsprits in places and swinging ourselves from yardarm to yardarm, pursued across the decks at one point by the bo'sun of a British steamer brandishing a stoker's slice and swearing that he'd 'ave our livers out, so 'e would, cheeky young 'ounds. Then about November the flood of grain would begin to slacken, and its place would be taken by Hungary's other export trade. Day after day we would see them climbing the gangplanks of the steamers moored along the Riva Szapáry: ragged, thin and often barefoot in the drizzle, their few belongings tied in bundles across their shoulders, the surplus rural population of the great Hungarian estates. In those days Hungary was run as a huge outdoor museum of feudalism, its landless labourers more wretched and downtrodden than the

Negro slaves of the Mississippi plantations. The emigrants seemed not to know where they were bound for: Brazil, Canada or Madagascar, it was all one to them so long as they were getting away from the sordid, overcrowded villages of gentry Hungary. The more socially aware of the Hungarian magnates (or so we were told by Magyar fellow-cadets) actually ran emigration agencies to disencumber their estates of surplus human livestock.

We spent the first seven months of our first year at the Marine Academy learning the rudiments of the sailor's trade. In the spring of the year 1901, when the worst of the bora season was over, came our first sailing exercises on the open sea, tacking, beating and wearing up and down the Quarnerolo Gulf in an eight-metre naval cutter with two balanced lugsails, shivering in the chill spray thrown up by the wind off the Velebit Mountains. We also spent time in the local shipyards, learning the fundamentals of ship construction and sweating in the oil- and steam-laden atmosphere of a torpedo-boat's engine room as the Maschinenmeister instructed us in the mysteries of valve rods and exhaust boxes. Then, in May, once the weather had settled, we set off on the adventure most of us had yearned after for so long and spent so much time preparing for: our first voyage out of sight of land.

Our ship for this exercise, a ten-day training cruise in the Quarnerolo, would be the brig S.M.S. *Galatea*, aboard which we had already done our basic sail-drills. She was fitted out now for the new season and would spend the next six months as she had spent every summer for the past three decades, taking parties of forty or so cadets and their instructors out to learn how to handle a real ship on the open sea. We boarded her at eight bells on the morning of 10 May, marching across the cobbles of the Molo Valeria with our sea-bags on our shoulders. We reached the foot of the gangplank, and I paused for an instant to look up at the masts towering above me, with sails bent now to the spars waiting for a wind to fill them. I had by now a sound theoretical knowledge of it all, and knew how to lay aloft and handle sail while moored to the quayside in a calm harbour. But how would I fare on the heaving unruly sea? Had I chosen the right career after all? It was rather like pausing at the end of the high-diving board trying to summon up the nerve to jump. In the end the matter was resolved by a bellow from behind me.

'Look alive there, Prohaska! Stop dreaming about the cabbage-fields you Bohemian clod and get yourself aboard!' A petty officer's boot in the backside propelled me up the gangway and into my new life; into that alien, swaying, tar-reeking wooden shell which would henceforth be my world. An hour later the Fiume waterfront was falling astern as a steam-tug towed us out into the Quarnerolo, hoping to pick up a breeze away from the shadow of Monte Maggiore.

The naval training brig *Galatea* was already an old ship by the time I joined her: built at the Arsenal in Venice in 1845 and kept on in the Navy despite her age on account of her superb sailing qualities. She was a chip of a vessel to be sure, a mere 185 tonnes' displacement and about twenty metres from bow to stern. But her fine, sweet lines and her large spread of canvas made her a formidably fast and weatherly sailor, even if she was now beginning to show her age in the form of leaking seams and crumbling bolts. A vast amount of time and effort aboard wooden sailing warships was devoted to cleaning and painting; not just as a way of keeping their large crews busy but also because wooden vessels with hemp rigging were vulnerable to decay and needed as much attention as a Stradivarius violin to keep them in sailing condition. Most of this attention involved constant, laborious scrubbing and scraping, in effect slowly wearing the ship away. This was tellingly demonstrated to me about six one morning a couple of days out from Fiume as I knelt, bleary-eyed with sleep, pushing and pulling a great block of sandstone to scour my allotted section of quarterdeck. There was a sudden splintering noise – and I found myself staring in disbelief at the large hole through which my holystone had just disappeared. I had finally scoured through the last wafer-thickness of deck planking and the stone had crashed through to the deck below, narrowly missing on the way a warrant officer who now rushed up on deck and proceeded to kick me around for a few minutes on the grounds that I had tried to assassinate him. Later in the day, below decks, I found myself at work scraping layers of old paint off the side-planking for the Carpenter. The incrustation was so thick that the blade of the scaling iron would sink into it a finger's thickness without touching the wood beneath.

The *Galatea* carried a great deal of canvas for such a small vessel: eight square sails on her two masts, plus two jibs and a staysail on the foremast, plus two staysails and a large spanker on the mainmast, plus eight studding sails to be set on sliding booms from the lower yards in light airs. With no auxiliary engine she certainly needed all that lot, because the summer winds in the Adriatic are notoriously fitful. For the first five days or so we had every last pocket handkerchief set, and were constantly on deck bracing the yards round to catch every fickle puff of wind that rippled the glorious sapphire-blue surface of the water. Sometimes we glided along at a couple of knots; more often we sat and drifted with the sails flapping idly, our attendant dolphins gambolling around the bows as if to make fun of our impotence. Half-way through the cruise we were still among the islands – Lussin and Cherso and Pago with their bare limestone screes on the landward side, towards the blasting winter bora, and their grey-green forests of pine dotted with the black spikes of cypress on the seaward shores, sheltered from the mainland wind. It was only on the sixth day out from Fiume that a south-west breeze got up and we began to enjoy some real sailing at last in the open sea to westward of Lussin, bowling along under full canvas as the bow rose and fell, rose and fell through the sparkling cobalt waves. It was at this point, I think, that I finally decided that I rather liked this life after all.

The working day was certainly long: watch-on, watch-off plus all the hours between 5.30 a.m. and 7.30 p.m. when not on watch. Hammocks were slung either on the single, crowded main deck – noisy and disturbed because of the comings and goings of the watch on deck – or (if one was privileged in some way) on the lower deck below, which, though dark and airless, had at least the advantage of being relatively peaceful. Food was of the most basic sort: a half-litre of black coffee and ship's biscuit –

zwieback – for breakfast; dinner an Eintopf – potatoes and salt meat all boiled together in the single cauldron over the brick galley fire beneath the fo'c'sle; and supper that Dalmatian favourite, sardines with oil and sour wine, which we cadets found unspeakably nasty even though the instructors ate it with relish. Food at the Marine Academy was pretty spartan, but at least we ate it at tables with impeccably folded napkins, wineglasses and ornate silver cutlery. Here it was clasp knives and tarry fingers, crowded shoulder to shoulder along the narrow mess-tables – more accurately mess-planks – slung from the low deck beams.

There were thirty-eight cadets aboard: thirty-four from the 1900 year and four from the preceding year's intake to act as Captains of the Tops. There were three officers and eight or so NCOs to act as instructors. Our commander was Korvettenkapitän Ignatz Preradović, Edler von Kaiserhuld: a lean, sallow man in his early fifties with piercing, sunken eyes staring out of a face like a skull; a likeness which he enhanced by shaving his head so that if one looked closely one could see the sutures of the cranial bones beneath the parchment skin. Unmarried and ascetic in his personal habits – no one had ever seen him smile – Preradović was regarded with awe and some fear by those who knew him. A promising early career had been cut short in 1880 by a bullet in the liver, received while storming a village stockade in the mountains above the Gulf of Cattaro after the local tribesmen had raised an insurrection against Austrian rule. With the surgical techniques prevailing in those days it was a wound such as he ought not to have survived. But he did, and after being invalided out of the Austrian service he entered the British merchant navy and rose to become captain of an Australian passenger clipper, the *Guadalquivir* which made several record passages from London to Sydney in the early 1890s. He had rejoined our navy about 1895, but recurring bouts of jaundice had restricted him to training commands. Known throughout the k.u.k. Kriegsmarine as 'Ignatius Loyola', his devotion to the craft of seamanship was little short of fanatical. To him a rope coiled left-handed was a mortal sin, a sail furled lee-clew-first a rank heresy and a fouled anchor a blasphemy against the Holy Ghost. So far as Korvettenkapitän Preradović was concerned, the true habitat of homo sapiens was a wooden hull floating upon salt water, and all the rest – wives, children, agriculture, houses and so forth – were evolutionary mistakes. His first command to us on leaving Fiume, once we had slipped the tug-boat's hawser, was for each of us to come forward to the fo'c'sle rail in turn, draw up a bucket of seawater on a rope and pour it over our heads to signify that we were washing ourselves free of the land and its corrupting influences.

Eccentric though his opinions might have been, old Ignatius Loyola was a remarkably good tutor in seamanship, and had competent officers and NCOs beneath him. Before long we were all scrambling aloft to reef, furl and make sail as though we had never known anything else, the two masts working against one another to see who could get the job done first. Everything aboard the *Galatea* was done by drills; not from operational necessity – drills were quite unknown aboard merchant sailing ships – but rather from the need to keep us from under one another's feet. Compared with merchantmen, sailing men-o'-war had enormous crews, because of the necessity of fighting the ship in action as well as sailing it – and because of the need to have a certain surplus of men to replace the dead and wounded. If the crew were not to be tripping over one another all the time then drills were essential.

My station was the port watch, foretop division, second man out on the starboard topgallant yard: the second highest of the four yards on that mast. It was not a particularly easy station to reach in a hurry because we had to scramble up the topgallant shrouds to the cross-trees, where the ratlines ended, then continue aloft, all six of us, one after the other, by means of a rope ladder after we had let the four royal-yard men go up ahead of us. But at least once we had got there it was a relatively easy sail to work since, unlike the two below it, it had no reef-points to reduce its area if the wind got up. It was either set and sheeted home, or it was lowered to the cross-trees and furled. It was mildly alarming at first, to be lying across the yard on our bellies handing sail with our feet braced out on the footropes behind us as the mast swayed in great slow loops to the motion of the ship. But it was surprising how soon we became accustomed to it. Only Cattarinić and Tarabochia – who worked the royal above us – smiled patronisingly and remarked that we were not doing too badly for a lot of Bohemian ploughboys and yodelling Tyroleans.

The last day of the cruise found us becalmed again in the Morlacca Channel between the mainland coast and the island of Veglia, a few miles north-west of the town of Zengg. The previous day's breeze had dropped and the ship was now rolling slightly on a sea of glassy blue, lifted by a swell so gentle as to be barely perceptible. It was just after dinner. The port watch had spent the morning receiving instruction in naval gunnery, using one of the *Galatea*'s four bronze six-pounder muzzle-loaders, which so far as we could see had hitherto existed only for us to polish them. As a treat Gauss and I had been allowed to fire a blank charge, causing a satisfying 'boom!' and a picturesque squirt of white smoke – and had then been required to spend fifteen minutes of our precious lunch hour scouring out the barrel. We were off-watch now and taking the hour's after-dinner rest prescribed by service regulations. Some lay dozing on the deck planks, others had gone below out of the blazing midday sun to catch up on their sleep. As for me, I was leaning over the port bulwark in the shade of the forecourse, gazing absent-mindedly at the mountains of the mainland coast a couple of miles away. I noticed without attaching any particular importance to it that the Velebit range was wearing a cap of white cloud like a court lackey's wig. I also found it slightly strange that with the sun blazing down and the sails slapping languidly against the masts, the *Galatea*'s three boats had been hoisted in and secured with the gripes: long bandages of canvas which crossed over to hold the boats secure to the iron davits; also that two men should be at the wheel and that the studding sails should have been furled and sent down despite the lack of wind. A faint sense of expectancy seemed to hang in the air, although I could not put my finger on it precisely. Perhaps it was just sun and sea air and lack of sleep, I thought. I turned back to look at the coast once more – and noticed that a curious blurred white line now stretched along it as far as the eye could see in either direction. The line seemed to be moving towards us. At any rate, it had just engulfed a small offshore islet. What on earth could it be? Surely not sea-fog, on a day as fine as this. Suddenly I felt a vague twinge of disquiet. Ought I to shout an alarm? But the look-out – an instructor seaman – had said nothing, and I had no wish to be the laughing-stock of the 1900 Jahrgang for the rest of the academic year: 'the man who thought Venus was a masthead light'. I looked around, and saw that the two helmsman had laid hold of the wheel. Ought I to say something . . . ?

The bora squall hit us like an invisible express train: all the demons in hell galloping on the backs of panthers across the summer sea in a shrieking, howling mob. Within a couple of seconds the *Galatea* was leaning over with the sea pouring in through the gunports as the watch below swarmed up through the hatches in alarm and half-awake cadets slithered across the heeling, spray-scourged deck. Already the petty officers were bawling, 'All hands lay aloft!' above the screaming of the wind. The ship righted herself a little as her inertia was overcome and she began to move through the water, groaning in torment as the wind and spindrift lashed against her canvas. It says a great deal for the little ship's sailing qualities that she began to move without being dismasted. But we had to reduce the press of sail. Without thinking I swung myself up into the weather shrouds and began to climb, pressed flat against the rigging and blasted by the salt spray being driven horizontally across the sea. Somehow I reached the foretop, then the cross-trees. Stop here and wait for the royal-yard men to get aloft, the drill told me. But there was no stopping on the swaying, twisting rope ladder as the press of bodies from below pushed me upwards, and no way of seeing where I was going anyway because of the driving, stinging spray. In the end it was by touch alone that I found my way out on to the yard and began to grapple with the thrashing wet canvas as the men on deck hauled in the buntlines to spill the wind out of the sail. It fought back at us as though a couple of full-grown tigers were rolled up inside it. Above the roar of the wind I heard a cry, and caught a dim glimpse through salt-stung eyes of something falling into the seething white sea below. But there was no time to look or to wonder. Twice the wind snatched the sail from us, and twice we clawed it back until we had the better of it and were able to pass the gaskets around it in an untidy but adequate furl. All the time I had been working on the starboard, low end of the yard as it leant at about forty degrees to the horizontal. It was not until we and the cadets below us had reduced sail that the ship began to heel back towards vertical – though by that time the squall was passing and the press of wind was lessening anyway.

It was only as I was able to see properly and had leisure to think that I noticed something was not quite right. There was no sail above me: I was not on the topgallant yard but on the royal yard above it, which must have been lowered a couple of metres before I reached it. In the confusion and in my inexperience I had gone aloft all right, but not to my proper station. As I edged in along the footrope and prepared to go below the full ghastliness of my situation dawned upon me. I had been absent from my appointed post in an emergency. The bottom dropped out of my stomach as I realised the horrible import of my crime. I, an officer trainee, an aspirant to lead other men in situations such as these, had fallen down on my duty. Perhaps no one had seen... But the Captain of the Foretop was waiting for me as I clambered down.

'Prohaska, you stupid sod, where were you? I'll have you up in front of the Old Man for this!'

I had never realised until then just how much woe can be piled upon a single human head. It was as if all my fifteen years were but milestones along the road leading me towards the pit of scorpions into which I had just fallen, in a single moment of carelessness and indecision. All eyes seemed to be upon me: Prohaska the incompetent; Prohaska the dodger; Prohaska the man who could be absolutely relied upon to let people down; Prohaska the would-be seaman who could not even be trusted to find his way to his allotted station in an emergency, let alone do anything useful when he got there: the lumpen Czech peasant who had aspired to become a sailor when he should have become a minor provincial civil servant. I was a pile of filth, a running sore, a nothing ... We were mustered in the waist for the Captain to address us, now that the wind had passed to leave only a hazy sky and a short, confused swell. But the Captain was delayed a while because something was going on. The boats had been manned and lowered and were criss-crossing the sea to an accompaniment of a great deal of hand-waving and shouting through speaking-trumpets. The delay was ten further minutes for me to savour the exquisite wretchedness of my position; ten minutes before verdict, sentence and execution. I looked at the shot-racks, wondering whether I might break ranks to snatch a cannonball and leap overboard before the petty officers seized me. But before I could act on this resolution the Bo'sun's whistle called us to attention. The Captain would now address us from the roof of the officers' lavatory, his usual rostrum when he wished to speak to us. I tried to make myself as small and unobtrusive as possible, but I sensed that my classmates were eyeing me and licking their lips inwardly in anticipation of the spectacle to come. It was not any particular cruelty on their part or malice towards me: I was liked, and got on very well with most of them. It was rather the detached interest of the spectators at a crucifixion, or of the people who habitually read the divorce and bankruptcy columns in the newspapers: that universal, ghoulish human relish at notable beastliness being inflicted on someone else when it could equally well have been them. There was nothing personal in it, I came to understand later in life; in fact rather a sort of compassion at shared human frailty. But that was little comfort to me now. The worst of all was to see my comrades Gauss and Ubaldini look sorry for me – but still move away from me slightly, as if misfortune were contagious.

The Captain began. 'Cadets of the 1900 year, I will begin my remarks by saying that, over-all, what just took place was not a particularly impressive display of prompt action in an emergency. It was adequate, but no more than adequate to the situation. You took about twice as long over it as trained seamen should, and you wasted a great deal of time fumbling about trying to make neat harbour furls when you should have been concentrating on getting the yards lowered to reduce the windage aloft. Also I have to report that as a result of habitual conceit and carelessness on his part, we are temporarily one man short: Cadet Cattarinić, who disregarded the rule about never letting go of one handhold before taking hold of the next, and has now paid for his negligent bravado with a good ducking. He took a calculated risk it seems. But by the look of it his calculations were not very good . . .' There was a pause for laughter. 'When the boats have fished him out he will be paraded dripping before you as an example of what comes from unseamanlike showing-off. But what shall I say of two others of our number?' He fixed one glowing, madman's eye upon me and I wished for a thunderbolt to consume me. It was the slight pause for effect as the executioner unsheathes his sword to glint in the sun. '. . . Of Cadets Gauss and Prohaska, both of whom are to be congratulated on an exceptionally fine and seamanlike reaction to an emergency; something which has done a little in my eyes to redeem the rest of you.'

Holy Mother of God, was I dreaming this? Surely there must be some mistake . . . ? He went on.

'Cadet Prohaska, although stationed on the fore topgallant yard, made his way aloft to the fore royal yard without being ordered to do so, and Cadet Gauss who followed him aloft took his place. They realised, like the moderately intelligent young men that they are, that the thing to do in a squall is to forget drill evolutions and get aloft as high as possible to take in canvas, thus reducing the ship's turning moment and making it easier for the men below them to douse the sails. So far as I can see they alone among you have grasped what I have been trying to bang into your thick skulls these past ten days: that drills are indeed necessary to sail a warship, but that drills are not everything. They might suffice if we were soldiers and ships sailed on parade grounds. But ships sail the seas, and old Ocean knows nothing of drills. Let me say in conclusion that I am all the more impressed by the action of these two cadets because I understand that both are inlanders, whereas many of the rest of you come from seafaring families. If this is how they react then perhaps in future we should man the Imperial and Royal Fleet exclusively with Czechs and Viennese Jews. That is all that I have to say. You may return now to your duties. Dismiss.'

We dispersed, and I stumbled back to my work in a sort of semi-trance. It was all far too much for my little brain to take in. One moment a shameful defaulter; the next praised as a model cadet and exemplar of the seamanly virtues. My classmates regarded me now with the rueful look of those who consider that one of their number has gained an unfair advantage, not by chance – which might equally well happen to anyone – but by the exercise of personal qualities above the normal. I began to understand for the first time that afternoon that the world's acclaim and the world's condemnation are merely opposite sides of the same counterfeit coin, the one as worthless as the other.

For Max Gauss and me the net outcome of the cruise was a 'most favourable' marking on our personal dossiers. For Cattarinić though, for poor show-off Blasius Cattarinić, it was the rubber stamp DISCHARGED DEAD. His body was washed up a week later on the shore of Lussin Island not a hundred metres from his family home. Gauss, Ubaldini and I were part of the funeral party sent by steamer from Fiume to represent the Marine Academy. When we offered our condolences afterwards to the Dona Carlotta his mother we found her to be sorrowful, but less than broken with grief at her son's loss. We gathered that no male member of the Cattarinić family had died in his bed since 1783, and that any death other than by drowning or powder and shot would have been regarded as deeply dishonourable.

The end of the first year arrived, and Max Gauss and I were invited to spend the summer vacation at the Castello Ubaldini above the village of Topolizza, just outside Ragusa. This was the first time that either of us had visited the southernmost end of Dalmatia, that sun-baked land of limestone and sweet-scented macchia, with its vineyards and its balmy summer nights when the sound of the mandolin echoed through the narrow streets of the towns. It did wonders for my command of Italian – though at the price of stamping it for ever with the winged lion of St

Mark in the shape of that soft, lilting Venetian accent that one heard in those days all the way down the Adriatic shore as far as Corfu. We voyaged out among the islands in Ubaldini's little lug-sailed cutter, we swam and fished for octopus, and we made our way down the coast to explore the majestic fjords of the Gulf of Cattaro. I learnt to smoke, got drunk for the first time on the innocent-looking but powerful Curzola wine, and began to sprout a miserable failed-paintbrush growth which would eventually become a moustache. And I fell disgracefully in love with a cousin of Ubaldini's, a delicious black-eyed little flirt called Margaretta. She took me aside one afternoon during a picnic in an olive grove and allowed me to insert my hand inside the front of her blouse and touch her pert little breasts. She then announced the next day that she intended entering a Carmelite convent: a decision which I hoped had nothing to do with my inexpert fumblings of the previous afternoon. She later became a Mother Superior, I believe, and led a life of such exemplary piety that I understand she has recently been put forward for canonisation. If so, then it is a great pity that I shall not be here to see it and take satisfaction from the knowledge that I am probably the only man living to have groped a saint of the Church.

All in all it was a marvellous summer, the very high point of careless youth. Life was never as blithe again, nor perhaps ever could have been. I suppose it must seem to you now that old Austria at the turn of the century was a doomed empire, slithering helplessly towards catastrophe amid a baleful twilight illuminated by flickerings of lightning. Certainly at the time, people moaned and lamented that there had never been an epoch in the whole of history as awful as the present. But then Central Europeans had always said that and probably still do: 'I tell you these filthy Communists have starved us and reduced us to beggary – here, have another goose leg, your plate's empty.' No, I was around to see the old Danubian Monarchy in its last years, and I do not remember it as having been like that at all. In fact I recall that beneath the quotidian bellyaching there was rather a general mood of optimism. We lived after all in an easygoing, civilised, deeply cultured state which, for all its hidden poverty and oppressions, was still at its frequent best far more charming and gay than anything I have ever encountered since. Much of it was beautiful to look at, it was becoming more prosperous by the year, war was as remote as the planet Mars, and if the nationalities did bicker and snarl at one another there seemed little real malice in it. While I would not go quite so far as to say that only he who knew the ancien régime can ever understand the true sweetness of life, I have to say that an adolescence spent as a naval cadet in the Danubian Monarchy was a wonderful preparation for the trials that lay ahead, laying up a stock of pleasurable memories to tide me though the years that followed. I would often think of those summer days at Topolizza forty years later as I lay in a hut in Buchenwald among the dead and the near-dead, with the typhus lice crawling over me; and somehow it would all seem more bearable. Curiously enough my dreams during the months I spent in that terrible place were nearly always pleasant ones. The nightmares came years later.

4

HARBOUR WATCHES

We returned to the Marine Academy in September 1901 to begin the second year of our studies. Having mastered the basics of seamanship, we would now be initiated into the sacred mysteries of marine navigation. Some of my fellow-cadets found the whole business intensely baffling and (I suspect) never quite grasped it; learning only how to perform a series of actions – much as a parrot will learn a poem or an illiterate will forge a letter – without ever really understanding the sense of what they were doing. But for Gauss and me at least, the business of navigation presented no great conceptual difficulties. Gauss possessed that seemingly native Jewish facility with figures and abstract ideas, while I, though no great mathematician, had taken an interest in the subject for years past and understood the basics quite well before I even started the course. Others might blunder their way through the definitions of great circle and small circle; sensible horizon, visible horizon and rational horizon; observed, apparent and true altitude; might have their ship sailing along the crest of the Andes or through the forests of the Congo basin. But we two hardly ever contrived to put a foot wrong, so that the tutors eventually became accustomed to calling out wearily, 'Gauss' (or 'Prohaska'), 'come up here to the blackboard and show these numbskulls how it should be done.' All ship's officers in those days used to make a great song-and-dance out of navigation, to a degree where, aboard battleships, taking the midday observation on the bridge had become rather like high mass in St Peter's celebrated by the Pope himself, complete with acolytes holding sand-glasses and striking gongs as the sun reached the zenith.

But between ourselves, there is really not a great deal to it except for common sense and careful checking of calculations – and the awareness that one might always be wrong. A sound rule for longevity at sea in those days before RDF and radar was 'Better one good sounding than a dozen dubious estimated positions'. Aboard sailing ships dead reckoning had a way of turning out to be just that.

We also began our sea service in steam vessels that year: first in an old torpedo-boat attached to the school as a tender, then in the spring of 1902 aboard the cruiser *Temesvár* on a fortnight's voyage in the western Mediterranean. For the first time in my life I set foot on foreign soil, on the quayside at Cartagena. I shall never forget that first visit to a foreign port, traipsing in carefully supervised crocodile around the town's ancient monuments and all of us trying to sprout extra sets of eyes and ears to take in the sensations of this exotic new world where people did not have winter-grey Mitteleuropean complexions and wear clothes of loden green. This, we all felt, was what we had joined the Navy for.

When we arrived back from our cruise a War Ministry circular awaited us at the Academy. We were mustered in the main hall and the Kommandant announced to us that, in view of the k.u.k. Kriegsmarine's programme of expansion over the next ten years and the consequent need for junior officers, it had been decided by the naval Commander-in-Chief Rear-Admiral the Freiherr von Spaun, after due consultation with the Ministry of Finances, that on the 1899 Jahrgang's forthcoming ocean cruise in the late summer and autumn, room would also be made for a small number of particularly able cadets from the 1900 intake. There was intense excitement at this news: we all knew that the cadets of the 1899 year would be off in June for a six-month scientific voyage to the South Atlantic. But who would be the lucky ones among our year who would go with them? There would be room only for four second-year cadets. In the end the matter was resolved by the tutors putting forward ten names – mine among them – and then drawing lots. My heart stopped for a few seconds each time a name was drawn out of the Kommandant's cap, up there on the platform that hot June afternoon, then when it was read out the pent-up blood roared in my ears even more loudly than it had that afternoon in the olive grove as I had slid my hand over Signorina Margaretta's delicate little bosom. Max Gauss's name was called, and Tarabochia's, and a little-known cadet called Gumpoldsdorfer. But in the end Ubaldini and I were unlucky: the fourth place was taken by a Croat cadet called Globočnik. The name Otto Prohaska was drawn fifth.

It was a crushing disappointment. But there: the luck of the draw. At least my name had been put forward. And at least, even if we would miss Gauss for six months, Sandro Ubaldini would still be around. Youth is resilient, so I swallowed my disappointment, returned to my studies and after a few days had forgotten all about it.

Until one Sunday afternoon a week or so later. Ubaldini and I had been down to the steamer quay that morning to see Gauss and the other cadets off on their way down to Pola to join their ship. Globočnik had been missing, but this had caused no great consternation. He had been home for the weekend to see his parents who lived near San Pietro and was probably going to catch the train down to Pola. We returned to the Academy, and went exploring in the afternoon. Then at about 6.00 p.m., just after we had arrived back, an orderly stuck his head into our dormitory.

'Cadet Prohaska? Report to the Kommandant's office at once.'

An hour later I was clattering down to the steamer quayside in a fiacre with my hastily packed sea-chest beside me. It appeared that Cadet Globočnik and several other silly young idiots had been scrambling about the previous evening among the limestone rocks near his home and that he had slipped and fallen, breaking his leg, and was now lying encased in plaster in the Ospedale Civico. My name having been drawn fifth, I was reserve cadet and I would now repair with all haste to Pola Naval Dockyard, there to report aboard His Imperial, Royal and Apostolic Majesty's steam corvette *Windischgrätz*, currently preparing to depart on a six-month voyage to the South Atlantic.

Dawn the next morning found me leaning cold and stiff – I had been obliged to buy a ticket at the gangway and travel as a deck passenger – against the rail of the Austro-Lloyd coastal steamer as we puffed past the end of the mole and entered the wide, island-dotted, almost land-locked harbour of Pola, down at the southernmost tip of the Istrian peninsula. I peered into the light early-morning mist with eyes reddened by saloon smoke and lack of sleep. Ah yes, that must be her, riding at anchor off Fort Franz a little apart from the other warships. She could not easily be mistaken. This was 1902 and the vessels of the k.u.k. Kriegsmarine were going over from their nineteenth-century black-white-buff colour scheme – smart but not very practical in a Mediterranean summer – to a more businesslike but still rather unappealing olive-green, like unroasted coffee beans. But the vessel that I was looking at, an elegant three-masted sailing ship, was painted over-all in white. Austria-Hungary had no colonies, so white meant a ship ready to sail on a prolonged cruise in tropical waters. That distant hull would be my home, my world for the next half-year: would bear me across the oceans to who knew what adventures and what strange lands.

I landed at the Molo Elisabeth, collected my sea-chest and self-importantly hailed a fiacre to take me to the Molo Bellona, from whence (I had been told by the steamer's purser) I would be able to find a boat to ferry me across to the *Windischgrätz* lying at anchor. When I got there, there was a minor unpleasantness with the fiacre driver, who tried to over-charge me – and succeeded, since in those days sixteen-year-olds generally lacked the self-assurance to argue the toss with Pola-Italian cab drivers. Then I set out to look for a boat to take me out to my ship.

There was only one boat manned this early in the morning. Its crew of a couple of seedy-looking ratings sat on bollards – old naval cannon sunk muzzle-first into the quayside – and gossiped half-heartedly.

'Er . . . Entschuldigen Sie bitte . . .' I coughed.

One of the sailors turned to look at me. He was swarthy and unshaven, in filthy working rig. For a moment I suspected that perhaps a pair of robbers had stolen Austrian naval uniform to further their crimes.

'Ché?'

'Er, um . . . Scusi, può mi aiutare, per favore?'

'Verzeih – non capisco.' He shrugged his shoulders and turned back to converse with the other man, talking in an argot so dense that it resembled no human tongue, Germanic, Latin or Slav, that I had ever encountered. I persisted in German, which after all was supposed to be the language of our common service.

'Excuse me, I – said – can – you – tell – me – where – to – find – a – boat – to – take – me – to – S.M.S. – *Windischgrätz*?'

He turned back to me, clearly exasperated by these constant interruptions. 'I – say – you – kid, you – go – get – lost – now – leave – us – alone, yes?'

And of course, since I was not yet even a Seekadett, let alone a commissioned officer, he was probably within his rights in speaking to me thus. What should I do? As a putative officer I ought not to take this sort of insolence lying down. But what could I do? If I demanded their names and threatened to report them for insolence (but to whom?), instinct told me that I would be swimming in the harbour before the words were out of my mouth. There was nothing for it but to swallow the insult and wonder whether everyone was going to treat me like this over the next six months.

In the end a passing washerwoman who spoke some German directed me good-naturedly to a battered and rather unsavoury looking eight-metre rowing cutter moored some way along the quay and being loaded with cabbages and sides of beef. This was the morning Proviantboot about to make its rounds delivering the day's fresh provisions to the waiting galley cauldrons aboard the ships at anchor. It was 5.30 a.m. now. There was a sudden puff of white smoke from the harbour flagship, an old wooden frigate. As the boom echoed across the harbour the buglers aboard the ships began to blow 'Tagwache und zum Gebet'. Several thousand men were now groaning in their close-packed hammocks and stirring themselves to turn out on deck at the start of another day. As they did so I was pleading in some desperation with the coxswain of the provisions boat.

'But surely you can take me aboard since you're going there anyway? I'm joining the crew and I'm late already.'

'Not so easy, young sir. We're not supposed to carry passengers. Someone caught anthrax from the meat last year and there was an awful row. And who might you be anyway?'

'Otto Prohaska, second-year cadet at the Imperial and Royal Marine Academy.'

'Where's that then?'

'In Fiume.'

'Never heard of it. And anyway, how do I know you are who you say you are? If you were a stowaway or a spy or something you could land the lot of us in trouble.'

'Oh, please' I begged, almost in tears by now.

'Oh all right then, hop in, but when you get there don't tell anyone we brought you. We'll drop you at the foot of the gangway and you can do your own explaining. Here, let's have your chest.'

It was thus that I embarked on my first ocean voyage, crouched out of sight among bleeding sides of beef and nets of Savoy cabbages, being rowed across the early-morning harbour by four men complaining bitterly to the coxswain about having to lug along some snotty-nosed brat and his box. At last I was pushed out at the foot of the corvette's starboard gangway – the port one was not lowered – with my sea-chest after me. Then the Proviantboot pushed off and made its way forward to hail the officer of the watch and start transferring its stores by means of a net slung from the foresail yardarm. I was left to bump my belongings up the steps to the break in the bulwarks where the gangway led on deck. As I reached the top I paused to wipe my brow and gather breath – it was already getting warm. As I put my handkerchief back in my pocket my cap was almost blown into the water, and me after it, by a roar of anger somewhere between the firing of a cannon and the siren-blast of an ocean liner.

'WHAT THE DEVIL DO YOU THINK YOU'RE DOING HERE, YOU INSUBORDINATE YOUNG SWINE?'

I turned, dazed by the noise, and found myself looking up at a fearsome apparition, like a mustachioed ox walking on its hind legs and crammed into a tar-smeared suit of dungarees. I tried to salute.

'Er . . . excuse me . . . I mean, I obediently report.'

'SHUT UP!' He turned to a couple of equally filthy men who had just sidled up, attracted by the noise. 'It's a funny man we have here; a humorist. Well, take the bastard down below and chuck him in the dark arrest for twenty-four hours. Cadets using the officer's gangway indeed, never heard the like of it . . .' He turned back to look at me, suspicious now. 'Who are you anyway, and how did you get here?'

Without waiting for an answer he reached into his trouser pocket and pulled out a grubby, much-creased sheet of paper. He consulted it, eyeing me as he did so.

'Ah yes, don't tell me: you must be Globočnik.'

'But Herr . . . er . . . I obediently report that I'm not . . .'

'BE QUIET YOU MISERABLE LOUSE! Right, another twenty-four hours for reporting on board late. Away with him, I've got more important things to see to than stupid young sods who can't read a steamer timetable.'

This was my introduction to the *Windischgrätz*'s Bo'sun, Oberstabsbootsman Radko Njegosić. As his two acolytes frogmarched me towards the companionway leading below I had just time enough to see that the ship, so virginally white and swan-like when seen from a distance, was something far short of immaculate when viewed close-up. In fact from what I could see of it the upper deck seemed more like a cross between a farmyard and a building site than the deck of a man-o'-war: planks encrusted in coal-dust and cement; grease, tar and paint lying everywhere in pools and dribbles; fraying pieces of rope, scraps of canvas and carpenter's shavings accumulated in drifts against the bulwarks; workbenches set up and reels of rigging wire blocking every access. Dockyard workers in cloth caps and bowler hats wandered among this chaos, moving at the stately pace common to dockyard workers the world over, so slowly that one had to view them against some fixed object to be sure that they were moving at all. And everywhere unshaven, shabby-looking naval personnel, filthy with rust and soot and red lead, lounged about or carried things around with no apparent guiding purpose. Where was all that clockwork naval precision, that seamanlike smartness and the iron discipline of shipboard life that the instructors had banged on about so endlessly at the Marine Academy? If this was an ocean-going ship as conceived of in the Austro-Hungarian Fleet then I wanted an immediate transfer to the k.u.k. Armee... I was roughly shoved down the hatchway into the echoing, tar-reeking space of the battery deck, then down more steps on to the lower deck, then down another flight into the hold; finally down a dim, dark, cramped passageway which might have been a gallery in a mine for all the light that got through to it, and from the powerful smell of coal-dust that pervaded everything. We were down in the very nethermost bowels of the ship now, lit only by a dim candle-lantern in the passageway trying to spread its light through panes of glass so grimy that they could just as well have been sheets of cardboard. One of my escorts rattled a key in a lock. A ponderous iron-plated door squealed open and I was shoved into a murky recess which seemed to be about the size of a cupboard. But before I could examine it the door banged shut behind me and the key grated in the lock. I was in the dark-arrest, one of a row of cells between the cable tiers and the boiler room, down in the very lowest part of the ship just above the keel.

I have never been prone to claustrophobia, or very frightened of the dark. But here in this dismal little cell, in total darkness, far below the waterline, a sudden wild panic seized me. I banged on the massive door with my fists and shouted that I was innocent; that I was not Globočnik but Prohaska and that I could explain everything if they let me out. I demanded an interview with my divisional officer as laid down by the *K.u.K. Dienstreglement*, Volume 4, paragraph 268. There was no reply, only the noises of the ship above me and the sonorous booming of men working somewhere with riveting hammers, then the clanking of chain around a winch. I fell back, panting with effort. How could they treat me like this? I was a future officer, one of the most able cadets of my year; yet as soon as I put my nose aboard my ship, transported here in a boat full of cabbages, these ruffians laid hold of me like a common criminal and flung me into the ship's prison. Then fear and an overwhelming sense of loneliness took hold of me: a sixteen-year old, far from home, among strangers aboard a strange ship in a port which I had never set eyes upon until that morning, bound soon for lands which I had barely heard of. I was tired after my sleepless journey, and ravenously hungry. I sat down on what seemed to be a wooden bench and cried with vexation, then slumped for a while sunk in dejection. Was the rest of it going to be like this, or worse? Bigger fool me for not having paid more attention to Melville, R. H. Dana and all the other authors who had been trying to tell me that ships were in fact floating jails, manned by the refuse of mankind and ruled by the lash. Why had I not listened to them?

I have no idea how long I sat like that: time seemed to have been shut out of my cell along with the light. But after a while, being naturally of an inquisitive cast of mind, I began to explore my prison. It was about two metres long by a metre across by rather less than two metres high, so far as I could judge. It contained a rough wooden bench which took up about half the deckspace, a tin container of water, and a covered tin pail. It was only as I explored the latter receptacle with my fingertips that I discovered that someone had recently made use of it. Several centuries later there were footsteps in the passage outside. The door opened and a loaf of Kommisbrot was flung in – then the door slammed shut again and was locked before I could explain my innocence. I sat on the bench and gnawed ravenously at the bread, which was still warm from the ship's ovens. But then I thought again. I was in here for two days, and I had no idea when – if at all – the next meal would be. So I ate about a quarter of the loaf and wrapped the remainder in my jacket, then lay down on the bench and tried to get some sleep. But worry about my sea-chest haunted me. If these louts would fling an innocent youth into jail for nothing at all then they would most certainly not hesitate to rifle his belongings.

An indeterminate time later – in fact Wednesday morning at six bells – the door opened and a lantern shone in to reveal me blinking in the light, dishevelled and bleary-eyed. It was two ship's corporals.

'Right young fellow, on your feet and up on deck sharpish. The Bo'sun wants a word with you.'

'Excuse me, could you tell me what has become of my sea-chest? It came aboard with me and I'm afraid my belongings may have been stolen...'

I saw at once that I had said the wrong thing. There was a heavy silence. At last one of the corporals spoke, quietly.

'If you value your front teeth I wouldn't say things like that, my lad. There's no pilfering aboard a decent ship like ours and no one's going to thank you for suggesting there is. Your chest's probably down in the hold. Anyway, up on deck, let's have you.'

I clambered up the companionways with stiff, aching limbs and into the fresh air and soft early sunlight of a June morning. Bo'sun Njegosić was waiting for me on deck, shaved now and in uniform instead of dungarees. The ship was still in a dirty and disordered state, but I saw that during my time below some impression had been made on the chaos. More sailors were aboard now, and the work was proceeding in a more lively and purposeful fashion, to a point where even the dockyard staff were showing a certain animation.

'Good-morning young lad, and how are we today?' He smiled so that the freshly waxed ends of his moustache went up like semaphore arms. I hardly knew how to answer this apparent friendliness, which seemed to me suspiciously like the overture to another ferocious bout of bullyragging. And how was I supposed to address a senior warrant officer? Best to err on the side of politeness, I thought, with a giant like this.

'I most obediently report, Herr Oberstabsbootsmann...' There was a roar of laughter from the bystanders. I turned purple with embarrassment. 'I mean, Herr Bootsmann, very well thank you... Except that I'm not who you think I am. I'm...'

'...The lost Archduke,' someone chipped in, 'stolen from his cradle by gypsies. The heart-shaped birthmark will reveal all.' There was another burst of merriment. Oh God, I thought, why are these ruffians tormenting me? Is this voyage going to be one

73

long Calvary of humiliation and oppression? If it was then I would cut my wrists without further delay.

'No, no,' I spluttered when the laughter had subsided, 'I mean, I'm not Cadet Globočnik. He's in...' I was cut off by a bellow of fury from the Bo'sun.

'What? Not Globočnik? Then you're an impostor, you young hound: a stowaway like as not or a pickpocket evading the police ashore. I'll teach you to try your tricks on us! Over the side with you, and swim back where you came from...' His huge fists seized me by my jacket collar and the seat of my trousers and carried me struggling and screaming towards the rail.

'No! No! Please! I can explain! My name's Prohaska, not Globočnik! Just wait a moment ... Please!'

He dumped me gasping in the scuppers and stood towering over me, massive legs apart and arms folded as he regarded me with one bullock's eye, as if deciding whether or not to crush me beneath his enormous boot like a woodlouse.

'Prohaska, you say?' He reached magisterially into the breast pocket of his jacket and pulled out another sheet of paper, then studied it intently for some time, tracing the words with a forefinger the size of a belaying pin and forming them silently with his lips as he read. It was clear that German was not his mother tongue. 'Aha, I see now,' he said at length, nodding. 'Fair enough.' He tucked the paper back into his pocket. 'All right, Prohaska, get down below and change into your working rig, then back here on deck and go up for'ard to join the other brats. There's plenty for you to do. We're supposed to be sailing in ten days and the old tub still looks like a battlefield.'

'But Herr Bootsmann,' I protested as I stood up and tried to brush myself down, 'I have just been locked up in the dark for two days for something I didn't do. With respect, I feel that I must raise the matter with...'

'Eh? Oh, never mind that. You shouldn't have used the starboard gangway: you ought to know that by now.'

'But there was no other...'

'Makes no difference. And as for the other twenty-four hours, well you can have that gratis. Just put it down on account against your future crimes.'

'But I must protest...'

He laughed, and slapped me genially on the shoulder, almost knocking me off my feet. 'Don't worry yourself about a little thing like that, my son: a sailor who's never been in the lock-up is no sailor. Now, look lively and get to work or I'll send you back there – in irons this time.'

I decided not to argue the matter any further; just got down below, retrieved my sea-chest from the Captain of the Hold and changed into my working rig after finding my way to the grandly named 'Gunroom Annexe' which was to be my home for the rest of the year. In the end an elderly naval pensioner watchman led me there by the light of a hurricane lantern, me dragging my chest along behind me up ladders, down ladders and along narrow, dark, musty-smelling passages.

My first thought when we arrived was that surely there must be some mistake: minus its iron-plated door, the cell from which I had recently emerged would be a palace bedchamber compared with this dismal cubbyhole. We were way down below the water-line on a deck just above the ship's single propeller shaft, where the hull narrowed towards the sternpost so that the chamber was shaped like a truncated wedge. In a pure sailing ship it would have been termed the orlop deck, just above the hold and the ballast; but here aboard this auxiliary steam-ship, with its boilers, engine room and coal bunkers occupying the middle of the vessel below water, it was termed the after platform deck. It was mainly used for stores. The forward platform deck held the cable tiers and sail lockers, and also much of the space for provisions. The after platform was all provision rooms – apart from one which had been cleared to make room for us four: probably because it was too awkward a shape to be much use for storing anything except juvenile bodies. Since the gunroom a deck above had insufficient space for all the 'Marineakademikers' as well as the ship's regular midshipmen, we four 1900 Jahrgang cadets were to be stowed down here. The lowest of the low in the shipboard hierarchy – there would be no boy ratings coming on this voyage

– we had been given the most insalubrious and cramped accommodation this side of the ship's bilges.

About two metres across at its widest by just over two long, the gunroom annexe was not much over a metre and a half high, so that even the shortest of us could not stand up without bending his head below the deck beams. There was no light apart from a smoking candle-lantern, no ventilation and barely enough space to sling four hammocks together. As for furniture, our sea-chests would be chairs, tables, writing desks, wardrobes and dressing tables to us for the duration of the voyage. The only thing present in abundance was a thick, heavy smell compounded of tar, bilgewater, wet rot, grease from the propeller shaft and the many-scented effluvia from the provision barrels being stacked in the compartments around us. Even if I had not known as I stood there that the fish room was next door, I could perfectly well have guessed it. Our quarters for the next six months seemed uninviting enough that morning lying in harbour. But at sea they turned out to be far worse. We were thankful that the ship used her engine so infrequently, because when we were proceeding under steam the vibrations of the propeller shaft made the whole place shake like a cement mixer. Even under sail the constant working of the rudder against its post a few metres abaft made the compartment groan and shudder as if a constant, low-level earthquake were in progress. Water oozed in constantly through the bottom planking so that the chamber was permanently damp and mildewy like an old cellar. But there; youth is hardy, and no one in their right mind ever shipped aboard a sailing warship in expectation of comfort. Our voyage would be largely within tropical latitudes, so we would be on deck for most of the time. Likewise we were assigned to opposite watches – Tarabochia and Gumpoldsdorfer to the port, Gauss and I to the starboard – so there would usually be only two of us sleeping there at any given time. In a perverse sort of way I think that we gradually became rather proud of our cramped, gloomy, evil-smelling accommodation and would have resisted any proposal to move us anywhere better. After all, only real – how do you say? – 'hard-nut cases' could put up with quarters like that.

I changed into my working rig, folded my best uniform carefully and packed it away in my chest. Then I scrambled up towards the light, trusting to instinct to guide me up the right ladders. A few minutes later I had the satisfaction of seeing Gauss, Tarabochia and Gumpoldsdorfer pause suddenly in their work, scaling rust from a ventilator by the funnel, and stand staring open-mouthed as I sauntered towards them, whistling nonchalantly and with my hands in my pockets.

'Ciao, Burschen, wie geht's?'

'Prohaska ... Where the devil have you sprung from ...?'

'As you see, the Navy decided that it couldn't manage without me after all. The Commander-in-Chief sent his yacht up to Fiume specially to collect me. They chucked me into the cells for two days when I came aboard, but that was because they thought I was a Russian secret agent. In fact I understand ...'

'PROHASKA, YOU IDLE BASTARD! GET YOURSELF A HAMMER AND START CHIPPING RUST WITH THE OTHERS! MAUL HALTEN UND WEITER DIENEN!' It was Bo'sun Njegosić, in the main top above us. I thought it best to seize a hammer as instructed and get to work. Explanations could wait until dinner.

For the next ten days the *Windischgrätz* was an ant-heap of activity as the crew came aboard and the dockyard workers were chivvied and browbeaten into some semblance of activity after months of indolence. Before long the upper deck was like a country fairground, thronged with men from before dawn to long after midnight, working by the light of kerosene lamps as the cockchafers droned around the decks, attracted from the pinewoods ashore. Everything was done manually – 'Armstrong's Patent' as it was called in the British service. The ship possessed not a single steam-winch or donkey engine, so for entire mornings scores of men hauled away at ropes to sway the yards aloft into the slings – the lower ones were iron tubes and weighed several tonnes each – and rigged gantlines to send up the sails: great off-white worms of canvas brought up from the sail lockers below by processions of twenty or thirty men at a time, like

Chinese New Year dragons. Men traipsed around the capstan for hours on end as though in the grip of some melancholic obsession. Meals were hasty affairs of bread and tinned meat consumed sitting around the deck with hands foul with tar and paint, nails blunted and torn by sail canvas and harsh new rope.

We four second-year cadets were fortunate enough to avoid most of this toil and confusion. Being not yet fully grown, it was felt that the muscle power we could contribute when tailed on to a halyard was probably not worth the space we took up. So we were assigned to a relatively easy number, rowing the captain's four-oared gig to run passengers and messages between ship and shore. This was strenuous enough work to be sure: I should think that we rowed a good twenty or thirty miles each day, and when we were not rowing we had to sit out in the open, rain or shine, moored to the Molo Bellona awaiting orders. There was certainly no shortage of work running errands: the Captain and most of the officers were still berthed ashore, in the Marine Casino and around the town, and there was no telephone line rigged to the ship. We were at work from just after 6.00 in the morning to well after 11.00 at night, delivering messages around the Naval Dockyard and to the Marine High Command building, and to the ordnance depot and the victualling establishment on the Via Aurisia. More than once we were required to ferry lady passengers across to the ship late in the evening, and then back again next morning at first light before the Port-Admiral was up and about. We were required not to ask questions about these visits, but would not have done so anyway, since the ladies in question were invariably charming, tipped us generously and sometimes gave us a kiss each before they bustled ashore.

It was a curious sort of town, Pola: created by and exclusively for the Imperial and Royal Fleet. Stuck at the tip of the Istrian peninsula, down at the very end of nowhere, it had been the ultimate back of furthest beyond until the late 1840s: a torpid malarial fishing hamlet visited only by the occasional antiquarian come to view its immense Roman amphitheatre – bigger than the Coliseum – and the other mementos from its far-distant days of glory as the city of Pietà Julia. But despite its remoteness the place did unquestionably have a magnificent natural harbour: sprinkled with islands, surrounded by low, wooded hills and accessible from the sea only by a single narrow inlet. The Austrian Navy was looking for a more secure base after the events of 1848, when the insurgents in Venice had captured about two-thirds of the fleet in harbour, so the War Ministry had set to work in 1850 to turn Pola into the Monarchy's principal naval base.

It must have been a frightful dump of a place in those early days, before the railway branch-line came down from Divacca: a harbour, ships, a lot of half-constructed dockyard buildings – and very little else except sun, limestone and fever. The Polesaners were a surly lot by all accounts, in their baggy red breeches and pillbox hats. Half-witted from inbreeding and malaria, they spoke an opaque dialect that some scholars said was Italian corrupted by Croat, and others Croat corrupted by Italian. Even as late as 1870 (naval pensioners used to tell us) a dose of fever was the usual consequence of a stroll ashore among the pinewoods. The chief diversion for junior naval officers, we were told, was to stand around the town in a ring and all shout suddenly at the top of their voices, to set the donkey population braying in alarm. By 1902 the place had become a great deal more civilised, it is true. The malarial swamps had been drained, piped water had been installed, theatres and coffee-houses and quite decent hotels had been built. The town had two newspapers, one German and one Italian, and thousands of people were now employed in the dockyards and the naval depots scattered around the harbour. There were military-band concerts on Sundays in front of the Roman arch, the Porta Aurea, and a naval officers' suburb had grown up among the orange trees of the Borgo San Policarpo to accommodate wives and families. But it was still a one-company town; a cramped and suffocating little place even by the standards of Old Austria. There was no way out except by the slow, single-track railway line up to Divacca or by coastal steamer to Trieste and Fiume. Although their sole source of income was the k.u.k. Kriegsmarine, the townspeople despised the Navy and referred to us collectively as 'gli Gnocchi' – 'the Dumplings'. Postings changed infrequently, since Austria had no other naval bases to speak of, and promotion was in any case achingly slow in the Habsburg armed forces. People took to drink, seduced one another's wives, ran up gambling debts and shot themselves by way of diversion. Gossip flourished as in no other garrison town of the Danubian Monarchy, to a degree where Pola was known popularly as 'Klatschausen', or 'Tattletown'.

Even the main thoroughfare was a restricted, claustrophobic sort of place. One of the nicest things about the Old Monarchy was that just about every town of any size – even in Poland or Bohemia – had its corso: usually a chestnut-lined promenade where the officers and civil servants would stroll on summer evenings with their ladies on their arms, kissing hands and tipping their hats to other local worthies as they passed. But in Pola the corso was the Via Sergia, a narrow, dark chasm of a street in the town centre, running between high stone house walls like one of the sickly, damp alleyways of Venice. The Via Sergia was suffocating in summer. People had to jostle against one another there at the best of times, and during festivals like the Fasching period just before Ash Wednesday it was scarcely possible to move there for the press of bodies. The best thing about Pola, naval opinion agreed, was the highway leading out of it: the broad, flat, blue one.

One of Pola's principal buildings – in fact just about the only one of any note after the amphitheatre and the Temple of Augustus – was the Marine Casino at the corner of the Arsenalstrasse and the Via Zaro. It was quite a remarkable sort of place in its way: a combined club and hotel for naval officers ashore, with a restaurant, a café, a concert hall, a library, reading rooms and even a skittle alley, as well as noted sub-tropical gardens stocked with all manner of exotic trees and shrubs brought back from distant lands. It was much more impressive than most such officers' clubs in the Danubian Monarchy, receiving a sizeable subsidy from the Ärar each year so that the annual subscription could be kept low – in fact exactly the same sum for a rear-admiral as for a midshipman. The reason for this quite uncharacteristic generosity on the part of the Ministry of Finances was that up until the 1880s Pola had been so isolated from the rest of the world and so utterly devoid of amenities that the casualty rate among junior officers from drink, suicide and syphilis had alarmed even official Austria. Something had to be done to keep the younger men out of gambling dens and bordellos, so in the end the government had splashed out to build the Casino. I was myself destined to spend many happy hours there once I became a commissioned officer. Inside the Casino's doors all forms of naval hierarchy were suspended – saluting and so forth – and, in theory at any rate, the most recently commissioned Seefähnrich was equal to the Commander-in-Chief, constrained only (as the regulations put it) 'by the natural reverence that youth owes to age and experience'. It was certainly no mean or common place: Toscanini and Lehár conducted there, Caruso sang there and James Joyce gave English conversational lessons there for a while in 1905 or thereabouts. I was never one of his pupils, but brother-officers who were said that he was a decent enough sort of fellow but too shy and reserved to be much use as a language tutor.

A lot of our business as errand boys was with the Marine Casino since most of our officers were still lodged there. And it was there, in the breakfast room early one morning, that I had my first encounter with our commander on the forthcoming voyage, Fregattenkapitän Maximillian Slawetz, Freiherr von Löwenhausen. I had been summoned up from the Molo Bellona to carry a message for him, and honestly I think that a first-year seminarist called to an audience with the Pope could scarcely have approached it with more trepidation or shaken more at the knees than I did that morning. For 'der Slawetz' was a living legend within the Austrian fleet. Quite apart from anything else, there were precious few serving officers by 1902 who had ever heard a shot fired in anger. Our last real sea-battle had been in 1866, when we had mopped up the Italian Navy at Lissa, and since then there had been only occasional skirmishes like the Boxer Rising in China. Most of our officers, though professionally able and generally very agreeable people, had suffered the slow change that comes over any armed service after decades of peace: turning almost imperceptibly under the insidious influence of boredom and routine into uniformed civil servants, with wives and children and mortgages and more directly bothered about their pension entitlement than with the prospect of giving their lives for their country. But a few officers had seen action, and it was people like old Slawetz who kept the spirit of aggression and adventure alive.

He had been a young Fregattenleutnant in 1864, during the Danish war, aboard the gunboat *Kranich* in the North Sea. Sent inshore to reconnoitre off the island of Sylt one morning early in May, they had run up against the Danish gunboat *Arethusa* bound on a similar errand. There had ensued an hour-long duel between the two vessels: one in which Slawetz was swiftly promoted to command since the first Danish cannonball had knocked his captain's head off. After the two ships had battered away at one another for forty minutes or so without much result, Slawetz had tried to resolve the matter by ramming and sending over a boarding party. But the Danes were a resolute lot and the boarders were repulsed, so in the end the two much-dilapidated vessels had stood off and limped back into port to land their dead and wounded and prepare to fight again next day. There was fog the next morning when they came out, and the day after that news came that the Danish government had sued for an armistice. Slawetz came out of it with two wounds and the Order of Leopold. He had commanded an armoured frigate very creditably at Lissa two years later, and in 1875 had taken part in an expedition to Novaya Zemlya, nearly dying of starvation and eventually saving his sledge-party by a fifty kilometre forced march across the ice-floes. He had then gone off to Africa on his own account for a few years to explore and fight Arab slave traders around Zanzibar, and after returning to the Imperial and Royal Fleet had devoted himself to hydrography, being personally decorated with the Order of the Maltese Garter by Queen Victoria for his work in recharting the Sunda Strait after the Krakatoa eruption in 1883.

Slawetz was recognised as one of the finest seamen of his generation. And now I was to sail under him on his last ocean voyage before retirement. It was an awesome privilege: rather like having piano lessons with Beethoven. Certainly there could be no mistaking him as he sat there at his table reading the *Giornaletto*: the long, grey, forked Neptune-beard, the wrinkled brown complexion, the aquiline Red Indian chief's nose and the piercing blue-grey eyes. Dressed in rags this man would still have dominated a room full of royalty. His whole being radiated assurance and the habit of command. Saluting was suspended inside the Marine Casino, but still I wondered whether I ought perhaps to approach him on my knees and reverence him. As it was though he just looked up from his newspaper and smiled.

'Yes?'

'Ahmm... er... I most obediently report, Herr Kommandant....'

'Ah yes, you must be the message boy. What's your name, lad?'

'Obediently... I mean... I respectfully... Prohaska, Herr Kommandant... Otto Prohaska... Second-year cadet at the Imperial and Royal Marine Academy.'

'A Czech, are you?'

'I... I most obediently report that... er... yes, Herr Kommandant.'

'Bohemian or Moravian?'

'I most obediently report, Moravian, Herr Kommandant.'

He smiled. 'Good: we are fellow-countrymen then. I was born and brought up in Kremsier. Do you know it at all, by any chance?'

'Obediently report, that not at all, Herr Kommandant.'

He sighed wistfully. 'Well, that makes two of us. I haven't been back there since about 1870 and I doubt whether I'd be able to navigate my way around the place now. First voyage, is it?' I nodded dumbly, too tongue-tied to speak. 'Splendid, no doubt we'll get along well together. I've commanded a good many Czechs in my time and they always make first-class sailors. I dare say we'll turn you into one as well. Now, run along to the Hotel Città di Trieste with this note and hand it to Linienschiffsleutnant Zaleski. Present my compliments and tell him that I wish him to report here within the hour for an officers' conference.'

I found Linienschiffsleutnant Florian Zaleski, Third Officer of

S.M.S. *Windischgrätz*, in his rooms at the Hotel Città di Trieste: a decidedly one-star establishment looking out over the fish market in the square behind the Temple of Augustus. I enquired after Tenente Zaleski in my best Italian from the greasy-looking landlord scratching his belly behind the porter's desk, and was brusquely pointed up the dark stairs to Room 15. I knocked. No reply. I knocked again. Voices within. I knocked a third time, and the door opened to reveal a young woman brushing her long red hair. My eyes bulged and my ears rang to a degree where I was sure that she must be able to hear it as well. She was wearing nothing but a very diaphanous silk nightdress, and her figure beneath it was what would have been described in those days as 'ripe'. This was 1902, when even a glimpse of female ankle was regarded as mildly scandalous. So far my study of the female body had been conducted through the medium of Braille, so to speak, on my dancing partners at the Marine Academy and on Signorina Margaretta the aspirant nun in the olive grove the previous summer. And now this splendid creature stood before me... I gulped for air, blushing a deep plum colour. She smiled, went on brushing and regarded me with one long-lashed eye from between the strands of hair.

'Bitte?'

'I obedient... I mean, I... er... um... I...' The words refused to come out.

She laughed and leant back into the room, her body outlined against the light from the slatted shutters over the window. 'Schatzi, there's a boy to see you. I think he must be from the ship.' There was a muffled voice from within the room, 'Coming, Mitzi, tell him to wait,' and she turned smiling back to me. 'A moment, if you please.'

After a short while 'Schatzi' appeared: collarless, in his shirt-sleeves, with his braces hanging down, with a razor in his hand and with half his face covered in soap suds. This was my first sight of the man who would be my Divisional Officer for the duration of the voyage: commanding officer, instructor, spiritual mentor, moral guardian, father-confessor, banker and physician rolled into one. I knew already that he was a Pole from Wadowice in western Galicia, in his early thirties. But now that I had the chance of meeting him I had to say that he did not look in the least Polish: more Armenian or Turkish, with his hooded black eyes, black moustache and dense black eyebrows set in a smoothly rounded face the colour, shape and texture of a brown egg; certainly more Middle Eastern than Slav anyway. But I suppose that there was nothing too strange in this. Until the end of the eighteenth century southern Poland had shared a frontier with the Ottoman Empire and the Galician gentry had received a strong admixture of invaders, prisoners of war, merchants and settlers granted land by the Polish kings. In those days, there were even some Jewish landed squires around Lemberg; something quite unique in Europe since Jews had everywhere else been forbidden to own land.

Zaleski regarded me with half-closed eyes and took the proferred envelope, receiving my verbal message from the Captain. He nodded curtly.

'Very good then. Which division are you in, young man?'

'I obediently report, starboard watch of the mizzen division, Herr Schiffsleutnant.'

'I see. Well, in that case you'll be seeing a lot of me over the next six months, so watch your step. Abtreten sofort.'

I saluted, and he returned the salute with a glower and a negligent flick of shaving lather. Throughout this interview the delectable Fräulein – at least, I assumed she was Fräulein – Mitzi had been regarding me in amusement, standing behind the lieutenant with her bare arms clasped about his shoulders. As I descended the rickety stairs I wondered to myself whether this was what they had meant at the Marine Academy when they went on about setting a high moral tone for the younger generation of officers.

I was to appreciate over the coming months just how fortunate we were to have Linienschiffsleutnant Zaleski with us aboard the *Windischgrätz*. Despite his rather offhand ways he was regarded throughout the service as a very promising young officer who ought to have made Korvettenkapitän about 1899. I have often noticed that where Nature supplies a deficiency of some quality, she commonly does so in superabundant measure; so that (for instance) women who are given to physical aggression tend to be far more ferocious and violent than men. It was likewise with Zaleski. With the exception of my Aunt Aleksia my Polish gentry relatives had always struck me as being some of the most vapid, futile, aimless, utterly pointless semi-vertebrates that God in his inscrutable wisdom had ever allowed to crawl upon the earth: charming to be sure, and quite well educated, but about as devoid of initiative and purpose as any living creature can be and still manage to get up in the morning. Put the lot of them in a field with a sheep, a knife, a bundle of wood and a box of matches and they would infallibly have died of starvation as they sat there debating what to do. But Florian Zaleski was not at all like that: in fact his ability to size up a situation, decide what to do and act upon it were little short of phenomenal. The only reason that he was with us now, I learnt later, was because of an incident one night during the 1901 summer naval manoeuvres when he had succeeded in torpedoing the Blueland flagship, the old ironclad *Erzherzog Rudolf*, then caused considerable damage to his own torpedo-boat by scraping her over a sand-spit south of Sansego Island while making his escape. The court of enquiry had let him off over the damage to his boat – especially after he had dispensed a month's salary as bribes to local fisherman to perjure themselves that the sand-bar was a shifting feature. But the torpedoing was a more serious matter, since an archduke had been commanding the Blueland fleet. It was an unwritten rule of Habsburg war-games that the side commanded by a member of the Imperial House should always win; and here was this mere lieutenant daring to put a torpedo into his flagship, thereby causing the Archduke (had the torpedo had been a live one) to end up swimming for his noble life among a lowly mob of stokers and mess orderlies. It simply would not do. Zaleski had been unofficially sentenced to sit out the next two years of the stately promotion minuet, and he had elected to spend part of the time away from Pola by volunteering to sail with us aboard the *Windischgrätz*. Before long we had all formed the opinion that Pola's loss was our gain.

5

DISTANT WATERS

We were now five days away from our scheduled date of departure: Sunday, 15 June. The rigging work was complete and four hundred tonnes of coal had been loaded into the ship's bunkers: a filthy task which had lasted two days and which, even though it had been performed by mechanical elevator alongside the coaling wharf, had left the vessel and everything aboard it covered in a thin film of black dust. The ship was now visibly settling lower in the water as stores were loaded for our six-month voyage. Down they went, lowered through the fore- and after-hatches to be carefully stowed in tiers in the hold, all the various delicacies supplied to us by the naval victualling depot on the Via Aurisia: great casks of salt meat, innumerable bags of zwieback, sacks of flour and rice and macaroni and meal and coffee beans, cases of tinned meat, casks of oil and fish and dried fruit; all the items necessary to provide upwards of 350 men with their daily rations as laid down by regulations, for the most part in a tropical climate and aboard a ship without benefit of refrigeration.

If I had been a more experienced seaman and knew what sailing-ship catering was like on a long ocean voyage, a profound melancholy would have come upon me as I followed the Proviantmeister and a civilian auditor around the holds one morning, squeezing our way among the tiers of casks and piles of sacks in that gloomy cyclopean larder, carrying a clipboard and ticking off the items as we made our final check to satisfy the Ärar that none of the Emperor's stores had evaporated during loading.

'Salt beef ten tonnes; salt pork five tonnes; meat preserved fourteen thousand tins; biscuit thirty tonnes; flour ten tonnes;

rice three tonnes; beans five tonnes; dried peas five tonnes; lentils three tonnes; macaroni two tonnes; potatoes fresh five tonnes; meal two tonnes; salt fish dried one tonne; sardines in cask three tonnes; figs dried nine hundred kilograms; raisins dried five hundred kilograms; salt 1,500 kilograms; pepper seventy kilograms; bean coffee unroasted nine hundred kilograms; sugar nine hundred kilograms; olive oil one thousand litres; vinegar one thousand litres – why in God's name do they need so much vinegar? – sauerkraut in cask four hundred kilograms ... Ah, here we are at last: wine forty-five thousand litres; brandy one thousand litres. Prohaska – run up on deck and get the Provost. Tell him we need to unlock the wine room.'

The previous day two lugsailed trabacallos, brightly painted as farm-carts, had lain alongside the *Windischgrätz*. The great oak barrels had been swung aboard by tackles from the yardarm, as reverently as if each had been a casket with the relics of some saint, and had been lowered down the after-hatch to be manhandled aft and bedded down on the iron crutches in the wine room. The Provost brought the keys, and now we entered that holy place, its fragrance like the scents of the Indies after a morning spent among the strong and generally not very agreeable smells pervading the various provision rooms. There they lay on their sides, like Franciscan friars dozing after a good lunch: the great casks of Dalmatian red Patina purchased from a wine merchant in Novigrad who made a speciality of supplying the Navy. To the palate of a wine lover ashore it was cheap, coarse stuff barely fit for disinfecting drains; but for the Austrian sailor of 1902 the daily half-litre wine ration had an almost religious significance as it gurgled into his tin mug. Six months away from home, pitching and rolling among the sleet-swept grey seas of the Southern Ocean, it would remind our men of their far-off sunny homeland and its smells of pine and lavender: liquid essence of Dalmatia. Quite apart from anything else, after a few months at sea it would be the only item of our daily ration that we could possibly look upon with any relish. For the rest, sailing-ship fare was always basic and usually rather nasty. Food at sea was good to the extent that one chewed the stuff and swallowed it without noticing it. If one remarked upon it then this usually meant that it had gone off.

At last, with two days to go, loading of stores was completed. Schiffsreinigung now commenced, scouring and scrubbing and swabbing away the accumulated grime of the dockyard in preparation for our ceremonial departure. It was loathsome work for the most part. We cadets now exchanged scaling hammers and paintbrushes for scrubbing brushes and wire wool, wearing our knees raw as we scraped the ingrained mess of tar and paint off the decks and woodwork. One morning I found myself kneeling on the bridge working on the teak edging with a wire scourer and a bucket of that dreadful liquid known as 'sugi-mugi': a sinister-looking, viscid solution of caustic soda in water. The skin was already peeling off my hands as I ground away at the crust of old, flaking varnish. A huge shadow fell over me. It was Bo'sun Njegosić.

'Having trouble there, lad?'

'Bo'sun, there's something wrong with this stuff.'

'Oh dear, can't have that, can we?' He knelt down beside me. 'What's the matter then – burning your hands, is it?'

'Yes Bo'sun, look . . .' I dripped a little puddle of the fluid on to a bare patch of teak with a stick. We stared intently. After about ten seconds the wood began to change colour from pinkish-grey to a dirty dark brown. Njegosić nodded.

'You're right and all – cat's piss and that's the truth. It ought to be turning it black. Run along to the Painter's stores and tell him to chuck in another ladle of caustic. If the wood starts smouldering then we can always water it down a bit.'

The crew were mostly aboard now, ferried over from the naval barracks ashore by our steam-launch towing cutters full of men and their kitbags. Watch bills were being drawn up as shipboard routine began to form itself like a butterfly inside a chrysalis out of the amorphous toil of all hands at work throughout an eighteen-hour day. We were divided into two watches, port and starboard, of which one would always be on duty and the other off duty each four hours while at sea. The ship was also divided crossways, so to speak, into three divisions: foremast, mainmast and mizzen. All thirty-eight Marine Academy cadets were in the mizzen division under Linienschiffsleutnant Zaleski. Gauss and I were on the starboard watch of the mizzen division while Tarabochia and Gumpoldsdorfer were in the port watch. While not on watch or asleep all cadets would undergo their normal Marine Academy programme of studies. Linienschiffsleutnant Zaleski would give tuition in marine navigation, the Second Officer Linienschiffsleutnant Mikulić would school us in seamanship, while instruction in naval law and administration would be imparted by the First Officer, Korvettenkapitän Count Eugen Festetics von Szentkatolna. We would also receive tuition from time to time in particular subjects from the ship's passengers, her complement of scientists.

They were a distinguished company to be sure, our men of learning, seconded for the voyage from some of Austria-Hungary's most eminent scientific institutions. Chief among them – at any rate in his own estimation – was Professor Karl Skowronek of the University of Vienna's Department of Anthropology, one of the founders of the science of racial genetics and Europe's acknowledged leading authority on craniometry: the science of determining the origin of human populations by means of skull measurement. The Imperial and Royal Geographical Institute had provided Professor Geza Szalai the oceanographer, Dr Franz Pürkler the geologist and Herr Otto Lenart the natural historian. They had each brought their assistants, and also prodigious quantities of scientific apparatus packed in brass-bound boxes and wicker baskets: patent sounding-machines, seawater-collection bottles, specimen boxes, a crate of explosives for rock-blasting, thousands of jars and bottles for preserving finds in alcohol. The scientists were accompanied by an official expedition photographer, Herr Krentz, and a taxidermist, Herr Knedlik. There was also a supernumerary coming along whose exact functions were not clearly defined: a certain k.k. Hofrat Count Gottfried Minatello who (it appeared) was normally an official of the Imperial and Royal Foreign Ministry on the Ballhausplatz. He claimed to be an ethnographer, but it seemed that his functions on this voyage would be more of a diplomatic nature.

The scientists and their retinues arrived alongside, and we did our best to accommodate them as befitted their station in the cabins beneath the poop deck. The only one who caused us any trouble was Professor Skowronek, who had scarcely been aboard a couple of hours before he began to acquire the reputation of a know-all and a compulsive interferer. A tallish, bald, blond-moustached man in his early fifties, he wore even in Pola a pair of tweed breeches, puttees, a Norfolk jacket and a slouch hat which imparted a faintly comical effect when worn with a monocle. He had hardly arrived at the head of the gangway before he began complaining that the cabin space allotted to him was insufficient for his needs and, frankly, an insult to a scientist of his eminence. The Bo'sun demurred politely, saying that space allocations had been agreed weeks beforehand with the institutes concerned. The Professor replied that he would not argue with a ranker, and demanded to see the First Officer since the Captain was not yet aboard. In the end Festetics, always keen to avoid rows, had given way and allowed Professor Skowronek an extra cabin as a workroom – though privately he said that he had no idea why an anthropologist should need a laboratory. Herr Knedlik had been evicted and forced to double up with Herr Krentz down on the lower deck, where he had his darkroom. It turned out that not the least of the Professor's reasons for wanting so much space was that he had brought with him a small armoury of guns: at least four shotguns of various sizes, two light sporting rifles, and a very expensive Mannlicher hunting rifle with telescopic sights, powerful enough to knock over an elephant.

The Captain was piped aboard on the morning of Friday, 13 June, by which time the rest of us were engaged in a final frenzy of holystoning and varnishing. It had been announced that before our departure on the Sunday morning we would be inspected by the doyen of the House of Habsburg, the eighty-nine-year-old Field-Marshal Archduke Leopold Xavier, who had served with Radetzky in 1849. Although extremely short-sighted, the Archduke had been Inspector-General of the Fortress Artillery since about 1850 – which probably did much to explain why the guns installed in Austria's permanent fortifications were a byword for antiquity: some of them still bronze muzzle-loaders even in 1900. He had come to Pola to see that the guns in the fortresses around the naval base were up to scratch as regards obsolescence and, since he would be in town the morning we sailed, had been persuaded to overcome the House of Austria's notorious distrust of saltwater and pay us a visit before we left.

The Captain arrived from the Molo Bellona in his personal gondola. Ours was a German-speaking navy; at least on paper. But it had not always been so. Up until 1850 the language of command at sea had been Italian, and even when I was a cadet many customs still lingered on from the navy of the Venetians. In 1902 there was still a storage hulk rotting away in a corner of Pola Naval Dockyard which had begun its career as a forty-gun frigate under the winged-lion banner of the Most Serene Republic. Quite a number of the older and more conservative staff officers still used gondolas as personal transport in harbour. These were a simplified version of the ones used on the canals of Venice – without the ornate bow-iron – but every bit as cantankerous to steer with a single oar, as I discovered next morning when I was detailed to run the Captain's gondola back to the dockyard so that it could be laid up in the boat store for the duration of the voyage. The thing simply pirouetted around in the middle of the harbour for half an hour or so, with sailors lining the rails to jeer at my discomfiture, until a passing steam pinnace took pity on me and gave me a tow.

We were at work until late on Saturday night putting the finishing touches to our preparations, even sending a couple of men down in the dinghy with rags and bottles of metal polish to burnish up the few centimetres of copper sheathing that still showed above water. The figurehead of Field-Marshal Prince Alfred Windisch-Grätz had received its last licks of paint, the last flecks of gold leaf had been applied to the scrollwork around the ship's name beneath the stern cabin windows, the brasswork had been polished to an insolent glory worthy of a fairground steam-organ, the decks had been holystoned white as a tablecloth, and the lower masts and funnel – the latter now lowered – had been painted to a faultless buff yellow. Every last thing was in place and the ship reeked from stem to stern of carbolic soap and metal polish. We flopped exhausted into our hammocks at midnight – and at 4.00 a.m. were rousted out of them again by the buglers so that we could get ourselves into parade order. The worst-off in this respect were the twenty men of the guard of honour, who had to turn out in best whites, gaiters and the lot to present arms as the Archduke came aboard. Our guest was known to be a fanatic as regards the military dress regulations. In the end the men were dressed by their shipmates like windowdummies in a gent's outfitters, and had to remain standing up throughout the morning to avoid putting creases in their clothing.

At eight bells the ensign was run up at the stern and the ship's band played the 'Gott Erhalte'. We had twenty naval musicians with us for this voyage, for, whatever our shortcomings in the matter of naval technology, no self-respecting Austrian warship could go on an overseas tour and not provide high-quality musical entertainment wherever she called. High mass was celebrated on the quarterdeck at 10.00 a.m. by the ship's chaplain, Marinepfarrer Semmelweiss: attendance obligatory for everyone except the ship's handful of Jews and Protestants. Then at 11.00 a.m. sharp the festivities began.

Since Austria-Hungary had no colonies it was not every day that one of our ships left for distant waters. So in view of this, and since an archduke was visiting Pola, and since it was a Sunday in summer and everyone had the day off anyway, it had been decided to make a gala of the occasion as only Habsburg Austria knew how. By mid-morning the entire town had turned out to watch; apart, that is, from a few dozen Italian irredentists who had ostentatiously organised an outing to Medolino for the day and who had departed early in the morning in ten or so hired fiacres, followed by another twenty or so fiacres full of plainclothes policemen. It was certainly a glorious day: balmy earlysummer weather with a light but steady breeze from the east. By midday the waters of the harbour were crowded with boats of every size and shape: steamers, launches, yachts, rowing boats, canoes, skiffs, lateen-sailed brazzeras and tubby red-sailed trabaccolos flying the red-white-green Austrian merchant flag. The warships lying in harbour were dressed over-all and flying the black-and-yellow double-headed eagle flag of the Imperial House from their mastheads. Their orchestras were standing ready on the quarterdecks, sun gleaming on the brass of their instruments, while the crews were lining the rails in their best whites. At last a gun was fired from the shore to signal that the Archduke's boat had left the Molo Bellona.

'Right, all hands lay aloft and man the yards!' We scrambled into the mizzen shrouds and clambered aloft as we had done several times the day before in practice. Lines had been rigged from the lifts of the yards back in to the masts. With pounding hearts we shuffled out on to the yards, standing on the rolled canvas of the sails with our shoulders resting against the lifelines and one hand grasping the line, the other clutching the jacket sleeve of the man next to us. It was not reassuring, to stand there forty metres above the deck on a swaying, shuddering wooden curtain rod with only a thin rope between us and eternity. We tried not to look down. At last a whistle blew to signify that the Archduke's boat had come into sight. The bands aboard the ships struck up the 'Radetzky March', without which no official celebration in old Austria would have been complete. When it finished the guns boomed out in salute. Nineteen, twenty, twenty-one... At the sound of a whistle from below we let go of the man next to us, took our caps off and waved them three times as we cheered the 'Dreimal Hoch!' Then it was caps back on and edge gingerly back in to the mast to make our way down on deck. By the time the bo'sun's whistles shrilled to welcome our august visitor aboard we were all neatly paraded in the waist.

The Archduke Leopold Xavier was an impressive sight only in so far as it scarcely seemed credible that any living creature could be so decrepit and still move around on its own legs. The heavy white side-whiskers were of the familiar Habsburg pattern; also the protuberant lower lip, which had often caused it to be said among Army officers who had been chiefs of staff to members of the Imperial House that the only military use for an Archduke was to stand him beside one's desk as a pencil holder. What was non-standard were the narrow, rheumy, myopic eyes behind the thick wire-framed pebble glasses. The Archduke was reputed to have been extremely short-sighted even in youth, so what the old fool was like now scarcely bore thinking about: probably as blind as a mole and barely capable of distinguishing night from day. However, short sight or no short sight, he still insisted on inspecting the guard of honour: no mere formality, either, since he knew the *K.u.K. Adjustierungsvorschrift* by heart and regarded even the most hair's-breadth departure from it as equivalent to high treason. He made his way down the line of men, peering closely at each one in turn, snorting and hmmphing in disapproval as he did so. At last he turned to our GDO Korvettenkapitän Count Festetics, standing behind him in gala uniform with drawn sword.

'Herr Graf, why are these men dressed as sailors?'

'Er ... um ... I most obediently report, Your Imperial Highness, that they are dressed as sailors because ... er ... because they are sailors.'

'Eh? Stuff and nonsense: the Navy mutinied back in '48 and was abolished. These men are in fancy dress. Take them down to the cells and lock them up: twenty-five years' hard labour on bread and water in leg-irons for the lot of them. Subversive Italian dogs ...' He turned to the Captain. 'Tell me, Tegethoff, how is Ferdinand Max doing out there in Mexico now they've gone and shot him? Do you like bacon dumplings? Myself I prefer a nightshirt. I knew a man once who said ...' I finally lost track of this conversation as his two ADCs led him away beneath the bridge to inspect the wheel and the steering compasses. Meanwhile the Provost and the ship's corporals had arrived to arrest the guard of honour and take them below. After all, a field-marshal archduke is someone whose orders cannot be lightly ignored. They were kept there until after we had sailed, packed into the lock-ups to standing room only and highly indignant. In the end they could only be pacified by allowing them to clear up the remains of the buffet reception which had been held in the captain's saloon.

By mid-afternoon our illustrious guest had departed and we were making ready to sail. The anchor had been broken out from the bottom and was trailing on the harbour mud, just enough to prevent the ship from drifting in the breeze. There would be no laying out on the yards to loose sail: that had been taken care of already. The sails had been furled not with the usual gaskets – substantial lengths of rope with a toggle and becket at opposite ends – but with parcel twine. A line had been doubled along each yard on top of the furled sail, then rove through a block at the end of each yard to take it down to the deck so that pulling on the line would snap each thread in turn, like the perforations on a postage stamp, and allow the sail to fall. We were ready now, waiting for the order. It came at last.

'Anker auf!' Sixty men started to run around behind the capstan bars to lift the anchor clear of the seabed. The ship's twenty guns boomed out in salute, surrounding us with swirling clouds of dense white smoke.

'Focksegel und Vormarssegel los und bei!' The men forward hauled at the lines and the forecourse and fore topsail came tumbling down to be pressed aback against the mast by the breeze. Slowly at first, the ship's head began to pay off on the port tack.

'Alle Segel los und bei!' We hauled at the lines as the band struck up the 'Prinz Eugen March'. By the time the drifting white smoke had cleared, as if by the wave of a magician's wand, all seventeen sails were set, sheeted home and filling to the breeze as the ship began to move through the water and the anchor rose dripping towards the cathead. The whole performance had lasted perhaps thirty seconds. It was a shameless piece of theatre, the sort of spunyarn trick that could only be practised in a harbour with a steady summer breeze. But it had passed off without a hitch, and we all felt that it had been worth the hours of preparation when we heard the gasps and cries of admiration that went up from the boats gathered about us as the ship emerged from the smoke, heading for the harbour entrance a mile or so away. A paddle tug was standing by to help us out in case we got masked from the breeze in the lee of the Musil promontory, but in the event we were all right. Band still playing, we glided past the end of the mole, crowded now with cheering spectators in their straw boaters and picture-hats. Admission here had been by ticket only, reserved for families and friends of the crew so that they could give us a rousing send-off. We passed within a few metres of them. I saw that one young woman in a pale blue frock was waving and blowing kisses to Linienschiffsleutnant Zaleski standing on the wing of the bridge.

'Auf wiederschauen, Flori!' she cried, 'Arrividerci! See you in six months!' And he waved his cap and blew kisses back to her as we slid by. We were close enough for me to see that whoever she was, she was not Fräulein Mitzi: I knew that not just because the girl had black hair but because Fräulein Mitzi herself was standing a few metres further along the mole, also blowing kisses and waving farewell to the lieutenant. Zaleski spotted them both and managed to get down from the bridge just before they noticed one another. The last I saw of them as the mole fell astern, the two women were deep in conversation.

As we cleared the harbour entrance the guns of Forts Punto Cristo and Maria Theresa thundered in salute, then those of Forts Musil and Stoja and Verudela as we ran down the seaward shore. The last of the booming and cheering and music had not died away until we passed the Cape Porer lighthouse at the very tip of the Istrian peninsula. We had certainly been sent off in style. But still a faint thought crept across my mind like a high summer cloud as the shores of Istria fell astern: this is how a voyage begins; but who can say how and where it will end?

Once the Cape Porer lighthouse had sunk below the horizon we changed into working rig, folded and put away our best uniforms, and very quickly settled into that curious, almost trance-like state that characterises life aboard a sailing warship on a long sea-passage: watch on, watch off; each day beginning at noon and chopped into half-hour segments by the ringing of the ship's bell; half the men below and the other half on deck; each day very much the same as the one before it and the one to follow, except for the slow creep of one's duties around the clock face occasioned by the two two-hour dog watches in the early evening – specially inserted to give an odd number of watches in the day and prevent people going mad from routine. With 356 men closely packed into a wooden hull about seventy metres long by twelve across there could be no privacy and precious little free time, every single minute of the working day being filled with some activity whether necessary or not. In the blue and cloudless weather of a Mediterranean summer the passage of time was marked almost geologically; by such details as the fresh beef running out about the fifth day to be replaced by salt, and by the scientists – who were most of them clearly unused to sea-voyages – emerging from their cabins around the seventh day as they overcame their initial queasiness.

The wind was a steady, fresh north-easterly breeze for most of the time, so we made rapid progress down the Adriatic and then westwards through the Mediterranean. We doubled Cape Santa Maria di Leuca, the tip of the heel of Italy, on the third day out, Cape Passero on the fourth, and Cape Bon, the northernmost point of Africa, on the fifth. I saw none of these headlands, always passing them either at night, or when I was off watch asleep, or too far out to sea to catch sight of them. But I still noted the fact diligently. Common seamen aboard sailing ships, either merchant or naval, usually knew little and cared even less about the ship's position. They took navigation on trust as a mystery revealed only to officers, and so long as the ship eventually reached land without hitting anything then they were pretty well satisfied – in fact always seemed mildly surprised when the ship made port, as if this were some sort of unexpected bonus on top of their pay and rations. But not so we cadets: we were future officers, on this cruise to learn marine navigation, and we would keep ourselves fully briefed in the matter of our progress or our superiors would want to know the reason why.

The day before we sailed the GDO had assembled us for a brief conference in the wardroom. A map of the Atlantic Ocean was unrolled with our intended itinerary marked in blue crayon.

The ship would proceed to Gibraltar, and thence down the coast of West Africa as far as Cape Palmas. We would then cross the Atlantic to visit Pernambuco, at the north-eastern extremity of Brazil, whence we would sail diagonally across the South Atlantic to Cape Town. We would then sail back up the western coast of Africa, across to the Azores to take advantage of the prevailing winds, then back to Gibraltar and home. No precise times could be given for this voyage – sailing ships have destinations, not estimated times of arrival – but it was reckoned that it would take us until about December at the earliest and February at the latest. Naturally, we cadets hoped that it would be the latter since we would then miss most of the spring term at the Marine Academy. During this voyage all cadets would keep a personal diary and logbook of the voyage, paying particular attention to the ship's position at midday each day, meteorological conditions and the distance run in the previous twenty-four hours. Was that clear? It was, and we departed to the Purser's office to collect our nice shining new logbooks, bound in dark-blue oilcloth and provided for us gratis, courtesy of the Ärar.

We reached Gibraltar on 25 June, our tenth day out from Pola. It was good if not outstanding progress: an average of seven knots or so after a spell of calm weather south of the Balearic Islands. But then S.M. Dampfkorvette *Windischgrätz* was scarcely in the ocean-greyhound league. The best speed we ever logged under sail was about eleven knots in the South Atlantic with a Force 5 wind two points abaft the beam. All things considered the ship was not one of the Emperor Franz Joseph's better bargains. The k.u.k. Kriegsmarine was a navy permanently crippled by lack of funds and official interest. Back in the 1860s, under Admiral Tegethoff, the Austrian Navy had been a formidable force. But Tegethoff had died young, his patron the Archduke Ferdinand Max had been shot after trying to make himself Emperor of Mexico, and the fleet had gone into decline under a succession of weak commanders-in-chief. The old Emperor took little interest in the sea – in fact tried to avoid it as much as possible – and, because of the endless quarrels between Vienna and Budapest about the annual defence budgets, the Navy was left with so little money that by the early 1890s it had achieved almost shore-based status for lack of ships. What few vessels it did possess were a collection of obsolete old flat-irons, repeatedly and expensively modernised in a desperate attempt to give the k.u.k. Kriegsmarine at least the semblance of a credible fighting fleet.

The immense difficulty in getting naval estimates through the Imperial Reichsrat meant that a number of subterfuges were used to obtain money. One of these was a device called 'official reconstruction', which meant getting money voted for the repair of an old ship when in fact it would be used to build a new one. The *Windischgrätz* aboard which I was now sailing had been officially reconstructed not once but twice. Like the vampire, she had been born and died several times already. Originally launched at Trieste in 1865, she had been condemned as rotten and broken up in 1879, the engines, frames and fittings being used to build another, broadly similar ship under the same name. When a decade later this ship was found to be rotten too and broken up, quite a lot of her had been used by the Pola Naval Dockyard to construct the third *Windischgrätz*: still officially the same ship as that launched a quarter-century before but in fact rather like the proverbial five-hundred-year-old hatchet which has had three new heads and two new handles.

Despite the fact that she had been modernised somewhat at each reconstruction, the S.M.S. *Windischgrätz* launched in 1892 was a thoroughly obsolete vessel even as a cadet training ship. A standard three-masted wooden frigate of 2130 tonnes (the 'Korvette' rating was misleading since her guns were carried on a covered battery deck), she was equipped with a ponderous old two-cylinder compound steam engine which developed a nominal 1,200 horse power (in fact about half of that by 1902) even though the cylinders were each big enough for a man to stand up in. It drove a clumsy two-bladed propeller five metres in diameter. When not in use the propeller was disconnected from the shaft by a dog-clutch and hoisted by chain tackles into a trunk inside the ship's stern, so that its drag would not affect the ship's handling under sail. Likewise the funnel was telescopic and could be lowered into the deck so as to be out of the way of the sails. The screw was raised and the funnel lowered for most of the time I shipped aboard the *Windischgrätz*. We carried only four hundred tonnes of coal, the crude box-boilers were greedy consumers of fuel and the engine was monstrously inefficient. It had been fitted with a steam superheater about 1894 to try and raise its wretchedly low working pressure, but this was about as much use as fitting an oxygen supercharger to a lawnmower. We used the engine only on the most special of special occasions, for entering or leaving port in a flat calm. Otherwise it was ignored. Proceeding under sail and steam together was not advisable aboard the *Windischgrätz* with anything other than a stern or quartering wind, since otherwise the forces exerted by the sails seemed to counteract those from the propeller and make the ship virtually unsteerable. Coal-smuts spread over everything while we were steaming and the lower sails had to be furled and wrapped in special covers of impregnated canvas to guard them from sparks. All in all, the ship's steam propulsion was not greatly valued – especially by a captain like Slawetz von Löwenhausen, who clearly regarded 'hoisting the iron mainsail' as a personal defeat and a slur upon his professional standing.

There were other little touches of modernity aboard the *Windischgrätz*. There were two electric searchlights for example, one at each end of the bridge. But since the auxiliary engine which drove the dynamo to power these appliances took an hour to raise steam their presence was largely symbolic. The rest of the ship was illuminated by oil lamps and wax candles: the ubiquitous government Apollo brand which had once lit barrack rooms throughout the Old Monarchy but which had since been relegated to sailing ships since nowadays even provincial jails had electric light. There were two torpedo tubes however, on the lower deck at bow and stern and pivoting on a complicated system of sockets and metal slides let into the deck so that they could be brought to bear through ports on either beam. These were quite unimaginably useless for any purpose except training. True, I did carry out a successful torpedo attack myself from a sailing vessel, many years later. But that was in the dark from a smallish boat, using surprise and a considerable helping of good luck – not to speak of a modern torpedo. With the Whitehead 40cm model – effective range about five hundred metres – the chances of a three-masted sailing ship getting near enough for a shot were remote in the extreme.

But then the rest of the armament was not a great deal better, consisting as it did of twenty 15cm Wahrendorf guns firing through ports in each side of the battery deck: breech-loaders to be sure, but of such an antiquated pattern that they might as well have been muzzle-loaders. The twelve amidships were on slide mountings, the other eight mounted on wheeled carriages as at Trafalgar. We drilled diligently enough with them, and polished them lovingly, and carried out the Friday-morning ritual of clearing for action – the evolutions subsumed in the order 'Klarschiff zum Gefecht', running about with cutlasses and building sharpshooters' nests of sandbags in the fighting tops. But in reality it was pure pantomime in the year 1902, when battleship guns already had a range of twenty kilometres, when the first submarines were taking to the water and when the first aeroplane flight was only a matter of months away.

Virtually useless as a fighting ship, S.M.S. *Windischgrätz* was none too brilliant as a sailing vessel either. The two successive rebuildings had transferred rot spores from one ship to the next. Also the hull had been lengthened on each occasion to accommodate new boilers, and the scantlings were now too light, with the result that the hull worked constantly in any sort of a sea, making pumping out the bilge a twice-daily instead of a daily chore as it would have been aboard a more soundly built vessel. There were two knees down in our dark little cubbyhole above the propeller shaft: massive L-shaped brackets of grown oak used to connect the frame timbers to beams beneath the deck. One of these used to gape open from the floor as the ship rolled, then close, then open again like the yawning of a crocodile. It worried us a good deal during our first few days out on the Atlantic swell, but after we had brought the Carpenter down to look and he had boxed our ears for us we concluded that there was probably no harm in it. Max Gauss said anyway that he thought he remembered reading somewhere that eighteenth-century pirates used to remove some of the knees from their ships to make them more flexible and faster in a seaway. The rest of us thought it best for our peace of mind to believe him.

Work aboard the ship was hard. Sailing men-o'-war had abundant muscle power because of their large crews, but in consequence everything had been built as clumsy and massive as possible, with not the slightest thought given to labour-saving or economy of operation. For the past half-century merchant sailing ships had been dividing the topsails and topgallant sails in two so as to make sail-handling easier. But we still carried the old-fashioned single-sail versions with rows of reef-points for reducing sail area in a wind: a slow, arduous and often downright dangerous procedure when a gale was blowing. Sailing merchantmen had by now taken to clewing sails up to the yards; that is to say, pulling them straight up to the yards for furling rather like a venetian blind. But we still clewed to the bunt: pulling the two bottom corners of the sail up to the centre of the yard so as to make a great flailing paunch of canvas just where it was most difficult for the men on the yard to get at it. Down on deck the steel windjammers were now making use of modern labour-saving devices like brace winches, jigger capstans and even steam-driven donkey winches to ease the burden of work aboard. But we would have none of it: in fact spurned even simple aids to efficiency like ball-bearing races in the hundreds of blocks in our rigging. Everything was done by brute muscle power, putting sixty men on the capstan to raise anchor and tailing forty or fifty of them on to each brace when we wanted to wear ship. It was the first great illustration in my life of the truth that hard work is not necessarily effective work, and that laziness is one of the great motors of human progress. But that was always the way in the k.u.k. armed forces, and not just aboard its sailing warships: abundant cheap labour and no money. It was often said in officers' messes that if the British Army wanted a hut they just bought one from a civilian supplier for £5 and put a carpenter to work for two days erecting it. If the k.u.k. Armee wanted to achieve the same end they would take two hundred men and twenty horses, fell ten hectares of forest, spend two years sawing the planks and banging the hut together – then find that there was no money left in the cashbox for a door-lock and post a sentry to stop unauthorised persons from entering. The sentry would probably still be there twenty years later, long after the hut had burnt down or been demolished.

I suppose though that a great deal more could not have been expected of our men. This was the first time that I had been able to view an Austro-Hungarian warship's crew at close quarters over a long period, and the experience was most instructive. It was certainly a very strange navy that we operated there in the old Danubian Monarchy: eleven nationalities and as many languages packed together promiscuously into a single ship and despatched across the oceans as a sort of commercial traveller's sample of the Imperial and Royal Monarchy. All eleven were represented aboard the *Windischgrätz*, and also members of ethnic oddments like the Jews, the Gypsies and the Ladinischers of the South Tyrol who had not quite managed to qualify as separate nations. But if all the peoples of the Monarchy were represented, they were by no means equally represented. The great mass of the lower deck were Croats and Italians from the Dalmatian coast and islands, with a sprinkling of Slovenes from the top end around Trieste and also a few Montenegrin Serbs – Bo'sun Njegosić was one – from around the Gulf of Cattaro down at the extreme southern tip of the Monarchy.

I have often heard the opinion voiced – mainly in England – that some people like the Norwegians and the Danes and (of course) the English are 'natural seafarers', while other more southerly peoples like the Spaniards and Italians are a cowardly rabble who will run for the lifeboats babbling Hail Maries and trampling over women and children at the first sign of a gale. Myself, I think that this is palpable nonsense, and that given good training anyone can become a capable sailor. Quite the best seaman I ever shipped with was a Pole, the child of political exiles, born and brought up in Central Asia about as far from salt water as it is possible to get on this planet. But, having said that, there did seem to be certain areas of Europe in those days that produced large numbers of very able sailors: usually poor, overpopulated, rocky island-coasts like those of Sweden or the west coast of Ireland where an able-bodied young man's only hope of avoiding a life of poverty lay upon the water. And of course Dalmatia, that coastline of a thousand islands with its gnarled olive groves and its poor, stony fields laboriously terraced into the sides of the bare mountains. Forced to the sea by the poverty of the land, the Dalmatians practically spent their lives afloat, able to handle a boat almost as soon as they could walk and usually apprenticed to an uncle or a cousin aboard a sailing vessel from about the age of eight. Seafaring was a very international business in those days – sailors never bothered with passports – and before they were called up to do their four years' service in the Navy many of our men had already served aboard foreign merchant ships: British, German, Scandinavian, Russian, even American. They were a tough lot, our Croats: simple, taciturn and often barely literate; but at the same time sturdy, uncomplaining and remarkably skilful seamen.

As for the rest of the nationalities, they fitted themselves pretty well around the Croat majority. Engine-room crews and the technical branches generally tended to have a majority of Germans and Czechs, the two best-educated peoples of the Monarchy. There were a great many Italians in the electrical branch for some reason, and also a good few Hungarian artillery specialists. But generally the matter of nationality was never too obtrusive aboard our ships, until the last few months of 1918 when the Monarchy was on the point of collapse. As for language, we got by officially in German – though most of it would have been quite unrecognisable to a burgher of Göttingen – and unofficially in a curious patois called 'Marinesprache' or 'lingua di bordo', made up of about equal parts German, Italian and Serbo-Croat. German was only used on state occasions as it were: for giving and acknowledging orders or when superiors were looking. There was an old anecdote in the Navy, I remember, about a Croat sailor who was taking his qualifying examination as a gunner's mate and who had spent days learning the names of the parts on some piece of ship's artillery. He was now being examined by a panel of officers under the eyes of the master gunner, the Geschutzmeister, also a Croat.

'And what is this called?' the Herr Schiffsleutnant had asked, pointing to a component called the 'Backbüchsenpfropf'.

'G'samstmelde, Herr Lejtnaant, daas heisst där Bix-baxen-poff.'

The Geschutzmeister at once dealt him a box around the head. 'Budala! If I've told you once I've told you a hundred times – that isn't the Bix-baxen-poff, it's the Bax-bixen-poff!'

I never did really get to know exactly what our lower deck felt in the innermost recesses of their hearts about being in the Emperor Franz Joseph's navy in general and on this voyage in particular. But since most of them were seamen by trade I doubt whether it made any great odds to them. True, naval pay was meagre and the discipline irksome; but the food was probably more plentiful than aboard a merchant sailing ship and at least no worse in quality, while with our large crew the work was lighter. Also naval vessels put into port more frequently, usually had a doctor aboard, were more competently officered and kept to more regular timetables so that there was no danger – as was often the case aboard merchant sailing ships – of a nine-month voyage stretching to two or three years because the owners had changed their minds about cargoes and ports of destination. Sailing-ship men in those days were a fatalistic lot anyway. To them all ports were much alike, and wages something that accumulated almost by magic in the course of a voyage so that they could be blown in a single night on arrival. I remember how, months later, when we were rolling across the immense wastes of the Southern Ocean several hundred miles from land in any direction, we saw a group of albatrosses sitting in a circle on the great heaving grey waves as calmly as swallows on the telegraph wires. Our petty officer instructor Torpedomeister Kaindel, a Viennese, was leaning against the rail next to me.

'You see those birds there,' he said: 'they sit there like that for a day or so on the ocean, then they get up and fly a thousand miles to sit on some other part of it, exactly like the one they've just left.' The remark might equally well have applied to sailors.

Some believed that albatrosses were the souls of dead seamen: myself I often inclined to the view that seamen were the souls of dead albatrosses.

6

BEYOND THE PILLARS

We dropped anchor at Gibraltar on 25 June for a stay of three days. We were entertained by the Royal Navy, went to a reception at the Governor's residence, were kindly shown around the fortress galleries by a major of the Royal Engineers, climbed to the top of the Rock, bought souvenirs, sent postcards to our families, had ourselves photographed with the Barbary apes and, in a word, did all the things that naval cadets on shore-leave have done ever since there have been shores and naval cadets to take leave on them. Yet it all seemed curiously unreal now: a sort of stage backdrop to our normal existence, as if the scene-shifters would come on in a few minutes and clear it all away to be replaced with a set labelled 'Lisbon' or 'Madeira'. I often noticed that as I got older: how for sailors the only real world becomes their ship. Seamen have the reputation of being incurable wanderers, and perhaps in many cases the desire to travel does lead them – as it led me after all – into that way of life. But they very soon become the most confirmed stay-at-homes. The only difference is that they carry their home about the world with them like a snail's shell, and after a while feel distinctly uncomfortable if they venture far enough inland to be out of sight of its masts.

The Rock of Gibraltar fell astern as we made our way out into the Atlantic, beyond the Pillars of Hercules now. There was a distinct feeling that we had passed beyond the limits of the world as known to the Austrian Habsburgs, out into the great Sea of Darkness so feared by the ancients. We made slow progress for the first few days out of Gibraltar, often propelled more by the current through the Straits than by the wind. But even so the swell beneath the smooth sea was distinctly not that of the Mediterranean: great surging, slow ocean waves several hundred metres from crest to crest and that dark indigo blue that comes from unimaginable depth. Then at last the sails stirred and bellied solid: we had picked up the north-east trade wind – the Passat – and we were off, rounding the westward bulge of Africa about a hundred miles out to sea.

Our only landfall during those days was Madeira, where we lay briefly during a calm one Friday morning. The Captain had decided that, since we were near land and since the place looked uninhabited, we would make a regular jamboree of the weekly 'Klarschiff zum Gefecht' by firing broadsides, sending landing parties ashore and generally looking as if we meant it. I ended up in the ten-metre barge with Torpedomeister Kaindel as coxswain, in gaiters and full equipment – Mannlicher rifle, cutlass, bayonet, entrenching tool and the lot – to carry out a landing and capture a ruined tower standing on a knoll just above the shoreline. We had even taken our Uchatius landing gun with us: a ludicrous little miniature field gun on a wheeled carriage that looked as if it ought to have a cork in the muzzle, secured by a string, or perhaps eject a red flag with the word BANG! on it when fired. As we rested on our oars the *Windischgrätz* fired her first and only broadside of the voyage, shells wobbling and toppling lazily end over end as they emerged from the smoke to splash into the sea some way abeam. When the smoke cleared we heard the buglers aboard sound, not 'Reload and run out' but 'Damage parties on deck' and then 'Man the pumps'. We learnt when we got back aboard that the combined shock of half the ship's guns firing at once had had such an alarming effect on her structure that the Captain had decided not to repeat the experiment.

So the days passed as we sailed on into the tropics, the dolphins frolicking about our bows and flying fish now beginning to flop on to the decks to be caught and taken to the galley. They were not bad fried, I remember: rather like a red mullet. The ship went about her daily routine, we attended our classes when not on watch, and the time went by in well-run tranquillity. The weather was fine, so we spent most of our time on deck. The crew had few off-duty hours: chiefly Sunday afternoons and the evenings between about 7.30 and 9.00 p.m. But it was the recognised custom of the service that these hours could be spent by the off-watch men as they pleased, within the confines of naval regulations. Amusements were simple: chiefly lotto and music. The bandsmen would give a concert on the fo'c'sle deck each evening, weather permitting, and there were also the traditional songs of Dalmatia sung to an accompaniment of mandolin and piano accordion, and Viennese heurige songs. A great favourite among the latter repertoire was the 'Wiener Fiakerlied', which had been made famous a few years before by the comedian Girardi. It must have been strange for the ships that passed us in the evening calms to hear the clotted dialect of Vienna rolling across the Atlantic waves: 'I' hab zwaa harbe Raapen, mei Zeugerl steht am Graben . . .'

It was during these days out in the North Atlantic that we cadets began to follow the lower deck in forming our opinions of the local representatives of Habsburg Austria's twelfth nationality, the Imperial and Royal officer corps. We had fourteen of them aboard in all, or fifteen if one counted Father Semmelweiss. At the top of the pyramid of authority was the Captain, the redoubtable Slawetz von Löwenhausen: a semi-deity residing like the Mikado in his own suite of rooms at the end of the battery deck and only to be seen among the crew at Captain's Divisions on a Sunday morning before mass. Otherwise his domains were the bridge and the poop deck, where by tradition any sailor or junior officer also present had to stand at a respectful distance downwind of him. Such was the way with ship's captains in those days before wireless. Once we were out of port his authority was absolute, short of imposing the death penalty – though in certain closely defined circumstances he could even do that – and his burden of responsibility correspondingly enormous. Slawetz made a habit of dining four days out of seven with his officers and the scientists in the saloon, but he had no need to do so: the custom was that if he so wished he could dine there alone in solitary state every day of the voyage.

Slawetz's second-in-command, the GDO Korvettenkapitän Count Eugen Festetics von Szentkatolna, was one of the Imperial and Royal Navy's few representatives of the Austrian aristocracy. Minor titles – Edlers and Ritters and Freiherrs and so forth – abounded in our navy list, but anyone of the rank of count or above was something of a rarity. Festetics was a true specimen of the Habsburg imperial class, the people who had kept the whole ramshackle state going for three hundred years and who were now quite patently running low on the energy and self-confidence needed for managing empires. His name was Hungarian, but he himself was, like most of his class, devoid of any sort of national tincture: a colourless man from nowhere (Baden-bei-Wien to be precise) with no particular accent and frankly a rather insipid if amiable enough personality. He was generally agreed by the crew to be 'a nice man': courteous, easy-going, considerate of his subordinates' welfare in a rather off-hand sort of way, and scrupulously fair: 'ein echter Gentleman' as we say where I come from, borrowing the word from English since the qualities of decency and fair play are not ones that readily spring to mind in connection with the peoples of the Danubian Basin. A lean, elegant, slightly stooped, somewhat greyhound-like figure in his early fifties, his attachment to seafaring was perhaps questionable. He had served in the Marine Section of the War Ministry in Vienna for much of his career and had spent many years at court as Naval ADC to the Emperor and the ill-fated Archduke Rudolf, a post for which he was well suited by reason of his social connections and his faultless manners. He unquestionably knew a great deal about his job and had a very advanced theoretical grasp of navigation, corresponding on astronomy with several noted scientists of the day. But the suspicion remained that he was really a court-sailor with little instinct for the ocean. Our Captain tacitly recognised as much by converting the post of GDO into a largely administrative one, leaving Festetics in the office for most of the time to deal with the ship's voluminous paperwork, which he himself detested.

This meant that practical running of the ship devolved to the three watch officers, Linienschiffsleutnants Mikulić, Zaleski and Svoboda; each of them assisted by two Fregattenleutnants and a Seefähnrich as a sort of dogsbody and apprentice. For my part I was relieved that the officer of whom I saw most was my divisional commander Linienschiffsleutnant Zaleski: not just because he was reputed to be a good seaman and a fair if rigorous officer, but because the Second Officer Linienschiffsleutnant Demeter Mikulić, commander of the foretop division, was such an unpleasant alternative. We saw Mikulić when he was officer of our watch, and also when he took us cadets for classes in boatwork and anchor-handling, and most of us very soon took a considerable dislike to him. It was not that he was in any way a bad officer – in fact even his bitterest enemies spoke well of his skills as a seaman. It was rather that he seemed altogether too full of himself and correspondingly disdainful of others. A Croat from Spalato, though not a large man he was stocky and quite amazingly strong – I several times saw him tie knots in fingerthick iron bars for amusement. He was also a skilled boxer – and by no means averse to letting his subordinates know it. He had come into the k.u.k. Kriegsmarine not through the Marine Academy, which might have knocked some of the conceit out of him, but as a Seeaspirant at seventeen, after having served for a while in the American merchant service, aboard a sailing ship owned by an emigrant uncle. This had given him not only strongly American-flavoured English but also a voracious appetite for the stories of Francis Bret Harte and Jack London, whom he admired tremendously. Mikulić professed to be a social Darwinist: someone who believed that the fittest will not only survive but actually possess a sort of moral imperative to exterminate the weak. He would very much have liked (we understood) to have been mate of one of the notorious American 'Down-East' clippers, and his main complaint about the *K.u.K. Dienstreglement* with its long list of Draconian punishments for defaulters was not its harshness but rather that it set too many obstacles in the way of Austrian ship's officers exercising discipline Yankee-fashion, with fists and belaying pins over the head. Certainly the results of unofficial discipline à la Mikulić practised on ratings whom he had managed to provoke into insolence were sufficiently terrible to put even a giant like Bo'sun Njegosić in some fear of him. Swabbing the blood off the planks and sweeping up the teeth from the scuppers afterwards, we were thankful that the Imperial and Royal system of discipline, however stupid and pettifogging, at least gave us some protection against people of that stamp.

We cadets certainly needed all the protection we could get, because we were really in rather an invidious position aboard. For most purposes we were the lowest of the low; the youngest members of the crew apart from the ship's cat and subject to every harassment that the Bo'sun and his acolytes cared to pile upon us: run from one end of the ship to the other with rope's ends flicking at us, mastheaded in all weathers for the smallest offence and generally treated as of no consequence whatever. But at the same time we were also scholars required to apply ourselves to our studies for a large part of each day at the 'Borduniversität' on the poop deck, and to comport ourselves at all times like future officers and gentlemen. For the time being, however, the only tokens of our future membership of the Imperial and Royal sea-officer corps were (i) that we were allowed to use one – and only one – of the officers' lavatories under the stern, for which privilege we had to pay by cleaning out all the others; and (ii) that we were admitted to dinner and supper in the captain's saloon – though only in order to wait at table, usually after a hurried wash-down in a bucket on deck at the end of an afternoon spent blacking down the rigging. The Captain was concerned to develop esprit de corps between his officers and the expedition's scientists, and also to instil in us cadets that ethos of comradeship and polite behaviour to be found (he maintained) at its finest in the wardroom of a man-o'-war: a spirit which we were to imbibe by standing against the bulkheads hour after hour, napkins over shoulders, waiting to fill wineglasses and remove plates to the steward's pantry.

Most of the cadets professed to find these social evenings boring in the extreme; but being both of us of a curious disposition, Gauss and I quickly discovered that if we kept our eyes and ears open we could learn a great deal that was interesting and much that was profitable – particularly when retailed to the galley cook next morning. Before long Messrs Gauss and Prohaska were principal suppliers of raw news to that traditional shipboard industry the Galley Telegraph. We soon found that if we doled out our information in a controlled manner, so as to manage the market, and promoted one another's shares by carefully contrived leaks, we could wheedle a great many useful privileges out of 'Schmutzi' Heidl the fat, greasy potentate of the Mannschaftsküche: things like being allowed to dry clothes by the galley range and being permitted to bake horrible sticky compounds of dried figs, molasses and pulverised zwieback.

'Well, young sir, what is it today?'

'We're being diverted to Greenland: it's official. It's the Old Man and the Arctic exploration, you see? We're going to look for the magnetic pole.'

'Horse shit. Who told you that?'

'We got sealed orders at Gibraltar apparently: you can ask Cadet Gauss if you don't believe me. And Herr Schiffsleutnant Svoboda's wife is expecting again.'

'Again? That must be about their seventh and he's only thirty. If you ask me she ought to buy him a fretwork set for when he's home on leave. But . . .' (he lowered his voice), '. . . they had to get married, you know? Don't let on, but they say she's the Archduke Rudolf's illegitimate child, the Old Gentleman's granddaughter. But then Svoboda's not his real name either they reckon . . .'

'Can I leave these socks here to dry?'

'Bugger off out of my galley you insolent young . . . Oh all right, give 'em here then . . .'

And the days passed like dreams. The wind was steady northeast to east-north-east, so we ran before it with yards squared for most of the way, barely needing to trim sail at all apart from 'freshening the nip' – adjusting the ropes around the cleats and belaying pins – at the start of each watch and going aloft to slacken ropes because of the chafe caused by hemp rubbing against canvas in the same place day after day. At nights we greatly preferred to be on Svoboda's or Zaleski's watch. Linienschiffsleutnant Mikulić was a fanatical stickler for seamanlike watchfulness even when there was not the slightest need for it, as there usually was not in this steady, clear, trade-wind weather. He would insist that everyone remained on deck standing for the entire watch. Even so much as leaning against a ventilator would bring a vicious and unexpected kick in the backside. This was a sore trial when there was almost nothing to do except keep lookout and man the wheel. And when he chose to vary this waxwork-like inactivity – talking was strictly forbidden – it would usually be to give us some heartbreakingly pointless and stupid task, like picking old rope to pieces with our nails, or scraping a broomstick into shavings with a piece of broken bottle, or reducing a lump of scrap iron to filings with the aid of a worn-out file. Zaleski and Svoboda were much more sensible about night watches. So long as all the men were at their stations and sentries were posted each hour to wake them up when needed, they had no objections to us bringing blankets on deck and lying down discreetly for a few hours' much-needed sleep beneath the boats or behind coils of rope. Every now and then they would test our readiness by blowing a whistle – whereupon we would all spring up at once like a medieval painting of a cemetery at the Day of Judgement. But otherwise they were not needlessly strict in their understanding of discipline. It was a policy which I always tried to follow myself years later when I was a U-Boat captain in the Great War. No one ever let me down.

We sailed on around the coast of the Sahara, past the Canaries and the Cape Verde Islands, always keeping well out to sea to take full advantage of the winds. Not that the *Windischgrätz* was much of a performer under sail: we usually averaged about six or seven knots over a day's run, even with all canvas set. Square-riggers were always slow with a following wind because the mizzen square sails tended to mask the ones forward, thus obliging us to sail with studding sails boomed out for most of the time to increase the area of canvas presented to the wind. Really though, at around 1,800 square metres our sail area was not over-generous for a vessel of upwards of two thousand tonnes, while compared with the latest steel windjammers it was very inefficiently disposed, so that on almost any point of sailing at least one sail would be flapping useless, masked by those to windward of it. The corvette's hull form was not especially fine-lined, and anyway the fact of having auxiliary steam seemed to spoil her for sailing in some mysterious way: perhaps because the propeller aperture upset the after-swim to the rudder, perhaps because the weight of engines and coal bunkers amidships affected her balance in some subtle fashion. Her best sailing point was about twenty degrees abaft of the beam, when she might manage briefly to get above ten knots. But on all other points she was a mediocre performer; particularly bad beating to windward, when she became a thoroughly tiresome old packing crate, prone to fall off to leeward when close-hauled and extremely reluctant to bring her head round when tacking. But that was always the way with sailing ships: two apparently identical vessels, built to the same plans in the same yard, would often have completely different sailing qualities. When people nowadays go dewy-eyed over the romance of the old sailing ships and wax lyrical about their 'character', I who sailed aboard some of the last of them tend to think of phrases like 'The accused was described in court as a man of known bad character'.

Still, they undeniably looked splendid under full sail; I would be the first to admit that. And especially a vessel like the *Windischgrätz*, with a sail-plan which was decidedly old-fashioned even for 1902; which in fact would not have looked too far out of place in 1802. Even sailing merchantmen were becoming fewer by the turn of the century, as competition from the steamers began to bite, so the sight of a warship proceeding under full sail was a rare one indeed. We discovered as much on the sixth day out from Madeira when we were overtaken by an Elder-Dempster passenger steamer, the *Degema*, en route for Lagos. They came in close and her passengers crowded the rails to see us. At first we were rather flattered by this attention and waved our caps back at them from the rigging. But as they passed on to leave us coughing in their funnel smoke it occurred to us that perhaps their curiosity had been something less than totally admiring. Previously we had given no great thought to the fact that we were a sailing warship afloat in the age of battleships and thirty-knot destroyers. But now we suddenly became self-conscious, rather like a man who goes out wearing a well-cut but antiquated suit discovered at the back of a cupboard, and suddenly realises that the passers-by in the street and on the tops of buses who are turning to look at him are in fact laughing at him. But there: we would just have to get used to being a spectacle. Money was tight in the k.u.k. Kriegsmarine and allocations to buy coal in foreign ports were meagre to say the least of it. The wind was free, and we were to make as much use of it as we possibly could. What else could we expect from a government that had reputedly named our ship the *Windischgrätz* when it should properly have been *Windisch-Grätz* because the former counted as one word for sending telegrams and the latter as two?

We passed the Cape Verde Islands on 10 July, then pointed our bows due south-east to take us around the bulge of West Africa. The trade winds carried us forward a couple of days longer, then faltered and died as we entered the zone of tropical calms, the notorious Doldrums. The next five days were spent bracing round the yards to every farthing's worth of wind; sometimes gliding ahead at a couple of knots, more often lying still rocking to the slow, almost imperceptible heave of the ocean beneath us. Nine or ten times each day we would be inundated by tropical rainstorms drifting across the sea, for this was the height of the rainy season ashore. Once or twice we were narrowly missed by water-spouts, and on 12 July, perched in the fore cross-trees, I counted no less than twelve of them at once. As we reached 10 degrees north latitude we entered the malarial zone, as defined by the Imperial and Royal War Ministry in far-off Vienna. From now on, as long as we were within ten degrees of the Equator and less than fifty miles from land, each of us would take a daily dose of five grains of quinine, to be swallowed each morning at eight bells in front of the ship's surgeon, Korvettenarzt Gustav Luchieni. We were also forbidden to appear on deck during daylight hours without tropical headgear. For reasons of economy the k.u.k. Kriegsmarine had never issued a sun helmet for ship's crews sailing in the tropics: not even so much as the stylish and cheap straw hat favoured by the British and Dutch Navies. Instead we had to attach a white cloth flap to the back of our usual headgear to hang over the nape of the neck in the style of the French Foreign Legion or Henry Morton Stanley. The result was so ludicrous that after two days the Captain decreed that, except for landing operations ashore, we could dispense with the neck flap provided we kept our heads covered at all times while out in the sun. The flaps were thankfully returned to sea-chests and never appeared again while we were at sea. No case of sunstroke ever resulted as far as I know.

I gathered during my evenings waiting at the captain's table that our first African port of call would be Freetown in the British colony of Sierra Leone, after which we would proceed down-coast to Cape Palmas as planned. This caused some excitement; the prospect of our first landing on this continent which – seen from the spire of St Stephen's Cathedral – was nothing but one vast, unexplored expanse of desert and steaming foetid jungle infested with lions and elephants and cannibalistic tribesmen. We wondered whether even at Freetown we would have to venture ashore armed for fear of assegai-waving savages and herds of buffalo. Apart from our Captain, only Professor Skowronek had ever ventured into the African hinterland.

The Professor was certainly an ebullient, talkative character with more than a touch of the actor about him as he sat there at table and held forth each evening, reducing sailors and scientists alike to silence by his compendious knowledge of just about every conceivable subject. As I stood there behind him listening I began to wish that I might some day know even one-half as much about anything as the Professor seemed to know about everything. Yet somehow he managed to avoid being a bore: an immensely unlikeable man perhaps, but not tedious. Quite the contrary: even for those who heartily disliked him there was a kind of baleful fascination in listening to him hold forth. For many of those present I suspect it was an intense desire to see him caught out, disproved, refuted, conclusively shut up. But if that was the case then the onlookers were doomed always to be disappointed, because Professor Skowronek had a politician's gift for turning hecklers inside-out, as well as bullet-proof self-confidence.

'Of course,' he would say, 'I've travelled a good deal in the Dark Continent over the years. From the point of view of the anthropometrist it contains some of the most fascinating source-material on earth: peoples preserved in their primitive barbarism for thousands of years past, or in fact allowed to degenerate from lack of contact with Caucasians. In South America there's been so much racial mixture for so long that it's only in a few remote areas of the Amazonian jungle now that one can find pure pre-Colombian specimens. But Africa is unique: hundreds of tribal populations cut off until a few years ago from contact either with advanced civilisations or, for the most part, with one another; scarcely a trace of genetic admixture from the higher races. Fascinating. Did you know that the average Negro skull has twenty per cent less cranial capacity than that of the average Tyrolean? If he were born in Innsbruck the Negro would be classified as a microcephalous cretin? No wonder they never even invented the wheel.'

'Yes, Herr Professor,' said Linienschiffsleutnant Zaleski, laying down his fork, 'but what does that prove? I read somewhere a few months ago that the average Japanese, the average American Red Indian and the average Papuan have larger brains in relation to body weight than the average European. And anyway, what makes you so sure that the Tyroleans invented the wheel even if they do have larger brains than black men – or that they make use of their cranial capacity, come to that? Most of the Tyroleans I've met have been as thick as mutton . . .'

The captain banged his spoon on the table.

'Herr Schiffsleutnant, that remark was uncalled-for.'

'I apologise, Herr Kommandant.'

The Professor smiled. 'Yes, Herr Leutnant, I appreciate that your reading in the sphere of anthropometrics has been deep and extensive. But I also read an article recently, by my old friend Professor Lüdecke of Berlin, one of the world's most eminent authorities in the field, and he has proved conclusively what the rest of us have suspected for some time: that cranial capacity is but one of the many features that determine that innate creativity and nobility of spirit to be found among the Nordic peoples, and the ignorant baseness of the earth's lesser races. Convolution of the brain's surface is one factor; but more important is the distribution of the brain's total volume. In the Negro, you see, the frontal and temporal lobes are poorly developed, thus producing severely limited creative and inductive powers. Likewise there is a corresponding over-development of the basi-occipital area at the top of the spinal column: that part of the brain where the emotions and the sensual appetites are known to be located. It is a matter of common observation that the Negro cannot be controlled by appeal either to his intelligence or to his sense of honour, but only by physical chastisement and the denial of his baser desires. There is no disputing this: it is scientifically proven fact and to deny it is to deny both nature and the validity of the scientific process. The black man's sensuality and his intellectual and creative poverty are both as much part of his physical make-up as his dark fingernail roots and his woolly hair.'

'I see,' said Linienschiffsleutnant Mikulić, 'and do I take it, Herr Professor, that your system of cranial measurement can be applied elsewhere?'

Skowronek smiled self-deprecatingly and pushed his plate away from him before settling back in his chair.

'I am flattered, Herr Leutnant, by your characterisation of my ideas as a "system": I do not feel able at present to describe my working hypotheses in such terms. But I feel that in a few years' time they will have become a complete system of craniometry, a science in its own right, and once that has come to pass then yes, they will most certainly be capable of wider application. Given a sufficiently large body of data on which to base the tables and sufficiently sensitive measuring instruments, it should in principle be quite possible to classify the entire human race – or at the very least the populations of the European states – according to racial criteria. Once that has been done then I see no reason why, for example, it should not be possible to introduce eugenic policies, restricting population growth to the most worthwhile elements of society. I can also foresee that once the system had been elaborated it might be applied to the judicial and educational systems.'

'In what way, might I enquire?'

'Well, for applying a kind of sliding scale in the criminal courts for example. Someone whose cranial development assigns them to a lower category cannot reasonably be held to be as guilty of a crime as someone endowed with higher reasoning and moral faculties. The one might be flogged, the other fined or exposed to ridicule for the same crime. And in the schools, if we could predict on the basis of cranial formation how children would develop intellectually, then we could concentrate our educational efforts on those most likely to benefit from them and assign a purely vocational training to the innately stupid. Also I might tentatively suggest that some of the national conflicts of our own Monarchy might more profitably be resolved by recourse to science than to the sterile categories of politicians and bureaucrats. If we could classify the population of a territory like, say, Carinthia according to skull formation rather than the misleading criterion of whether the inhabitants speak German or Slovene, then perhaps populations might be exchanged and our affairs managed more efficiently. After all, once we are entirely, scientifically certain of what constitutes a race then we can prevent further race-mixing.'

'And am I to take it, Herr Professor,' the Captain asked, 'that this science of skull classification of yours can be applied to the whole of mankind? If so, then where does skin colour come into it? After all, I have seen very few black Swedes.'

'Of course, Herr Kommandant. To take your point about skin coloration first of all, I agree that it does have some bearing on racial classification. But not nearly as much as was once thought. Fifty years ago it was assumed, broadly speaking, that skins became darker the further one went down the evolutionary tree. But that seems to apply only up to a point. True, your Scandinavian is fair-skinned and blue-eyed and our African Negro or

Australian Aborigine is black. But the Bushmen of the Kalahari desert are generally acknowledged to be some of the lowest specimens of the human race so-called: not only subsisting on a barely imaginable level of barbarity but also anatomically different even from Negroes, to the extent that half-breeds resulting from couplings between them and members of higher races are as barren as the offspring of a mare and donkey-stallion. But whereas one would expect them according to theory to be coal-black they are in fact a dirty yellowish hue. No ...' he tapped his head with his forefinger, '... the answer lies in the cranium, no question of it. Once we have established beyond question what features of skull formation make a Swede a Swede and a Bushman a Bushman then I think that the category homo sapiens may be ready for a little revision – and not before time either. The so-called human race is long overdue for a sorting-out into subspecies.'

'But Herr Professor ...' It was Father Semmelweiss the Chaplain: a timid, pinkish-faced young man who usually avoided controversy wherever possible. 'But if you "sort out" the human race, as you put it, on earth, what happens in heaven?'

Skowronek laughed tolerantly. 'Reverend Father – is that how I am to call you by the way? As an agnostic rationalist myself I have no opinion on the matter: I am a scientist and my competence ends, I am afraid, about ten kilometres above sea level ...' Everyone laughed and Father Semmelweiss blushed and tried to sink into the collar of his soutane. '... But allow me to say that if your "Kingdom of Heaven" exists, then when we get there we may find that it is already organised along national-racial lines ...'

'What a bore then,' Zaleski interjected; 'that means there'll be customs posts I suppose: "Kindly open your bags for inspection – there's been a lot of harp-smuggling recently, what with the duty on catgut being higher on this side of the frontier."' There was laughter around the table. But Skowronek was not embarrassed or put out: clearly he was quite used to dealing with objectors.

'Quite possibly, Herr Leutnant, quite possibly. Sadly we scientists must always face the prejudice and facile mockery of the ill-informed. But still we press on. Anyway, if you gentlemen will excuse me I must go to my cabin. We land at Freetown tomorrow I believe – and for me at least the serious scientific work of this expedition begins.'

We caught our first glimpse of Africa next morning, about an hour after dawn. It had been pouring down in torrents during the night and Gauss and I, port and starboard look-outs respectively at the fo'c'sle rails, were dressed in oilskins, shivering in the watery early-morning chill after the clammy heat of the previous evening. Visibility was about half a mile, but away to eastward we could sense the brooding presence of the great, mysterious, barely explored continent; could (we fancied) detect a faint organic, rotting-leaves smell in the air. I stood bored rigid on the wet deck: not a ship or any other object in sight on the greyish-blue disc of sea. Then suddenly I noticed him. Damn him – he had crept up on us bows-on without me seeing him.

'Boat off the port bow!'

The entire watch rushed to the bulwarks to peer over as Linienschiffsleutnant Svoboda came running up the fo'c'sle ladder. It was a native dug-out canoe, about eight metres long and needle-sharp at each end, paddled by a single man even though we were several miles offshore. As it turned broadside on I saw that along its black side were painted in letters of orange the words NO MAN LIKE GOD! The paddler stopped a few metres below us and stood up. He was a tall, well-built black man, stark naked except for an Eton collar and old top hat adorned with stripes of red and blue paint. He stooped, and held up an enormous bunch of bananas for us to inspect. As he did so he raised the top hat with his free hand and treated us to a smile like the sudden lifting of the lid over a piano keyboard.

'What-ho old beans, an' good-mornin' to you. Ah am Sir Percy fram W1.'

This, then, was Africa at last.

Sir Percy from W1 came aboard to sell us his bananas, complaining bitterly as he did so that business was bad now that the Boer War was over and the troop-ships were no longer calling.

Gauss and I tasted our first bananas. Cadet Gumpoldsdorfer also bought one, but ate the skin and threw the centre overboard. He suffered terrible stomach pains later on. We cheered him up by assuring him that he had cholera and would certainly be dead by nightfall.

The calm lasted for the rest of the morning. In the end, in sheer frustration, we fired up the boilers, raised the funnel and let down the propeller to enter Freetown harbour under steam; to the inexpressible disgust of our Captain, who regarded using the engine as an affront to his professional competence. Perhaps it was a good thing that we had done so, however, because the entrance to Freetown harbour might have been tricky under sail that particular day. The place was certainly picturesque enough to look at – from a distance at any rate – with the densely wooded hills sweeping down to the bay, their tops lost in the rainclouds. But at this season of the year there were all manner of freakish down-draughts bouncing down from the mountains to cause difficulties. Just as we were preparing to anchor below Fourah Point another rainstorm struck us, accompanied by a minor typhoon. Soaked to the skin, we struggled to release the bower anchor from its bed in a downpour so torrentially solid that even breathing became difficult. It cascaded down the funnel to put out the boiler furnace, and it was only by struggling to get tarpaulins over the hatch gratings that we prevented the ship from being flooded below decks. But at last the anchor plummeted into the waters of the bay and the chain clattered through the hawse-pipe, just as the rainstorm was passing and the clouds were scurrying away like the remnants of a defeated army through the forests above the town. We had arrived, we were told, at the start of the miniature dry-season – that is to say, a period of occasional breaks in the incessant rain – that lasts in these parts from about the middle of July to the middle of August. Even so, we sensed that so long as we were anchored here we were going to need our daily dose of quinine.

We were three days at Freetown: more than enough as it turned out to sample that town's rather limited attractions. The off-duty crewmen piled ashore in the liberty boat almost as soon as the anchor had been dropped, all but a few of them paying their first visit to black Africa. In those days hardly anyone in Austria had ever seen a black person: perhaps the odd footman in the retinue of some Viennese magnate, but certainly no more than that. So there was an intense curiosity to see what these exotic people were like in their natural habitat; and in particular, among the lower deck, to sample the unbridled sensuous passions and musky delights of African women; a scientific curiosity which was not in the least blunted by the surgeon's pre-embarcation lecture on venereal diseases, even accompanied as it was by luridly coloured charts and by a sick-bay attendant demonstrating the fearsome tools used in their treatment, rather like the Spanish Inquisition showing the prisoner the instruments. We cadets were sheltered to a large extent from these unsavoury matters, but we gathered next day that the tour of the town's brothel quarter had proved a great disappointment. The local drink was poisonous, the survivors reported, the climate ashore was like a hot face flannel while as for the girls, they not only smelt fusty, like a wet haystack, but were also rather prim, being for the most part Church of England or Methodists of some description and not in the least happy about jig-a-jigging with a lot of Papists unless they received a ten per cent surcharge.

We cadets were kept under close supervision for most of the visit, working aboard the ship until the second afternoon when we were ordered to change into our best whites to attend a garden party at Government House, up on a hill above the town and just below an enormous military hospital built that size (we understood) to take the fever cases. It was infernally hot and humid even if the rain had let up for a few hours. But our bandsmen did their excellent best – Strauss, Zeller, Millöcker and the lot – sweating like so many boiled puddings in their high-collared tunics. The Governor and his wife made small-talk with us and were delighted to find that we spoke such creditable English; likewise the representatives of local society, the ladies dressed in voluminous petticoats and flounces and ostrich-plumed hats which must have been perfect torment to wear in such a climate. Most of the people of Freetown, we understood, were the descendants of slaves set ashore from ships captured by the Royal Navy. But there were also guests from among the inland tribespeople: dignified blue-black Muslims from up on the plateau and Mende chieftains from the interior. Among them were two splendid-looking girls of about sixteen, the daughters of an inland chief, who were at boarding school on the Isle of Wight and home now for the holidays. Gauss and I talked to them about the weather and this and that, admiring as we did so the patterns of scars on their cheeks. As we chatted one of the sisters rolled up her eyes, sighed and ran her finger around inside the collar of her high-necked blouse.

'But surely, miss,' I said, 'having lived in this country all your life you must be used to the heat?'

They both laughed. 'Oh, it's not so much the heat, it's these clothes, you see? When we're home from school in our village our mama makes us go about naked like the others. She says that unmarried girls wearing clothes leads to immorality.'

It was only on the last afternoon of our visit that we cadets were given a couple of hours' liberty to look around Freetown unsupervised, while the drinking dens and houses of ill-repute were closed for the afternoon. It really was a most curious place and not in the least how I had imagined Africa: not a grass hut in sight but only ramshackle, muddy streets – Clarence Street, Hanover Street and Bond Street – of brick and clapboard houses with cast-iron lamp posts and helmeted English-style policemen strolling their beats among the refuse and the water-filled potholes. Vultures were everywhere: much smaller than I had imagined, and really quite extraordinarily shabby-looking fowl when walking about on the ground picking around among the rubbish. Gauss and I made our way down the main thoroughfare, Kissy Street, from the clock tower towards the wharf where the boat lay that would take us back aboard. We were going to have to hurry, because out to sea a great mass of indigo clouds announced the approach of yet another rainstorm. There had been nothing worth buying as souvenirs, so we had done little except take a few snapshots with my camera and send postcards to our families from the main post office, dropping them into a red-painted pillar box with the VR monogram. We were generally rather disappointed with the place as well as being exhausted by the mournful, clammy, grey heat. As we hurried down the street we stopped, and gazed in wonderment. The shack was called 'Refreshing Bungalow' and outside it was a hand-painted sign so magnificent that despite the imminent downpour I just had to write it down in my notebook. It read:

BUNGIE THE SYMPATHETIC UNDERTAKER

Builder for the Dead, Repairer of the Living,
Supplied with hearse and uniform at any moment.
Been born sympathetic, promise to carry out this great
Sympathetic function,
To bury dead like good Tobias of old.

Undertaker's advice:
Do not live like a fool and die like a great fool.
Eat and drink good grog.
Save small, pay honest debts: that's the gentleman.
Then be praying for the happy death.
Bungie will do the rest by giving you decent funeral,
With small discount – that's Bungie all over.

This advertisement impressed us both greatly, and we reached the jetty only just in time to avoid a drenching which would probably have put the pair of us in need of Mr Bungie's discounted sympathy within a few days. Death and funerals seemed to be a major preoccupation in Freetown, the whole place suffused with a morbidity that was almost Viennese in its gruesome relish. But I suppose that this was only to be expected in such a pestilential climate. Years later when I was briefly seconded to the Royal Navy at Gosport I talked about West Africa with a naval pensioner who had served on the anti-slavery patrols from Freetown half a century earlier. He told me that the orders for the day had once read 'Port watch will go ashore at eight bells to dig graves; starboard watch will work as usual making coffins'.

We departed from Freetown on 17 July amid a downpour

almost as intense as the one that had greeted our arrival. Everyone was back aboard safely, and, apart from a great many aching heads and a number of anxious young men examining themselves for the first sores and discharges, no one seemed any the worse for our courtesy call. Professor Skowronek had arrived back a few hours before we sailed. He had set off inland with a party of five men as soon as we arrived and had now reappeared with his assistants carrying a padlocked wooden box. It was only a couple of days after we sailed that the news began to spread through the lower deck that the box contained six or seven human skulls which the Professor had now cleaned and arranged along one of the shelves in his laboratory, which was kept locked most of the time. This caused some consternation: it is a longstanding superstition among seamen that to sail with dead men's bones aboard brings bad luck.

We had also acquired living freight at Freetown. The Foreign Ministry emissary Count Minatello had been ashore on the second day, wearing a white suit and an outsize solar topee with a neck cloth hanging down the back, just to be on the safe side. He had stayed two days in Freetown's one cockroach-infested hotel and had come back aboard accompanied by a young black man: a slim and self-consciously elegant fellow with a straw panama, a gold-headed cane, a monocle and a cigarette holder, and also a gaudy tropical flower in his buttonhole. This mysterious passenger said nothing to anyone and disappeared as soon as he came aboard into a spare cabin, where he took his meals. Rumours soon spread via the galley that this personage was in fact an illegitimate son of our Captain, fathered on an African princess twenty-five years before when 'der Alte' had been exploring in Africa. But this was discounted by the more geographically literate on the grounds that Slawetz had been in East Africa, not West. In the end the matter was resolved by Max Gauss, who had been detailed to clean the cabin and had found a very splendid gilt-embossed visiting card which he showed to us. It read *Dr Benjamin Saltfish MA (Oxon) D. Phil (Harvard). Foreign Minister of the Federated Kroo Coast State.* We had no idea what he might be doing aboard our ship. But we did know that on the last day of our visit the cipher books had been taken out of the ship's safe, and that Linienschiffsleutnant Svoboda had gone ashore to send a number of very long telegrams in code from the post office on Kissy Street. Something was afoot.

7

VACANT POSSESSION

We spent the next five days working our way down the Liberian coast well out of sight of land. Both watches had been ordered to stand by for landing operations, but as yet there was no indication where we were heading. All that we cadets knew, as a result of our daily navigational exercises, was that when the ship finally hove to and dropped anchor about mid-morning on 22 July 1902 we were rolling in the long Atlantic swell some three miles off an unknown, anonymous stretch of coastline about four degrees north of the Equator and seven degrees east of the prime meridian. It lay there in the distance, flattish and bland-looking, as I climbed to the top of the foremast, wedged the telescope into the shrouds, wiped the sweat from my brow and peered into the steam-fogged eyepiece. Yes, there it was: a line of dark green forest – palm trees as far as I could make out – above a boulder-strewn shore, a beach of dark yellow sand, then a white strip of foam where the ocean waves crashed on to the strand. I traversed the telescope to eastward a little – and my heart leapt within me much as those of the early discoverers must have done: the Portuguese who had first arrived on this coast five hundred years before. That mysterious fleck of white that I had noticed from on deck was nothing less than a castle: a small fortress perched on a bluff above the mouth of a river. Across the river, among the palms, I could even make out the thatched roofs of a native village. This was Africa at last then, the veritable Dark Continent, still only half explored in those days and pregnant with every adventure and marvel that a sixteen-year-old could imagine sitting on the winter evening in snowbound

Moravia, reading about gold and ivory, slave traders and savage potentates, piracy, treasure and the whole works. A few more hours now and I would be setting foot on its shores to sample its wild mysteries.

My landing was in fact delayed until the next day by bad weather: more rainstorms sweeping in from the Gulf of Guinea. But by sneaking into the chart room that evening while the officer of the watch was busy I did at least discover a little about the mysterious shore off which we were lying. The castle, I learnt, was an ex-Danish trading post called Frederiksborg, about ten miles to the west of Cape Palmas, and the river whose mouth I had seen was called the Bunce, whence the name of the native village, marked on the maps as 'Bunceville'. The place was located, at least nominally, just within the boundaries of the Republic of Liberia. Or to be more precise, within a triangle of dotted lines marked as 'Disputed region: boundaries still (1901) awaiting settlement'.

Early next morning, the weather having cleared for a while, one of our eight-metre cutters was lowered to make for the shore under the command of Fregattenleutnant Rodlauer. The purpose of the mission was to take soundings. A sand-bar ran right along this coast about a mile out to sea, and, although it was lower opposite the river mouth than elsewhere, it was described in the pilotage guide as having less than four fathoms of water over it at high tide and as being liable to shift. If there turned out to be enough water the *Windischgrätz* would try to anchor in the mouth of the Bunce; if not then we would have to lie anchored offshore and ply with the land by boat: probably no bad thing anyway since the pilotage guide described the shores of the Bunce Creek as 'low-lying and unhealthy'.

It certainly turned out to have been unhealthy for Rodlauer and his crew: the survivors returned to the ship a few hours later looking very sorry for themselves, in a native surf-boat propelled by nine or ten naked black paddlers and painted with the grimly apposite motto WHAT MAN CAN DO, THAT MAN DOES. They had run into breaking seas while going over the bar and the usual thing had happened: the coxswain had panicked and let the boat get carried forward by the surge until she was moving at the same speed as the wave and the rudder ceased to work. The breaking sea had then got under her stern, the bows had fallen into the trough and dug in, and over she had gone, flinging twenty men into the water with the boat on top of them. Luckily for them the surf-boat had been on its way out to escort them in – the natives had tried to wave them back out of danger but Rodlauer had taken no notice – and sixteen half-drowned survivors had been picked up. Rodlauer and three seamen were missing. One body was washed up on the beach that evening, another was found half-devoured by a shark the next day, but Rodlauer and the remaining sailor were never seen again. It was a salutary lesson. The Captain decreed that henceforth all boats communicating with the shore would carry a local pilot to guide them through the surf, however injurious this might be to the prestige of the white race – though Linienschiffsleutnant Mikulić swore in private that he would be damned if any nigger was ever going to tell him how to manage a boat.

This meant that over the next couple of weeks we saw quite a lot of the local seafaring population. It had been decided that there was not enough water over the bar for the ship to enter the river safely, so we remained anchored about two miles out and communicated with the shore by boat. This meant that throughout our sojourn off Frederiksborg there were always native pilots aboard who had arrived with one of our boats or were waiting to guide one back. We came to know them pretty well and, after getting over the initial strangeness of having black men sitting around an Austro-Hungarian warship, quite came to like them. They were certainly a cheerful lot, these Kroo-men as they called themselves – though in fact they were members of the Grebo, a sub-tribe of the Kroo people who inhabit that part of the West African coast. They had earned a living for generations past aboard European ships and were therefore quite used to the white man and his odd ways. In fact quite a number of our Kroo-men had served aboard the ships of the Royal Navy's West African Squadron and had been given names like Union Jack, Jimmy Starboard, Masthead Light and Honesty Ironbar. Some of them had even acquired a smattering of German from having worked a couple of years previously on contract to the government of German South-West Africa, handling surf-boats through the breakers at Swakopmund. Most of the time though they used Krio, the local version of the Pidgin English, which was spoken in those days all along the western coast of Africa. It sounded very strange to my ear at first, but it was surprising how quickly I became used to it. I suppose that using English as a foreign language myself I had no preconceptions about how it ought to sound, and being young I treated the whole thing as a wonderful lark instead of an affront to my dignity. At any rate, Max Gauss and I had soon been appointed as semi-official interpreters in Krio.

I made my first trip across to Frederiksborg as a member of a landing party the morning after Fregattenleutnant Rodlauer's disaster. Our boat was carrying the Kroo-man Jimmy Starboard as pilot: an ugly bandy-legged fellow of about twenty-five with a great towering mass of wool on top of his head and teeth filed to points. His first action on boarding the eight-metre cutter rolling and pitching on the swell alongside the *Windischgrätz* was to unship the rudder – 'pass-all no bloody good shit' as he described it – and fling it aside in favour of a spare oar lashed over the stern. He also bade us empty out the water barricoes and lash them beneath the rowing benches as buoyancy, just in case. He seemed to know what he was up to, but as we neared the roaring breakers – invisible from the seaward side – it was with a distinctly uneasy, fluttering feeling in the pits of our stomachs. Luckily the officer in charge of our boat, Fregattenleutnant Andreas O'Callaghan del Montespino, was a diffident sort of young man and not inclined to assert white supremacy just for the sake of it. If he had been then he would probably have ended up drowning the lot of us.

We could not see where the waves were breaking over the bar, but we could hear them and feel their surge as we drew near. The men lugged grim-faced at the oars as I sat in the stern next to our pilot as interpreter of his orders to the crew. He was standing, legs braced in their ragged shorts, muscles tensed, gripping the oar loom and scanning the sea ahead of us with a look of intense concentration, searching for a break in the waves and the flat patch that follows two or three successive rollers. The sea was beginning to push us forward now as well as the steady creak, creak of the oars in their rowlocks. Suddenly he yelled, 'Go! Wan-two, wan-two!' I signalled the crew to double their stroke as they braced their feet against the stretchers and strained their backs to shoot the cutter ahead. Six, seven, eight strokes – the stern began to fall into the trough as the wave surged ahead of us. 'Back all-man oar like hell!' The rowers dug their oars in to back water and slow the boat as Jimmy Starboard wrestled with the steering oar to keep our stern to the following wave. It lifted us up as it raced beneath our keel. 'Go 'gain now – wan-two wan-two!' We shot forward again in the wake of the breaker which had just done its best to broach us and roll the boat over. Twice more we did this: forward then stop, forward then stop again. Until at last we realised that we were safely through; that the growl of the surf was behind us, that the boat's motion was easier and that we were now protected to some degree from the Atlantic swell by the sand-bar which we had just crossed. Jimmy Starboard grinned at us with his pointed teeth and wiped the sweat from his brow. The only trouble was that we would have to negotiate the breakers each time we wanted to travel between the ship and the shore. The surf never lets up along the West African coast, and there are plenty of sharks and barracuda lying in wait for those who treat it without due respect.

Not that there seemed to be very much to make our recent perilous journey worthwhile, once we had arrived in the smoother waters of the river mouth. By African standards it was indeed a creek rather than a river: barely a hundred metres wide. Certainly the shore hereabouts was picturesque enough: very much the tropical strand as I had always imagined it; surf thundering on a beach of ochre sand littered with rust-red boulders; boats drawn up above the high-water mark; waving coconut palms; and further up, half hidden among the foliage, the first of the village huts, their palm-thatched roofs blending most pleasingly into the dense green of this rain-saturated landscape. A few people stood on the beach on the Bunceville side of the river to watch our arrival: naked black children, and women wearing headscarves and shapeless but brilliantly coloured cotton dresses. It looked a scene of immemorial peace and tranquility. As we drew nearer I saw that some way into the river mouth on the Frederiksborg side there was a derelict stone jetty below the castle. I also saw that the castle perched up on the bluff among the trees was itself virtually a ruin: windows gaping empty, roofs evidently fallen in and patches of the white plaster crumbled away to expose the masonry beneath.

Our party was to land below the castle while the other boat, commanded by Fregattenleutnant Buratović, would land at the jetty at Bunceville. Father Semmelweiss was with them. They had work to do, burying the dead men washed up after the previous day's accident. As for us, fifteen in all (Jimmy Starboard had bidden us goodbye and jumped overboard to swim ashore as we neared Bunceville), the purpose of our expedition up to the castle was not immediately obvious since the place had clearly been deserted for years. But we had brought our rifles and cutlasses with us, Fregattenleutnant O'Callaghan wore his black-and-yellow sword-belt, and after we had moored and formed up on the stone quayside we set off up the winding, cobbled roadway with a bugler in front of us and an Austrian naval ensign carried on a staff.

Snakes basking in the sunshine slithered out of our way in alarm and bright green lizards with red ruffs scurried into the bushes on their hind legs as we marched up towards the castle, perhaps a kilometre from the jetty. It all seemed to be a great deal of ceremony on behalf of an abandoned shell of a building, for as we climbed up towards the gateway, already sweating in the clammy morning heat, we saw that the rusty cannon which protruded from the embrasures in the battlements were leaning at all angles, their carriages having long since been eaten away by termites, and that creepers were at work breaking up the walls. The roadway was still in reasonable condition, apart from the odd tree root forcing up the pavement, but the echoing gate-arch was empty except for the skeleton of a dead goat, picked clean by vultures. Massive iron hinges were still mortared into the walls, but the gates were no more. Over the archway, eroded by years of rain and sunshine, was a coat of arms and the inscription FREDERICVS IV REX DANIORVM AEDIFICAVABIT MDCCXXVII.

So the place had been built in 1727. But how long had it been deserted? For several decades at least, to judge by the scene that greeted us as we entered the courtyard. The African bush was rapidly reclaiming its own. Young trees the thickness of my waist were cracking the walls while creepers and shrubs of every sort grew in profusion from the empty doors and window arches. Only the cellars below the castle remained intact. Gauss and I ventured down the stone steps that led to them from the courtyard: gloomy, dank-smelling vaults closed off by massive iron grilles. Peering into these doleful, echoing caverns – which somehow neither of us had any great wish to explore further – and looking at the ponderous locks on the gratings, we realised that whatever merchandise this trading station had once traded in, it had certainly been kept under very close guard while awaiting shipment. Despite the heat we were both shivering slightly from an unaccountable chill by the time we rejoined the others.

But we were not here as tourists: Fregattenleutnant O'Callaghan evidently had orders to carry out. The party were told off by twos to conduct a quick survey of the fortress and its surroundings, and then to report back to the courtyard in half an hour's time. Meanwhile Gauss and I were handed the ensign on its staff and told to go up on to the battlements and find a secure place in which to fix it. We clambered up on to the walls by means of a flight of stone steps and made our way along to one of the bastions facing the river mouth; the only one whose flat roof had not so far succumbed to the assaults of rain and white ants. Several cannon still pointed out to sea, standing on cast-iron carriages. At last we found a hole in the stone pavement suitable for holding the base of the staff.

'Obediently report, everything ready, Herr Leutnant,' we shouted down into the echoing courtyard.

'Very good: wait up there and raise the flag when I give the order.'

We waited as the men returned from their brief exploration of the castle and formed up in the courtyard below, in the clear patch in the middle where the flagstones had not yet been displaced by the invading bushes. When everything was ready a petty officer bellowed, 'Hab 'Acht!' and boots crashed on the stones as the men came to attention. Fregattenleutnant O'Callaghan drew his sword and the bugle shrilled out the 'Generalmarsch' into the muggy, insect-chirping air as the grey parrots rose squawking in alarm from the trees round about the castle. Gauss and I raised the ensign. It fluttered limply in the faint sea breeze as we jammed the base of the staff into the hole in the stones. The lieutenant raised his sword to his sweating forehead in salute as the men presented arms. The red-white-red ensign of Imperial Austria was flying over the battlements of Frederiksborg. A few moments later a crackle of shots came to us from across the river. Landungsdetachement Buratović was firing its three salvoes over the graves of the sailors drowned the previous day. In its way each party was taking possession of territory in Africa.

Many had done that already, by the looks of it. Before we left Frederiksborg to return to the cutter moored at the jetty Gauss and I accompanied two sailors to look at what they had discovered in the bush behind the castle. It was an old cemetery: row upon row upon row of moss-covered headstones leaning drunkenly or toppled over among the undergrowth. One row near the front consisted of taller and more elaborate gravestones than the rest. We scraped the moss from some of them with our cutlasses: SEPTIMUS VAN HELSEN, GOVERNOR, MAY 1735, JORG EBELTOFT, GOVERNOR, DECEMBER 1735, PEDER SVENSEN, GOVERNOR, MARCH 1736, JENS KARSTEN, GOVERNOR, APRIL 1736, and so on, and so on. It was clear that promotion prospects in the Danish West Africa Company had been excellent in those days. We had quinine now, and all the resources of modern tropical hygiene aboard a warship riding at anchor a couple of miles offshore, well out of range of the mosquitoes that Professor Koch had recently proved were the true agents of malaria. But even so, as we smelt that curious sweetish-decaying, mouldy-leaves odour of the African coastal swamps wafting up to us from the river, we devoutly hoped that we would not be staying too long on this coast.

Back aboard that evening I was detailed to wait at supper in the saloon, barely given time to change out of my sweat-soaked best whites. This particular evening it was Count Minatello's turn to hold forth, since Professor Skowronek had been paddled ashore that morning and had still not returned. The Count had been ashore himself earlier in the day to talk with the chief men in Bunceville, dressed fit to kill in an all-purpose explorer's outfit such as could only have been supplied by a Viennese department store: another outsize pith helmet – khaki drab this time – a lobster-like carapace of spine-pads and cholera belts, khaki breeches and high lace-up boots that must have taken his valet the best part of a morning to lace up for him and the best part of an evening to unlace again. It was raining again as supper was served; cascading down like theatre curtains outside the open cabin windows as the thunder rumbled and sheet lightning flickered in a murky, aqueous twilight such as might prevail at the bottom of a pond. The all-embracing damp seemed even to dim the oil lamps hanging from the deck beams above the table, swinging their yellowish light in slow circles over tablecloth and cutlery as the ship rolled on the never-ending swell.

'Frederiksborg,' said the Captain, 'don't I remember that name from somewhere? Remind me, Herr Graf, wasn't there some business or other around here back in '64?'

'Yes Herr Kommandant, there was – though you might reasonably be forgiven for not recalling a great deal about it. I can assure you that it took us quite some time to unearth the details from the Foreign Ministry archives.'

'Didn't old Subotić of the *Erzherzog Leopold* sink a Danish vessel here and capture the castle or something like that? I don't remember the details because I was up in the North Sea during the Schleswig-Holstein business, but I did hear something about it when we got back to Pola.'

'Yes Herr Kommandant, perfectly correct: it appears that in May 1864 Fregattenkapitän Giovanni Subotić von Mastenwald,

Captain of the Imperial-Royal frigate *Erzherzog Leopold*, did indeed land men at Frederiksborg and take a Danish palm-oil schooner as a prize of war. But as to capturing the castle, there seems to have been precious little left to capture since the Danes had abandoned the place several years before. According to our treaties registry, the Danish Crown built Frederiksborg in the 1720s after acquiring the place from the Swedes by the Treaty of Utrecht, the Swedes having acquired it in 1697 by the Treaty of Rijswijk from the French, who had been ceded it in 1656 by the Dutch, who had captured it from the Portuguese about 1630. It was a slave-trading station at first, like all the other trading forts along this coast; but in 1780 the Danes abolished slavery and they never found any real use for the place thereafter, apart from a little trading in palm oil. They appear to have tried selling the castle to the British about 1850, but the British had no use for the place either and thought that it might be on Liberian territory anyway. So the Danish government just abandoned the castle about 1860: removed everything usable and left the rest to crumble away.'

'But forgive me, Herr Graf, am I not correct in thinking that there was a fight here in 1864 even though there was no garrison in the castle?'

'Hardly a fight, or even a skirmish – though perhaps Fregattenkapitän von Subotić may have liked to make it seem as if there was one. I have researched the matter as thoroughly as I could in the War Ministry archives, even consulting the *Erzherzog Leopold*'s logbook, and it appears that what happened was in fact quite undramatic. In April 1864 the frigate was returning to Pola from a scientific cruise to South American waters. Off the coast of Brazil the *Erzherzog Leopold* fell in with a Hamburg ship which informed Subotić that Austria and Prussia were at war with Denmark and told him – quite erroneously – that a Danish squadron was cruising between the West Indies and the coast of Africa. In order to avoid them Subotić crossed the Atlantic to the West African coast and made his way up it, keeping close inshore so as to have neutral ports nearby. On 6 May he sighted a Danish merchant ship off Cape Palmas and followed her to

Bunceville where he found her two days later loading barrels of palm oil for a soap factory in Esbjerg. A landing party took the vessel as a prize and she was later towed out to sea and set on fire as there was no way of getting her back to Pola. But before he left the Bunce River, Subotić sent a landing party ashore to raise the Austrian flag over Frederiksborg, claiming it in the name of the Emperor Franz Joseph.'

Slawetz chuckled. 'Yes, yes, that sounds like old Subotić: always claiming this that and the other for the House of Habsburg. He even laid claim to New Zealand once, I believe, when he was with Wüllerstorf aboard the *Novara*. If you'd put the man down in a bordello in Tangier he'd have climbed on to the roof with a flag and claimed it for Austria.'

'Yes, Fregattenkapitän Subotić does appear to have had rather a penchant for claiming colonies. I gather that he caused us a great deal of trouble with the French about 1872 when he claimed Madagascar. But in this case it appears that the claim was based on something slightly more substantial than a hot-headed naval captain running up the flag over a derelict slave-trading fort – yes, young man, a little more wine if you please. It seems anyway that his next action after claiming Frederiksborg was to cross the river to Bunceville and conclude a treaty with the local potentate – a man called King Horace Christian Goliath – by which he ceded the Austrian government full territorial rights over a stretch of coastline extending from Cape Palmas up to the Cess River, a distance of about a hundred kilometres.'

'But was this Goliath fellow entitled to sell it?'

The Count smiled. 'My dear Herr Kommandant, my impression of the affair is that for twenty bottles of schnapps and a sack of beads the black-faced rascal would have sold Subotić the entire African coastline from the Cape of Good Hope up to Gibraltar. But what does that matter? I was present myself as a junior secretary at the Berlin Colonial Conference in 1884 and I assure you that many of the African territorial claims recognised by that gathering were every bit as insubstantial as this one, or even worse. The Portuguese, I recall, went into the conference claiming about two-thirds of the African land-mass on the strength of long-lost Jesuit missions and tales of treaties concluded four hundred years earlier with Prester John and the Monomotapa. The wonder is not that they lost so much of what they claimed but rather that they managed to have so much of it recognised. No, my dear sirs: the difference between the other European powers and ourselves was that while they sent gunboats and soldiers to enforce their claims in West Africa, Austria dithered and dallied. The result is that Britain and France and Germany – even Italy, would you believe it? – now have large and profitable estates in Africa while we have nothing. Just think what we might have done if we had shown a little more resolution. That old rogue Leopold of the Belgians is now one of the richest men in the world from exploiting the rubber and diamonds of the Congo. What might Austria not have done as well – if she had not sat by the wall in Berlin and watched the others, like the girl at the ball with spots and bad teeth who never gets asked to dance?'

'So why, in your opinion, Herr Graf, did we not take part?' asked Korvettenkapitän Festetics. 'My father was a diplomat at the time, in our embassy in Paris, and he used to say that we could have taken our share if we had wanted; that we were in no weaker a position than Germany and a good deal better placed than the Italians and Portuguese.'

'True, Herr Kapitän, very true. No: myself I have to say with all proper respect that it was largely because of our beloved Emperor. Remember if you will that he lost his own brother in the Mexican fiasco, shot by a republican firing squad. I am sure that that experience has given him an abiding distrust of colonial adventures. Also we had problems of our own in the early 1880s with Bosnia-Herzegovina, and – with all due respect to yourself – the constant, enervating arguments with our Magyar partners.' (Everyone nodded vigorously in agreement with this; even Festetics). 'No, it was not that no attempts were made to found Austrian colonies – Tegethoff's claim to Socotra and Baron Overbeeck's attempt to annex Borneo for example. It was rather that whenever these claims looked likely to involve us in conflicts with other countries the Emperor and the Ballhausplatz invariably took alarm and backed away. We even gave way to the Dutch over Borneo, for God's sake. A most edifying spectacle I can assure you: one of Europe's Great Powers being faced down by a few million cheese farmers living in a swamp. No, gentleman, it was a most uninspiring period in the Monarchy's history – and one that I sincerely hope we shall soon bring to an end.' He paused to light a cigar, conscious of the effect his last remark had caused around the table. It was Slawetz who spoke first.

'But Herr Graf, forgive me if I do not quite understand you. You say "bring to an end", but how can we do that? As I understand it the dispositions of the Berlin Conference as regards Africa were final. Surely we are twenty years too late to be making territorial claims, especially here along the West African coast?'

'Not quite, Herr Kommandant, not quite. Permit me to explain. The Berlin Conference laid down "effective occupation" as the main criterion for a territorial claim in Africa – which is why the Portuguese lost so much of what they said was theirs. But it did allow claims to be registered as "pending" where there was no other power involved. And just such a claim was in fact registered by Austria-Hungary in respect of this stretch of coast off which we are now lying, on the strength of Fregattenkapitän Subotić's annexation of Frederiksborg and his subsequent treaty with King Goliath. The file was mislaid in the Foreign Ministry registry after the conference and we simply forgot about it. But it remains in an annexe to the Berlin Convention and, so far as we are aware, no one has ever questioned it.'

'But what about the British and the French – not to speak of the Liberians? I gather that Liberia is little more than an American protectorate, so might the United States not also have something to say on the matter?'

Minatello laughed at this. 'True, the British have just proclaimed a protectorate over the Gold Coast, while the French, we understand, have claimed the coast from Cape Palmas eastward to Elmina. But the French have never done anything to enforce that claim, apart from establishing an outpost at Abidjan, while the British have their hands full at present annexing the territory inland of the Niger delta. The latter have made it abundantly clear that they have no interest in this coast: English palm-oil traders have been nagging London for years past to declare a protectorate, but they have never received anything except refusals.'

'And Liberia?'

'Liberia, my dear Herr Kommandant, is not a country but a figment of the diplomatic imagination: a pseudo-state established by a few hundred American mulattoes whose authority barely extends outside their capital. The Kroo Coast has been in rebellion against them for years. No, the trouser-wearing niggers of Monrovia are the least of our problems. The country is so impoverished that a few years ago, when a German gunboat was threatening to shell Monrovia in retaliation for some outrage or other, the local white merchants had to pass the hat around to raise an eight-hundred-dollar indemnity. There is a Liberian navy, we understand, but it consists of a single armed yacht which, when it set out to chase a British steamer some years ago over an alleged customs violation, ran out of coal and had to be towed back into port by its intended victim. No, gentlemen: the so-called "Liberian Republic" is a null; a sham; the emptiest of ciphers. True, the Americans support it, but nowadays only in the most distant manner possible. Our ambassador in Washington assures us that the USA would not lift a finger to protect Liberia's alleged frontiers; in fact might not be unhappy to see the entire country taken off their hands by a civilised power.'

'Do I take it then, Herr Graf, that you yourself favour the acquisition of k.u.k. colonies in Africa?' asked Festetics.

'Most certainly. This is the age of colonial expansion, and in my view any European Great Power which declines to take part in the race will rapidly cease to be a Great Power. Colonies confer prestige, as the Italians have found – since frankly the only conceivable use of places like Eritrea is to make the Kingdom of Italy look a faintly less risible entity that it would otherwise appear. People ask: Can the Austro-Hungarian Monarchy afford to acquire colonies? My answer to them would be: Can it afford *not* to acquire them?'

'But why in Africa, and why on such a small scale?'

'Herr Kapitän, there are two possible routes for Austrian expansion. One is into the Balkans and the Near East as the Turkish Empire falls to pieces, towards Salonika and the Aegean. We have already gone some way down that road in occupying Bosnia-Herzegovina. But what have we got for our trouble? Only a few pigs and plum trees to compensate us for having acquired several million brigands and cut-throats. A drive into the Balkans makes us enemies of Russia, and that puts us in the pocket of Berlin since we need the good will of the Germans. But outside Europe, that is an entirely different story: virgin territories, packed with good and useful things, and populated by simple children who can be taught to love and revere the white master instead of shooting at him from behind boulders. Small-scale? Undeniably. But every oak tree was once an acorn. Was not Rudolf of Habsburg once laughed at as "Rudolf of Habnichts Burg"? We have been left behind so far in the race for colonies, it is true. But that race is only beginning, and many who started behind the others may emerge as winners. The Berlin Conference was but the entrée at the banquet, I suspect. Look at the Portuguese Empire in Africa: quite patently on its last legs and awaiting partition among the Great Powers. And after that perhaps the Dutch East Indies with their fabulous riches, a territory larger than the whole of Europe ruled by a silly little country with neither the means nor the will to exploit it. Then there is the Ottoman Empire in the Levant, falling apart already, and China and South America thereafter. No, gentlemen: the main courses have yet to be served, I am sure of that. All that Austria must do now is secure herself a seat at the table. She once made herself a Great Power not by fighting but through peace treaties and judicious use of diplomacy. Might she not do the same once more? You have all seen it I am sure: the inscription over the gate in the Hofburg, A.E.I.O.U. – AUSTRIA EXTENDITUR IN ORBEM UNIVERSUM, or ALLE ERDE IST ÖSTERREICH UNTERTAN if you prefer that version. The empire of Charles V on which the sun never set. It was so once: why not again?'

The meal ended, the company dispersed and I was left with the other stewards to clear the plates away. The rain was still thundering down outside the cabin windows with a steady, obsessive, manic intensity, to a degree where I was beginning to have visions of the Atlantic Ocean overflowing its banks. Up on deck water cascaded from the sodden, flapping awnings and gushed out of the scuppers as if from the gargoyles around a cathedral roof during a thunderstorm. It was all intensely melancholic there in the fading grey light of evening: the lone ship rocking on the swell at the centre of a universe reduced by the relentless downpour to a diameter of a few metres; a weeping, soaking, gurgling, incessantly drumming world where speech itself seemed to be swallowed up in the noise of the pouring rain.

The ship's boats had been turned on their sides against the davits to prevent them filling with water and breaking their backs. Yet down below in the murky light of the oil lamps two parties of men were getting ready to leave next morning on expeditions ashore. The one party, led by Fregattenleutnant Bertalotti, was to accompany the geologist Dr Pürkler on a mineral-prospecting tour in the jungle behind the coastal plain. The other party, consisting of fifteen men under Fregattenleutnant Hrabovsky, was to take one of the ship's cutters up to the limit of navigation of the Bunce River, about forty kilometres inland, and there set off on foot to make contact with one of the Grebo hill-tribes whose chief was reported to be unhappy at the prospect of French rule. Each expedition would take about five days to do its work and return to the ship, but since the inland country was stiff with disease extra precautions would have to be taken to safeguard the men's health. Both parties were paraded outside the sick-bay early next morning to be administered their daily dose of quinine by Dr Luchieni. But before Luchieni could serve out the little glasses of the bitter fluid Professor Skowronek appeared and an argument began behind the closed door of the surgeon's office. In the end the men received their daily dose of anti-malarial prophylactic mixed with a dark brown liquid of the Professor's own devising, which was supposed to protect them against yellow fever as well. The Professor had been working, he said, for some years past on the problems of the Negro race's apparent immunity to that disease and whether this resistance could be transferred to white people. Luchieni was clearly unhappy. But he was a diffident young man, and Skowronek was pulling rank, pointing out that his own degree was from Vienna University while Luchieni's was from Cracow; also intimating that he was a personal friend of the Kriegsmarine's Chief Medical Officer the Freiherr von Eiselberg and how would it look if a junior naval doctor were judged to have been obstructing the course of science? In the end Luchieni capitulated. After all, the men were getting their daily dose of quinine mixed into the Professor's vile-smelling potion, so what did it matter? It could do them no harm and might possibly do them some good. Each man in turn was duly required to knock back a glass of the unspeakable fluid – and receive a little package, carefully labelled in the Professor's own hand, containing ten doses of the mixture, to be taken each morning under the supervision of the expedition's leaders. The men swore that they would rather have yellow fever; but naval discipline is naval discipline, so there was no fear that they would not take their medicine as ordered.

Over the next few days, once the expeditions had left, we spent a good deal of our time plying in boats between the ship and the shore at Bunceville. In this way I became quite well acquainted with the citizens of the putative Federated Kroo Coast State, soon (it seemed) to become Austro-Hungarian West Africa. Very early in our stay we were visited by Bunceville's only white resident, Mr Jorgensen, the local agent of a Danish company which still bought palm oil from this coast in exchange for bottles of Schiedam trade gin (in fact potato spirit), cotton cloth and the short, heavy, clumsy flintlock muskets still known locally as 'Dane-guns' which the natives used for hunting and tribal warfare. Mr Jorgensen was about sixty, but looked much older after forty years spent marinading in gin and malaria on this disease-ridden coast. But he retained his Danish facility with languages – German, English, French and a half-dozen African tongues – and he certainly knew his way around among the local tribes. He warned us from the outset to keep all our belongings aboard securely under lock and key, since the Kroo-men's reputation as seafarers and ministers of religion was equalled only by their fame as thieves and drunkards. He told us of the incident a few years before which had led to the German gunboat threatening to bombard Monrovia. A Bremen passenger steamer en route for the Cameroons had lost her propeller off the Cess River and been driven ashore. The local Kroos had shown the utmost courage and skill in rescuing the passengers and crew from the surf – but as soon as they got the unfortunates ashore had plundered them of all their belongings and the very clothes from their backs before setting to work to strip the wreck of everything movable. The survivors had been left to walk to Monrovia barefoot and near-naked. The Kroos took the view – reasonably enough, I suppose – that plunder was their legitimate reward for having risked their lives saving people from the sea, but the Imperial German government had not taken the point.

Certainly the local Kroos were not much to look at compared with some of the up-country black people we had seen at the Governor's garden party in Freetown. The Mandingo tribespeople I had met there were marvellously handsome and surpassed even Montenegrins in their easy, regal grace of bearing. The Kroos though were generally an ugly lot: short and bow-legged with the excessively developed shoulders and over-long arms which come I suppose from a lifetime spent paddling surf-boats. Their noses were flat and shapeless, their complexions were greyish-black and their teeth were usually filed to points. Each of them also carried three parallel scars on the bridge of his nose: the 'freedom mark' which Mr Jorgensen said was a relic of the slave-trading times when the Kroos had been energetic middlemen in the trade in human flesh, and had themselves been guaranteed immunity from the slave dealers. Altogether they seemed pretty unlikely candidates to become subjects of the Emperor Franz Joseph. But I suppose on reflection that they were no more outlandish than Bosnian Muslims or some of the more exotic sub-tribes of the Transylvanian Alps.

Although a few of them like Union Jack knew some German already, most of the time they spoke Krio with us. It fascinated me to listen to it, once I had got used to the sound. But then I suppose that the k.u.k. Monarchie, with its wealth of made-up languages – not just our own lingua di bordo but also Armee Slawisch and Sparkasse Deutsch – had given me an abiding interest in such argots. I soon came to admire Krio for its admirable economy and its amazing flexibility, features totally lacking in languages like Polish and Czech which had been taken in hand by the scholars in the late Middle Ages and locked for ever into rigid grammatical structures based on Latin. I was charmed by the way in which (for instance) the word 'chop' could be used without modification for the noun 'food' and the verb 'to eat'. Or the way in which the conditional mood was indicated by starting the sentence with ''Spose' and the genitive case by the verb-turned-particle 'belong'.

The Kroo surf-boat paddlers who came aboard the *Windischgrätz* were certainly a friendly and cheerful set of men; much more animated than the rather morose black people we had met in Freetown, and forever making up impromptu rhymes in Krio. One custom that particularly appealed to me was that whenever they were paddling their boats, even in the most fearsome surf, they would always sing to keep time, dipping and raising the paddles to the rhythm of chants apparently made up on the spur of the moment and usually of a satirical nature. I well remember one they sang the day they transported Slawetz von Löwenhausen and me across to Frederiksborg to conduct an inspection.

> 'Capting, good man, dash we ten bob.
> 'Spose he dash we, we no wet him.
> Capting rich man, Kroo-boy poor man.
> Four, five half-crown dash poor blackman.
> Hib hib hurrah! God bless you all!'

Perhaps it was as well that these men were locally engaged civilians: also that the Captain was slightly gun-deaf in one ear.

The fact that they were civilians and not naval personnel did not spare the Kroo-men from summary justice at the hands of the officers aboard. As on the memorable morning when the officer of the watch, Linienschiffsleutnant Mikulić, caught – or believed he had caught – Jimmy Starboard pilfering a tackhammer, the property of the Ärar and valued at two kronen. Mikulić felt that African natives aboard a European ship ought go be kept in a barbed-wire pen amidships when not working, and objected very strongly to their being allowed to wander about the decks at will. He had strong opinions on these matters, derived in a large measure from his reading of Jack London and other such authors, and was always holding forth in capital letters about 'The Negro Race', 'The Yellow Peril' and similar ideas popular around the turn of the century. He had been prowling about for several days trying to catch one of the Kroos pilfering, and now he had succeeded.

'Put that hammer down, you thieving nigger villain!'

Jimmy Starboard put down the hammer and stood facing his accuser – to receive a punch in the face that sent him staggering. But that was clearly intended to be no more than the prologue to the spectacle. A crowd was gathering as Mikulić took off his jacket. The black man was not naval personnel, but so much the better: if he did not fall under naval discipline then naval discipline could not protect him from an exemplary thrashing at the hands of a consummate expert in beatings-up. Mikulić got to work, and landed a few almost playful preparatory punches on Jimmy Starboard's head and chest. The Kroo-man made little effort to protect himself or even to dodge the blows.

'Come on you black ape, defend ourself so I can beat the daylights out of you. What are you monkeys made of?' The lieutenant came up close and made a few more jabs, mocking his victim a little before proceeding to beat him to pulp.

But taunting a Kroo-man was not a wise thing to be doing: roughly comparable to standing behind a wild ass and thrashing its hindquarters with a willow switch, or resting one's chin against the breech of a heavy-calibre naval gun about to fire. Jimmy Starboard clearly took a good deal of provoking, but when he struck he had no need to do so a second time. The punch lifted Mikulić clean off his feet and sent him crashing against the fo'c'sle bulkhead, where he lay slumped unconscious as the Kroo-man bent solicitously over him and wiped his face with a wet cloth amid a circle of wondering onlookers – just as Bo'sun Njegosić arrived to explain that he had lent Jimmy Starboard the hammer to tack a patch over a leak in his boat. Mikulić regained consciousness in the sick-bay and was not seen again on deck for three days or so. When he returned to duty he thereafter avoided the Kroos as if he had not noticed them. The incident was never referred to again. Somehow I doubted though whether it had been entirely forgotten.

8

THE OSTRICH-MEN

On the seventh day of our stay the rain let up sufficiently for us to pile into the boats and land at Bunceville in style: all of us in our best whites with rifles and full equipment – laid on the bottom boards for the moment just in case the boats got swamped in the surf. The Captain and officers accompanied us in the steam pinnace, resplendent in fore-and-aft cocked hats and gold epaulettes. Count Minatello was present, but Professor Skowronek was not with us, having gone ashore the previous day on his own with his Mannlicher hunting rifle: a choice of weapon that surprised us, since this part of Africa was relatively well populated and devoid nowadays of any game larger than bush-pig and a few of the smaller antelopes. But we would not miss him today; our purpose ashore was clearly diplomatic rather than scientific, to judge by the size of our landing party: upwards of a hundred men in all.

On closer acquaintance Bunceville town turned out to be not nearly as picturesque a place as I had imagined from what I had been able to see of it from the rickety landing stage. We disembarked and formed up behind our ship's band and the Imperial and Royal ensign, then set off to march up the main street. Our officers and Count Minatello were borne in front of us in litters slung from poles and carried on the shoulders of native bearers. As for the rest of us, we splashed our way along, trying to keep in step and also to avoid bespattering our gaiters and immaculate whites in the huge, muddy-red puddles. It seemed the entire district had turned out to watch us as we marched along, rifles slung at shoulders. The band paused to change their sheet music, and a cheer went up from the crowd: 'Long lib Australia!' We looked at one another as the cheer spread along the street. Ought someone to correct this misapprehension? But we shrugged our shoulders and marched on. To these simple people one lot of white sailors must look very much like another, so we decided to leave it at that for the moment.

Bunceville itself was rather a sordid settlement from what we could see of it: a sort of half-way stage between the traditional palm-thatch architecture of this part of Africa – which at least decayed gracefully in the rain-sodden climate – and the sub-European world of corrugated iron, clapboard and laterite brick as represented by Freetown. It was more African than the latter place, but not much more: in fact reminded me rather of photographs I had seen of small towns in the southern states of America: a sign perhaps that the despised Americo-Liberians of Monrovia had in fact had some influence further down the coast. But over it hung that characteristic, rather pleasant West African village smell compounded of wood smoke, pepper and palm oil, and in the middle of it, the place's largest building was an open-sided hall with a palm-thatch roof and a raised floor of beaten earth. This was the palaver-house, and the dignitaries of the region were waiting there for us to commence the palaver: the local King, Matthew Neverwash III; his Prime Minister, who (we learnt) rejoiced in the name of George Buggery; a range of lesser chieftains and their followers; and our erstwhile passenger Dr Benjamin Saltfish, Foreign Minister of the Federated Kroo Coast State, elegant and watchful as ever sitting on the dais beside the King. He reminded me rather of a lizard I must say: perfectly still, but always alert and occasionally flicking out its tongue to catch a passing fly.

Compliments were exchanged, and the officers and Count Minatello took their place with King Matthew on the dais. Meanwhile the rest of us were ushered into the palaver-house to sit cross-legged on the mat-covered floor – and not before time too, since it had just started to rain once more. Prestige in these parts was gauged by the number of a man's retainers, so we had been brought along merely as walking tokens of the Captain's and

Count Minatello's importance. Once we had stacked our rifles and cutlasses – within easy reach, just in case – we would have no further part in the negotiations. But this was Africa, and before diplomacy could commence the inner man must be refreshed. When we were all settled down and silent the King clapped his hands above his head and called out, 'Pass chop!' At once thirty or forty attendants came in bearing steaming dishes of rice and of a glutinous, rich concoction called 'palm-oil chop' which seemed to be chicken stewed in a sauce of palm oil, pepper and chilli. It was fiery stuff – even our goulash-hardened Magyars choked on it – and very difficult to eat with the fingers and not get our uniforms dirty. But we did our best until indigestion and burning mouths got the better of us. Gin was provided to settle down the meal: "Spose chop plenty too-much hot, grog lie him down-sleep insida belly,' as it was explained to us. The gin was served, I noticed, in tumblers marked 'Elder-Dempster Shipping Co. Ltd, Liverpool': the booty (I supposed) from some recent Kroo exploit in marine salvage.

As we ate and drank, our leaders parleyed with King Matthew and his ministers. They were certainly a strange-looking set of people. I had expected that they would be wearing long robes of some kind, like the tribal chieftains I had seen in Freetown, but instead they were dressed in a grotesque collection of cast-off European clothing, the wearing of which seemed to confer prestige in these parts. In Freetown the dress of the local notables, though over-elaborate and no doubt hideously hot in the climate, was at least a passably accurate copy of the London fashions of about fifteen years before. But here the costume appeared to have been assembled by looting rummage sales and rag-dealers' yards across the whole of Europe. I suppose that much of it must have come from plundering ships wrecked on the shore; at any rate, there seemed to be a good deal of seafaring dress among the tweed Norfolk jackets worn with necklaces of beads, and the evening trousers worn with bare feet, and the straw boaters and deerstalker hats that perched on top of mounds of woolly hair.

Most popular of all though among King Matthew's retinue were old military uniforms, as if the court and cabinet of ministers had furnished their wardrobes by stripping the dead after a battle. Mr Jorgensen told us later that one of his most profitable import-lines was old military clothing bought up cheap in Europe and brought out here by the shipload. The best times, he said, had been the early 1870s, when the French Republic had been selling off the gaudy uniforms of the recently defunct Second Empire. The King was wearing an old Zouave tunic covered in grubby gold braid, while his Prime Minister George Buggery had an elaborately frogged and gilt-buttoned hussar jacket to complement his silk opera hat (worn closed) and tweed plus-fours. No wonder Foreign Minister Saltfish – immaculately dressed as always – had about him the distant air of a man who would prefer not to be too closely associated with such a vulgar crew.

The preliminary palaver went on for a good two hours, during which time we grew stiff from sitting cross-legged. The incessant, steady thundering of the rain upon the thatch and the splash of the run-off into the mud around the palaver-house made it difficult for us to catch much of the negotiation up on the dais, which seemed now to have resolved itself into a three-cornered bargaining process between Count Minatello, George Buggery and Dr Saltfish: a prolonged haggle that eventually turned around the question posed by the Prime Minister: "Spose Krooman sell you we country, how much you dash we?" – which I suppose is in the end what most diplomacy boils down to, once one has stripped away the pourparlers and démarches. At last, about mid-afternoon, it became clear that an agreement had been reached acceptable to both high contracting parties. The Count motioned to the Captain, who motioned to Linienschiffsleutnant Zaleski, who motioned to a petty officer, who motioned to a group of sailors, who thankfully got up and went to the back of the palaver-house. This was the high point of the negotiations: the exchange of dashes.

Over the previous week I had come to learn a good deal about the complex etiquette of dashing. At the top of the scale of munificence came 'topside dash': that appropriate as between rulers. Below this came 'gen'lemen dash': generous but more modest, such as a master might give to a servant as a mark of especial favour, then 'man dash': normal everyday presents. 'Boy dash' was regarded as adequate but rather on the niggardly side, and at the bottom of the scale came 'piccaninny dash', which if offered to an adult would constitute an insult and quite probably lead to homicide. The presents that would now be exchanged were in the topside-dash category, to signal that agreement had been reached. The sailors brought a brass-bound wooden chest up to the dais and opened it. It was a handsome example of the new wind-up gramophones, built by the Österreichische Gramofon Gesellschaft of Vienna. The sailors set up the horn, wound up the machine, placed a shiny black record on the turntable and carefully lowered the needle on to its spinning surface. There was a hiss for a few moments, then music. It was a military band playing the Schrammel brothers' march 'Wien bleibt Wien'. Its insufferable jaunty frivolity filled the palaver-house as the King and his ministers gazed at it in wonder. At last the record ran down and the music faded back to a hiss. It stopped, and the melancholy drumming roar of the West African rain surged back like a temporarily repelled sea. The King spoke at last.

'Ostrich white-man palaver bokiss plenty good. But him nowhere 'smuch good like Edison Drum Phonograph.'

It seemed that, far from being a stranger to such European marvels, King Matthew had built up quite a collection of recordings – Caruso, Nellie Melba and others – after retrieving a phonograph from a wrecked ship off Cape Palmas. He was of the opinion that as far as tonal quality went the gramophone still had a good deal of ground to make up. The 'Ostrich white-man', by the way, was George Buggery's interpretation of the maker's name-plate on the gramophone. He could read quite well, since he was a Methodist lay preacher when not being Prime Minister, but he was unaware that German was not the same as English.

The rest of the dash consisted of various trifles like an Austrian staff-officer's patent-leather shako with a gold rosette, a portrait of the Emperor, a loden jacket and other such baubles. They were courteously received. The dash from King Matthew's side consisted of a specially built surf-boat with the words HURRAH

FOR FRANKS JOSEPH painted along each side in yellow and blue lettering. Then, gifts having been exchanged, the substance of the draft treaty was reached. In return for an annual subvention of fifty thousand Austrian kronen in gold, twenty cases of trade gin and treatment for his gonorrhoea (the 'cock-humbug' as he called it) King Matthew Neverwash III of the Coast-Grebos was graciously pleased to commit his lands and people in perpetuity to the care and protection of Franz Joseph the First and his heirs, Emperors of Austria and Apostolic Kings of Hungary. The treaty would be drawn up that same evening and signed the next day.

I was among the crew of paddlers entrusted with getting the surf-boat back to the ship. It was certainly a most timely present, since we were now a boat short. The eight-metre cutter that had been capsized in the surf on our first day had later been washed up on the beach near Frederiksborg. But it had been badly knocked about against rocks on the beach and was eventually written off as beyond repair. The surf-boat was about the same size, and the Carpenter said that he thought we might be able to turn it into a proper pulling boat by fitting thwarts. As it was the gunwales were kept apart by strongbacks, like a big canoe, and it had a large open space amidships so that it could carry palm-oil casks. The eight or ten paddlers knelt around the side with their feet braced in rope strops while the helmsman stood in the stern with a steering oar. Heavily built of mahogany to stand rough landings on the beach, she had a widely flared bow and stern to ride the surf: a rather odd craft to naval ways of thinking, but no doubt capable of being made into something useful.

We had to sit up most of the night restoring the neatness of our uniforms after their soaking in sea-spray and splashing with street mud. Tomorrow would be a great day in the history of the Imperial and Royal Monarchy: the official proclamation of its first overseas colony. We were all keenly conscious of the solemnity of the occasion as we formed up there next afternoon on the field in front of the palaver-house in Bunceville. A flagpole had been erected for the occasion and the house and the huts round about had been decorated with red-and-white and black-and-yellow bunting. It was the beginning of a momentous chapter in the annals of our venerable Empire, we all of us knew that. Even our professional prospects as future career naval officers suddenly seemed a great deal brighter, for we all knew, young as we were, that the possession of colonies would make it necessary for Austria to build a proper navy at last instead of the miserable semi-coastal fleet with which we had been stuck since the 1870s. Count Minatello had already been talking grandly at supper the previous evening of dredging a channel through the bar to Bunceville and turning the place – soon to be renamed 'Leopoldstadt' – into the principal port of West Africa. After all (he said), what had Singapore or Hong Kong been but fishing hamlets until they had been taken in hand by an enlightened and energetic colonial power?

The treaty had been signed – or in the King's case thumbprinted – in the palaver-house and the dignitaries had emerged on to the field. Count Minatello and Fregattenkapitän Slawetz von Löwenhausen climbed up on to a wooden platform. The official proclamation was to be made inaugurating the colony of Austro-Hungarian West Africa. It had been drafted the evening before in German, but since few of the Emperor's new subjects knew any German as yet Dr Saltfish had obligingly translated it for us into Krio. It made odd reading. Since he was more impressive to look at than Count Minatello – in fact more impressive than just about anyone we could think of – our Captain had been given the job of making the proclamation. It was a job to which his sonorous, booming sea-captain's voice was well suited: no 'I say, can you hear me at the back?' It began most imposingly.

'In the name of Franz Joseph the First, by the Grace of God Emperor of Austria and Apostolic King of Hungary; King of Bohemia, Dalmatia, Croatia, Slavonia, Galicia, Lodomeria and Illyria; Archduke of Austria and Grand Duke of Cracow; Duke of Styria, Carniola, Krain, Upper and Lower Silesia and the Bukovina; Prince of Siebenburg; Margrave of Moravia, Count of Salzburg and the Tyrol; King of Jerusalem and Holy Roman Emperor of the Germanic Nation, be it ordained . . .' He paused, and adjusted his reading spectacles. 'Herr Graf, for God's sake, I can't read out this gibberish...'

'You must, Herr Kommandant,' the Count hissed back, 'you must.'

'Oh, very well then... ahem... Be it ordained... er... All boy belongina place, you savvy. Big fella massa Franz Joseph he come now. He strong fella, plenty warboy belong him. He take all him place. He look out good alonga with you fella. He like you fella plenty much. 'Spose you work good 'long new-fella massa, he look out good alonga with you. He give you gentleman dash an' more good chop. You no fight other fella black boy other fella place. You no chop man no more. You no steal mammy belong other fella boy. Else new fella massa he send steam-boat full him war boy, he come black-boy place make all kinda no-good shit, he humbug you pass-all bad. Now you give three hellova big cheer belong new fella massa...'

He took off his cocked hat and flourished it in the air.

'Hoch der Kaiser und König! Hoch der Kaiser und König! Hoch der Kaiser und König!'

We presented arms as the crowd cheered. The band played the 'Gott Erhalte', and the red-white-red flag of Imperial Austria was run up the flagpole to flap languidly in the tepid breeze. The natives of Bunceville cheered lustily in that curious high-pitched ululating way of theirs – though from what I could hear of it they still seemed to think that we were Australians. Fireworks began to crackle around the field amid the cheering, the Geschutzmeister having virtually emptied the pyrotechnics locker to put on a suitable display. Signal rockets hissed into the sky as the townspeople fired off their dane-guns with bright flashes and clouds of white smoke. Flocks of parrots ascended screaming from the trees around the field as the vultures flapped heavily into the air from the hut roofs, rudely disturbed from their afternoon siesta and no doubt wondering what all the fuss was about. Mere birds, how could they know that Austria-Hungary's great colonial adventure had just begun?

Over the next couple of hours, before the rain swept in once more to put an end to the celebrations, a great deal of gin, palm wine and small chop was consumed on the field in front of the palaver-house. The band was playing the 'Erzherzog Albrecht March' as Father Semmelweiss tried his best in his inadequate English to convert King Matthew Neverwash to the Catholic faith. I suppose that as local representative of Europe's principal Catholic monarchy he felt that he had to try, but by the sound of it he was not getting very far. The local people were mostly adherents of one brand or other of Methodism, varied from time to time by the odd human sacrifice, and Father Semmelweiss was in any case someone who would have had difficulty converting the crew of a sinking ship to the use of lifebelts. In the end the best that he could get was an assurance that Frederiksborg Castle would be given to the Austrian Jesuits to set up a seminary.

Towards the end of the party Dr Benjamin Saltfish sidled up to me, cross-eyed and giggly with gin. He knew that I spoke English rather better than most of the other cadets and he seemed to feel a wish to confide in me. He spoke English well, with a slight American accent and idiom which I supposed came from having been educated at college in Monrovia as well as at Harvard University.

'I like you, boy. Union Jack says you're a pretty bright sort of kid by all accounts.'

'Thank you, Your Excellency, I am flattered by your high opinion of me.'

He paused for a while, thinking. 'Yes, certainly smarter than the rest of the dumb white cockroaches, that's for sure . . .'

'Excuse me, Your Excellency, but I do not quite understand . . .'

He laughed and threw his arm round my shoulder, turning me aside from the rest of the crowd as his voice sank to a confidential undertone.

'You Austrians must think we black folks are pr-e-t-ty dumb, that's for sure, selling our country to you for a few bottles of square-face gin and a gramophone and a general's hat and suchlike trash. But I can tell you now, we ain't no-way near as stupid as you think. Tell me kid, why do you think we asked you here? Tell me that.' I found this question embarrassing. But an Austrian officer had to be his country's ambassador when abroad, so I tried to frame the answer that I believed would be expected of me.

'I imagine, Your Excellency, that your King and the people of the Federated Kroo-Coast State had heard of the Dual Monarchy's unequalled reputation for maintaining harmony and tolerance among diverse peoples, and took the view that as subjects of our Emperor you would be treated on a footing of equality with all the other nationalities that comprise the great family of peoples gathered under the Habsburg sceptre.'

He laughed uproariously at this. 'No, kid, not quite. We chose Austria after a lot of hard thinking, that's true enough. We looked at the British: but then we remembered the Hut Tax up in Sierra Leone, making the black folks pay them money so they'd have to work for the white master to earn it. We thought about the French – but we kind-of didn't take too well to the notion of having Molière and Racine stuffed down our throats and our young men being rounded up each year for the Chasseurs d'Afrique. We didn't think too much of the Germans either with their dog-whips, nor the Italians, nor the Belgians chopping picaninnies' hands off because their pa hasn't collected enough rubber. We asked the Danes, but they said they were trying to sell off their colonies, not get themselves any more. So in the end we fixed on old Austria. And do you know why? I'll tell you: because of all your precious Great Powers Austria's the weakest; just strong enough to keep the other white cockroaches out of our hut-thatch, but not strong enough to give us any humbug about taxes and conscription and all that kinda shit.'

I was deeply shocked by this, so much so that for some moments I was unable to speak.

'But Your Excellency, you and your fellow-countrymen have just cheered the Imperial flag as it was hoisted... I do not understand...'

'Sure: with the Monrovia niggers sending soldiers down the coast to burn our villages and rape our women we'd be glad to see any flag fly over us so long as it's not theirs. But anyway, what's to say we don't like you fellas? Your music's pretty good, and we might even start learning German one day if we feel like it; maybe even have a governor here and a few policemen if your old Emperor can afford it. But get this . . .' He stared into my eyes with his own slightly yellowed whites. 'No man makes a Kroo work. See this?' He pointed to the triple scar on the bridge of his nose. 'The freedom mark. We Kroo-men work hard for the white master – but only for money and good chop, not because he whips us and humbugs us. No man in this world makes a Kroo do anything.' He smiled and slapped my shoulder genially. 'Think of it as a partnership if you like it that way: we give you a colony to make you look important back in Europe, and you keep the other Europeans off we country.'

'Excuse me, Your Excellency, but so far as I understand it all the other peoples of Africa thought that – until it was too late. What is to prevent us from sending ships and soldiers in a few years' time to make you do as we say? Austria-Hungary is a good deal stronger a power than Liberia, I can assure you.'

'Make us do as you say? But that's rich. From what they tell me your old Emperor can't make people do as he says an hour's train ride from Vienna. No sir: if the white masters in Vienna try humbugging us any we'll just write and complain to the other white masters in Budapest. That'll make them stop and think, you can be sure of *that*.'

I was deeply shocked at this display of utter duplicity from one of the most educated representatives of a people who had just elected, of their own free will, to seek shelter beneath the wings of the two-headed Habsburg eagle. But I must confess that I still felt a certain sneaking admiration for this young man from such a backward and remote country who had so coolly and accurately sized up the political realities of a far-distant empire which he had certainly never visited.

'Your Excellency,' I said at last, 'what is there to stop me going and reporting what you have just told me to Count Minatello and my captain? They would be deeply concerned that you should have said such things on such an afternoon as this.'

He threw his arm around my shoulder. 'Boy, no one would believe you. No one ever believes kids or black folks. But don't take on so: I kind of like you. There's plenty of white people have been good to me over the years, and I reckon we can be good friends yet. Just don't go around giving yourself airs that you're any smarter than us because it ain't so. Our King Matthew and your Emperor Franz Joseph they're both kings; only one of them's a bit darker than the other, that's all.'

We rode at anchor off Frederiksborg until 6 August, by which time the 'Summer Dries' had advanced to a point where the rain poured down for only about half of each day – though always during my watch on deck. We could have weighed anchor and departed the day after the hoisting of the flag over our new colony, since for the moment there was nothing further to be done but notify Vienna of the annexation. Count Minatello had been rowed across on the following day to a passing Elder-Dempster steamer bound for the Gold Coast. He carried a sealed diplomatic pouch with a coded telegram which would be despatched to the Imperial and Royal Foreign Ministry once he reached Accra. I had helped Linienschiffsleutnant Svoboda encode it the evening before. It read:

BEG TO INFORM YOU K.U.K. PROTECTORATE OVER KROO COAST
PROCLAIMED BUNCEVILLE NOW LEOPOLDSTADT I AUGUST
STOP DEPARTING SOON STOP SEND TROOPS AND
ADMINISTRATORS STOP

LONG LIVE THE EMPEROR AND KING EXCLAMATION

FGKPTN SLAWETZ VON LOEWENHAUSEN
S.M.S. WINDISCHGRAETZ
OFF FREDERIKSBORG 2/VIII/02

Once that task had been performed there was nothing further to keep us from continuing with the purely scientific part of our voyage and departing for Brazil – except that one of our two exploration parties had failed to report back on the appointed day. Dr Pükler's geologists had returned without mishap, laden down with boxes of specimens and none the worse for their five days in the jungle except for a man who had been stung by a scorpion and one with an infected cut on his arm (in this microbe-laden climate the smallest scratch turned septic within a couple of hours). Whatever was in Professor Skowronek's anti-fever cocktail, it seemed to have worked pretty well, because they had otherwise remained in perfect health despite working in dense rainforest which even the natives avoided as disease-ridden. But of Fregattenleutnant Hrabovsky's party there was no word. We waited for them – and waited. In the end canoes were sent upriver from Bunceville to see what had become of them. They found nothing but the expedition's eight-metre cutter abandoned below the first cataract in the river about forty kilometres upstream. Of the fifteen men there was no sign. In the end, rather than delay the whole expedition on their account, the Captain decided to sail without them, leaving instructions for them to catch a steamer to the German colony of Togoland when they got back and make their way home from there. King Matthew's counsellors said that they were unlikely to have come to any harm. The inland Grebo were Christians, but one of their chiefs was known to be very wary of the French, who were encroaching on to his territory, and might have detained Hrabovsky and his men thinking them to be a survey party from Senegal.

The disappearance of Landungsdetachement Hrabovsky cast a shadow over us all as we tramped round the capstan on the morning of 6 August to break out the anchor and set sail. We were not sorry to be leaving the Kroo Coast. We were sick of the endless rolling on the swell: always very trying aboard a sailing ship riding at anchor because the masts accentuate the roll when there is no canvas set to act as a damper. And we were thoroughly tired of the enervating laundry-room heat and the constant rain. I had opened my sea-chest the day before, to be greeted by an overpowering smell of mildew. Fungus was growing over the deckheads, despite the wind-sail ventilators rigged on deck, and the ship was rapidly being taken over by insects: notably the huge West African cockroaches from on shore – insolent great brutes the size of dates which fluttered around every lantern and scurried away with incredible speed when one tried to crush them with a boot heel. They ate everything, but it seemed that they particularly relished paper – books, letters, charts and anything else they could reach – and also the hard skin from sailors' feet, so that before long the watch below had to sleep with their socks on to prevent their soles from being chewed down to the quick. The cockroaches were soon known by the lower deck as 'Staatsbeamten' – 'civil servants' – because of their ability to multiply, their uniform appearance and their love of paper. Linienschiffsleutnant Zaleski, who hated form-filling above all else, set us to work one evening to trap as many of them as we could with the aid of candle-lanterns. After we had caught several hundred of the insects he made us release them in the ship's office, then locked the door for the night in the hope that by morning they would have munched their way through the ship's entire stock of official forms, thus freeing us from scribbling for the rest of the voyage. It was a good idea, but unfortunately there was something in Austrian Kanzlei-Doppel paper which was not to their taste. Instead they merely contented themselves with devouring the petty-expense claims.

While we were claiming new territories for the Noble House of Austria Professor Skowronek had been busy ashore on his scientific investigations, roaming about inland with his assistant and a couple of native bearers to carry his guns. It was not until the final day of our stay that he came aboard with a large hessian bag, looking very pleased with himself, and went below at once to his cabin. Several of us were already growing suspicious of the Professor's methods of collecting specimens; particularly after the British steamer which had collected Count Minatello had kindly sent us back a parcel of old newspapers, as was the custom among ships in those days. Among them was a copy of the *Freetown Bugle* from 19 July, two days after we had sailed. An item read:

RIOTS OVER SORCERY

It was reported today by the Commissioner of Protectorate

Police that armed clashes took place on 16 July near Moyamba between rival gangs from the Mende and Farkinah tribes after it had been discovered that graves in Moyamba's Church of England mission graveyard had been desecrated the previous night by persons unknown. According to reports the skulls had been removed from several corpses, although the rest of the remains had apparently been left untouched. The villagers seem to have blamed the neighbouring tribe and clashes immediately broke out between gangs armed with spears and bush-knives, leaving seven people dead and many injured. Order has been restored by a force of Protectorate police led by Major Williamson, and investigations are now proceeding into possible witchcraft. Several local medicine men are reported to be assisting the police with their enquiries.

On the morning we left Frederiksborg, just before we got under way, the officer of the watch sent me below with a message for Professor Skowronek. I knocked on the door of his workroom. 'Bitte!' I opened the door – to be enveloped in a cloud of evil-smelling steam. As the murk cleared I saw that the Professor was in his shirtsleeves boiling something in a cauldron over a stove. It was monstrously hot despite the cabin scuttle being open, but he seemed to be too absorbed in his work to mind. I saw that it was true after all: a row of six human skulls sat grinning on a shelf while a seventh lay draining on the bench, shining ivory-white while the ones on the shelf were a dirty brown, as if they had been buried for years in leaf-mould.

'Ah, come in young man, come in. And how are we today? A message from Leutnant Svoboda, thank you. Tell me, young man: what's your name?' He was gazing at me with a penetrating look; not at my face, I soon realised, but at the top of my head.

'Prohaska, Herr Professor; Ottokar Prohaska. Second-year cadet of the Imperial and Royal Marine Academy.'

'I thought so. Prohaska: a Czech I suppose?'

'My father is a Czech, Herr Professor. My mother is a Pole.'

He smiled knowingly. 'Just as I thought: the typical Czech skull tends to be of more mesaticephalic type as a result of Alpine-Dinaric influence while the typical Pole has a cranial index of around eighty-three from Baltic admixture. This fellow though...' He picked up the clean white skull from the bench, '... This fellow here is of typical lower negroid type, do you see?' He picked up a sort of large Vernier scale made of boxwood from the bench and clamped it across the skull. 'Ah yes: facial angle about sixty degrees; spheno-ethmoidal angle almost a straight line; foramino-basal also extremely shallow; index of about sixty-eight average and as low as... let me see... yes, I would say as little as fifty-five over the temporal axis. Not much to be expected in the way of creative intelligence from *that* individual when he was alive I think. Some of those up there however...' He pointed up at the row of skulls on the shelf: '... are getting near to low-grade Europeans: possibly Mandingos or members of some other such Berber-influenced tribe. When they were alive I would have expected them to have worn clothes and to have shown some glimmerings of creative ability in crafts like pottery and weaving. These Kroos here though are completely worthless specimens from a eugenic point of view: fit for nothing but paddling canoes as human engine rooms. I was not in the least surprised to see them aping – I use the word advisedly – the fashions of Europeans when I was in that detestable hole of a village of theirs, Bunceville or whatever they call it. They are a people patently incapable of any creativity or originality whatever. Without the redeeming influence of the white race they would still be sunk in a squalor so beastly as to be scarcely imaginable.'

'But, with respect, Herr Professor, Cadet Gauss and I have worked a great deal with Kroo boatmen over the past couple of weeks and they have always struck us as very cheerful, witty, intelligent people.'

He frowned at me: clearly he was not accustomed to being contradicted, least of all by sixteen-year-olds. 'Parrot learning, young man: monkeys in red jackets and pillbox hats capering to the music of the white man's street-organ. Without the European to imitate they would be even more sullen, morose and generally maladroit than the rest of the Negro race. Myself, I suspect that this general incapacity may have much to do with the early closing of the cranial sutures in negro children, preventing much development of the brain after the age of about three; but as yet I have not accumulated a sufficient body of evidence to prove that hypothesis. But I must get back to work . . . Here, take this up on deck and empty it overboard for me, will you?' He reached into the steaming cauldron with a pair of wooden tongs and fished out another skull, steaming and pouring water like a boiled pudding. He placed it in the sink to drain, took the cauldron off the stove and handed it to me. I peered into it – and felt a sudden intense urge to vomit. It was filled with a mass of boiled-off flesh. Both skulls had evidently been attached to living people only a couple of days before. I managed somehow to get up on deck and shoot the contents of the cauldron overboard to the sharks before I was sick. I was off my food for some time afterwards. Somehow boiled salt pork at dinner appealed to me even less than usual that day.

9

CROSSING THE LINE

The passage across the Atlantic to the coast of Brazil took us the best part of a month, even though the linear distance was not much over two thousand miles. The trouble was that a passage from Frederiksborg to Pernambuco necessarily took us through that belt of calms, the Doldrums, which extends for about ten degrees each side of the Equator. The only way to get across the Atlantic in fact was to sail southwards as best we could until we were below the Equator, then hope to pick up the northernmost edge of the south-east trade winds to get us across to South America, then turn north-westwards again to cut in to Pernambuco. If we had tried doing this north of the Doldrums we would have stood a good chance of getting ourselves jammed behind Cape São Roque, the north-easternmost tip of Brazil, and found ourselves fighting against wind and current for months on end to reach our destination. So we crawled and dawdled and drifted south-westwards for eighteen days until we picked up the breeze. It was a frustrating time. For most of those days my personal logbook read, 'Distance run in past 24 hours: 2 miles,' and on 11 August it actually noted 'Distance run: minus 1 mile,' since we seemed to have drifted astern in the night.

It was also very hard work. I know that people nowadays imagine sailing-ship men toiling like lunatics while rounding the Horn, and then lolling around for the rest of the voyage bored witless with inactivity. But it was not like that at all. True, working the ship in the Roaring Forties could be very hard, but it was at least exhilarating hard work, with the ship surging along at twelve knots for days on end with no more trouble to the crew than laying aloft to handle sail. In the calms though the work was just as hard, bracing round the yards to catch every fleeting puff of wind – and often with nothing to show for all our toil in terms of distance sailed. The watch on deck had to be at the ready for the entire crossing, whether the sun was making the pitch ooze and bubble from the deck seams or whether the tropical rain was pouring down in torrents from clouds that seemed to take a malign satisfaction in hovering just above us, as if they too were trying to relieve the boredom by doing their best to drown us all. Tempers soon became frayed as the sun glared down from the brassy sky and up from the mirror-like sea; while the sails hung limp as tea-towels and the rubbish thrown overboard after breakfast was still floating under the taffrail at noon.

For us cadets there was no respite whatever. We were back on the two-watch system now, after a spell during our stay at Frederiksborg when we had been put on to three watches: two off and one on. When we were not on deck, either trimming sails or waiting to trim sails, we had to attend our full daily quota of classes. Since we were in different watches it was only during instruction that Gauss and I saw much of our mess-mates Tarabochia and Gumpoldsdorfer. Tarabochia was much improved now, we both felt, from the rather obnoxious youth he had been when he had joined the Marine Academy. Perhaps the death of his crony Cattarinić the previous year had sobered him. I never much liked him, but he had become at least tolerable company, now that our own grasp of seamanship and our nimbleness aloft had nearly caught up with his own. Poor Toni Gumpoldsdorfer though was a sad case, and one that grew sadder as the weeks passed by. In himself he was a most likeable boy: genial, kind-hearted, polite and almost impossible to offend as well as being decidedly handsome; an earnest, rather slow, blond, blue-eyed youth from near Klagenfurt in Carinthia where his father was a doctor. But somehow his great personal amiability only seemed to make matters worse. In fact as the voyage progressed the rest of us were increasingly at a loss to explain how 'der Gumperl' had ever managed to get into the Marine Academy at all, let alone be selected to come on this expedition. Max Gauss took the view that it was a case rather like that of the 'mathematical idiots' one sometimes reads about: people who can instantly give you the square root of 297 to four places of decimals, or tell you that 19 February 1437 was a Wednesday, but who are incapable of tying their shoelaces or of being sent out on their own to post a letter.

Gumpoldsdorfer seemed to do well enough in navigation classes; at least, his own solutions to Linienschiffsleutnant Zaleski's problems were not noticeably more wrong than anyone else's. It was just that he seemed totally, painfully incapable of making the link between theory and practice. The poor lad was about as devoid of common sense as anyone I have ever come across: in fact one could well have defined common sense as the opposite of what Toni Gumpoldsdorfer would do in any given circumstances. I well remember the first sea-watch he stood after we sailed from Pola. He had been entrusted with the half-hour sand-glass and it had been explained to him in the simplest terms possible that every time the glass ran out during the four-hour watch he was to turn it, then strike the ship's bell once for every half-hour elapsed since the start of the watch: two bells after one hour, three bells after ninety minutes and so on up to eight bells and the end of the watch, thus giving (Bo'sun Njegosić added to make matters entirely clear) a total of thirty-five strokes of the bell during the entire four-hour period. Gumpoldsdorfer had nodded to signify that he understood, and we went below to our hammocks. We had hardly got to sleep when the entire watch below were roused out of their hammocks by the strident clang-clang-clanging of the ship's bell. Bleary-eyed men in their underpants rushed up the companionways to seize buckets, convinced that the vessel was on fire – then saw Gumpoldsdorfer by the bell-house, tongue clenched between his teeth with concentration, counting up to the thirty-five strokes which would signal that it was now the end of the first half-hour of the middle watch.

In short, if there was any way of making a pig's ear of any job whatever, Gumpoldsdorfer would assuredly find it; and his calf-like, apologetic bewilderment afterwards only served to make matters worse since it was so difficult for anyone to get really angry with him. 'Ach so: dürft'ich nicht so machen?' – 'Ooh-er, shouldn't I have done that?' – became a sort of catchphrase among the cadets of the port watch. Yet, as I have said, he was an immensely well-meaning boy and impossible to dislike, so we all made allowances and covered up for him as much as we could, treating him like a mildly half-witted relative – but still taking good care to stand well away from beneath him when he was working aloft.

We cadets were mustered one sultry, windless morning in mid-August, in mid-Atlantic somewhere north of the Equator, to receive further instruction from Bootsmann Torpedomeister Kaindel in the workings of the 40cm Whitehead torpedo. The *Windischgrätz* carried eight of these devices, with two trainable tubes on the lower deck for discharging them. We were now assembled around the bow-tube studying the firing mechanism. We had learnt about the torpedo itself at the previous lesson, using an example sliced down the middle with the working parts painted in various bright colours to make them more visible. But now it was to be the real thing: we were actually going to fire one. Normally this should only have been done in harbour, for fear of losing the torpedo. But there would be no danger of that today: the ship had moved barely a hundred metres since dawn, and anyway a rowing cutter was standing by to retrieve the weapon at the end of its run, which had been set for about four hundred metres. Gauss was commander for the purposes of this exercise; I was trainer, cranking a brass wheel to line the tube up with numbers on the semicircular slide let into the deck; and Gumpoldsdorfer was in charge of loading. Tarabochia and another cadet would push the torpedo into the tube from its trolley and Gumpoldsdorfer would shut and lock the door behind it, then signal that we were ready to fire the small charge of black powder which would blow the torpedo out of the tube like a cork from a bottle.

'Right!' shouted Kaindel, 'load the torpedo!' Tarabochia and his assistant grunted with effort as they slid the greasy bronze body of the torpedo – which weighed four hundred kilograms – off its trolley and into the tube.

'Torpedo home!' Gumpoldsdorfer shouted. There was a pause and a heavy metallic clunk as the door shut and was locked.

'Door locked – ready to fire!'

Well, I thought, I heard the lock so he must have got *that* right at least. Gauss squinted through the sights at the target, an empty cask bobbing in the sea about three hundred metres off our port bow.

'Train tube forty degrees!'

I cranked the wheel officiously to traverse the tube: thirty degrees . . . thirty-five degrees . . .

'Tube trained to forty degrees!'

I yanked at the brake lever to hold it steady, though there was no need whatever since the ship was as steady as a cathedral in the flat calm. There was a pause, then Gauss tugged on the lanyard. There was a jolt and a muffled poom! as the charge fired. We rushed to peer out of the port in the ship's side as the white smoke cloud drifted away – and saw that the torpedo was lying about ten metres off our bow, wallowing placidly like a sleeping porpoise. The boat's crew got a line about it and it was hoisted back on board as we ran up on deck to see what was wrong with it.

'Probably motor failure again,' said Kaindel. 'I tell you, these things are as finicky as a lady's watch. I don't know why we bother with them . . .' He stared. There was a terrible silence. At last he roared, 'Cadet Gumpoldsdorfer, you imbecile – come here!'

'What's the matter, Torpedomeister?'

'Look, you triple-distilled cretin, look . . .' Kaindel was pointing, his finger quivering with rage like a water diviner's rod. We looked. The plywood clamps which secured the torpedo's two counter-rotating propellers during transit were still in place. They should have been removed after the weapon had been hoisted up from the store, before it was placed on the loading trolley – and it was Gumpoldsdorfer who should have removed them. He blushed crimson, but instead of guffawing the rest of us hid our faces in embarrassment, trying to look somewhere else. He got a four-hour mastheading, and when he came down he had to refill the torpedo's compressed-air reservoir, which had needed to be bled since the motor's starting level had been tripped on firing and there was no other way of deactivating the thing. It was a large reservoir to charge with a hand-pump and the working pressure was eighty atmospheres, so the poor fellow was still at it next morning.

We crossed the Equator on 20 August, two weeks and a mere five hundred miles after leaving Frederiksborg, at about 20 degrees west longitude since our Captain was sure, from his long study of wind patterns, that at this season of the year the belt of calms would be at its narrowest about there. He was right as it turned out: next day we would get a faint breeze that would allow us to ghost southwards sufficiently to pick up solid south-easterlies. But we were not quite there yet, so the afternoon of the crossing could be given over to that traditional maritime saturnalia, the 'Equatortaufe'.

Gauss and I got the horseplay off to a start that morning. I had found Gauss on deck with a telescope, unscrewing the objective lens. 'Watch this,' he said. He stretched a hair across the middle of the lens, then carefully screwed it back into place. 'Now, follow me.' He stuffed the telescope down the front of his jersey, jumped into the mainmast shrouds and began to climb aloft, towards Toni Gumpoldsdorfer perched at the masthead. He had been sent up there an hour or so earlier to watch for the smoke of passing steamers. We had been at sea for two weeks now without seeing another vessel and were getting lonely, as well as being anxious to post letters home and replenish our stock of reading matter – especially now that the gunroom's copy of *Josefina Mutzenbacher*, that classic of literature pour la main gauche, had fallen to pieces at last from the combined effects of cockroaches and steamy adolescent breath. We found him jammed in the shrouds, dazed with sun and the glare from the glassy sea. A slight breeze was blowing, but we were still only making a knot or two through the water. Gauss prodded him awake.

'Equator in sight, Gumperl!'

'Eh? What . . .?'

'I said Equator in sight, you chump. Here, look.' Gauss handed him the doctored telescope, carefully presented to him so that the hair was parallel to the horizon. Gumpoldsdorfer peered into it – then, before we could stop him, turned to shout down to the deck:

'Equator in sight, dead ahead!'

The officer of the watch was Linienschiffsleutnant Svoboda, a tiny figure on deck by the funnel. He looked up at us.

'What did you say?' he shouted.

'Obediently report, Equator in sight, Herr Leutnant, dead ahead!' There was an ominous pause, then:

'Cadet Gumpoldsdorfer, come down here on deck. I want a word with you.'

We looked on aghast as Gumpoldsdorfer scrambled down on to the deck and saluted. Svoboda asked him something. Gumpoldsdorfer proffered the telescope. Svoboda snatched it, strode to the side and peered through it – then came back and hit Gumpoldsdorfer over the head with it. We neither of us said anything. There was no need: we both felt utterly rotten and despicable. The worst thing about it was that Gumpoldsdorfer treated the whole business as a splendid joke and congratulated us on our ingenuity. The best we could do was break out one of Gauss's precious pots of plum jam from his sea-chest that evening and share it with our victim.

The real Equator – at least, as observed by sextant – came into sight at noon that day. An announcement was made from the bridge, and at four bells sharp King Neptune and his entourage came aboard: Bo'sun's Mate Josipović and a collection of the ship's more dubious characters. There was Neptune's wife: the Gunner's Mate wearing a wig of spunyarn and the make-up of a Spalato whore. There was Neptune's chaplain: the Carpenter dressed in a cardboard bishop's mitre with a shot-rammer as a crozier. There were Neptune's daughter – Steuermatrose Kralik wearing breasts made of canvas stuffed with oakum and painted pink – Neptune's personal physician – a sick-bay attendant armed with a sinister-looking syringe exuding soap bubbles – and Neptune's bank manager: the Paymaster's clerk carrying a cashbox and a pair of carpenter's pincers for extracting fines.

They were paraded round the deck to the music of drum, bugle and accordion, and then the fun began. All those who could not show a certificate proving that they had crossed the line were subjected to various indignities in tubs of water, shaved on collapsing chairs with an enormous wooden razor and finally daubed with various colours of paint. The passengers were exempt – that is, unless they wished to join in – but not the officers. But as it happened only the hapless Fregattenleutnant O'Callaghan had not crossed the Equator before, so he was the only member of the wardroom to be ducked, lathered, scraped and red-leaded that afternoon – which ordeal, it has to be recorded, he suffered with exemplary good humour. The only doubtful case was the Chaplain. He had not been across the line before, it was true. But he was not quite a member of the crew and anyway, even the most case-hardened sceptics among the lower deck had doubts about the propriety of daubing an ordained priest's private parts with Rote Minium paint. After all, who knew what ill luck might follow? In the end Father Semmelweiss sat at the break of the poop deck watching the blasphemous rituals taking place below him, much as a rather timid missionary from Rome might have watched a gang of Vikings sacrificing horses and prisoners of war, smiling nervously and keeping an eye all the time on the gate leading out of their encampment. At the end of it all we got our certificates – beautifully calligraphed; I had mine for years afterwards – and that was that. We cadets were now probationary blue-water seafarers. The only thing necessary to complete our initiation was to round Cape Horn east to west, which would give us the right to spit into the wind and to drink the Emperor's health with one foot resting on the wardroom table. Perhaps next year or the year after, we thought to ourselves...

On 23 August, 4 degrees south of the Equator, about half-way between Africa and Brazil, the sails suddenly began to fill. We had picked up the south-east trades. We sailed due south for two days, until the wind was nice and steady, then turned westward towards Pernambuco to bowl along at a regular eight or nine knots. We had seen Africa: now we were going to look – albeit briefly – at South America. For me, however, although I had no way of knowing it at the time, our stay at Pernambuco would mark a milestone in my life a good deal more important than crossing imaginary lines on the ocean or setting foot on new continents.

The name Pernambuco was rather misleading: Pernambuco was the most north-easterly province of Brazil, and the port that we would visit for five days was in fact known to its natives as Recife, situated on an island and connected by bridges to the Brazilian mainland. I am not quite sure how it came about that the name of the province came to be attached to its capital city, but such was the usage in those days among seafarers. I suppose that it scarcely mattered: the shores of the world before the First World War were dotted with towns that existed entirely for sailing ships and their crews, their positions determined by the winds and by the now long-vanished trades they existed to serve: Hobart and Canton, Iquique and Port Victoria – now often no more than faded names, where the desert winds blow across the crumbling wharves and rusty corrugated-iron shacks where once thousands of seamen on shore-leave would gather to brawl, drink and whore away their accumulated pay. Pernambuco in 1902 was not in the first division among these sailor-towns, but it was certainly well up in the second, handling most of northern Brazil's trade in coffee, sugar and cotton. When we arrived there that September morning we counted no less than fifty-eight ships in harbour, sailing vessels and steamers alike. It was only with difficulty and a good deal of bribery that we eventually secured a berth on the far side of the harbour, towards the bar, anchored between two other warships: the French armoured cruiser *Denfert-Rochereau* paying a courtesy call, and an American sloop here on a debt-collecting expedition.

We dropped anchor, the sails were furled in an impeccable harbour-stow, the upper yards were sent down and the topmasts were housed. Harbour watch-bills were posted, a month's accumulation of sea-grime was cleaned off until we were in a fit state to receive visitors and, these chores having been completed, the boats were swung out and lowered to be moored to the booms, ready to receive the first batch of liberty men now busy on the lower deck shaving themselves and pressing their best whites ready for a run ashore. The shore-goers were paraded at the start of the first dog-watch to be inspected by the Bo'sun and the officers of the watch, and, having been pronounced fit for human consumption, were ordered to form up at the Paymaster's desk to receive their accumulated pay and allowances in golden twenty-kronen pieces. That ceremony over, they were then allowed to pile into the boats and row ashore to discharge the back pay and pent-up energies accumulated during nearly two months at sea.

By all accounts they would have no problem finding amusement in Pernambuco. So far the only sizeable towns we had visited were Gibraltar and Freetown, both God-fearing, sedate and rather dowdy places ruled by the British Crown. Pernambuco however fitted into none of those prim categories: was in fact regarded as something of a nautical frontier-town, altogether too lawless and debauched a place at any rate for a group of adolescent naval cadets to be let loose in it unsupervised. We were kept aboard ship and set to work on various menial tasks of painting and cleaning under the supervision of Linienschiffsleutnant Mikulić, who was himself in an even nastier mood than usual from having been given the daytime watches. We four second-year cadets were sent down into the dimly lit cable tiers and given the heart-breaking task of rubbing the rust and old paint off the spare anchor chains, link by link, using sand and old pieces of canvas: about as frustrating a corvée as can well be imagined. We were still at it next afternoon as the liberty boats arrived back at the ship carrying the first batch of survivors from the previous night's razzle. We sneaked up to steal a look at them through an open skylight as they came aboard: a scene somewhere between the Retreat from Moscow and Géricault's 'Raft of the Medusa'. The seventy or so walking wounded, casualties of brawling and local rum, were given first aid where necessary by the sick-bay attendants, then stumbled or were carried down to the lower deck to sleep off some of the most murderous hangovers in the history of the Austrian fleet. We were put to work later scouring the battery deck above them, and it diverted us no end to hear the howls and curses from below when one of us dropped a scrubbing brush on the planks.

The cadets got their turn to go ashore on the third day of the visit, ferried across in the ten-metre barge wearing our best whites with dirks at our belts and with the Captain's parting instructions still ringing in our ears to comport ourselves like future Austrian officers and representatives of Europe's most august and most Catholic ruling house. Not that we had much chance of doing otherwise: as soon as we had disembarked we were surrounded by a strong and vigilant escort of petty officers led by Linienschiffsleutnant Svoboda – whose name, we recalled ruefully, is Czech for 'freedom' – and Fregattenleutnant Buratović who was in a bilious temper after having been denied leave as punishment for having turned out late on watch. In the end the only concession to shore-leave as generally understood by seafarers was that we were not manacled ankle-to-ankle and escorted by guards with fixed bayonets. We trooped around the cathedral, the botanical gardens, the provincial assembly, the presidential palace, the museum of antiquities ('noteworthy collection of pre-Colombian pottery artefacts') and the rest of the sights: all very colonial-Portuguese with their crumbling ochre-painted façades and the wealth of blue-and-white ceramic tiling. Despite the closely regulated character of our tour and the considerable heat I decided that I rather liked Pernambuco – or Recife as I suppose I ought to call it now. It was poor, dirty, crowded and rather shabby, I have to admit. But this was the tropics as I had always imagined it: almost the Spanish Main of pirate stories, given a little imagination. Compared with the mournful, damp, fever-haunted drabness of Freetown this place fairly hummed with life and shimmered with gaudy colours like a parrot's wings. As for its inhabitants, growing up in the pinkish-grey uniformity of Central Europe had never even begun to prepare us for a world where there could be quite so many gradations of colour. It was as if the city had been designed as a sort of selection chart for human skin pigmentation, rather like those folders one gets from decorator's shops with the little shiny oblongs of paint colours. There was everything in these teeming streets, from West African blue-black through chocolate brown and Chinese heliotrope to Indian copper, Portuguese cinnamon and north-European pink. We gaped in wonderment at the shabby splendour of the people and their costumes: colours which would have looked vile under northern skies, but which here seemed as perfectly right and God-ordained as the plumage of the bright birds fluttering among the jacaranda trees in the municipal park. If this was the world outside Europe then most of us concluded there and then that we had chosen the right profession – particularly when the great dark eyes of the girls out with their mamas in the jardim botánico turned furtively in our direction. They and we were both well-chaperoned now. But in a few years we might be back here as junior lieutenants, wearing the black-and-yellow sword-belt and free of officious petty officers.

We were herded back aboard as evening fell. Two cadets had managed to give our escorts the slip. but naval police pickets were now out after them. As for the rest of us, it would be back to working rig tomorrow morning, and with it the endless tasks of care and maintenance aboard a sailing ship. The remainder of the crew had been given their forty-eight hour passes and gone ashore the day before. Some of the weaker of their number were already being brought alongside to be laid out like so many logs on the lower deck as the convalescents from the first shore party began to hobble about, pale and hollow-eyed. I was cadet of the side on the second dog-watch the next evening, from 6.00 to 8.00 p.m., standing ready to receive any distinguished guests via the starboard gangway. It looked like being a tedious two hours since all the routine calls had already been paid. The local medical officer had come aboard just after we anchored to carry out the necessary health inspection – that is to say, parading up and down the lines of men at a brisk trot before signing a form declaring our ship to be free of yellow fever, smallpox, bubonic plague, cholera, anthrax and other such trifles. The Provincial Governor and his family had come aboard the same evening to be entertained in the captain's saloon, and the local Bishop, Monsignor Fernandes, had paid his visit the next day. The officers of the French and American warships had come aboard for drinks that evening, as was the custom in a foreign anchorage, and that was about it: social visits over for the rest of our stay. The Captain had thankfully changed into his shore-going uniform and had been rowed ashore in his gig the next morning, to disappear none knew where. The scientists were all ashore, Professor Skowronek to give a lecture to the local Eugenics Society on 'The Evils of Race-Mixing' – rather late in the day, we all agreed after our tour of Pernambuco. As for the officers, they had all dispersed to take up invitations to stay with families up-country for a couple of days: all, that is, except the wretched Fregattenleutnant Buratović, who was still serving out his penance for arriving late on watch.

All was now as quiet as only a sailing ship can be in harbour. I was standing by the rail, wondering whether I could risk leaning on it unobserved as I watched the sun sink towards the forest-covered hills of the mainland. It was boring here, but undeniably rather beautiful as the first lights started to twinkle ashore. Suddenly there was a voice from below. A boat had come alongside. It was Seefähnrich Kolarz in the ship's dinghy.

'Ahoy there – is that you, Prohaska?'

'Hello Kolarz,' I said, stepping out on to the grating at the head of the gangway. 'What's up?' I had detected a certain note of urgency in his voice.

'It's the Captain: we've lost him.'

'What on earth do you mean, lost him?'

'There's a rumour on the waterfront that something terrible's happened to an Austrian ship's captain somewhere in town. Only I don't know what – or where. Or at least, everyone says they know what and where, but I don't know Portuguese so I can't make head or tail of it. Can you get the officer of the watch?'

I ran below and knocked on the door of Buratović's cabin. He was in his shirtsleeves, reading an old and very dog-eared copy of the risqué Viennese journal *Pschütt*.

'What the blazes do you want, Prohaska?'

'I obediently report, Herr Leutnant, that Seefähnrich Kolarz is alongside and says something's happened to the Captain ashore, and please can you come up on deck?'

Buratović groaned and put on his jacket. 'Really,' he grumbled, 'this is too much. Can't a fellow even get a bit of peace below in harbour of an evening? I tell you it's worse than being in jail, being an officer aboard this ship. Just one damned thing after another...' He followed me up on deck and the matter was explained to him from below.

'Well then, Kolarz, if you don't know, is there anyone else who's got any idea where the old fool is or what's become of him?'

'Obediently report that no one seems to know for sure, Herr Leutnant. And certainly no one over there speaks any German.'

'Oh God, that means someone's going to have go over and look for him. Well, I can't for sure, since I'm the only officer aboard... Prohaska, you look an intelligent lad: go below and get a picket of naval police, then go ashore and look for the Captain.'

'With respect, where, Herr Leutnant?'

'For God Almighty's sake, you half-wit, if I knew where I'd scarcely be sending you to look for him, would I now? Search the place street by street if you have to. By the sound of it there should be a fuss going on, if he's been run over by a tram or something like that. If that fails then try the local hospitals.'

So thus it came about that one September evening in the year 1902, just as the brief tropical dusk was settling over the port city of Pernambuco, I, a sixteen-year-old naval cadet of the Austro-Hungarian Monarchy, found myself leading a naval police picket consisting of eight burly, mustachioed Dalmatian sailors armed with rifles and fixed bayonets. It was an unenviable task that lay before us. None of us spoke Portuguese, and the part of the city that lay before us, crowded on to its island, was a dense network of ruas and avenidas crossing at right angles. Short of knocking on each door in turn and enquiring whether there was a capitano austriaco inside injured or otherwise indisposed, there was nothing for it but to shoulder our way through the waterfront crowds and search the place street by street, trusting to luck to lead us towards our commander.

We certainly got some strange looks as we entered the sailor-town area. I was extremely glad not to be here on my own at nightfall, as drinking dens squirted gouts of drunken brawlers on to the streets. On one street corner a ring of cheering seamen surrounded a knife fight while on another a crowd of revellers was watching a French Matelot, minus his trousers, dancing the sailor's hornpipe. As for the inhabitants of this quarter of the city, even a well-brought-up youth like myself from Central Europe scarcely needed to be told what trades were plied in these streets: certainly nothing much to do with cotton, coffee or sugar at any rate. We passed down one such thoroughfare just as I was beginning to wonder at what point we could decently give up this search of an unknown city in an unknown language looking for we knew not what. Then I saw a small crowd further on, gathered around the doorway of an ornate but rather shabby-looking two-storey house: a sort of coagulation of the bustle in the street. They were standing around peacefully enough and one had a hurricane lamp, so I concluded that at least it was not another fight. We elbowed our way through the onlookers to the centre of the circle. Five or six men with a lamp were stooped over a recumbent figure in the doorway. As I approached one of them got up from feeling the victim's pulse. He spoke English.

'Well Jim, looks like 'e's a goner, sure enough.'

'He'? But the figure was a large woman in a long black silk dress with a multiplicity of petticoats... Then they moved aside, and I saw that the woman had a familiar long, forked grey beard. Surely not...? It was: the eyes of Fregattenkapitän Maximillian Slawetz, Freiherr von Löwenhausen goggled at us unseeing in the light of the kerosene lamp. The man called Jim turned to me.

'And 'oo might you be, young sir?'

'Cadet Otto Prohaska, sir: Austrian steam corvette S.M.S. *Windischgrätz*, lying at anchor in the outer harbour. I fear that this man is our Captain.'

'Was your Captain, you mean. It looks like 'e died of an apoplexy, as far as I can see.' I saw what he meant: Slawetz's face was

182

a dirty blue-purple colour and a thin dribble of bloodstained foam trickled from one corner of his mouth. 'Anyway, did I 'ear you right as saying you're from an Australian ship? You don't sound like an Australian to me, son.'

'No. But that is because we are not: we are Austrians, you see? Au-stri-ans.'

He looked at me, evidently not quite believing me.

'Well, that's as may be. All I can say is, it's a nice old carry-on sendin' a young feller like you out here to collect your capting from the doorway of a knocking shop.'

'Can we take him inside, out of the street?'

'Not much chance of that, young sir: it looks like 'e was taken bad inside and they just dumped him out 'ere so's not to 'ave trouble with the police later. They've shut up shop in there and we can't get 'em to open up. They ain't answering no one. If you asks me you'd better get him back to your ship as best you can and 'ope no one asks no questions.'

So with the help of Jim and his companions we procured an old door, laid our revered commander on it wrapped in a borrowed bedsheet, then carried him back to the quayside on our shoulders before rowing him across to the ship. Here was responsibility at last, I thought to myself: four hours before I had been a snotty-nosed cadet scraping old paint off an anchor chain like the lowliest of drudges; and now here I was coming alongside the foot of the starboard gangway, about to inform the officer of the watch that our boat was carrying the body of our Captain, dressed as a woman and felled apparently by a stroke suffered in a brothel. It was at this point, I think, that I discovered that juniority can also have its satisfactions; notably that of performing one's duty to the letter in the full knowledge that the fearful complications that will result are outside one's own competence and will have to be dealt with by one's superiors.

There was a frightful fuss next day of course: boats scudding between ship and shore like skimmers on a summer pond carrying officers to send urgent telegrams to Vienna and receive urgent telegrams back from Vienna. As for myself, I had unwittingly achieved a lower-deck celebrity such as few junior cadets can hope to attain, endlessly questioned over every detail of what 'der Alte' had been wearing when we found him – was it just beads as some said, or artificial pearls? – and generally playing the man of the world to a gaping audience, as if for me discovering senior officers dead in travesty in the doorways of Brazilian bordellos was all in a day's work. In the end it was all smoothed over, as these things tend to be in the armed services. The local police were splendidly corruptible, so there was no nonsense about our sailing being delayed by an inquest. The ship's surgeon carried out a cursory autopsy which confirmed the cause of death as a brain haemorrhage suffered 'in the course of intense exertion', and that was that: funeral booked for the next afternoon on account of the hot climate.

It remained only for a few details to be cleared up for the purposes of the Austrian death certificate, and for the Captain's clothes to be collected from the bordello where he had left them. This task fell to Linienschiffsleutnant Zaleski, partly because he knew Portuguese fairly well, and could thus take a statement from the madame of the establishment, and partly because (it seemed) he was already a personal friend of that lady from previous visits to Pernambuco. To my surprise he detailed me to accompany him, in order to take notes and act as a witness to the statement. I asked no questions about this: with Linienschiffsleutnant Zaleski one soon learnt never to ask any questions. All I was to do was to collect a notebook and pencil, and a holdall for the Captain's clothes, and join him to be rowed across the harbour in the gig.

The Casa de Refrescamento was a murky sort of place, much as one might expect from the trade carried on there. It was midmorning, so the establishment had closed for a few hours now that the last pale-faced citizen had crept home after the previous night's debauch. A lady or two stretched and yawned on the balconies over the street, but it was an elderly coloured cleaning woman who answered the bell and let us in, then ushered us into the tiled hallway. The manageress came out and greeted us both, then took the lieutenant by the arm and pointed him towards her parlour. Was I to wait in the hallway? I was not: before I knew what was happening the two of them were propelling me up the stone stairway towards the first-floor landing, then opening a door.

'There, Prohaska, I'll be about forty minutes I should think. There's no need to accompany us: I'll dictate the statement to you afterwards. In the meantime occupy yourself usefully.'

I was stricken with a sudden panic. 'But Herr Schiffsleutnant...'

'Get in there and shut up. Enjoy yourself and that's an order.'

The door slammed shut. I turned around bewildered. She stood there with her back to the slatted sunblinds. She wore a petticoat, but only from the waist down. She was a dark-haired, rather pretty girl about the same age as myself. I blushed and stammered, fumbling for the doorknob to escape.

'Desculpe senhorita... er... Não falo bem portugues...'

She smiled. 'Proszę, nie trzeba się przejmować.'

I stopped, puzzled. 'But you speak Polish. I don't understand. How did you know...?'

'Leutnant Zaleski told me. And I speak Polish because that's what I am: Stefania Odrzutek from Krzemieniki in Galicia; otherwise known as Donha Rosa Amelia of the Rua Amílcar Carvalho.'

'But what are you doing here...?'

'Fucking, mostly: people don't come to bordellos to read the newspapers.'

'How did you get here?' I had heard all about the South American white-slave traffic, of course: the popular press of Central Europe in those days was stuffed with lurid stories of innocent young girls who had been chloroformed on their way home from piano lessons and had woken up in waterfront brothels in Buenos Aires, the victims of procurers with names like Glückstein and Apfelbaum, abducted to Latin America without any hope of even making their whereabouts known to their grieving parents.

'Oh, I just came over from Genoa on the steamer like anyone else,' she said.

'Were you alone? Did they drug you and lock you in your cabin?'

She laughed. 'No, silly: there was eight of us travelling from Lemberg. And they didn't lock us up. We came out on proper contracts.'

'Did you know what you were coming here to do?'

''Course we did: Herr Grünbaum went through it all with us first. We could do it three hundred times a day at two kronen a time in a military establishment; or eight times a day at fifty kronen a go in a better-class house in Lemberg. Or we could come out here – the better-looking ones that is – on twenty-five times five hundred escudos plus board and lodging free, which works out about fifteen per cent better. Also we get a clothing allowance, and a free medical inspection every week, and Wednesday afternoons off, and overtime Sundays after mass and saints' days. So altogether it's not too bad a deal really.'

'It sounds like a very bad deal to me. . . .'

'That's because you're a man – well, almost – and posh. For a girl like me it's the only way out. Honest, the only life I'd have had back in Krzemieniki'd be far worse; some smelly peasant using me like a cow and giving me babies every year, then expecting me to lug buckets of water through the mud from the village pump when I'm nine months gone.'

'But the degradation, and the risk of disease . . .'

'Disease? half the people in our village were wiped out the year before last with typhoid, and they're just as dead as if they'd died of the pox and made some money out of it.'

'. . . And the uncertainty . . .'

'Don't talk to me about uncertainty; the only certainty I ever had back in Galicia was the certainty of being shit-poor for the rest of my life. No, out here I don't have to go around with icicles hanging from my backside half the year, there's wine to drink and nice dresses, and some of the clients aren't too bad: at least, they give me presents sometimes . . .' She giggled. 'There's one coffee planter I've got my eye on. He likes me, I think – at any rate, he keeps coming back. I think I might marry him and turn respectable: go to mass in a black mantilla and set up societies for fallen women. I might even be so rich I can turn up in Vienna one day and pass myself off as a comtessa. Anyway...' she turned to me, 'I don't suppose you're here to talk about the trade, so let's get on with it.' She lay back on the couch and rolled down her petticoat. I looked round in desperation at the door. She saw this, and smiled. 'First time?'

I nodded glumly. 'Why didn't you say so then, silly? Here, let me help you...'

She was very kind to me in a businesslike sort of way, Stefka Odrzutek from the village of Krzemieniki in eastern Galicia. As might have been expected with a sixteen-year-old for the first time, the process was over almost before it had begun, and I lay gasping and confused beside her like a fish landed on a riverbank as she stroked my hair. It was mid-morning and business was light, so she could take a little more time than was usual in her tightly scheduled working day. Then she helped me get dressed and pushed me out on to the landing, giving me a parting kiss and wishing me luck for the future. Linienschiffsleutnant Zaleski stood there waiting for me, leaning against the balustrade with folded arms and regarding me quizzically with those half-closed black eyes of his. I blushed crimson. Coming from a good bourgeois home in a rather prudish little provincial town I was frankly unused to this matter-of-fact attitude to fornication.

'Well, was she all right?'

'I... er, um... obediently report that yes, Herr Schiffsleutnant.'

He smiled faintly. 'Nice girl, that Stefka: I knew you'd like her. Anyway, let's be going.'

I stood stock-still. I felt in my pockets. A sudden ghastly realisation dawned upon me: I had not so much as a copper farthing upon me. Terrible visions began to float before my eyes: a row in a foreign language with the madame downstairs; the naval police being called; being marched off under escort to be thrown into the ship's lock-up; Captain's Report and a marking to be carried in perpetuity on my service dossier, perhaps even reported back to my parents: 'Sentenced to four days' dark-arrest after an altercation in a local bordello. Arrested after allegedly attempting to leave without paying.'

'Herr Schiffsleutnant, I obediently report that . . .'

Zaleski smiled indulgently. He seemed to know exactly what was on my mind.

'Oh, don't trouble yourself about that, Prohaska. I've paid already.'

'But Herr Schiffsleutnant . . . How can I reimburse you . . . ?'

'Don't bother. It's a birthday present.'

'Herr Schiffsleutnant, I obediently report that my birthday is in April.'

'I know; but it happens to be mine today. Anyway, look on it as a health measure, if you prefer it that way. Accumulation of the generative fluid over a long period causes it to rise up into the brain and obscure a man's reasoning faculties. It's a scientifically established fact.'

So we made our way back aboard: one statement taken, one set of clothes recovered and one virginity lost. I felt rather odd about it for some time afterwards. Quite apart from the fear of having caught something unpleasant there was a vague feeling that it ought not to have been like that; that the skies should have opened and trumpets sounded. But I suppose everyone feels that. As for Stefka Odzrutek, I have not the faintest idea what became of her. I hope that she married her coffee planter after all; but I suppose that in the end she went like most of her kind to a pauper's grave, worn out with disease and ill usage – which is pretty well what she would have done if she had stayed in Poland, though at least in Brazil she would not have two world wars crashing through her life like demented steamrollers. I only knew her for perhaps fifteen minutes, but her memory still lives on with me: her courage and enterprise, and how she managed to bring far more humanity than she needed to have done to her rather unappetising trade.

The funeral took place that afternoon, and was by common consent one of the grandest spectacles the city of Pernambuco had witnessed in years. The whole population had turned out to watch the cortège make its way from the quayside to the abbey cemetery over on the mainland. We borrowed a gun carriage from the local garrison, but all the rest we provided ourselves: the ship's band; the immaculately turned-out company of sailors slow-marching behind the gun carriage with rifles reversed; the velvet cushion on top of the flag-draped coffin with Slawetz's decorations pinned to it, and his cocked hat and sword resting beside it. It was what the Viennese call 'ein' schone Leiche', and greatly appreciated by the local people, who were no mean connoisseurs of funereal pomp themselves. The effect was only spoilt on the way back from the cemetery when the skies burst in a torrential downpour. By the time we reached the quayside the low-lying city's drainage system could no longer cope and fountains of sewage were gushing from the drains and manholes, to lie steaming gently in the sunshine once the clouds had passed. The ship's surgeon took alarm and ordered everyone back aboard at once, fearing an outbreak of typhoid or even cholera. Linienschiffsleutnant Zaleski, Gauss and I were the last to embark, having stayed at the quayside to make sure that no one was left behind. We ourselves would have to wait for the gig to come across to fetch us since the last boat had been too overloaded to take us aboard.

'Better have a drink and a bite to eat while we're waiting,' said Zaleski. 'We're sailing tomorrow for Cape Town so it'll be a month or more of salt horse and zwieback. You young fellows had better get a bite of something decent while you can.' We took his advice, and accompanied him to a waterfront bar whose landlord he knew. There Gauss and I partook of an iced-coffee, coconut and rum drink which he recommended to us, and I sampled some delicious little canapés of fish offered me by the landlord: salgadinhos or something like that. At last the gig arrived and we went back aboard, saying goodbye to Pernambuco as we did so.

We arrived to find the ship in an unsettled mood. Not only had we just buried our Captain, an event roughly equivalent aboard ship to the death of a monarch, but a batch of telegrams from Vienna had arrived in our absence. One of them appointed the

GDO Korvettenkapitän Festetics to the post of Captain for the rest of the voyage. And as if that news were not sufficiently disturbing, another telegram informed us of the fate of Landungsdetachement Hrabovsky, sent off into the jungles of West Africa seven weeks before. It appeared that they had turned up eventually at Bunceville. What was left of them, that is: two emaciated survivors borne in litters and raving with fever – malaria, black-water, yellow fever, dengue and the whole works. The party had started falling sick on their fourth day out, they said, and had died one by one. What had gone wrong? Why had Professor Skowronek's anti-fever cocktail worked so well for one party and not at all for the other – not even against common malaria even though it contained their daily dose of quinine? It was a complete mystery and one for which – quite uncharacteristically – the Professor could offer no explanation whatever.

10

DOWN SOUTH

Not that I was much disposed to think about the appointment of our new captain, or the sad fate of our exploration party. In fact by eight bells on the evening before we were due to sail from Pernambuco it was beginning to look as if I might shortly be on my way to join the unfortunate Hrabovsky and his men. First it was nausea, then violent stomach cramps and vomiting, then sweating and shaking, finally partial paralysis. There was considerable alarm as they carried me down to the sick-bay. Could it be cholera, contracted from the overflowing sewers on shore? But surely even cholera took a couple of days to develop? By that stage though I myself was out of the argument as my temperature soared towards the mainmast lightning conductor, raving in delirium as Dr Luchieni placed ice-packs on my forehead and applied mustard plasters to my feet. It was only next morning, after we had weighed anchor and left Pernambuco, that it was realised that what I was suffering from was no more than acute food poisoning; contracted probably from the fish canapés in the waterfront bar.

That was small comfort to me though, because for the first ten days of our voyage into the South Atlantic I was feeling very low indeed and officially convalescent, sitting in a wicker armchair on the poop deck with blankets around my legs and sipping beef tea. Even after the sickness had passed I was frightened that it had done for my naval career, because it had affected the nerves of my face and left me with a permanent, slight but maddening flutter in my left eyelid which took several months to fade away completely. My other preoccupation during my time as a convalescent was to pore over the medical textbooks in the sick-bay and examine myself at least once every hour for the various lumps and discharges that would signal that I had acquired another, more sinister souvenir of Pernambuco to go with my shuddering eyelid. But I had been lucky, it seemed, so that was the end of the matter until I next went to confession; which would not be until Christmas.

I was thankful though to have escaped standing watches for at least the first ten days of our South Atlantic passage, because the work was turning out to be very hard indeed. The trouble was that, in sailing diagonally between Pernambuco and Cape Town in the interests of scientific research, we were also sailing the wrong way, against the prevailing winds and current. The normal procedure for a sailing ship to get from the one place to the other would have been to have sailed down the coast of South America with the south-easterlies on the port beam, down to about 40 degrees south, then turned sharp east to catch the strong westerly winds of the Roaring Forties and scud across the Southern Ocean with yards squared to the wind before turning north-east to get to Cape Town on the Benguela Current. But that would have negated the purpose of our expedition to these waters. The Academy of Sciences and the Pola Hydrographical Institute wanted a detailed profile of the South Atlantic seabed along a straight line drawn between Pernambuco and the Cape, so our ship would now have to spend week after weary week beating to windward, yards hard up against the shrouds and lugged laboriously round at the start of each watch as we wore ship and went on to the opposite tack, heaving to every couple of hours to take another sounding. Dr Szalai's patent sounding machine now took over the ship – and his seawater-collecting bottles and his aneroid barometer and his wind machine. It was all valuable work I suppose: at any rate, we added a Löwenhausen Ridge and a Windischgrätz Deep (5,684 metres) to the map of the world; where for all that I know they remain to this day along with Franz Joseph Land and Lakes Rudolf and Stefanie, last visible evidences of an empire long since evaporated into thin air.

None the less it was achingly hard and weary work even for a crew as large as ours. S.M.S. *Windischgrätz* was not a sparkling performer to windward by any manner of means: about six and a half points off the wind was the best that she could manage, and even then she tended to make leeway like a paper bag. Also she had a rooted reluctance to pay off on to the new tack when we tried going about, which is why we always preferred to wear ship: putting up the helm and turning downwind to circle round on to the new tack rather than pointing up into the wind. The linear distance from Pernambuco to Cape Town is about 3,300 miles; by the time we had finished, our accumulated log tally was 5,700. It was a weary, monotonous passage marked by a constant frustrating sense that we were working hard just to stay in the same place, like a man running up a down-escalator. Watch after watch the ship would foam along close-hauled at about four knots with the yards braced around as far as they would go and everything trembling, surging up and down, up and down over the great long waves of the open ocean, sometimes a kilometre from crest to crest.

Even below decks there was no relief. The ship's structure, never too robust at the best of times, had been badly affected by several months of alternate soaking and scorching in the tropics. Timbers and planking were now working quite noticeably. Still, this was not entirely without its advantages, as we discovered about a week out from Pernambuco when we set to work on the sack of Brazil nuts which Gumpoldsdorfer had purchased in the local market. These were not Brazil nuts as you see them in the greengrocers' shops in this country in the weeks before Christmas; those sad grey-brown segments of fossilised orange. These were Brazil nuts just as they had dropped from the forest trees, still encased in a rough, round woody case of such adamantine hardness that no hammer and cold chisel borrowed from the carpenter's workshop could make any impression on its stony surface. We gazed at the sack of nuts in despair, down there in our airless little cubbyhole on the platform deck – until Tarabochia pointed suddenly at the great oaken knee, yawning and closing to the rolling of the ship as it had done all the way from Pola. The same idea struck us all at the same moment. We waited until the gap had opened to its fullest extent at the extremity of the roll, then quickly pushed a nut pod beneath it. The ship started to roll the other way. The knee groaned softly and began to close. There was a sudden crack like a rifle shot, and the knee closed completely on to the massive oaken beam underneath. When it opened again on the opposite roll it revealed an oily, round, fragrant cake of mashed Brazil nut mingled with fragments of pod and shell. In the end we solved the problem by jamming a piece of timber underneath the knee to restrict its closing to just the amount necessary to crack the nut pods without crushing them. For the next few days we gorged ourselves on Brazil nuts – until one evening the Provost turned up in the passageway accompanied by the Carpenter and his mate. The occupants of the gunroom two decks above had reported that the ship's structure was beginning to break up around them.

There was not much else to remark upon during those thirty-five days at sea. We were well away from the shipping lanes most of the time, so it was only on a couple of occasions that we even so much as glimpsed sails or steamer smoke on the horizon. The rest of the world might as well have ceased to exist: nothing but sun and sky, wind and waves. It was about this time that I first began to notice a certain discontent aboard. Grousing is as natural to seamen as prayer to monks, and if the crew has ceased to grumble this is usually a sure sign that something is badly wrong aboard a ship. But now the grumbling had taken on a poisoned, aggrieved note under the pressure of labour aboard a rather ill-found ship sailing day after day against the wind and the waves. There was also a noticeable malaise following the death of our Captain – who had been held in almost religious awe by officers and men alike – and by the news of the loss of Hrabovsky's exploration party. There was a feeling that the ship's good luck had turned sour, and perhaps (some said) that this might have some connection with Professor Skowronek's row of skulls grinning on the shelf in his laboratory. After all, they were the skulls of Africans, and everyone had heard stories about the operation of the ju-ju ...

As for our new Captain, feelings were mixed. Everyone agreed that he seemed a decent enough sort. But little was seen of him except at Sunday divisions, and he seemed not exactly to be impressing the ship with the stamp of his personality – if indeed he had one. Day-to-day running had passed to Linienschiffsleutnant Mikulić, now the acting GDO, and to the other senior officers. As for Mikulić, he left us in no doubt that while he held it the post of Gesamt Detail Offizier would be very much an active one and not that of a glorified ship's clerk as it had been under old Slawetz. He intended to run the vessel his way, and his way evidently owed a good deal to the notorious American bucko-mates he had read about and claimed to have sailed with. The result was frequent use of the rope's end to encourage the men toiling on deck to brace round the yards as we wore ship. Shipboard life was rough to be sure, but this was the 1900s and not the 1700s and our men were skilled professional sailors – most of them long-service men – and not some collection of San Francisco waterfront refuse dumped aboard by the crimps just before sailing. They put up with it for the time being, contenting themselves with drafting letters to be sent to Viennese newspapers and Socialist Reichsrat deputies when we reached Cape Town. Even so, ill-feeling grew and spread like dry rot through the timbers. If all the officers had been as harsh as Mikulić things might not have been so bad. But in the absence of a firm hand on the bridge rails, each ran his own part of the ship as he pleased: Mikulić arbitrary and exacting; Svoboda rather too lax for most people's taste; only Zaleski and Fregattenleutnant Bertalotti (who was now Fourth Officer) regarded as good, firm, competent all-round officers of the watch.

One consequence of the removal of Slawetz von Löwenhausen from the captain's cabin was that Professor Skowronek now came into his own as busybody-in-chief and resident Besserwisser. Two weeks out from Pernambuco things had come to such a pass that Bo'sun Njegosić had curtly told him to go away and mind his own business when he had caught him trying to supervise a party hoisting a boat to the davits. Skowronek had tried to have Njegosić arrested on the grounds that he, Skowronek, was a reserve army captain and was not going to be talked to like that by some hulking lout of a Serb. The matter had gone to the Captain and, to everyone's disgust, the Bo'sun had been forced to apologise to the Professor. Skowronek had wisely decided not to interfere directly in the running of the ship after that, but he still managed to add to the general air of irritation by striding about the decks at all hours giving his opinions on how best the sails ought to be trimmed and other such matters.

Table Mountain came into view on 12 October 1902, to the inexpressible relief of all aboard. The crossing had lasted thirty-five days, but it had seemed like as many months. A tug came out to tow us into Cape Town docks. The Boer War was only a few months finished, and the South African economy was experiencing a boom now that the Boer Republics were no more and the wealth of the interior was being opened up to rational plunder. The ships were packed at the wharves like cigars in a box. We would certainly never have made it under our own power, since the tug had to shove us into a free berth endways like a book on to a library shelf. As soon as we were moored to our wharf in Victoria Dock the Captain decreed a spell of shore-leave, despite sybilline mutterings from Linienschiffsleutnant Mikulić that in many cases the shore-leave might end up being a prolonged one. He was all for keeping the men on board throughout our stay with sentries posted on the fo'c'sle ready to shoot any man trying to get ashore. But this idea was dismissed as being impracticable in the early twentieth century – as well as being very bad public relations during a courtesy visit. So the liberty men went ashore and we cadets set off on the usual round of visits: the Governor's residence, Table Mountain, Adderley Street, the old Dutch Castle, the zoological gardens, a wine farm, etc., etc.

It was certainly a pleasant few days ashore for us. Cape Town was an attractive city with a climate like that of Naples, while the inhabitants were hospitality itself, laying on endless visits and outings for us at no cost to ourselves. I suppose that in those days before wireless, stuck there down at the very tip of Africa – a sort of Pola on a continental scale – they must have welcomed the diversion of entertaining a large party of well-conducted and often rather handsome cadets from the navy of a major European power. For our part we did our best as ambassadors of our distant empire: made all the right noises of admiration when things were shown to us, were impeccably polite and, if we yawned at times, contrived to yawn internally. And we did manage to pay them back a little for their kindness, since our excellent ship's band gave a series of much-applauded concerts in the municipal park; performances which brought tears to the eyes of many in the audience, since a high proportion of Cape Town's commercial class were in fact Austrian Jews who had come out here as pedlars and made good. People kept coming up to us and telling us in heavily Yiddish-flavoured German that although they had left Brünn in 1858 they still regarded themselves as loyal subjects of the House of Habsburg, and cherished the hope of retiring to 'the old country' one day. It was all further proof, if any were required, of the old adage that the only real Austrian patriots were the Jews since they alone among the peoples of the Monarchy had no other nationality.

It was not until we were preparing to sail on 17 October that it became clear that Linienschiffsleutnant Mikulić's forebodings about shore-leave had not been far wide of the mark. No less than seventy-three men had failed to report back aboard. The Captain spluttered and swore, and Zaleski and Svoboda were despatched ashore with naval police pickets to try and round up the stragglers. Meanwhile Festetics – taking me along as interpreter – hurried to City Hall to try and persuade the local authorities to set up roadblocks, search trains leaving Cape Town, send out the Cape Mounted Police and Hottentot trackers with bloodhounds to comb the scrub of the hillsides and so forth. It was hopeless: the authorities were sympathetic, but said that with wages so high in the diamond fields and gold mines following the recent war they doubted whether we would have much success; not when the agents of the mining companies were prowling Cape Town docks trying to induce seamen to desert. Our men, they said, were probably in Kimberley or Johannesburg by now. They promised to do what they could, but said that magistrates up-country were usually the local mine managers and were unlikely to be very helpful.

This meant that we sailed the best part of a division short, since in addition to the seventy-three men missing in Cape Town we had already lost four men by drowning off Frederiksborg, fifteen in the rainforests of the Kroo Coast and one man who had failed to report back aboard when we left Pernambuco. In those days all sailing ships on a long voyage could expect some losses by desertion and death, but this was ridiculous. Having to work a sailing ship with only 250 men instead of 350 would have made a merchant skipper snort in derision: most such ships of our tonnage would have sailed with forty-odd crew to handle a much larger sail-area. But naval discipline is cumbersome and slow to adapt to changed circumstances, and a ship which has lost nearly a third of its crew is going to find things difficult even if it was heavily over-manned in the first place. The *Windischgrätz* had got used over thirty years to doing things in a particular manner, and it would not willingly change its habits, like a millionaire who has suddenly been obliged to get by on half a million a year and feels himself to have become a pauper. The end result was more work for everyone and correspondingly lowered morale.

For me there was another change to my circumstances that morning in Cape Town harbour as we made ready to put to sea. I was supervising the hoisting-in of one of our eight-metre cutters: the one that had carried Hrabovsky's party up the Bunce River, which had been brought back abandoned and which most of the crew now tried to avoid if they could as being infected with bad luck. A telegraph boy appeared at the foot of the gangplank.

'Telegram for Mr Prohaska!' Well, that must be me: the only other Prohaska aboard, an able seaman, had been among those who had not returned from leave. I seized the brown envelope and tore it open. It was from my father.

CADET OTTO PROHASKA S.M.S. WINDISCHGRAETZ CAPE TOWN
16/X/02

REGRET INFORM YOU MOTHER DEAD AFTER SHORT ILLNESS STOP

PROHASKA
HIRSCHENDORF

I stared at it for some moments. My mother had been in poor health for some years past, but it was still quite unexpected. Yet I felt no particular grief – except perhaps at my lack of grief. We had been strangers for years, but even so ... I made a mental note to speak to the Captain when I came off watch and get permission to go ashore for an hour or so before we sailed, to send a telegram of condolence and perhaps arrange for a mass to be said in the Catholic cathedral. But my duties on deck got the better of my good intentions, and I only remembered about it when I put my hand in my jacket pocket and felt the telegram – by which time the cloud-covered top of Table Mountain was falling below the horizon astern of us.

What had diverted my mind from my mother's death was the surf-boat: the one given us by King Matthew Neverwash III as our topside dash that day the treaty was negotiated at Bunceville. It had given us endless trouble as we considered how to turn it into a replacement for the lost eight-metre cutter. At first it had seemed a reasonable substitute, except for being double-ended. But after detailed inspection the Carpenter had shaken his head sadly. In his opinion the only way to turn it into an acceptable pulling-boat would be to dismantle it completely and rebuild.

'The trouble, Bo'sun,' he had explained to Njegosić, 'is that the thing's not really a boat at all, just a big paddling canoe. Oh yes, she's strongly enough made: very good quality timber and nicely put together, all pegs – not a metal fixing in her. But build thwarts into her for rowers – that's a different story. The frames are too light so she'd flex all the time, and the centre of gravity's too high if you ask me: all right for paddlers kneeling round the gunwale but dead wrong for oarsmen sitting two-by-two. No, the tub's a paddling canoe and if you try making anything else of her you'll end up spoiling her and not get anything very good in return.'

So the surf-boat lay upside-down unused. Always enterprising, Linienschiffsleutnant Zaleski had tried manning her with paddlers once for a trip around Cape Town harbour, but there had been complaints from the Harbour Master that having naval seamen 'peddling abite the horber lak a lot of Keffirs' was undermining the prestige of the white race, so the experiment was abandoned. In the end we resolved to take the thing back to Pola and present it to the Ethnographic Museum in Vienna, who could dispose of it as they pleased.

Our next port of call was to Luanda, the capital of the Portuguese colony of Angola, though we would make a brief stop on the way at Swakopmund to exchange courtesies with the German Governor of South-West Africa. After our transatlantic exertions it looked like being an easy passage up the west coast of Africa. The prevailing wind was south to south-easterly and the powerful Benguela Current would push us along well past the mouth of the Congo. North of Swakopmund our course would take us along the sinister, silent coastline of the Namib Desert: the 'Skeleton Coast' or the 'Coast of Dead Ned' as it was known to sailors in those days; a stretch of shore with a particularly lurid reputation for swallowing up ships and men among its ever-shifting sand-bars and the sea-fogs and vicious currents that swirled over them. Such were the fears for our safety, since we proposed making a landing there for the benefit of our scientists, that the Governor at Swakopmund provided a naval gunboat, S.M.S. *Elster*, to escort us as far as Mossamedes in Portuguese territory.

It was certainly a desolate enough looking part of the world as we sailed past it a few miles offshore. Seen through binoculars from the masthead it was a monotonous, level streak of khaki-coloured sand dunes with a white streak of surf below them. Every few kilometres one could make out the half-buried remains of one of the countless, mostly unknown ships that had piled up on this arid coast over the centuries, usually leaving their crews to die of thirst and starvation amid the pitiless dunes. The German gunboat captain told us that years before, about 1880, a Portuguese sloop had entered a shallow bay on the Kaokoveld coast north of Cape Cross to scrape her bottom free of weed, and had been trapped in a matter of days as a sudden change in the current threw a sand-bar across the mouth of the lagoon to seal her in. The vessel could still be seen, he said, several kilometres inland now, permanently docked amid the sand dunes with most of her crew still aboard. A few had eventually managed to reach Mossamedes on foot, but had returned several months too late to be of any help to the rest. He said that he had sailed this coast for five years now, endeavouring to chart it, and the more he knew of it the more it frightened him.

In view of such tales it was with a certain trepidation that we prepared, five days out from Cape Town and a few miles north of the mouth of the Hoteb River – or to be more accurate, the dry bed of the Hoteb River – to put a landing party ashore on the coast of this eerie wilderness. The ship would anchor a couple of miles offshore after finding a likely route in through the surf and we would row ashore in two cutters. It would not be a lengthy visit: the main purpose was for Herr Lenart the botanist to collect specimens of desert shrubs – perhaps with any luck an example of that extraordinary plant the wellischia, which flowers once every other century. Professor Skowronek would also go ashore, he announced – though for the life of us no one could see why, since from an anthropological point of view the Kaokoveld must surely be as devoid of interest as the far side of the moon. All the same he clambered down the swaying rope ladder into the cutter heaving on the swell, followed by Gauss and I, who had been detailed to act as gun bearers for him. He was taking the heavy Mannlicher with the telescopic sight and also a powerful shotgun. This excited us. The Namib Desert might be one of the driest places on earth – it rained there about once every twenty years the German captain said – but it was said to have a surprising amount of wildlife: jackals, lions, wildebeest who migrated down the shore from time to time in vast herds, and also the occasional elephant. I looked at the heavy rifle and thought what a nice present an elephant's foot or even a tusk would make for my aunt in Vienna.

In the event we landed without too much difficulty behind a

sheltering sand-spit, helped by the fact that the wind was blowing off the land that morning and subduing the coastal surf a little. We hauled up the boats, men were detailed to guard them and recall us by bugle if the wind changed – we were taking no chances in this dreadful place – and we divided up into two parties: the bulk of the men with Herr Lenart, who wished to search a square kilometre of dunes for plants, and us two with Professor Skowronek. We took our water bottles, shouldered the guns and set off after him into the coastal dunes, heading northwards up the shore.

It was heavy going. Not only was the hot wind out of the desert rather like standing by an oven door, it was laden with mica dust as well. The sun glared up off the sand; the mica crystals stung our eyes and gritted between our teeth; and our feet sank in at every step since the endless accumulation of salt from the sea-spray and the lack of rain to wash it in meant that the surface layer of sand had formed a brittle crust like icing sugar, not quite strong enough to bear our weight. Meanwhile the wind moaned across the dunes with a sad, hollow sound like someone blowing across the neck of a bottle. Before we had gone a kilometre our throats were already shrivelled by the parching wind and the sun's glare. We had only a half-litre bottle each. Suppose this insufferable know-all contrived to get us lost in the dunes? We would be dead of thirst within a day. That many before us had come to grief on this coast was demonstrated by the quantities of sun-bleached flotsam which had accumulated on the seaward face of the dunes: driftwood, old cordage and all manner of detritus from centuries of shipwrecks. One board bore the voc brand of the Dutch East India Company which (I remembered from my naval history lessons) had been wound up in 1799. Before long we came upon the remains of a ship's boat, cast up above the high-tide mark and lying embedded in the sand. Gauss and I hurried forward to examine it – and recoiled to stand in silence when we saw that beside it was lying what remained of one of its occupants, Dead Ned in person, now nothing more than a half-buried jumble of sand-polished bones and a desiccated pair of leather shoes. The Professor laughed as he disinterred the skull with his boot and kicked it aside, remarking as he did so that the owner had obviously been of Caucasian stock and was therefore of no interest to him since he already had more than enough specimens of that particular type.

We moved on, back into the dunes now and both of us in a thoughtful frame of mind after what we had just seen. After half an hour or so the Professor stopped suddenly and pointed down. It was footprints in the sand; fresh ones by the look of it: splay-footed to be sure and probably barefoot but undeniably human. There had been about four of them we thought. But who could it have been in this God-forsaken place? Shipwreck survivors making north in search of help? Diamond smugglers? The *Elster*'s Captain said that there was a good deal of illegal diamond-prospecting going on now along this coast, among people foolhardy or avaricious enough to brave its terrors. On balance Gauss and I inclined towards the shipwreck theory – in which case we must catch up with them at once if the hand of Providence had sent us here to be the means of their rescue. The Professor disagreed, though, and said that diamond prospectors were more likely: probably armed and dangerous. Either way we were suddenly filled with the lust of the chase, thirst and dead men's bones forgotten for the moment. Four and a half months is a long time for two adolescents to be cooped up aboard ship. We had gone to sea in search of adventure? Well, castaways or smugglers, here was adventure for the taking. We set off in pursuit.

When we finally caught sight of them among the dunes we saw that they had stopped to rest. There were four of them: a man, a woman and two children. But they were neither shipwreck survivors nor illicit prospectors. They were near-naked, crinkly-haired, flat-faced and a coppery-yellow colour like tarnished brass pipes, the woman with pendulous breasts and enormous hypertrophied buttocks. They were eating something: a dead seal pup we later discovered. The Professor motioned us to wait and crawled off among the dunes, taking the rifle with him. What could he be about? Surely these people could mean no harm: we could see even from here that they carried no weapons beyond a single spear... Two shots rang out in the hot, arid air, then a third. We ran to find Skowronek. When we reached him he was kneeling over the man's body at work with his hunting knife. The woman's corpse already lay headless, bleeding into a dark patch in the sand.

'Gottverdammt: The two pups got away into the dunes. I'd have liked at least one of them so that I could test my theory about skull-suture formation... There, that's done it...' he dropped the severed head into the hessian bag to join the woman's. I saw that Gauss had turned a livid butter colour, and I felt rather unsteady myself. But the Professor was in a high good humour.

'Strandlopers: the most primitive race in Africa; lower even in evolutionary terms than the Kalahari Bushmen. I'd been trying for years to get specimens without success. A Boer in Cape Town tried to sell me a pair of skulls, but I'm pretty sure they were Hottentots. And now I only have to walk a couple of kilometres and I stumble across a pair of them; male and female too, of the same age. On that basis I can work out a completely authoritative index for this particular racial type. Working from a single specimen is always bad science in my opinion...' He had noticed our pallid faces. 'No stomach for this kind of fieldwork? Come, my young friends...' He slapped my shoulder. 'To a scientist nothing is disgusting, not even cutting off heads. One soon becomes used to it.'

'But Herr Professor,' Gauss stammered, 'these were people...'

'People? Not a bit of it. It's really game-hunting, of no more consequence than shooting a pair of baboons and removing their heads to mount on the wall. In fact I've got a good mind to ask Herr Knedlik to stuff and mount this pair. It should be quite possible to remove the skin without damaging the skull. Yes, I'm sure I shall now that I think about it.' He laughed. 'Pity I couldn't get the offspring as well, then you lads could have had a stuffed Strandloper head each to take back as presents for your parents. That'd be a fine souvenir from the Dark Continent now, wouldn't it?'

Gauss and I reported the matter to Linienschiffsleutnant Zaleski as soon as we got back aboard. He reported it to the Captain, and the Captain reported it to the skipper of the *Elster*, who reported it to the Governor when he returned to Swakopmund. There was no end of a row: shooting in German South-West Africa without a valid game licence was a serious offence, punishable by a fine of up to 250 marks or three months in prison. The case was eventually referred to the very highest levels in Berlin, we heard; but in view of his personal admiration for Professor Skowronek's work the German Kaiser closed the matter by paying the fine out of his own pocket.

We spent two days in Luanda, of which there is not a great deal to be said. It was a sleepy, shabby Portuguese colonial town, like an African version of Pernambuco: the same Jesuit churches, the same tilework and the same atmosphere of seedy gentility. We laughed up our sleeves at the Portuguese colonial empire, glad to have discovered at last an imperial set-up even more decrepit than our own. It was perfectly plain to the very dullest intelligence (we all agreed) that Portugal's African empire was now on its last legs and would shortly be divided up among more vigorous nations.

On the morning of our departure Gauss and I were ashore on a couple of hours' leave after accompanying the Captain on a visit to the governor's residence. Since there was very little else to do we were taking a stroll in the botanical gardens and admiring the local girls – though from a distance, since they seemed to be even more tightly escorted here than in Brazil. We were also keen to discover the source of a curious noise which had echoed over the town throughout the hours of daylight ever since we had arrived: a brass band playing a relentless ooomp-ooomp-parp-ooomp-parp tune; the same couple of bars over and over and over again. Surely they could not possibly be so bad that they needed two entire days to practise the same fragment of music? We had just found someone who knew enough German to explain it to us. Luanda in those days was a penal colony for metropolitan Portugal – the man told us that half the people in the place were convicts and the other half ought to be. But the conditions of imprisonment were fairly relaxed, and the prisoners were allowed out of jail during the day to earn wine- and tobacco-money by doing odd jobs around the town – among them playing to entertain the public in the municipal parks. The convict brass band had recently mutinied – a frequent occurrence here we were told – and the prison governor had decided to punish them by making them stand in the prison yard for three consecutive days and play the same piece of music over and over again.

There were other convicts at work even as we spoke, sweeping the pathways in the botanical gardens. These must have been more hardened offenders, because they were manacled in pairs, ankle-to-ankle. Gauss and I strolled past two of these dungaree-clad felons, scarcely noticing that they were Africans – until a familiar voice rang out. 'Why, Mass' Ottokar – Mass' Max – What you do here?'

We stopped and stared in disbelief: the two convicts were none other than Union Jack and Jimmy Starboard, our Kroo boatmen from Frederiksborg. They were thin and wretched-looking, but all smiles at meeting us. Once we had got over our initial surprise at finding them here they explained how they came to be in Luanda. Shortly after we had sailed from Frederiskborg in August they and eight others had signed up to work for a year as surf-boatmen at Lüderitz in South-West Africa. But on the way the German steamer carrying them had run on to a sand-bar off Cabinda and broken her back. They had been rescued, but only the Europeans had been sent on to their destinations. The Kroo-men had been brought to Luanda and thrown into jail as illegal immigrants until such time as someone could be found to take them back home. What jail – officially the 'assisténicia publica' – was like for black men in Angola was demonstrated to us by Jimmy Starboard, who opened his jacket to show his ribs already sticking out beneath the skin, which had lost its healthy shine. The food was wretched, they said, and what little there was consisted of manioc, which was very poor stuff – in fact mildly poisonous – for men used to a rice diet at home. One of their number had already died and another was in such a bad way that he could no longer walk. Union Jack said that it was only charity from passers-by that was keeping them alive.

Something had to be done. Gauss and I rushed back aboard the *Windischgrätz* and reported to the officer of the watch, who by good luck happened to be Zaleski. He went immediately to speak with the Captain. After all, these men were Austrian subjects now. Whatever else might have been said of Korvettenkapitän von Festetics he would never have knowingly left one of his men in the lurch. He went ashore to speak with the prison governor, and the upshot of it all was that by the time we sailed we had gained nine extra crew members to make up for some of those we had lost at Cape Town. It was not too bad a bargain: the Kroos were all experienced seamen and the Portuguese authorities had demanded only moderate bribes from us for their release. And anyway, they could earn their keep aboard by working that wretched surf-boat until we called back at Frederiksborg. For the time being they were signed up as locally engaged ordinary seamen and kitted out in Austrian naval rig – in which it must be said they looked very smart, except that they had to use hairpins to hold their caps on top of their mounds of fuzz.

But we would not be returning to Frederiksborg this voyage: while the Captain was ashore negotiating the release of the Kroo-men an urgent telegram arrived for us. He came back aboard in an extreme hurry, without even stopping to salute as the bo'sun's whistles trilled at the head of the gangway. He rushed straight to his cabin and immediately convened an urgent officers' conference. There is always something deeply satisfying in watching the officers engaged in a military panic: the urgent messages, the hurried consultations and the doors slamming up and down corridors. It was only towards evening that the momentous news began to trickle out from the conclave in the captain's saloon: we were not going to sail on up the coast of Africa at all; we were going to cross the Atlantic and sail home by way of the Pacific and Indian Oceans after rounding Cape Horn.

The news was received with wild excitement by the gunroom. What the lower deck must have made of it could only be guessed at, since we would not be home in Pola before about June now instead of at New Year as planned. But for us cadets it was cause for jubilation. Here was luck indeed: we had set out for a six-month voyage to the South Atlantic, and now here we were about to circumnavigate the globe. We had already seen Africa and South America; now the atolls of the Pacific and the scented islands of the East Indies would be added to our itinerary. We would miss the entire spring term at the Marine Academy, yet still have it credited towards our studies. It all seemed simply too good to be true.

Just before we weighed anchor, Captain Festetics mustered the crew in the waist and addressed them from the bridge. His Imperial Royal and Apostolic Majesty had certain urgent diplomatic and scientific tasks to be performed in South American waters and, since there was currently no Austrian ship nearer than the West Indies, it was his pleasure that we should extend our voyage to perform these errands for him. However, Festetics was a fair-minded man, so he concluded his address by calling forward our nine Kroo-men, who had only just come aboard, and asking them whether they wished to accompany the ship to Pola and be repatriated once she had paid off, or go back to West Africa now by steamer? The Kroos replied that it was all the same by them: they had just set their thumbprints to the ship's articles and for a Kroo it was a point of honour to stay with the ship for the duration of the voyage. They had no very exact notion of where Europe was, but they felt that they might as well see the place while they were about it.

The passage from Luanda to the Falkland Islands went like a dream: nineteen solid days of perfect ocean sailing in the southern spring, with steady south-easterlies blowing at an unvarying Force 6 on our ship's most favourable point, about two points abaft of the beam. We cracked along day after day at a regular eight or nine knots, creaming through the Atlantic swell as though engines were driving us – but without the noise and smoke and vibration and the stokers toiling away below in front of the glowing furnace-doors. It was gloriously exhilarating, to come off watch still in dry clothes and turn in to one's hammock, knowing that when one came back on watch four hours later the ship would still be bowling along at the same speed with all her canvas drawing, exactly as she had been on the previous watch and the watch before that. It was a true 'soldier's wind': one that required the minimum of work on deck for the maximum of miles covered each day.

For us cadets there was not a great deal to do except attend to our navigational studies and carry out routine chores like streaming the log at the start of every watch: a matter of keen interest now and subject of a good deal of bet-placing since we were all curious to find out exactly how fast the *Windischgrätz* could sail. Not that the measurements were very precise: our only means of gauging speed out of sight of land was still what it had been three centuries before, a quadrant-shaped block of wood the size of a quarter of Swiss cheese and weighted with lead on its rounded edge. This was attached to a reel of light line and would be heaved over the poop-deck rail by one cadet while another held the reel and a third stood by with a small sand-glass. The officer of the watch would count the number of knots in the line that slipped over the rail while the sand was running out, and from this he would work out our speed. It was a crude means of measurement, so I cannot say how accurate the reading was at the start of the afternoon watch on 4 November when the ship was found to be touching eleven and a half knots: her best speed ever under sail alone. Nor can I say whether this speed was maintained for long, because at the start of the next watch Cadet Gumpoldsdorfer heaved the log overboard without first making sure that Cadet Tarabochia was holding the reel. Speed measurement ceased thereafter for a day or so while the Carpenter made us a new one.

They were glorious days, that South Atlantic passage. I would idle on deck during the night watches, half hypnotised by the sounds of a great ship sailing at speed on the open ocean with a strong, steady wind: the slow, rhythmical creak and groan of the masts and spars above me as the ship rose and fell over the great, long waves, the steady rustle of foam as the bow sliced through the water, the high-pitched choir of the wind in the vast web of cordage aloft – steel-wire rope gave a very different note from hemp, I noticed – and below it all, like the boom of the very largest pipe on some great cathedral organ, so low and sonorous that one felt rather than heard it, the steady humming basso profundo of the wind in the sails. I could stand there and fancy that I had ceased to be; had become one with the wind, the ocean and the vast arching sky.

We sighted the odd sail or two on the horizon as we came near the shipping lanes, and once we fell in with a Norwegian steamer to exchange greetings and newspapers and check our chronometer against theirs; a constant preoccupation with sailing ships on long voyages in those days before wireless time signals. Meanwhile there was not a great deal to do, except to make our preparations for the ordeal that lay ahead.

Despite our excitement at the prospect of sailing around the world, we all of us secretly dreaded rounding Cape Horn, even in the middle of a southern summer. We all knew its evil reputation as a graveyard of ships, and those of our number who had been around it before, like Tarabochia aboard his father's ship and a number of fo'c'sle hands, spared nothing in telling us of the trials that lay ahead of us: gales that raged for months on end; sleet and ice even at mid-summer; mountainous grey-bearded waves rolling right around the world with no land to break their fury; the Antarctic ice lying in wait on one side and the savage unlit rocks of Tierra del Fuego on the other. We said nothing in reply, only set to work with a will to make our ship ready for whatever awaited her. Every last one of the hundreds of blocks in the rigging was checked and greased. Every last splice was gone over and every footrope replaced. Every one of the ratlines was renewed, served and tarred. Our sails – fibres slightly weakened now by months of tropical sun – were sent down and new storm-fast canvas swayed aloft to replace them. The steering gear was overhauled and greased, the deck planks were recaulked and the contents of the hold were restowed and bedded down with dunnage. As we neared the Falklands and 50 degrees south latitude every last item of gear below decks was made fast. The final, irrevocable step as we left Stanley, the earnest of our determination to do or die, would be the lashing-down of the ship's boats on deck. There was no point doing otherwise: if the ship were to be swamped or knocked over by the seas off the Horn – as so many had been before us and would be again after us – then there would be no time for launching boats. And anyway, what chance would an open boat full of survivors stand amid waves so frightful that even a fully rigged ship could not live in them? That is why so little wreckage was ever picked up from the hundreds of sailing ships that went missing in the Southern Ocean: all their loose gear had been so firmly lashed down that nothing was left to bob to the surface.

11

ON THE TREADMILL

In the event, we might have saved our ourselves the trouble and lashed the boats down before we reached Port Stanley, because there was very little there to make it worth the bother of lowering them to go ashore. A liberty boat left for the town when we dropped anchor there on the morning of 15 November, amid the driving mist and drizzle of an early Falklands summer. But when it came back an hour later it had most of the liberty men aboard, glum-faced, damp and thoroughly fed up. Nothing, they reported: a void; utter desolation; Siberia without the gaiety – or even the consolation of vodka, since this was strict evangelical Protestant territory and drink was frowned upon. In the end it was only the Captain and the GDO who went ashore, to visit the telegraph office and see whether there were any messages for us. There were none, so next day we set sail for the Horn. We were soon below 50 degrees south, and daytime work on deck ceased '50-to-50' as was the custom aboard sailing ships rounding the southern tip of South America.

Not that there was a great deal to be done anyway. Everything that could be attended to about the ship had been attended to already. All that we could do was prepare ourselves and our personal effects as best we could. Oilskin suits which had scarcely been brought out since we left Pola were now dug up from the bottom of sea-chests – and were usually found to have stuck together, as was the way with oilskins. They had now been recoated with a mixture of linseed oil and boot polish, and hung all about the ship with broomsticks through the arms as if to scare away the albatrosses who were now gliding along just astern of us: the drab yellowish-brown suits of armour in which we would ride forth to do battle with the elements. We also tried to prepare ourselves internally. Once we were out of Stanley harbour and heading south-westwards the Chaplain celebrated Sunday mass beneath a tarpaulin stretched across the waist. I perceived that there was a good deal more solemnity among the congregation than was usual at this service, and I had also noticed the evening before that there was an unusually long string of penitents waiting outside the office that had been rigged up as a confessional booth. Poor Gumpoldsdorfer took it all very seriously indeed, making out his will and sealing this into a bottle along with a last letter to his parents and one to his sweetheart in Klagenfurt. The rest of us tried our best to jolly him out of this graveyard mood, but he said that he had premonitions of disaster and was going to leave the bottle on deck so that it would float free when the ship foundered. He had been very depressed ever since the log-streaming incident, and seemed quite immune to anything that Gauss and I might do to try and cheer him up.

All things considered, it was rather a let-down for us to round the eastern end of Staten Island on the morning of 17 November, reduced to foresail and double-reefed topsails and with the entire watch on deck encased in oilskins lashed with ropeyarns at wrist and ankle – only to find ourselves gliding across a calm, sunlit sea with a steady north-westerly breeze coming off the Andean cordillera. Never mind, Festetics announced from the bridge, his voice emerging from between the brim of his sou'wester and the upturned collar of his oilskin coat, never mind: the Horn is deceptive as a quicksand. It may be fine now, but just you wait a couple of hours and see what devilry it'll be throwing at us. In fact we'd better put another reef in the topsails now just to be on the safe side. So we lay aloft, working up a fine old sweat inside our oilskins in the warm sunshine, and put a third reef in the topsails, fastening the pendants so securely that not even a West Indian hurricane could have dislodged them. Our speed fell to about three knots as a result. Yet the fine weather continued: the sun shone, the sea was no rougher than in the Adriatic on a spring day, the wind continued to blow steadily from the north-west – even veered north-north-west for a while – and the albatrosses continued their lazy soaring and swooping astern, regarding us curiously with their bright boot-button eyes. The promised gale did not come: the barometer remained steady and even rose a little towards midday. Yet still we ambled on down to 52 degrees south, to take us clear of the Horn and the notorious Diego Ramirez Islands, then turned towards the Pacific, our speed falling to about two knots as the wind came forward of the beam. Just before we did so the look-outs sighted a great mass of sail coming up fast over the northern horizon, back towards the Falklands. She had closed with us in half an hour or so. It was the *Paderborn*, one of the big five-masted Hamburg nitrate clippers of the Ferdinand Laeisz line. She was a splendid sight as she strode past us under full canvas – even royals set – and making a good eight or nine knots. As she passed by we saw signal flags fluttering from the halyard on the gaff.

'Gauss,' said the Captain, 'what are they saying?'

Gauss squinted through the telescope, then leafed through the code-book. 'I obediently report, Herr Kommandant, that the signal is "Do you require a tow?" '

Festetics fumed and spluttered like a true Austrian about the Pfiff-Chinesers and their confounded Prussian arrogance. But like a true Austrian he did nothing about it, and we continued to dawdle along at a couple of knots under storm canvas until the long Antarctic summer twilight fell, by which time the *Paderborn*'s sails had long since disappeared below the southern horizon.

We were still sailing like that the next morning as the glass suddenly started to fall. Blue-black clouds began to boil up over the western horizon as the wind hauled round ahead of us. The storms would soon be upon us – yet we were still well to the east of Cape Horn. We had missed our chance. When the Captain went below I saw Linienschiffsleutnant Mikulić tear off his sou'wester and fling it on to the bridge deck to dance on it with rage, inveighing most luridly in German, Croat, Italian and English against feather-brained Viennese aristocrats who ought to be ladies' maids and not sea-captains. Although nothing was said in public, most of those aboard shared his opinion. Naval discipline was naval discipline, but the lower deck (they declared) had still not had their brains taken out and replaced with boiled cauliflowers like the soldiery. Before long the entire ship was saying that it knew all along that the way to tackle the Horn was to do what the big German had just done: crowd on all the sail she could carry and batter down south-westwards on the starboard tack to the very edge of the pack-ice, then turn to make the port tack up into the Pacific.

By midday this was all largely academic. The westerly gales – or, to be more precise, one long gale – hit us, and for the next five and a half weeks we bade farewell to discussion, speculation and even thought as S.M.S. *Windischgrätz* struggled to claw her way to windward around the Horn. The sea is a very unforgiving place for fools, and having been given our chance and failed to take it we would not be offered another. For in the world of the Southern Ocean, south of 50 degrees, the terms 'winter' and 'summer' are very relative indeed. In the Drake Strait, between Cape Horn and the Antarctic ice, the weather is normally vile and the only discernible difference between winter and summer is that in summer the snow falls as sleet while in winter it freezes the rigging to glazed ice and turns the sails into sheets of plywood. In fact I often heard it said in later years by old sailing-ship hands that they preferred a winter rounding of the Horn, because the edge of the pack-ice, though it extended further north, was more solid and because one occasionally got spells of southerly or even easterly wind off the Antarctic.

But for us it scarcely seemed to matter after the first week or so of battling against the westerly gale and the constant brutal procession of great fifteen-metre waves rolling beneath and over us on their way around the world, the shrieking wind stripping salt spray from their crests to fling it in our frozen faces like splinters of glass as we struggled aloft in the weather rigging to handle sail: occasionally to let some out when the Captain felt that the wind had eased a little; more usually to take it in to the bare minimum necessary to keep our head to the seas as we drifted eastward, losing whatever meagre headway we might have made to westward. Each wave seemed exactly like the last in its towering menace; yet every now and then one would come rolling towards us which seemed intent on being our last, making us all hang on and shut our eyes tight in the hope that, if it happened, it would all be over quickly. During the thirty-eight days we were in the Drake Strait I imagine that several of these monsters must have hit us twice, having rolled right around the world in the meantime. Yet somehow the ship contrived to ride over them. Being a warship she had more freeboard than a deep-laden merchant sailing ship, which meant that at least the decks were not swept by the seas the whole time. But this slight advantage in dryness was more than offset by the fact that being rather high in the water – and perhaps lacking the momentum imparted by two thousand tonnes of Cardiff coal – made the *Windischgrätz* very liable to fall off when trying to go on to the opposite tack. Yet we would still wear ship every watch – usually losing in the process a good mile of whatever paltry westing we had managed to make on our last board. Korvettenkapitän Count Eugen Festetics von Szentkatolna was a decent man, but he would have done well to have heeded the remarks of Captain Preradović aboard the *Galatea*, to the effect that the sea recognises no drill manoeuvres. Because that is precisely what we were trying to do in those weeks: endeavouring to defeat the Cape Horn greybeards by recourse to the service regulations.

After five days of trying vainly to beat to windward under sail alone we fired up the boilers and tried using the engine to push us forward. It was hopeless: under steam alone the clumsy old two-cylinder engine was nowhere near powerful enough to drive the ship and its towering mass of spars and cordage into the eye of a westerly gale; especially when the propeller was being lifted out of the water for several seconds as we plunged into each wave trough. The best that it could do was hold the ship in the same place while the boiler furnaces devoured coal by the tonne. But when we tried using the engine to assist the sails the results were even more depressing, since the ship would no longer steer properly and kept trying to turn broadside-on to the seas. Apart from consuming upwards of seventy tonnes of coal, two days of trying to round Cape Horn under steam proved only that if S.M.S. *Windischgrätz* was ever going to get into the Pacific, she would have to do it under sail alone.

Sailing in those terrible seas was an exhausting process. We had a large crew compared with the sailing merchantmen that we glimpsed from time to time through the gale-driven murk, engaged in the same process as ourselves with greater or lesser success. As I have said, we were somewhat higher in the water than they were and thus rather less wet. But the size of the crew brought its own problems – like overcrowding and the press of cold, constantly wet, increasingly evil-smelling humanity on the dark, heaving lower deck. Freeboard or no freeboard, seas still swept the decks every few minutes and poured through the gunports in the bulwarks, forcing us to leap for the shrouds to prevent ourselves being washed overboard with them as they roared back to join the ocean. Half-frozen wetness became the normal condition of everything as water cascaded down the companionways and trickled in through the gunports in the battery deck, which, although battened shut and caulked with oakum, could never be made completely watertight. Before long hot food became a distant memory as the galley range was put out for the tenth time by waves pouring down the chimney and the Cook refused to go on trying to light it. As for our own dank little cubbyhole down on the platform deck, I think that a grave could scarcely have been more cheerless than that pitching, rolling, water-slushing box, lit only by a candle-lantern and with its walls constantly oozing and dribbling as the ship groaned and creaked her way across the roaring waste of waters.

By about the middle of December there could be no further argument: we had all died and gone to hell to spend the next quarter-million years trying to round that cursed cape, condemned to walk a sort of nautical treadmill until we had cleared our collective tally of fornication and petty theft; for ever wet, for ever cold; for ever hungry and exhausted; for ever hauling at the braces on the slimy, wildly heeling decks to lug our ship round on to the next tack on this road to nowhere; for ever wearing ourselves out to stay in the same place. All things considered, it was perhaps as well that the permanent sleet and low cloud made observations difficult; because when a sight of the sun or stars could be snatched through a gap in the grey murk scudding along above us, then the positions obtained had a depressing tendency to hover about the same longitude for weeks on end: sometimes 66 degrees west, sometimes 67, once even 68 degrees – but then back to 65° 40 or 64° 30 as we fell off once more to leeward.

We could perhaps take a certain chill comfort from the fact that others were even worse off than ourselves, because on 10 December we fell off so far to leeward after three days of raging westerly gale that we found ourselves east of Staten Island, in the relatively calm water where the last islands of the archipelago of Tierra del Fuego form a kind of breakwater against the fury of the ocean. Here we found not only large numbers of albatrosses and cape pigeons resting on the waves, but also a number of battered vessels which, like ourselves, had spent weeks trying to fight their way into the Pacific. One of them was a four-masted Liverpool barque, the *Toxteth Castle*, leaking badly and with her fore topmast gone. She had been short-handed to start with, it seemed – twenty-five crew of whom eight were apprentices – and a wave had swept her deck the week before to carry away half of an entire watch. In addition one man had been lying three weeks with a crushed leg, another was in a coma after falling to the deck, and a third had a smashed skull from being brained by a falling block when the fore topmast went. They had been down as far as the edge of the ice in their efforts to make westing and several of the nominally able-bodied men had frostbitten fingers and toes to prove it. Only eight men and boys were now fully able to work the ship, so canvas was being handled a half-sail at a time.

We learnt all this because the *Toxteth Castle* signalled for a doctor as soon as she saw that we were a naval vessel (very few merchantmen carried doctors in those days). Fregatternarzt Luchieni and I went across to her in the Kroo surf-boat, since it was the only one we had that was not firmly lashed down. The scene that greeted us in her fo'c'sle was of a misery such as I have scarcely witnessed outside of a concentration camp. The place stank like a sewer with gangrene and unwashed bodies. Everything was growing mildew and the crew were suffering from scurvy, worn out and half starved now that even the rations were running low. They already had a look of wolfish desperation about them. There was no possibility of transferring the injured, so Luchieni took off the gangrenous leg on the fo'c'sle table beneath a dancing hurricane lamp as I held the face mask over the man's nose and mouth and Jimmy Starboard dripped chloroform on to it. Luchieni amputated a few frostbitten fingers and toes as well, for good measure, but there was nothing to be done for the other two injured men except to hope that they would die quickly. On our way back to the gangway we spoke with the Captain. Luchieni asked him via me why he had not put back to Port Stanley to land the injured men.

'Oh no, I couldn't do that: the owners wouldn't like it at all – harbour fees and so forth. Company profits would be reduced and the shareholders would be unhappy.'

'But Captain, this ship is so completely unseaworthy and has only eight men left to work her. Where will you go now?'

'Back to try the Horn again, once we've rigged a jury mast. The owner's agent wouldn't sanction repairs even if we put back into Stanley. Anyway . . .' he straightened his back and stuck out his chin, '. . . we're British: the Bulldog Breed never gives in.' I looked back along the deck at his miserable crew – most of them Portuguese and Scandinavians – and wondered what they would say about being sacrificed on the altar of company dividends and national honour if the matter were put to the vote. In the end Luchieni waved aside the Captain's request to leave a bill for his services, saying that they were only what common humanity demanded, and a present from the Austrian government. It was only when we got back aboard that he told me that he doubted whether the bill would ever get paid if he had left one. And he was right: we did enquire when we were at Valparaiso, since the captain had given us a letter to post to his daughter, and we were told that the *Toxteth Castle* had been posted missing off the Horn about mid-December, ourselves having been the last to see her. I can only hope that the tears of the owners and shareholders were dried in some measure by the insurance cheque.

But we were not in much better case ourselves as we sailed out once more from behind the jagged pinnacles of Staten Island. A mood of sullen hopelessness was spreading through the lower deck. What were officers for if not to get us through situations like these? People began to mutter openly that 'der Festetics' should either put on all the sail we could carry and let us crack on through the seas down to the icefields if necessary, or admit defeat and turn to run with the westerlies into the Indian Ocean and towards Australia. We all knew that summer – such as it was – was short-lived in these latitudes. Before long the southern autumn would be upon us and the gales and blizzards would begin in earnest. By the week before Christmas, after a further ten days of futile attempts to beat to windward, matters came to a head. Linienschiffsleutnant Mikulić and a delegation of officers went to seek an interview with the Captain. It would now be the Pacific or death. The wind had eased a little and veered west-north-west, so what better time than now? We dragged ourselves wearily aloft and let out all sail except the royals. The sails banged like cannon as the gale filled them – but they held, and the ship began to surge through the waves, her bows pointed south-west. We were heading for the Antarctic ice.

That decision was very nearly the end of us. After a day and a night of sailing, and two topgallant sails blown to shreds, we found ourselves among the same howling, heaving wilderness as before – but this time with sinister-looking blocks of pack-ice surging among the waves and a bone-numbing chill in the air. We were down at the edge of the summer-rotten icefields. Just after the start of the morning watch on Christmas Day a yell came down to us from Tarabochia, lashed to the head of the foremast on ice-watch. We thought that it must be an island at first, as we peered with red-rimmed eyes into the freezing gale at the shape dimly visible through the snow in the morning half-light. But then we saw that the island was slowly rising and falling with the waves. It was a huge, low iceberg, dead ahead and much closer than we had thought: too close now for us to alter course and sail around it! In panic the Quartermaster put down the helm and we came up into the wind with a crash which made me think for a moment that we had run head-on into the thing. The whole ship shuddered and groaned as blocks rattled and the yards clattered back against the masts. Being taken aback like this in a gale was one of the most dangerous things that could befall a sailing ship. The masts in a square-rigger are braced to take strains from astern and either side, not from dead ahead. In the event I think that we only escaped being dismasted because the iceberg was sheltering us from the wind a little. At any rate we somehow managed to brace round the yards and get her head across on to the port tack before the masts were shaken out of her, hurtling past the end of the ice mountain so close-in that we could feel its freezing breath as we rushed by.

We were clear, but something dreadful had plainly happened to the foremast: a damage party was on its way forward over the icy decks. Something had also happened down below, to judge by the commotion coming up through the hatchways. I scrambled down the companionway ladder on to the battery deck – to find fifty or so men engaged in what seemed at first to be a kind of bullfight. Then I realised: a Wahrendorf gun had broken loose, the ringbolts that held its breeching ropes jerked clean out of the timbers by the sudden jolt as the ship had lurched over on to the port tack. The thing was now slithering and careering across the slippery-wet deck as the ship rolled through the seas. One good roll to allow it to gain momentum and it would crash out through the ship's side and let the sea come pouring in to sink us. What could I do but watch in fascinated helplessness as Njegosić and his men chased the three-tonne monster, trying desperately to get a line around it and slow it down? It smashed against the mainmast and slowed down as the ship reached the end of her roll; paused with a sort of sinister deliberation; then began to trundle backwards as the ship started to roll the other way. There was an anguished scream, and the men rushed forward. By the time I managed to get there to help them get a belay on the weapon it had slewed around and skidded to a halt. The gunner's mate had jammed a handspike beneath its wheels to hold it while we got a hawser around the carriage and back to the mainmast. Then I saw the cause of its sudden slowing-down. Gumpoldsdorfer was trapped beneath the carriage, his blue eyes staring stupidly as blood oozed from the corner of his mouth. It had run over him and crushed him. Broken white ribs protruded from his torn oilskins and a smear of blood had been wiped for two or three metres across the deck planks like a snail's track. He was quite dead: still apart from a little twitching. Some witnesses said afterwards that it had been an accident; that he had slipped on the deck, had fallen and had been unable to scramble aside in time. Others said that he had deliberately thrown himself in front of the careering gun to slow it down. Either way, der Gumperl was dead. In our situation there was neither the time nor the means for elaborate funerals; only the Captain and Father Semmelweiss and one or two cadets on the ice-crusted poop deck, bracing themselves into the shrouds to keep their footing as the canvas-wrapped bundle slid into the grey waves some way north of the edge of the Antarctic pack-ice. I have often wondered idly in the years since whether the sea in those latitudes is so cold down in the depths that he lies there still, frozen in everlasting youth, with his great blue eyes staring up at the translucent ever-moving ceiling above him. I suppose not. But he did achieve a certain limited immortality in later years – though not under his true name – as the principal character in an 'Approved Reading Text for Use in Junior Schools'. It was entitled *The Brave Cadet Who Gave His Life for His Ship* and was used as a reading exercise in Austrian schools right up until 1918. He could have done worse I suppose.

After that little encounter with the ice – one that we really ought not to have survived – it was back to reduced canvas once more and drifting to leeward in a newly freshened gale. We had nothing to show for our hair's-breadth escape but a badly damaged foremast and a hull that was now leaking profusely from all the seams which had opened under the brutal strains of the ship being taken aback. The *Windischgrätz*'s lower masts were in fact riveted tubes of iron plate. The foremast had buckled under the strain of being forced backwards – it had had to take most of the wind – and had burst open one seam. We had fished it: splinted the buckled section with wooden spars bound tightly in place with hawsers, but it could only be a temporary repair. The shrouds had been damaged as well – some torn bodily out of the chain plates where they were fixed to the hull – and they would have to be repaired in harbour. But even so we still spent the rest of the year 1902 trying to claw our way to windward in a last despairing attempt to round Cape Horn. We actually glimpsed it a few miles to north-westward in the early light of 28 December: a low, anonymous-looking twin-humped island just visible through the spray and driving rain about four miles off. I would not have recognised it myself, but several men who had been this way before swore that this insignificant hummock of rock was in fact the southernmost point of the Americas. From what I saw of it, it seemed to be a great deal of trouble that we were taking for such a meaningless dot of land. But after a couple of minutes we were denied even that, as we wore ship to take us away from the land – and were blown back eastwards again by the gale.

It was during our final attempt, on the morning of 29 December, that I was look-out at the head of the mainmast, wedged into the shrouds and stiff with cold and weariness as the mast described great fifteen-metre circles in the sky. The gale had got up again, but I cared not a button any longer. It was getting on my nerves now, the shriek of the wind in the rigging: not a steady 'wheee' noise but a slow-ululating 'wheee-whooo-wheee' as the masts rolled into the wind, then away from it, then into it again. I tried to look to westward into the driving snow. A large four-master was dimly visible about two miles to the south-west, sailing before the wind from the Pacific into the Atlantic – lucky devils. I turned to shout down to Fregattenleutnant Knoller on deck.

'Sailing ship in sight, Herr Leutnant, four points off the starboard bow! About two miles off!' I turned back to look at the four-master. A snow-squall obscured her – and when it cleared she was gone. I rubbed my eyes and stared again. No, there could be no doubt about it. I slithered down to the deck, almost fighting the wind which was trying to push me back up the shrouds.

'Are you sure?'

'Positive Herr Leutnant: she was there one moment and gone the next.'

We altered course to where I thought the ship had been – and caught a glimpse of an upturned lifeboat drifting away on the waves, too far off for us to retrieve it. We had to lower a boat: the air trapped under oilskins might keep survivors afloat for five or ten minutes. But who would go? In the end it was Union Jack and the Kroo-men in their surf-boat. They had suffered cruelly from the cold these past five weeks and I think that they actually welcomed the chance to work up a little animal heat by paddling, even if it meant getting themselves drowned in the process. The Captain would have refused, but they insisted, saying that no Kroo-man was ever frightened by waves. So we lowered the surf-boat on to a patch of oil dribbled from the officers' lavatories and watched them paddle away, singing one of their songs as they went to keep time. We expected that we had seen the last of them, but half an hour later they reappeared, visible for a few moments at a time on the wave crests. It took us the best part of an hour from getting them within hailing distance to floating a line down to them on an empty cask so that we could haul them in. When we finally got them aboard to be taken below and revived with schnapps we found that they had not managed to save any human lives from the foundered ship, only a cream-and-black pig which they had found swimming on the spot.

As for the rest, though, nothing. We never did discover her name. I suppose that it was the usual Southern Ocean story: the stern rising not quite fast enough to clear a particularly steep following sea; or the helmsman letting the wheel slip so that the ship broached to on the first wave, was knocked over on her beam ends by the second and had her hatch covers smashed in by the third to send her to the bottom. Hundreds of sailing ships went missing like that over the years: no survivors, no wreckage and only a terse note a few months later in Lloyd's List to mark their passing: 'Last spoken by S.S. *Valdivia* 24 August 1901, 52° 41' S. by 69° 52' W.'

As for the pig, the sole survivor of this nameless tragedy, we had no idea how he had come to be swimming after his ship had foundered beneath him. Sailing ships homeward bound from Australia in those days before refrigeration usually carried a fair amount of livestock; but in such weather all the animals would have been securely tethered in the manger under the fo'c'sle deck and should have drowned with everyone else. All we could surmise in the end was that our pig had been brought up on deck to meet the butcher just as disaster struck. In the circumstances we all felt that it would be tempting providence quite outrageously to contemplate eating him ourselves. So we christened him 'Francis' after the discoverer of the Drake Strait and thereafter allowed him the run of the ship, able to wander wherever he pleased like a sacred cow in Benares. Try as we might, we never could housetrain the creature, so even Linienschiffsleutnant Mikulić was obliged to put up with slithers of pig dung on his immaculately scrubbed decks.

On the last day but one of the year 1902, Captain Festetics was forced to admit defeat. There was no other choice; not with an exhausted and sullen crew, a badly damaged foremast and a hull now leaking so copiously from weeks of battering that the well was being pumped out every hour. The Carpenter and the GDO had made a survey of the hold that morning and reported that as things were it would only be a matter of time before we sprang a plank below the waterline and foundered. So at midday we put the helm up, squared the yards to the wind and ran for the Falklands. It was now six weeks since we had sailed from those islands. All we had to show for our battle with wind and weather was three dead: Gumpoldsdorfer, and two sailors who had simply vanished overboard one night; a badly battered, leaking ship; and a thoroughly depressed crew: demoralised not so much by the work and the weather – those would have been bearable – as by loss of faith in their leaders. It was a shabby business, after all, for a lavishly crewed naval vessel to have failed to round the Horn when ill-found merchant ships crewed by a few dozen men and boys were doing it all the time. We had been beaten and we knew it.

We limped into Port Stanley just as the light was fading on the last day of the year 1902. We might attempt it again if the weather moderated – it had suddenly turned fair as we neared the Falklands – but we were in urgent need of repairs first. It certainly looked though as if we had come to the right shop, because we could see in the long, low southern summer twilight that Stanley harbour and the coves round about were littered with derelict ships, the walking wounded from the everlasting Battle of Cape Horn. Many of them had quite evidently been here for years, to judge by their lichen-greened masts and the dark rags of kelp that festooned their sides. When the Captain and the GDO went ashore next morning to enquire about repairs we discovered why it was that the place was so strewn with abandoned vessels. Ship repair at Stanley was a monopoly run by two Scotsmen, the Guthrie brothers; and their charges were so high that many captains of storm-damaged ships, once they had telegraphed the likely repair bill to the owners, were instructed either to make jury repairs themselves and get the ship home as best they could, or failing that to run their vessel ashore in some out-of-the-way cove and repatriate the crew by steamer.

Needless to say, once we had telegraphed Vienna with Messrs Guthrie's estimate, the reply came back that there was no question of the Ärar sanctioning repairs at the exorbitant price being demanded. But that was not all; a second telegram had arrived from Vienna: one in code, and so lengthy that the cost of sending it would have comfortably paid for our repairs and left us with cash in hand. Once more the rumours began to spread via the galley telegraphic office. And this time they turned out to be reasonably accurate, because when we left Port Stanley on 2 January it was not to attempt rounding the Horn once more. Instead we were to head for the Chilean town of Punta Arenas, at the easterly end of the Magellan Straits, and proceed from there to carry out a survey of the waters around Tierra del Fuego.

The most cursory glance at the large-scale map in Max Gauss's sea-atlas showed that if this was indeed what we were going to do, then we were going – how do you say? – to have our work cut out. Because, compared with the five-hundred-kilometre coastline between Staten Island and Cape Pilar at the western end of the Magellan Straits, even the intricate 'Inselgewirr' of Dalmatia seemed a simple and straightforward affair. I suppose that in the whole world only the coastline of Norway and perhaps that of British Columbia can compare with it in sheer complexity: a fiendishly convoluted turmoil of channels and fjords separating innumerable jagged islands. But neither of those two coasts are as long as the southernmost extremity of South America, where the Andes finally plunge beneath the sea. Neither do they have the terrible gale-driven seas of the Southern Ocean crashing against them where the west wind meets the Andean cordillera and is forced through the gap between it and the Antarctic ice. Nor do they have the cold, nor the ferocious currents – the tidal range at Punta Arenas is about fifteen metres – nor the total absence of any aid or comfort on a shore which was in those days unlit, unmarked, only scantily surveyed and without any human presence apart from a handful of nomadic Indians.

That terrible coast was as much a graveyard of ships as the shores of the Kaokoveld. But there the bones lay in the open for years on end, embedded in the shifting sands. Here the casualties mostly lay on the sea-bottom, below the cliffs where the seas rolled across the entire Southern Ocean to smash against the rocks with such fury that columns of spray would be flung a hundred metres into the air. A few made it somehow into the relative shelter of the fjords to run aground. But their end was usually a miserable one, their crews marooned to die of starvation and cold and the ships left to rot away in the coves, posted missing at Lloyd's in the belief that they must have foundered at sea. Every summer, weather permitting, the Chilean Navy would despatch a gunboat down the coast to see what new wrecks had accumulated over the previous year, sending boats in to identify them if the seas allowed. Sometimes they managed to pick up a few survivors. But for most it was a miserable end down at the very extremity of the world, cut off from the rest of mankind as completely as if they had been wrecked on a distant planet. Right up until the First World War the sailing directions for Tierra del Fuego used to ask ship's captains to stand in near to the coast if possible and look out for castaways marooned in the coves. The very names on the map spoke foreboding: Desolation Island, Useless Bay, Starvation Cove, Terrible Inlet, Port Famine. Captain Fitzroy and his men aboard H.M.S. *Beagle* seventy years before had tried to instil a little manly optimism by dotting the map with a collection of red-faced Hanoverian Englishmen – Hardy Inlet, Duke of York Island, Cockburn Channel and the Brunswick Peninsula. But their beef-eating heartiness could do little to dispel the gloom that seemed to hover over the region. Even on a sheet of paper Tierra del Fuego still managed to look menacing, like the splinters of a shattered bottle waiting for someone to step on them.

I have to say though that the Land of Fire did not look particularly threatening as we approached Punta Arenas early on the morning of 5 January. During the night we had rounded the Cape of the Ten Thousand Virgins – Linienschiffsleutnant Zaleski had commented that he never knew there were that many – and entered the Magellan Straits on the tide. What we saw ahead of us was a flat, even shore backed by a line of low, grass-covered bluffs inland: rather like the seaward slopes of the Falklands but less wild to look at. We would have sailed up to Punta Arenas, but a head wind and the turn of the tide compelled us to use the engine to take us up to the anchorage below Sandy Point.

The renowned 'Southernmost Town in the World' certainly had little enough to recommend it apart from that distinction. But it did at least seem to hold some possibilities of adventure for naval cadets who had just spent three months at sea, because in appearance it was very much the wild South American pampas-town of our adolescent reading: wood and corrugated-iron shacks below bare, reddish hillsides; dusty windswept streets; and a cemetery full of pompous tombs far more splendid than the habitations of the living. There was a square with a statue of El Liberador Ambrosio O'Higgins, and a single bleak bar called the

Hotel Antárctica. Since there seemed to be so few opportunities for us to come to any harm in this place – once the local bordello had been placed under guard, that is – we cadets were graciously allowed a few hours' shore-leave. Gauss and I were aboard the first liberty boat to go ashore, at four bells before the town had started to wake up. It was quite unsettling at first, to stand on a firm wooden jetty after three months of constantly heaving decks: every bit as strange in its way as being aboard ship for the first time. I took three or four steps – and promptly fell over.

At the head of the jetty Gauss and I buttoned up the collars of our jackets against the blustering, eye-watering Antarctic wind and set off for the town centre. It really did look a most frightful hole of a place. I was intent on finding the church so that I could arrange to have a mass said for the repose of my mother's soul. It was almost four months now and I wanted to settle the matter just in case I never had another chance. We needed someone to give us directions, but it was early morning and the town square was empty – apart from a poncho-clad figure huddled on the steps of the Banco Chileano de Patagonia. We walked up to him – then hesitated. He might well be waiting to rob the place when it opened, so authentically villainous did the man look. But there was no one else about to ask, so Gauss (who thought well of himself as a linguist) approached him with a disarming smile and a small stock of Spanish carefully mugged up the evening before from Linienschiffsleutnant Zaleski's phrase-book.

'Perdone, señor, dónde está la iglesia católica más cercana?'

The man stirred and grunted, then looked up at us: an authentic gaucho with a flat, swarthy, high-cheekboned face and greasy handlebar moustaches – the sort of fellow in stories who flicks his thumbnail behind his front teeth, exhaling a blast of garlic-scented breath, and addresses the narrator as 'amigo' or 'hombre' in a threatening sort of way. He stared at us in puzzlement, then flicked his thumbnail behind his front teeth, exhaling a blast of garlic-scented breath.

'Qué, hombre?'

We could almost hear the upside-down question mark. At

what stage would the knife or the revolver be produced from among the folds of his poncho?

'Er . . . estoy buscando una iglesia católica. Amigo mío quisiera celebrar una misa por madre sua . . . um . . . recentamente decada.'

The man continued to stare at us in a rather hostile fashion. 'Extranjeros? Gringos? Breeteesh? Alemanos?'

'Non Alemanos, er . . . marinos austríacos . . .'

He stared at our cap badges – then broke into a wide, gap-toothed grin. 'Abär daas iss woonder-baar!Ik heiss Jovo Matajcić. Ik komm' auss Rijeka. Ik waar auk Osterreikischer Maatrose – Ess-Emm-Ess *Zezog Abrek*.'

So there we were: not ten minutes ashore into Spanish Latin America, down at the far end of the earth and the first person we ran into was a Dalmatian Croat ex-sailor who had once served aboard S.M.S. *Erzherzog Albrecht*. There was something faintly depressing about it really, as if we were dragging the Danubian Monarchy around the world with us like a dog with a tin can tied to its tail: 'Austria Extenditur in Orbem Universum' as Count Minatello had justly observed a few months before.

In the Bar Antárctica, out of the wind, Señor Matajcić explained to us that there were a great many Dalmatians in and around Punta Arenas, enticed out here in the 1890s as gold miners by a Viennese Jew called Julius Popper. For a few years there had been something like an Austro-Dalmatian colony across the Magellan Strait in Porvenir. Herr Popper had even issued his own silver coinage: Matajcić showed us an example with the word POPPER on one side and a crossed pickaxe and shovel on the other. But the Fuegian gold rush had fizzled out after a few years amid suspicions that what little gold-dust had been found had in fact been placed there by Herr Popper to boost his own shares. In the end a disgruntled miner had walked into Popper's tent and shot him dead. The company had collapsed shortly afterwards, leaving the dalmáticos to earn their living hereabouts as stevedores and as hands on the sheep-ranches up in Patagonia.

We arranged the requiem mass with Señor Matajcić's assistance, then wandered about Punta Arenas for a while before making our way back aboard. None of the other cadets had had much joy out of the place either. Women were almost unknown down here, drink was hideously expensive and mutton was the main item of diet. Others, however, seemed to have had more success in finding diversion. Throughout the day the town had shaken at intervals to the boom of explosions up on the hillsides. It had been Professor Skowronek and his assistants at work, collecting anthropological material, disinterring the bones from an old Patagonian Indian cemetery with the help of dynamite. The Professor had also made contact with the local governor and offered to pay handsomely for a pair of skulls of pure-blooded Fuegian Indians, reported by Darwin to be among the lowest and most brutal specimens of the human race and perhaps even the long-sought missing link with the apes. The Governor had replied that meeting the Professor's request should be no problem: colonisation of Tierra del Fuego was proceeding apace – powerfully aided by measles and smallpox – and Indian skulls were a commodity in abundant supply. Would the Professor like his specimens fresh or dry, so to speak? The Professor replied that if possible he would like to be able to attribute the skulls to a known and attested source. No problem, said the Governor: there were currently two pure-blooded Fuegian Indians, a male and a female, in jail in Punta Arenas for drunkenness. No one would miss them. The two heads were simmering in the Professor's cauldron that evening as we prepared to sail. He was very grateful and donated two hundred kronen in gold to the local natural history museum by way of thanks.

12

MISSING PERSONS

When we set off on our journey through the Magellan Straits at first light on 6 January we were proceeding under steam alone, with the topgallant masts and spars sent down to reduce the windage. We were also carrying an extra officer, Tenente Rodriguez-Crichton of the Chilean Navy, who was acting as our pilot. In its own way the winding Magellan Strait was quite as treacherous as the passage round the Horn – as could readily be seen from the number of wrecks that littered its shores. The Chilean government, fed up with having to rescue the crews, had recently ordained that all ships using the strait should carry a pilot. Quite apart from anything else the pilotage fees were a nice source of income for a hard-up government.

We began to see, as we steamed down the wide and apparently innocent strait, just why it was that pilots were necessary. Rocks lurked everywhere beneath the surface of the tortuous channel. Constantly shifting sand-bars crept out from the promontories while sudden, powerful cross-currents made it necessary to have four men at the wheel the whole time. The currents on the ebb were so strong – nine or ten knots at times – that all we could do when the tide turned was drop anchor and wait for the flood. Steaming at night was too dangerous to contemplate in such waters, so our progress was halting. We passed Port Famine, so-called because the first batch of Spanish settlers here had all died of hunger and cold in their first winter. But when we doubled Cape Froward with its whitewashed stone cross we came upon a new hazard: tendrils of kelp drifting from the rocks in the current. Several times a day the weed would wrap itself around the propeller and we would have to drop anchor, raise the propeller frame and send men down in the dinghy to cut the weed off with hatchets. It was a danger to be taken seriously: several of the steamer wrecks that lay in the shallows along the sides of the strait had got their screw fouled with kelp and been driven ashore by wind and current.

It was from Cape Froward that we got our first distant glimpse of the Darwin range to southward, its peaks covered in snow and the pale sun gleaming on the glaciers which crept down its sides to crumble into the fjords. Then the weather closed in again: constant westerly gales and freezing drizzle. We saw no sign of human life after rounding the Cape, apart from a British steamer which passed us going the other way. But Tenente Rodriguez-Crichton told us that just because we could see no one that did not mean there was no one about. Even in 1902 the Fuegian Indians were sufficiently far from having been pacified for ships anchoring in the Magellan Straits to be warned to keep a strong deck-guard at night in case of attack. Only a couple of years before, the Tenente told us, a Chilean gunboat had been sunk off Darwin Island after the local Indians had crept up in their canoes one night and tossed a stick of dynamite through an open cabin window. The best way of forestalling trouble, he advised us, was to post two sharpshooters on the fo'c'sle with instructions to pick off anyone they saw as we passed by. We thought that he was joking – then realised that he meant it. Korvettenkapitän Festetics was a humane man and would hear of no such thing, even though Professor Skowronek and Linienschiffsleutnant Mikulić had been strongly in favour. In fact, when a small bark-canoe emerged from the snow flurries one morning when we were anchored off Santa Ines Island, the Captain even allowed the three occupants to come aboard to barter otter pelts for cigarettes. They were certainly uncouth-looking creatures: short, with straight greasy black hair and flat features. Despite the wind and icy rain they were naked except for a flap of otter skin each and a short mantle of the same material, which they took turns wearing. All in all I think that, with the possible exception of Hungarian farm labourers in the 1930s, I never saw such woebegone and utterly wretched-looking creatures. As they puffed cigarettes three at a time amid a circle of wondering onlookers I saw Professor Skowronek eyeing them from behind the mainmast, trying to judge whether their skull proportions matched those of the heads presented to him by the governor in Punta Arenas. After all, one could never entirely trust these Latins . . .

On 10 January we turned the corner at Cape Pilar and began to feel our way gingerly down the Pacific coast with its terrifying chaos of islands and channels. We were in luck with the weather at least: the gales had abated the day before, so only moderate seas swirled and crashed among the tangle of rocks. But why were we here? Day after day we edged southwards towards Cape Horn, exploring every navigable bay and channel as we went, trying always to keep land between us and the Pacific, since being driven on to a lee shore in a Cape Horn gale was a fate so terrible as to beggar imagination. We seemed though to be doing no surveying in the formal sense: no soundings or triangulation anyway, just investigating every wreck we came across on the shore. Usually it was a cursory inspection carried out by telescope from the foretop.

'What is she, look-out?'

'Obediently report that it looks like what's left of a wooden four-master, Herr Leutnant. Been there about five years by the looks of it: there's very little of her above water anyway.'

'Wooden-built you say? No interest there, then. Slow ahead and let's get moving – I don't like the look of those clouds to westward.'

Thus we crept down the coast over the next two weeks, scraping past rocks and risking our lives from being embayed in the countless inlets, each of which looked exactly like all the others. Where the ship could not safely go the boats were sent in, tossing precariously on the swell. When gales blew up we sought shelter in the lee of the islands and sent parties of men on foot through the beechwoods and over the low granite hills to the Pacific shore. Sometimes they came across iron-built wrecks, which seemed to be of particular interest to our Captain for some mysterious reason. They would try to establish the wreck's identity, but usually there was little left to go on but a collection of sea-battered flotsam flung up above the high-tide mark in the coves. More than once our exploration parties came across the remains of survivors huddled in the lee of the rocks where they had vainly sought shelter from wind and spray. Our men did the decent thing in such cases and gave them Christian burial if there was time. There was hardly ever any means of identifying these unfortunates: we supposed because the corpses had been found later and plundered by wandering Indians.

It was intensely depressing to have to wander like this, inventorising the contents of the vast maritime cemetery scattered in this baffling maze of fjords and channels. It was said that before the place was properly charted by Captain Fitzroy and others at the beginning of the nineteenth century the crews of ships lost in these waters would go mad with fear as they spent week after week nosing into channels that turned out to lead nowhere. And as we worked further south, into the Beagle Channel between Gordon and Navarino Islands, it was all too easy to see why, as the terrifying black mountains of the cordillera loomed above us in the drizzle and low cloud, and the ship's bow ground and bumped its way through drifting pack-ice from the glaciers. The whole terrible landscape seemed utterly inimical to the human species, and a three-master no more than an earwig about to be crushed beneath a giant's boot. What madness had brought us to these regions? I began to wonder. Why did men risk their lives battling the seas off this desolate cape and the rock-bound channels inside it? Were there not graves enough ashore?

It was only on the tenth day out from Punta Arenas that I began to get some inkling of what we were doing in these waters. I was waiting at supper in the captain's saloon, served there for the first time since we left Port Stanley as Festetics had been ill with bronchitis for a week and confined to his stateroom. It had been another weary, frustrating day of wind and sleet and we were now rocking at anchor in an inlet on the east side of the Brecknock Peninsula. It was cold and damp despite the saloon stove and everyone was downhearted. The only crew members who seemed unaffected by the transition from tropical heat to sub-Antarctic chill were the cockroaches who had joined us at Frederiksborg. They now looked set to evict us all in a few weeks' time and take over the ship, despite every form of fumigation that officers and scientists could devise. It was widely believed on the lower deck that they were spreading the epidemic of skin rashes that was beginning to affect the crew; but more probably that was just the result of six months on searations: already several months too long, to judge by the peculiar taste of some of the salted meat that was now appearing on the mess-tables and the inevitable weevils in the flour and biscuit. A weekly dose of sauerkraut was keeping scurvy at bay, but not for much longer to judge by the dull metallic flavour which that vegetable had recently started to take on. Only the good red Dalmatian Patina remained in the condition in which it had left Pola, back in that now almost forgotten world of sunshine, warmth and calm blue seas.

As usual, Professor Skowronek seemed in disgustingly good spirits, quite unaffected by weeks of dismal weather and bad food.

'Well, Herr Kommandant, no luck today either it seems?'

'As you observe, Herr Professor, no luck today.'

'Perhaps it would help us all if we had some idea of what we were looking for? As a scientist I have to say that the past two weeks have been a complete waste of time from a research point of view. Herr Lenart here has collected some interesting botanical specimens, I understand, but as for the rest of us we have been unable to do anything much except sit in our cabins and write up our notes. We had no marine archaeological brief from Vienna when we set out, and none of us is qualified in that field, so why the sudden intense interest in recent shipwrecks? Are we undertaking a survey on behalf of Lloyd's, perhaps?'

'I agree, Herr Professor, that it must be frustrating for you learned gentlemen to have the scientific part of this voyage temporarily suspended in favour of its diplomatic mission. But please bear with us a little longer: our government is very anxious that this search should be carried out and there was no

Austrian naval vessel nearer to Tierra del Fuego than ourselves. Our orders came from the very highest quarters.'

Professor Skowronek snorted. 'I see: the very highest quarters. I suppose that means that the hunt for the Lost Archduke is on again? When will the Hofburg ever grow tired of this futile search and leave it to the Viennese gutter press?'

Festetics pursed his lips and hesitated, prodding at his food, but Skowronek persisted.

'Oh come on now, Herr Kommandant; we're none of us fools, and even the seamen on the lower deck have long since realised what the purpose of this "survey" of ours really is. It's the Archduke Johann Salvator, alias Herr Johann Orth, again isn't it? There's no point denying it any longer, I think.'

Festetics smiled weakly. 'Quite so, quite so, Herr Professor; you must forgive me. There was nothing particularly secret about our purpose in these waters as it happened. But you will no doubt appreciate that after having myself spent so many years at court, the habit of discretion dies hard where members of the Imperial House are concerned.'

'By your leave, Herr Kommandant,' said Fregettenleutnant Bertalotti, 'might you perhaps enlighten the younger among us a little as to the details of the Johann Orth affair? I remember the broad outlines, but since I was a child when it happened . . .'

'By all means, Herr Leutnant: you must forgive us old greybeards for talking so familiarly of long-distant events and assuming that everyone else here knows the story. The Archduke Johann Salvator – or Giovanni Salvatore to give him his baptismal name – was one of the archdukes of the Tuscan line of the House of Habsburg; born in Italy, but brought up in Austria since his early childhood. I knew him fairly well when I was a young naval ADC at court: a talented, even brilliant man in many respects, but . . . well . . . artistic in temperament, musical and frankly somewhat eccentric at times. He also had strong views – particularly on the organisation of the k.u.k. Armee – and since he was a serving officer these soon brought him into collision with our beloved Emperor and the Archduke Albrecht.' Festetics almost genuflected and crossed himself at this point: among black-and-yellow officers of the older generation the late Archduke Albrecht occupied a position rather like that of St Peter in the Catholic Church. 'Anyway, in 1885 or thereabouts there was a considerable fuss because he had agreed to accept the throne of Bulgaria without the Emperor's consent. I'm a sailor myself, not a politician, so I am not entirely clear as to the details, but there were also stories going around in Vienna some years later to the effect that he had been involved in the ... er ... unfortunate events at Mayerling. At any rate, the upshot of it all was that early in 1890 he renounced his title, becoming plain Herr Johann Orth, then left the country and studied marine navigation with the aim of becoming a merchant captain. Once he had obtained his master's ticket he arrived in England, where he chartered a three-masted iron-built barque, the *St Margaret*, and set sail for Valparaiso with a cargo of cement. I understand that he took a sailing master with him, a Captain Sodić, and a crew of Dalmatian seamen: likewise his companion, a certain Fräulein Milena Stübel of the Viennese light operatic stage. It was a difficult passage it seems. Disagreements between Herr Orth and his sailing master were frequent, until at Montevideo Captain Sodić and about half the crew left the ship. The ex-archduke seems to have engaged new hands and set sail from Rio de la Plata on 12 July 1890. They were sighted off the Horn in bad weather on 31 July, but since then neither the *St Margaret* nor any of those aboard her has ever been heard of again. Finish; the end; posted missing at Lloyd's on 30 November 1890.'

'Except,' said Professor Skowronek, 'except that every couple of years someone turns up claiming to have met the archduke or one of his crew.'

'Precisely, Herr Professor; and sends a very long, rambling letter about it to the Imperial Chamberlain's office, usually written on pink paper for some reason. And the Chamberlain's office forwards it to the Marine Section of the War Ministry with instructions to dig out the files and investigate the matter yet again. I am afraid that the realities of deep-water seafaring are not very clearly understood in Viennese official circles. When I telegraphed the k.u.k. Ministry of Finances from Port Stanley a couple of weeks ago about the estimate for repairs and our difficulties off the Horn I got the reply "Suggest you wait and try rounding the Horn in summer." I mean to say . . .'

'Have there been many such investigations, Herr Kommandant?'

'Several, I fear: all completely fruitless. The corvette *Fasana* came here late in 1890 to conduct a search – though looking for what precisely God alone knows: myself I'm convinced that the idiots in the Imperial Chamberlain's department must think that the Drake Strait is only about as wide as the Danube at Florisdorf. In 1891 the *Saida* conducted a search of the Beagle Channel, and the *Donau* five years ago. But the result was the same in each case. And now we have been diverted here for yet another attempt to find that which is now certainly beyond human reach.'

'But this all took place twelve years ago. Why the sudden renewal of interest?'

'The main reason, Herr Professor, is that a Dalmatian sailor called Fabrizzi has turned up claiming to be a survivor from the *St Margaret*. I interviewed the man myself when we were in Punta Arenas – though he refused to come aboard for fear that he would be arrested for perjury and taken back to Austria. Myself, I believe the man to be a fraud. But his name tallies with one on the vessel's crew list, and he certainly seems to have gathered quite a convincing amount of detail about the ship and her master – also highly discreditable stories which, I might add, he is threatening to sell to the press in Europe unless substantial sums are paid to keep him quiet. He says, in brief, that the *St Margaret* in fact rounded the Horn in early August 1890, but suffered so badly from the weather that she later ran aground in fog in a cove somewhere along this coast – he is being deliberately vague about where exactly. He maintains that Herr Orth and the crew survived, and that he and several others left them and set out in a boat through the channels to reach Punta Arenas – except that the boat capsized in a squall somewhere near Dawson Island and that everyone but Fabrizzi was lost. Vienna has got wind of this man's story through our consul in Montevideo, so that is why we are now trying to verify it: by scouring the coasts of this awful desolation looking for a ship and a man who have been lying at the bottom of the sea these past twelve years.'

'With respect, Herr Kommandant, why can you not just tell Vienna this? Surely they must respect your professional opinion as a senior naval officer?'

'Unfortunately, Herr Professor, senior naval officers a good deal more senior than I have been telling the court this for years past. We have told them repeatedly that ill-found ships with inexperienced captains, attempting to carry unstable cargoes the wrong way around Cape Horn in mid-winter, are more likely than not to sink on the way. But they will have none of it, I'm afraid: in the Hofburg's view members of the House of Habsburg simply do not drown like other people.'

'But surely, after so many years even the Imperial Chamberlain's office must realise that Herr Orth perished years ago, with not a single man of his crew reliably reported alive?'

'Indeed they might. But every time the matter looks like being closed some new clairvoyant in Madrid or some foolish American society woman will claim to have seen Herr Orth in a dream or met him wearing dark glasses and a false beard on the promenade at Cannes. And I am afraid that this time the tales of Signor Fabrizzi – and also certain vague stories from Chilean otter hunters, I believe – have come to the ears of a large Viennese insurance firm which eight years ago paid out a very considerable sum of money on a life-assurance policy in respect of Herr Orth. They strongly suspect fraud, I understand, and are sending out an investigator by steamer to Buenos Aires. In fact he may well have arrived there by now and be on his way to Punta Arenas. The Chamberlain's office and the War Ministry are both intensely anxious that if there *is* anything waiting to be discovered then the Imperial and Royal Navy should discover it first and not a civilian detective.'

'So in a word, Herr Kommandant, back to the search tomorrow?'

'Perfectly correct, I'm afraid: back to the search tomorrow at first light.'

We resumed our laborious hunt as promised at dawn the next day, bumping our way through the ice-floes along the Beagle Channel towards the English mission station at Ushuaia: the most southerly human settlement on earth in those days before the scientific outposts in Antarctica. We rounded Navarino and Hoste Islands, then returned to the Brecknock Peninsula where we had started three days before. Numerous wrecks had been sighted and a few investigated more closely, but most were too battered by the sea to be identifiable any longer. The best preserved was a British clipper, the *Etruscan Empire*, which had been dismasted and run aground on Hoste Island two years previously. We knew this, because the passengers and crew – unusually in such cases – had taken to the boats and managed to make Ushuaia a few days later with only a few of their number dead from exposure. We sent parties across to the wreck, but not for the purposes of investigation. Our errand was nautical cannibalism: dynamiting the wooden hulk then hacking the debris to pieces with axes and saws to feed our own boilers. After two weeks of steaming the channels we were down to our last few tonnes of bunker coal. The wood was to get us back to Punta Arenas.

The *Windischgrätz* dropped anchor once more off Sandy Point about midday on 17 January. Almost before the ship had stopped moving in the water the gig had been lowered and the Captain had gone ashore to send a telegram to Vienna: SEARCH FRUITLESS STOP COAL NEARLY GONE STOP DOUBT INFORMATION STOP AWAIT INSTRUCTIONS STOP FESTETICS. The reply came back within the hour: INFORMATION VERY REPEAT VERY RELIABLE STOP MENTIONS BAY WITH WHITE CAIRN STOP COAL AND CONTINUE SEARCH STOP. It drove Festetics into an unusual display of temper.

'Bay with white cairn, indeed. The imbeciles must think that the coast of Tierra del Fuego is the length of the Prater Hauptallee. There must be dozens of bays with white cairns.'

Coaling took place over the next two days: an unspeakably filthy, back-breaking task which involved using the ship's boats to bring four hundred tonnes of coal across in bags from the coal company's wharf at Punta Arenas, then manhandling them aboard. It was not good Cardiff steam coal; only the inferior, dusty Australian stuff which had been all that our coaling imprest authority from the Ärar would run to. The original four hundred tonnes taken aboard at Pola had been intended to see us to Cape Town and back, and the Ministry of Finances was very reluctant to forward us the means to purchase more. But it was coal at least. We tipped the last bag into the bunkers, then thankfully hosed down the ship and ourselves to clear it of the grime that the wind had distributed into every last corner. We would be off again next morning to resume our futile search for Johann Orth.

But before we left Punta Arenas there would be an evening free for a little socialising. Visits from European warships were not frequent, so the cream of Arenacian society came aboard that evening to be plied with drinks and small-talk in the wardroom.

Among our visitors was an English missionary, Mr Lucas-Bridges from the station at Ushuaia, who was in Punta Arenas for a few days on business. He was rather stiff about alcoholic drinks, and also about being aboard a warship of a Catholic power. Apparently he had read the invitation as 'Australian' and not 'Austrian'; a mistake which caused him no little puzzlement when he first came aboard. But once he had got over his initial surprise he was quite affable, and a mine of information about this desolate region of the earth. He was talking with the Captain and Linienschiffsleutnant Zaleski as I brought up a tray of drinks.

'Yes, the work of the mission is going quite nicely – no, thank you, not for me young man. The only trouble is that before long we shall have no natives left to convert.'

'Then I must congratulate you on your success, Mr Bridges. Might I perhaps interest you in coming next to Dalmatia to spread a little Christianity among my sailors?'

'Oh no, Captain, it's not that we've had any great success in bringing the Indians to God: quite the contrary in fact. It's just that they are dying off so fast now from measles and pneumonia that before long there won't be anyone left to hear the gospel. I gather that your people – the Salesian Brothers, isn't it? – are closing down their mission station on Dawson Island because of the lack of people to preach to. They had considerable success at first I understand in getting the Indians into clothes and learning to work for money, but then they just started to curl up and die by the hundred. If it isn't disease it's gin and repeating rifles. I gather that some of the settlers over in Fuego have been giving bounties for strings of Indians' ears in order to clear the land for sheep. But there, we must look on the bright side I suppose: they were going to die anyway once they came into contact with white people, and through our efforts at least a few of them have been saved from eternal damnation. After all, who are we to question the inscrutable decrees of God's Providence?''

There was an uncomfortable pause in the conversation for a few moments. It was Zaleski who spoke first.

'I see, Mr Bridges. And are all the Indian tribes as unresisting as these poor people whom you have described?'

'Oh no, not a bit of it. The Alcaloofs over on the Brecknock Peninsula for example: they're an utterly savage lot and totally unwilling to open their hearts to the good news of Christ's saving grace. We've got nowhere at all with them despite many years of trying to make contact. They've managed to get guns from the white men, and they may even have white men leading them. There's been talk for years past of a European called John North living among them . . .' A sudden dead silence fell over the wardroom.

'Excuse me Mr Bridges, but what was that name you just mentioned?'

'Why, John North. It's only hearsay of course, but there's some talk of him being an Italian – though to me it seems a rather peculiar sort of name for an Italian, I have to say. As for myself though, I don't attach too much weight to these tales. There was a half-caste called "Squire Muggins" some years ago who was supposed to be leading raids on the sheep stations over in Fuego. But he turned out to be six or seven different people.'

'But this man John North, Mr Bridges: what else do you know about him, if I might ask?'

'Not a great deal really, Captain. He's said to have been a

sailor: perhaps shipwrecked, perhaps a deserter, I can't really say. We first heard of him round about '96. But nobody that I know has ever met him, apart from a few of your dalmáticos here in Punta, and they say little enough about anything to outsiders. I'm sorry not to be able to help you, but I just don't know any more about him – if he exists at all, that is.'

As soon as the reception was over and the last guest had gone ashore the Captain and Zaleski tumbled into the gig and rowed ashore to try and make contact once more with the sailor Fabrizzi. They found him after an exhaustive search of the bar at the Hotel Antárctica. He suddenly became very non-committal, however, when the name John North was mentioned.

'I might know him, I might not: that's all I'm saying. I've heard stories among the Dalmatians over in Porvenir, but I couldn't tell you anything for definite. No, I couldn't say where the *St Margaret* went ashore: all those rotten inlets look alike. I couldn't lead you back there – at least, not without a sight of gold to jog my memory. You have to remember we were three days away from there when the boat went over and the Indians fished me out of the water, half frozen to death. That sort of thing affects a man's memory.'

When they got back aboard the entire lower deck were turned out of their hammocks and paraded to be questioned whether any of those who had been look-outs during our fortnight's search remembered a cairn of white rocks at an entrance to a cove. In the end Steuermatrose Christ remembered that during the forenoon watch on the fifth day, on the southern side of the Brecknock Peninsula, he had seen through his telescope a cove with a cairn of white rocks – and the wreck of a ship on the beach. He had reported the sighting to the officer of the watch, Linienschiffsleutnant Svoboda, but because of mist and rain it had been decided not to bother with a closer investigation. The place was checked against the record in the log, and in the end the location was narrowed down on the chart to an inlet called Starvation Cove, leading in from Hopeless Bay behind Cape Despair. The names seemed to augur particularly well for our forthcoming visit.

Our two-day passage back to the south side of the Brecknock Peninsula very nearly added another name to the long tally of ships lost in the waters around the southern tip of South America. South of Dawson Island, in the Cockburn Channel, the wind had veered northerly for a while on the second morning to a degree where topsails had been set to help the engine push us against the six-knot current. Despite the breeze the water in the channel was remarkably calm, so the battery-deck gunports had been opened to give the ship a much-needed airing between decks. We were nearing the vast black bulk of the Darwin cordillera, below the twin peaks of Mount Sarmiento where the Cockburn Channel turns west to become the Magdalena Channel. The icy draught of the glaciers was detectable even here, kilometres away. The ship steamed along, engines thumping and hissing steadily below. Then suddenly, without the slightest warning, slam! – a great freezing blast of air howling down from the Sarmiento glaciers caught us broadside-on. Before we knew what was happening we were sliding across the decks as the masts were pressed inexorably towards the water by a roaring torrent of air so solid that it was like struggling against a river in spate. Yells of alarm came from below decks, where water was pouring through the open battery-deck ports. Too frightened to think, Gauss and I scrambled into the weather shrouds of the mizzen to lay aloft – in fact almost walk aloft – and take in sail. We got to the mizzen cross-trees somehow, and on to the yard to claw in sail. But it was hopeless: we hung there in the screaming wind as the yardarms touched the water. The ship was going to sink. We closed our eyes tight, waiting for the freezing water to engulf us. Then, slowly, the ship began to right herself to an accompaniment of sail canvas banging and flapping itself to pieces. Down on deck someone had had the presence of mind to let fly the sheets and spill the wind from the sails, even though the sails would now flog themselves to destruction. We did what we could to make fast the threshing rags of canvas – the mizzen topsail and spanker had both blown out of their bolt-ropes – and then made our way back down on deck, trembling in every limb. The first officer we met was Linienschiffsleutnant Mikulić, who had given the order to let go the sheets. His knees were trembling visibly and his face was the sickly white colour of uncooked dough. 'Well done,' he said as we passed him to go below and clear up the mess. Gauss remarked afterwards that we must indeed have been close to death for Mikulić to thank anyone afterwards.

The pump was working for most the next day to clear the ship of the tonnes of water that had come aboard during our near-capsize. We emerged from the Magdalena Channel into the Pacific to be greeted by a raging gale, and only just made it around the western end of the Brecknock Peninsula before running into the calmer waters in the lee of Stewart Island. We were in a kind of trance now, passed beyond fear and into resignation. We knew perfectly well that we were all dead men, doomed to sail in these fearful waters until we went on to the rocks and were smashed to pieces, or until we met another williwaw even more violent than the one that had just knocked us over in the Cockburn Channel. A curious robotic state had taken over the ship, turning us all into clockwork automata. We knew now that this coast would be our grave: that if we ever found Captain Orth and the *St Margaret* it would be because we had gone to join them at the bottom of the sea.

It was on the morning of 22 January that we finally found Starvation Cove, marked by a rough pile of white rocks at its entrance. The boats were lowered to take search parties ashore, Gauss and myself among them. Not that there was a great deal to see. The wreck was certainly the remains of an iron-built three-master answering roughly to the dimensions of the *St Margaret*. And when the tide went out we saw that the hold of the wreck was filled with a solid mass of cement, the bags long since rotted away to leave their solidified contents stacked on top of one another. There was a good deal of wreckage ashore, though it was difficult to say whether all of it came from this particular wreck. There were the remains of a hut built from spars and tarpaulin, on the edge of the cove where the evergreen beech trees met the shore. Beside it were five graves in the shingle, with rocks stacked over them and marked by crosses of decaying driftwood.

There was also a path leading away among the trees, uphill from the cove. It was Max Gauss who saw it first. It was a faint trackway, but by the look of it it had been made by Europeans – several trees had been cut down with a saw – and it had been in use until quite recently. There were even faint wheel-ruts in the mud where a hand-barrow had been pushed along it sometime during the past few months. In view of the urgency of our mission it was resolved that exploration parties would be sent inland that very afternoon, even though the weather was closing in once more.

I was detailed to accompany Linienschiffsleutnant Zaleski's landing party of ten men, whose second-in-command was to be Fregattenleutnant Knoller. We were to carry three days' rations, and also – in view of the ferocious reputation of the local Indians – rifles, cutlasses and three hundred rounds of ammunition each. By the time we had kitted ourselves out aboard and returned to the cove the rain had turned to wet snow and a gale was blowing. We tramped miserably up the trackway through the threshing, dripping beech forest among the granite boulders, snow collecting on the shoulders of our jackets and dripping from our packs. Why were we doing this? What were we looking for? Any fool could see that this faint trackway through the forest had been made years ago by prospectors or hunters, not by missing archdukes whose bones had long since been picked clean by the fish a hundred miles out in the seas off the Horn. We were not going to find Johann Orth; but the Alcaloof Indians might find us – in fact might well already have done so. As we laboured miserably upwards through the forests we all of us had a curious feeling that we were being watched, and several times we thought we glimpsed figures flitting among the trees ahead of us. Perhaps they were just waiting for dusk to fall before they sprang their ambush . . .

It was already getting dark as we emerged from the beech forest on to a sort of sub-Antarctic tundra mixed with clumps of dwarf trees. How much longer would be have to wander like this, cold and wet and utterly miserable? At the very least, when would Zaleski give the order for us to make camp so that we could light a fire and warm ourselves? We stopped suddenly – and listened. I was at the head of the party with Zaleski while Knoller brought up the rear. Zaleski held out an arm to motion us to stop. But we had stopped already of our own accord. It was about fifty metres ahead in the semi-darkness, somewhere over the edge of a bluff of boulders above the pathway; obscured by the roaring of the wind in the trees below us but still perfectly audible. It was a piano accordion, and a woman's voice singing. A sudden indescribable thrill of fear ran through our party, leaping from man to man like St Elmo's fire in the rigging. The song that she was singing was the waltz 'Frölich Pfalz, Gott Erhalt's' from the immensely popular Karl Zeller operetta *The Bird-Seller*. Something close to panic broke out. It was the gloomy terror of this desolate place, I suppose, and the accumulated nervous strain of months of sailing in these terrifying seas; of the graveyard of ships which we had just spent three weeks exploring, the dark mountains looming above us and the savage enemies who might be closing in on us. At any rate, our collective nerve suddenly snapped. Whatever spirits had enticed us to our deaths on the shores of this God-forsaken wilderness, they were now about to manifest themselves to us, after first mocking us with the music of our distant homeland. The wind dropped a little. They could be heard quite plainly now, not far away . . . We were just on the point of breaking and running back towards the ship in terror. It was Zaleski who held us.

'Steady there I say – stay calm!'

'But Herr Schiffsleutnant, it's ghosts! It's the Lost Archduke, that's what it is, come to haunt us . . .'

'Ghosts my arse! Listen a moment, will you? Did you ever hear a ghost who sang as badly as that?'

We stood still and listened. Certainly he had a point: the piano accordion was in acute need of tuning, while the voice was that of the sort of woman who gets herself classed in amateur choral societies as a 'borderline contralto' not because of her ability to reach low notes but because she never quite manages to reach the high ones. Surely the sirens of antiquity would at least have taken singing lessons before they set about luring sailors to their death on the rocks?

'Knoller, you stay here with the men. Prohaska – do you believe in ghosts? You Czechs are all supposed to be rationalists.'

'I ob-b-bediently report that, n-n-no, Herr Schiffsleutnant.'

'Good man. Follow me then: we're going to get to the bottom of this.'

We set off through the trees, and turned a sharp bend around the bluff to find ourselves on a miniature plateau. Zaleski stopped and gripped my arm. Ahead of us, invisible from below, was a light. It was a hut. Inside it a dog was barking fit to choke itself. The music stopped. A door opened to reveal the lamp-lit interior of the cabin, and a man with a rifle stepped out.

'Qui va?' He reached into the hut and brought out a hurricane lamp. We walked forward to present our compliments. 'Down there, down there, I say . . .' He took the dog by the collar and dragged it back towards the doorway. 'We have visitors it seems, Milli.' He turned back to us. He was a shortish, thick-set man in his fifties, heavily bearded and dressed in a seaman's guernsey and pilot-cloth trousers.

'Do we have the pleasure of addressing Señor John North?'

He looked at us suspiciously: clearly he was unused to visitors.

'Perhaps. Who are you?'

Zaleski replied in German. 'Linienschiffsleutnant Zaleski and Cadet Prohaska of the Imperial and Royal steam corvette *Windischgrätz*. At your service.'

The man replied in German, but with a marked Italian accent.

'I see. So you have come for me at last. Well, all I can say is that you've been long enough about it. Better late than never though I suppose. Please come in. Our dwelling here is a humble one to be sure, but to us it means more than all the castles and palaces of Europe.' We stooped to enter the low doorway. It was indeed a gloomy hovel, constructed of logs, old ship's timbers and tarpaulin and surrounded by heaps of assorted chandlery: mounds of rusty anchor chain, piles of old hawsers, assorted ship's ironmongery, a couple of bower anchors and an upturned lifeboat. Surely the man must have required help to drag all this up from the cove?

'Milli? Allow me to introduce Linienschiffsleutnant Zaleski and Cadet Prohaska. Herr Leutnant, Herr Kadett . . . May I present Señorita Milli Stübel?'

Milli stared at us dimly. She was a fattish, exhausted-looking woman in middle age with blowsy, straggling faded blond hair and heavy, not particularly intelligent features. She was incongruously squeezed into a much-patched Tyrolean dirndl costume several sizes too small for her. She got up unsteadily on varicose-veined legs and blinked at us mistrustfully. She too was plainly unused to callers.

'Schani, who are these men?' The voice was pure lower-class Viennese; the accent of Faworiten or Ottakring. So this was the notorious dancer and soubrette Milli Stübel, for whom the Archduke Johann Salvator had renounced his titles and who was supposed to have drowned with him off Cape Horn. By the looks of it he was unwise to have done the former and she exceedingly unwise not to have done the latter.

'They are Austrians, my love. They have sent a ship after all these years to take us back home, just as I always told you they would.'

She eyed us suspiciously. 'Are they police?' She turned to us. 'I 'aven't done nothing wrong. It was all his idea . . .'

'No, no, my dearest. They are naval officers. A warship is waiting for us down in the cove.'

'Oh Schani, I'm frightened. Suppose they . . .'

'Hush there my love: don't be frightened. Put some coffee on the stove for our guests now.'

She turned, still muttering, to put a blackened enamel coffee pot on the stove: a cast-iron bogie-stove of the kind one used to find in merchant ships' fo'c'sles and which seemed to have the peculiar property of always being out. The chimney was an iron pipe that led up through the tarpaulin-covered board roof. The hut was truly a dismal enough den: draughty, leaky and grimy, with its only furniture a ship's-cabin table, a few chairs, a bunk bed with some ragged blankets – and an old and battered piano accordion. Sheet music lay about, and a few framed prints adorned the sooty walls: mountain scenes, and the lithograph 'A Stag in the Clearing' which marked this place down as a Viennese household much as the mesuta nailed over the door used to distinguish Jewish huts in the villages of Poland. There was a greasy, musty ambience of frying pan and damp clothes. Zaleski spoke.

'Señor North – or Herr Orth perhaps?'

The ex-Archduke smiled. 'By all means: call me Herr Orth if you prefer it. The news seems to have leaked out, and anyway it scarcely matters now.'

'Herr Orth, we heard you playing as we came up the trackway, and Fräulein Stübel singing. It was from Zeller's *Vogelhandler* was it not?'

'Why yes. Do you know the piece?'

'I saw one of the first performances when I was a cadet: in Vienna in 1891, if I remember rightly. So how is it that . . .?'

'I understand: when we disappeared the previous year. Well, Herr Leutnant, we arrived here in the middle of 1890, as you must have guessed by now. I assume that our friend Fabrizzi has been talking. For some time past he has been trying to blackmail me during his visits here, threatening to denounce us to the authorities. And I suppose that Señor Lopez the otter hunter has been to the Austrian Consul in Valparaiso as he said he would. Yes, we came here in – let me see – August 1890. Our ship managed to round Cape Horn after a difficult passage, but we were badly knocked about and were eventually driven to seek shelter in the cove below, where we ran aground in a sinking state. Everyone got ashore, and Fabrizzi and the Mate set out in a boat to try and reach Punta Arenas. But while they were away the crew got their hands on bottles of spirits and fighting broke out. They were English wharfside rats whom we had recruited in Montevideo when Sodić and his men abandoned us. In the end five of them were dead, and the remainder set off in a boat to follow Fabrizzi and the Mate. We never saw them again. Fabrizzi managed to get back to us a few months later, after having nearly drowned, and offered to get us to civilisation. But by that time Milli and I had changed our minds and decided to stay here.'

'Changed your minds, Herr Orth? Then what had been your original intention if I might ask? I had always understood that the *St Margaret* had been bound for Valparaiso.'

'That is true. But we were only carrying cargo to pay for a further passage, to the South Seas, where I hoped to find a suitably isolated island on which to establish my headquarters. My intention was to sit there and wait until the political situation in Vienna had resolved itself to our advantage, whereupon Herr Johann Orth would reappear on the world's stage. I had decided upon this plan shortly after the Crown Prince shot himself at Mayerling. But there: if temporary isolation from the rest of mankind was what we sought, then what better place could we have found in the entire world than the Brecknock Peninsula? I soon made the local Indians my subjects, by using my contacts to procure them rifles and my experience as an army officer to teach them how to employ them to good effect. And it was I who sought to develop the place by bringing that confounded swindler Herr Popper out here to dig for gold. During all these twelve years those encrusted idiots in the Hofburg have believed me to be dead. But now the hour has come to prove them wrong. The period of waiting is over. By this time next year all Vienna will lie at our feet.'

'But Herr Orth, I fear that you may be ... may perhaps be under a certain misapprehension as to the purpose of our visit here ...'

'Fiddlesticks: I know perfectly well why you are here. My Indians have been watching your ship along the coast these past three weeks, and my agents had informed me of your arrival at Punta Arenas before you had even dropped anchor. Oh no, there is not much goes on in these parts without Johann Orth getting to know about it, I can tell you. You and your men have been shadowed by my followers ever since you landed at Starvation Cove. You would never have been allowed to reach this place alive if I had not known of your purpose in coming here and instructed my faithful Alcaloofs to give you safe passage.' He turned to Milli Stübel. 'Anyway, Milli my dearest, shall we give them a sample now?'

The fat woman simpered complacently at us as Herr Orth pulled out a thick, dog-eared sheaf of music paper from a tin trunk. He set it up on a music stand, then slipped his arms into the shoulder straps of the accordion, which wheezed horribly like a bullock with emphysema. He smiled, and Milli curtseyed to us. She had just set up a wooden frame with a row of cowbells hanging from it. The performance was about to begin. Orth turned to us.

'Herr Leutnant, young man: you will be able to tell your grandchildren that you were present at the first public performance of the operetta to end all operettas, the piece of musical theatre that knocked Strauss, Millöcker, Suppé and the rest into a cocked hat. I give you *The Tyrolean Maiden of the Andes*. A note, Milli...' He squeezed the box to give a rather flat A; a lugubrious honk like a motor-car horn. Milli Stübel replied with an A-verging-on-G, and we were off.

It must have lasted the best part of an hour altogether, I suppose. It only seemed much longer, there in that dismal shack down at the very end of the world as the sleet drove against the window panes, the Cape Horn gale moaned about the hut and the wet beechwoods threshed below us. I supposed that Fregattenleutnant Knoller and his men could not be having too cheerful a time of it waiting for us down there, huddled under a flogging tarpaulin and trying to coax life into a fire of wet beechtwigs. But even so their lot was still greatly to be preferred to ours, as the accordion groaned and Milli Stübel howled her way through what must surely, in its entirety, have been one of the flattest musical entertainments ever written. I was not and never have been the possessor of super-sensitive musical ear, and dreadful amateur musicians were one of the great hardships of life aboard a naval vessel in those days. But even so I had never before come across anything quite as dire as this ludicrous confection of bad tunes and flaccid libretto. It concerned (we gathered) a Tyrolean countess forced by cruel but unspecified circumstances to emigrate to South America and start a new life as a milkmaid in the Andes, wearing a dirndl skirt and yodelling as she would have done back home, but against a background of tempestuous Latin-American music, llamas, Inca princesses and so forth. And that was just Act I; in Act II a Hungarian nobleman, likewise forced by cruel circumstance to emigrate to South America and become a gaucho, rescued her from a flock of marauding condors which were trying to pull her from a mountain ledge, and promptly fell in love with her. But after that I am afraid that we rather lost track of it all as one dire tune followed relentlessly upon the heels of the last, delivered in the style of the Alps or the Andes or the Hungarian puszta as circumstances dictated. It was a complete dog's breakfast of a story, such as even a master of the genre, a Lehár or a Kálmán, would have been hard-pressed to make anything of. But in the hands of Herr Orth and his companion it was a purgatory all of its own; an entertainment roughly comparable to an afternoon in the dentist's chair.

It is only by listening to a solid hour or so of really awful music that one comes to understand what distinguishes bad music from good: the stodgy, earth-bound tunes that never quite manage to get both feet off the ground at once; the melodic lines that never lead anywhere but end by wandering round and round in circles until they fall down dead; the horrid little ornaments fixed on to dreary music in an attempt to liven it up, like those plastic scrolls and rosettes which amateur decorators tack on to old Utility furniture and which merely serve to underline its lumpen gracelessness. What we got that evening in the shack was only a sample, I understood: the full three-act entertainment would have lasted nearly four hours and involved a cast of thirty, as well as hundreds of extras and a full orchestra. What it would have been like if ever staged scarcely bears thinking about: 'Wagner Comes to Bad Ischl' is probably not far off the mark anyway. Its aim, we gathered – apart from making Herr Orth a millionaire of course and establishing him as the world's greatest composer of light operas – was to relaunch Fräulein Stübel's career on the Viennese stage after an absence of some twelve years.

'Of course,' he confided to us as we sat afterwards dazed and bewildered, 'that was the real cause of the trouble at Mayerling you know? Rudolf and I were working together on something like this back in '89 when he took up with the Vetsera girl. I was writing the score and he was doing the libretto. Several of Vienna's leading impresarios were very interested. But of course, once that minx had attached herself to him and heard about the project, what did she want but the female lead, even though she couldn't sing a note? There was a quarrel about it in the hunting lodge that evening and she snatched the manuscript from his desk and threw it on to the fire – she was a pretty little thing, I grant you, but spoilt and bad-tempered as they come. He threatened her with his revolver, she tried to snatch it from him, and it went off and killed her. Anyway, when the smoke had cleared and he saw that she was dead, Rudolf put the pistol to his own head rather than face the row with his old man.'

'I see, Herr Orth; most interesting. Thank you both for a most memorable performance, but Cadet Prohaska and I must now return to our ship.'

'Glad to hear that you liked it. Rather good isn't it?' He paused for some moments. 'Well, where's the contract then?'

'Er . . . the contract? . . .'

'The contract from Herr Karczag at the Theatr an der Wien. I keep up with the Austrian papers, you know? There isn't much that goes on in Vienna that I don't know about here in Tierra del Fuego I can tell you. My emissaries have shown the draft score and libretto to Herr Karczag. So where's the contract?'

I saw Zaleski glancing nervously at the rifle in the corner. Our own weapons were outside.

'Oh yes: the contract. Where's the contract, Prohaska? I told you to bring it.'

'I obediently report, back at the ship, Herr Schiffsleutnant.'

'Imbecile! That means that we shall have to go back and fetch it. Herr Orth, Fräulein Stübel – we must take our leave of you now. I am afraid that there has been a small misunderstanding aboard our ship and that this young fool here has brought the wrong papers. We must return and bring it back here tomorrow

255

for you to sign. But may we perhaps persuade you to return to Austria with us?'

'No, no thank you: it will take at least six months to engage the cast and rehearse the piece, not to speak of preparing the sets. Milli and I will return instead by steamship in time for the start of rehearsals. The whole production must be ready for the start of the Christmas season. But perhaps you may take this back with you ahead of me, to show them that I am not dead after all...' He reached down the front of his guernsey and pulled out a gold medallion on a chain. He took it off and handed it to Zaleski. 'There, Herr Leutnant: a token from Herr Johann Orth, if any should doubt that you met me, or that it was really me whom you met.'

I looked at the medallion. It was a rather nice communion medal of ornate design. On the reverse was engraved in copperplate script: ARCIDUCA GIOVANNI SALVATORE, 12A IUGLIO 1859.

So we said our farewells and left to rejoin Knoller and his men encamped among the dripping beech trees further down the hillside. Had we dreamt it all? As we walked down the trackway from the hut in the blustering wind and snow Zaleski muttered to himself.

'Mad: completely barking mad the pair of them...'

We saw the others huddled around the dim, flickering light of a hurricane lamp.

'Well, you certainly took your time,' said Knoller. 'What was going on up there? It sounded like a variety cabaret. We've been freezing down here. You might have asked us in. If there's a worse place than this for weather in the whole world then I've yet to see it. Who were they anyway? Escaped convicts? Lunatics? Hermits? I thought there were supposed to be only a few Indians around here.'

'Otter hunters, that's all: an old chileano and his wife. He claims to be half Swiss, so that's the reason for the piano accordion. We just couldn't tear ourselves away from them. But then I suppose they don't get visitors very often down here.'

'I don't wonder at it. Anyway, let's get back to the ship before we all catch pneumonia. I'm frozen.'

We arrived back at the cove, sodden and weary, just before dawn the next day, having got lost in the forest on the way back. As we rowed out to the ship Linienschiffsleutnant Zaleski was unusually quiet, and as soon as we came alongside he jumped to the gangway ahead of us and climbed up on deck to disappear below in search of the Captain. It cannot have been a lengthy interview, because at 5.45, just as I was warming my numbed hands around a tin mug of coffee at a mess-table on the battery deck, there was a bellow down the companionway.

'Cadet Prohaska? The GDO wants you up on deck!' There was no arguing with such a summons, even when wet, exhausted and chilled to the bone. I hurried up on deck to where Linienschiffsleutnant Mikulić was waiting. He was not in a good temper.

'Befehl, Herr Leutnant?' I saluted.

'Prohaska, do those niggers of yours down below understand you and you them?'

'I obediently report that fairly well, Herr Leutnant.'

'Good. And how much German do they know how to jabber?'

'I obediently report that not a great deal as yet, Herr Leutnant.'

'Splendid. Well, get the buggers up here at once to man that jungle canoe of theirs. Then go to the Armourer and bring a stout wooden box: a rifle-box should do nicely. Also a few picks and spades from the Bo'sun. We're going ashore to do a little gardening.'

The nine Kroo-men turned out as ordered, indigo-black with cold and misery, and were despatched to man their surf-boat at the falls. The items requested were loaded into it, and we set off across the grey morning waves to the wreck of the *St Margaret*, leaving our own ship at anchor rolling on the swell. We landed on the shingle beach and made as indicated by Mikulić towards the tumbledown hut and the row of graves beside it.

'Very well, let's start with this one. Prohaska – tell these men to dig.'

They did not have to dig far: the bodies had not been deeply buried after that drunken knife-fight twelve years before. When we had uncovered the first lot of bones Mikulić produced a tape measure.

'Metre eighty-two: far too tall. Try the next one.' In the end we had uncovered three skeletons before Mikulić found one that met his requirements as regards height. 'Metre seventy-two: that should do nicely. Well, what are you all waiting for? Get him into the box.'

There was not a great deal to put in the box, only a sad collection of bones, a pair of leather seaboots and a rust-clogged clasp knife. We also found some coins: a couple of Argentinian ten-peso pieces and a few English copper pennies, the latest of which was dated 1889. To my surprise Mikulić took these and flung them into the forest. Before we put the skull in the box he took it, knocked off the dirt, fitted the jawbone in place and regarded it critically from the side.

'Yes, yes: I suppose that with a little imagination . . . Come on, let's get back aboard.'

As we were pushing off from the beach there was a shout from the edge of the woods. It was a woman's voice. 'Herr Leutnant! Wait!'

It was Milli Stübel, limping down the beach towards us on her bad leg. Her hair was wet and straggling and she looked in every way the personification of misery.

'Herr Leutnant, take me with you, please . . .' She seized Mikulić's arm. 'Take me with you . . . Don't leave me here to die in this 'orrible place. I didn't do nothing wrong, honest I didn't. It was all his idea about the insurance and the ship and all. I never saw a gulden of the money. They can put me in jail if they like, just so long as I get to see Vienna again and me mum and sister. Take me back with you, pl-e-e-ase.'

Mikulić's reply was characteristically sharp and to the point: a vicious blow in the face that sent her staggering back to sit down in the water. She got up sobbing hysterically as we drew away from the beach. The last thing I saw of her she was kneeling in the shallows wailing and wringing her hands to us in supplication. I had to look away from her, towards the ship. Within the hour we were weighing anchor to leave the shores of the Brecknock Peninsula.

13

WCSA

It was the last week of February 1903. We had been drifting like this for ten days now, sails hanging as limp as tea-towels while we drifted in the flat calm, the ship heaving slowly to the long Pacific swell. So far the world's largest ocean had certainly lived up to its name. We had enjoyed fair winds from Cape Pilar to Valdivia, where we had landed Tenente Rodriguez-Crichton after four weeks aboard, during all of which time he had kept the meter ticking, so to speak, thus accumulating considerable sums for the Chilean state treasury in the form of pilotage fees. Nor had we fared too badly on the passage up to Valparaiso, where we had spent two days and carried out a number of urgent running repairs to make good some of the damage that we had suffered in the waters around Cape Horn. But since we had left Valparaiso on 5 February, bound for the Peruvian port of Callao two thousand miles up the coast, the late-summer calms had set in to a degree where most days the *Windischgrätz* made more progress from being drifted northwards by the Humboldt Current than from being blown along by the wind.

It was all intensely frustrating: day after day after day of the same glassy sapphire-blue sea with the drab line of the Atacama Desert shore in the distance and, beyond that, the brown and mauve ramparts of the Andes with their snow-covered summits. For engineless sailing ships, one of the great hazards of this interminably long Chilean desert coast was that of getting too close in a calm and being slowly rolled inshore by the swell to smash up among the breakers, unable to claw out to sea again because of the lack of wind and unable even to drop anchor because of the steeply shelving sea-bottom. We were intent on staying at least four miles out to sea to avoid this peril. True, we had an engine of sorts. But it took us at least an hour to raise steam, and in any case we were down to our last few tonnes of bunker coal after our recent tour of the channels around the Magellan Strait. No further coal could be obtained at Punta Arenas because our coaling imprest authority under the 1902 naval estimates had been exhausted, and the Ärar would sanction no further delegated expenditure. But never mind, they had cabled back, they were still able to purchase Austrian-produced coal under the 1902 allocations, so we were to expect a chartered steamer from Europe laden with five hundred tonnes of Bohemian coal – purchased and despatched at a mere four or five times what it would have cost us to have bought the coal in Punta Arenas. For reasons of chartering, the coal would be delivered to await us in the Chilean port of Concepción. We never did see that coal though – which is scarcely surprising since there is no Chilean port of Concepción: only a Chilean city of that name some kilometres inland and served by the port of Talcahuano: presumably a geographical distinction too fine to have shown up on the small-scale maps of South America available in the Ministry of Finances. We arrived at Talcahuano late in January, but of Austrian steamers and Bohemian coal they knew nothing. The mystery was not solved until 1926, when I was serving in the Paraguayan Navy – in fact commanding the Paraguayan Navy – and came across a vast heap of coal lying on the wharfside at a place called Concepción, on the Paraguay River about three thousand kilometres inland in the middle of the Gran Chaco. They told me that it had been brought there many years before by lighters from a ship lying at Buenos Aires and that, since the town enjoyed tropical weather all year round, no one had any idea what to do with it; not even the townsfolk, who normally stole anything moveable. I used it to some profit over the next few months to fire the boilers of river gunboats. It was a curiously comforting feeling, to know that even from beyond the grave the old Austrian Monarchy was extending a bony hand to help me.

The other great navigational hazard for sailing ships along the West Coast of South America – the WCSA as everyone called it – was a much less dramatic one than being driven ashore in a calm. It was simply that of overshooting one's port of destination and being unable to regain it because of the current and the lack of wind. It was a fatally easy thing to do: all the ports on this coast – Iquique, Tocopila, Caldera, Antofagasta – looked much alike from the sea even in daytime, and lighting of the coast was minimal, so it was quite easy to mistake one for another. This was dramatically illustrated to us in February by the strange affair of the *Reine Clothilde*.

She caught up with us and overtook us in a morning calm just after we had left Valparaiso. The *Reine Clothilde*, 2,340 tonnes, was a big four-masted steel nitrate clipper belonging to the Société A. D. Bordes of Bordeaux. She passed us very slowly in the barely discernible breeze. But she overtook us all the same, ghosting along under full canvas at perhaps a knot or so while our ship was barely moving at all. They were splendid-looking vessels, those big French square-riggers: quite the handsomest of sailing ships in my opinion, with their graceful pale-grey hulls and the black-painted top strake with its row of fake gunports. The *Reine Clothilde* was in ballast that morning after unloading Welsh coal at Valparaiso. It was galling for a man-o'-war to be overhauled by a merchant vessel, but there was some compensation for us at least in the magnificent spectacle as she glided past within hailing distance, her elegant masts and vast spread of bone-white canvas – all of it drawing perfectly – quite dwarfing our more old-fashioned and ill-arranged rig. It was also pleasant for us to be able to speak to another ship and exchange news after so many months away from Europe.

'Good-morning *Clothilde*. Permit us to observe that you look a splendid sight.'

'Thank you, you are most generous. Would you like some French journals? We have made a fast passage, so they are only a very few weeks old. And may we perhaps also carry some messages for you?'

'You are very kind. Where are you bound for?'

'For Iquique, to load nitrate.'

'Splendid. When you arrive, would you be so kind as to contact the Austrian Consul and get him to telegraph a message ahead to Callao for us? We had a rough time off the Horn and need to reserve a drydock for repairs.'

'Most certainly: it will be our pleasure.'

So a boat was lowered and the message was delivered to the *Reine Clothilde*'s captain, the boat returning with a bundle of newspapers which we fell upon and devoured like so many famished beasts: even those of us who could not read a word of French. By midday the French vessel's mastheads had disappeared over the horizon to northward.

We thought no more of this meeting until late in February, when we were ourselves approaching the latitude of Iquique. A call went up from the look-outs.

'Sail in sight, dead astern!'

As the hull came up over the horizon we saw that it was a Bordes nitrate clipper. Torpedomeister Kaindel broke off his instruction class on the quarterdeck to launch into his usual peroration about the A.D. Bordes line: about how everyone at sea referred to that shipping company as 'the Jesuit Navy' because anyone with any pretensions to being well informed knew that it was in fact a front organisation for the well-known religious order. When Gauss and I had asked him what possible interest the Society of Jesus might have in the bulk-nitrates trade, Kaindel had merely looked knowing and remarked that that just went to show you how cunning they were. Kaindel was a true Viennese: like all Central Europeans an avid enthusiast for the most fantastic and improbable theories of conspiracy. In that particular milieu the only explanation that is never accepted for anything is the simple and obvious one.

The ship drew closer on the light breeze, then overtook us – and we saw to our astonishment that she was the *Reine Clothilde*. Her captain was not in a good mood.

'Nom d'un nom! We were unable to deliver your message because the putain current, it carry us past Iquique in the night and take us as far almost as the frontier of Peru. Voilà! – We must pick up the trade winds and beat three thousand miles south to encounter the westerlies once more near the Île de Pâques, then sail back up the coast. Ptui! Five thousand miles to return to where we are before! Ah, to have an engine!'

Apart from small incidents like these – and a narrow escape from being wrecked by a tidal wave at Taltal – the tenor of life aboard the *Windischgrätz* during those weeks was monotonous in the extreme. While at Valparaiso, thanks to the constant swell in the roads, we had been unable to heel the ship and had therefore been able to staunch only the more accessible leaks. Pumping went on day and night now, eight men constantly cranking the great cast-iron wheels to keep down the water level in the ship's well. Also the food was bad and getting worse. We had taken on fresh provisions wherever we had called, but the staples of diet aboard were still the rations that we had loaded at Pola eight months before. And as we climbed slowly back from polar latitudes towards the tropics it was becoming more apparent with every passing day that something had gone badly amiss in the Imperial and Royal Navy Victualling Depot the previous summer. Perhaps they had made up the embalming fluid incorrectly, or perhaps the meat had been off even before it went into the casks. At any rate, when I accompanied the officer of the watch down into the hold on 18 February to inspect the provision barrels we found that several of them were groaning gently from the pressure of gas inside them, making little squeaking mews like a sleeping cat dreaming of mice. The Carpenter was sent for and instructed to spline the casks. He splined the first – and the result had us all up on deck in about five seconds flat, followed by the entire watch below, driven from their hammocks by the unspeakable stench erupting from the hold. It was as if all the charnel-houses, all the cesspits and all the tanneries of the world had opened their doors at the same moment. The only thing I have ever come across even remotely comparable were the Carso battlefields in the summer of 1916. The very air itself seemed to vibrate from the smell with a faint musical note, like telegraph wires in the wind. Within a couple of minutes the entire crew had taken refuge upwind on the poop deck, gasping for breath.

In the end the only way of getting someone to go down into the hold and remove the offending cask was to bribe Union Jack and the Kroo-men with twenty-gulden pieces. They went below with their faces wrapped in camphor-soaked handkerchiefs and got a sling around it so that we could hoist it up on deck and tip it overboard. We then set to work getting the other suspect casks of salt meat up from the hold and over the side. When they were a safe distance astern we sank each of them with rifle fire from the poop. It was most diverting to watch the fins of our attendant sharks slicing towards the burst casks in the hope of a good meal – then see them turn around and rush away in terror once they got a whiff of the contents.

Over the next few days a great quantity of condemned provisions went overboard – including the barrels of sauerkraut which had in theory been all that stood between us and an outbreak of scurvy, but which had now deteriorated to a point where even scurvy seemed preferable to eating the stuff. The daily diet resolved itself into a monotonous affair of zwieback, beans, rice, olive oil, tinned meat and not much else, since the dried fish and other such stores had gone mouldy months before off West Africa and had been tipped over the side. Tempers were short and everyone was in a peevish mood; especially Linienschiffsleutnant Mikulić, who now became positively dangerous to approach. His duties as GDO relieved him of watch-keeping and us of his company for much of the time, but he would still intervene with his fists in the daily management of the ship at the smallest provocation.

The one small compensation for being aboard a sailing ship becalmed off the coast of Chile was that we were at least able to supplement our rations by fishing. The cold Humboldt Current teems with fish and we sometimes had to do little more than lower a basket into the water to provide ourselves with a supper of sardines or anchovies. We cadets also fished a good deal on behalf of Herr Lenart, helping him to carry out a survey of the marine life of the eastern Pacific. This helped somewhat to vary the monotony of the daily round – especially the morning off Tocopila when we had cast the lines in the hope of catching a large specimen of tunny mackerel for the taxidermist to stuff. Almost as soon as we had baited the hook and trailed it astern there was a violent jerk on the line. But as four or five of us hauled it in to the mizzen chains we saw to our dismay that what we had caught was not a tunny mackerel but a large and very angry squid with a body the size of a rolled hammock and tentacles three or four metres long: one of the ferocious 'jibias' which prowl these waters and which are the terror of the local fishermen. The thing writhed and fought there for about five minutes, changing colour like a railway signal in its anger as its tentacles coiled around the shrouds like pea tendrils and it squirted at us with its brownish-black ink. In the end it snapped the line with its parrot beak and departed. Herr Lenart was annoyed at losing such a fine specimen, but as for the rest of us – who would have had to get it aboard – we were not at all sorry to see the back of the creature.

By early March the calms had become so constant that desperate measures were being taken to move S.M.S. *Windischgrätz* towards her destination. The boats had been lowered and we were towing the ship northwards in the hope of picking up the south-east trade winds, which at that season extend to about 15 degrees south of the Equator. This was particularly hateful drudgery. The ten-metre barge with her forty oarsmen sitting double-banked was a clumsy enough old tub in her own right. But pulling her through the glaring summer sea with two thousand tonnes of ship trailing astern was a labour so back-breaking, so exquisitely tedious that no prison governor in Europe would have dared to prescribe it as a punishment. It was like being a galley slave, but without even the compensation of rapid motion through the waves to make up for aching muscles and blistered hands. We lugged at the oars beneath the midday sun as Linienschiffsleutnant Mikulić abused us from the fo'c'sle through a speaking-trumpet and threatened to disrate the petty officers if they could not get more effort out of us. The hawser dipped and tautened, dipped and tautened as the ship crept forward a metre at a time across the shimmering pool of molten lead on which we were floating. After two days of this one of the older long-service ratings, Steuermatrose Baica, fell dead of heart failure while heaving at his oar. Several men were down with sunstroke. One of them was a young Czech seaman called Houska, towards whom Mikulić had taken a particular dislike. Houska was rather plump, and very fair-skinned. He took the towing under oars very badly: fainted three times in one morning until Mikulić finally lost his temper and gave him a cut across his bare back with the knotted rope scourge which he had taken to carrying of late, but which until now he had never actually dared use on anyone. This was going too far in the year 1902: Houska was left lying unconscious on the fo'c'sle deck as the surgeon wiped the cuts on his back with iodine. Meanwhile Mikulić was tactfully led below by the Bo'sun and his assistants, swearing most villainously and practically foaming at the mouth. The scourge was discreetly dropped over the side and the matter was smoothed over – for the time being. The general opinion among the lower deck however was that if the Captain had any backbone at all he would never have permitted 'der Mikula' to wander about with such a thing in the first place.

When relief from this purgatory came the next day it was from an entirely unexpected quarter. There had been a faint southerly breeze just after dawn and the ship had made a few miles' northing to about the latitude of Arica, where the coast bends in towards the Peruvian border. We were now only six hundred miles from Callao: less than two days with a fair wind. But as things stood by about mid-morning the passage might well take us the rest of the year, because the breeze had died once more to leave us becalmed. Before long, we knew, the boats would be lowered and it would be another back-breaking day of four hours at the oar followed by four hours at the pump followed by four hours at the oar ... About 10.30 a call came down from the look-out at the masthead, perched there half-insensible with sun and exhaustion:

'Steamer in sight, three points off the port bow!'

It was indeed a steam-ship. We crowded to the rail to look: we had not seen another vessel for the past three days. But as the mystery ship altered course towards us I saw through the telescope that she was no merchant steamer but a small warship: a large gunboat or small cruiser, painted white with a buff funnel and with a blaze of gilded scrollwork at her bow. Well, that was good to know: merchant-ship captains with schedules to meet would not be inclined to waste time socialising with foreign warships, but another naval vessel would certainly stop to exchange news and reading matter with us. We all dived into our sea-chests and began scribbling postcards to our families.

Within twenty minutes the mystery ship had closed with us and was steaming on a parallel course about eight hundred metres abeam. We could see the stars and stripes fluttering from her gaff as she steamed past. Why were they not coming alongside? Did they think we might have smallpox aboard? And why were they apparently cleared for action? Good God, they were training their guns at us... There were two sudden bright orange puffs of flame, and the ship was lost for several moments in a cloud of white smoke. The two shells and the crash of their firing reached us at the same moment. One hit the foremast just below the cross-trees with a brilliant red flash and a deafening bang. The crew scattered in panic as hot shell-splinters peppered the decks and the fore topgallant mast and sails crashed down in a tangle of rigging. The second shell went through the middle of the spanker sail to burst in the sea far beyond us.

There was pandemonium as men ran about trying to reach their battle stations and the bugles blared 'Clear for action'. The Captain stood on the bridge, staring in disbelief. Zaleski, though, who had been standing beside me on the poop watching the American ship's approach, seized a mess tablecloth which had been hung out to dry and scrambled into the mizzen shrouds. I have no idea what the world record is for the climb from the poop deck of a three-master to the mizzen truck, but I imagine that if there is one then Zaleski still holds it. Festetics awoke from his horrified trance to shout to him to come down. But within ten seconds he was clinging to the masthead with one arm and frantically waving the tablecloth with the other. Meanwhile men were swarming up on deck with rifles from the small-arms racks. Zaleski yelled down to them to stand fast and not to shoot back. Confused and frightened by the bewildering turn of events, everyone stood still and looked up at him uncertainly as he came scrambling back down through the rigging, then at Festetics on the bridge shouting something about running out the port battery – then at the American gunboat which had gone about and had now closed to three hundred metres to steam past with her starboard guns trained at us, ready to fire. There was dead silence. A voice came to us across the water, amplified by a speaking trumpet.

'Do – you – surrender?'

Festetics seized our own speaking trumpet from its hook, clearly preparing to shout some bravado back. But before he could do so Zaleski had leapt up the steps of the bridge and snatched it from him, shouldering the Captain aside.

'What is the meaning of this outrage? We are the Austrian corvette *Windischgrätz*. Are Austria and the United States at war? If so we have heard nothing about it.'

There was silence for a few moments – then the American vessel suddenly ran her engines astern to stop. At last a voice came back across the water. The note of puzzlement was detectable even at that distance.

'The who?'

'The Austro-Hungarian steam corvette S.M.S. *Windischgrätz*, on passage from Valparaiso to Callao. I think that perhaps we should discuss this. Can we lower a boat to come across?' It seemed that a debate was taking place on the American's bridge. At last the reply came.

'OK: send someone over. But don't try anything funny. We've got you covered and we'll put two shells through your waterline if you start monkeying around.'

While this exchange was taking place Festetics had been trying to wrest the loud hailer from Zaleski's grasp. 'Herr Schiffsleutnant, I must insist that you give me the speaking trumpet. We must reply to these people in kind . . . This is an outrage . . . Pure piracy... The honour of the Monarchy will not permit such an insult to go unavenged...'

'Herr Kommandant, by your leave... Please wait a moment... We must go across to talk with them...'

'But this is a flagrant breach of international law, to fire on us without the slightest provocation. We must return their fire... Buglers – sound "Prepare to fire"!...'

Zaleski seized him by the lapels of his jacket. 'With respect, Herr Kommandant, shut up. You see those guns there trained on us? They're modern quick-firers with high explosive shell. If we so much as sneeze at the Americans they'll blow this old packing crate to splinters inside a minute...'

'Zaleski, have you gone mad? This is rank mutiny...'

'Prohaska, come with me. Lower the port cutter, you men, we're going across to talk with them.'

'Herr Linienschiffsleutnant, you are under arrest!'

'With respect, Herr Kommandant, be quiet: the rest of us want to live a while longer.'

So we rowed across to the U.S.S. *Tappahannock* under a white flag of truce, to be met at the gangway by the Captain and his First Officer with an armed guard. The Captain was a stocky, barrel-chested little man with his cap rammed down squarely onto his head and his neck bulging over the high collar of his tunic. They saluted us curtly, and looked at Zaleski with extreme suspicion. It was true that he did not greatly resemble most people's idea of an Austrian.

Zaleski saluted. 'Delighted to make your acquaintance.' He extended his hand. 'Florian Zaleski, Senior Lieutenant in the Imperial and Royal Austro-Hungarian Navy, currently Second Officer of S.M.S. *Windischgrätz*. My Captain has sent me across to parley with you. And with whom do I have the honour...?'

'Thomas H. Dahlgren, Commander US Navy. This is my First Officer Lieutenant Kowalsky. I must now ask you to hand me your sword.'

Zaleski smiled. 'My sword? Ah, there now, I forgot to bring it with me. Will you perhaps accept this in lieu?' He fumbled in his jacket pocket and produced a pearl-handled penknife. Lieutenant Kowalsky smiled, but I saw that Dahlgren sensed that he was being made fun of. I had divined already that he was not an unduly bright man, and also very full of himself. He snorted angrily.

'Very droll. Well lootenant, I guess you'd better do some explaining mighty quick.'

Zaleski smiled disarmingly. 'With respect, Captain, explain what? You have just fired upon us and not we upon you.'

'Now see here, Lootenant Zabiski or whatever your name is. Are you or are you not the Peruvian frigate *Arequipa*?'

'Good heavens no: what on earth can have given you that idea?'

Dahlgren's neck bulged even more about his tunic collar. 'I see. Then why the hell are you flying a goddamn Peruvian flag?'

'Excuse me, but I do not quite understand. We are flying an Austrian naval ensign.' He looked across at our ship. Her foremast was a sorry tangle of fallen spars and cordage and the spanker now sported a great rent in the middle where the shell had passed through it, but the red-white-red flag was still hanging limply from the gaff peak on the mizzen. Dahlgren thrust his bull-face into Zaleski's with the look of a tourist who knows that he is being swindled by a bazaar stall-holder but is still trying to keep his temper.

'The – goddamn – Peruvian – flag – is – red – and – white – with a – goddamn – badge – in – the – middle: understand?'

'Ah, but so is ours. The difference, if you will permit me to explain, is that the red and white stripes of the Peruvian flag run vertically – so – while those on ours run horizontally. Also the badge is rather different in each case.'

In the end the matter was resolved by reference to the international flag code-book brought from the ship's office. Dahlgren stared at the two flags for some time, like a dog presented with an equation. He tried for a while to maintain that we probably were the *Arequipa* after all – anyway we looked kinda foreign. But at last he stumped away to stand the ship down from action stations, growling something about being a fighting sailor and having no time for all this diplomatic jawboning stuff. Lieutenant Kowalsky was left to parley with us.

Once Commander Dahlgren had left, Zaleski suddenly became quite charming and amenable about the whole affair, as if being fired upon without warning and having half our foremast brought down was really no trouble to us at all.

'Mistaken identity, my dear Lieutenant, mistaken identity. A perfectly understandable confusion. It could have happened to anyone. But please tell me, why did you fire upon us?'

'We've been out from San Diego for the past month looking for the *Arequipa*. They had another revolution in Peru and her crew mutinied back in January. The guys aboard her hadn't been paid for a year, so they took off as pirates, stopping every ship they met and robbing them. They stopped a whole lot of Yankee ships, so Washington sent us and the *Memphis* down here to find her. You sure enough look like her picture in the recognition book, but we're sorry for shooting at you all the same.'

'Think nothing of it. But Kowalsky, that is a Polish name I think? Or perhaps Czech?'

The lieutenant smiled broadly. 'Why, how did you guess that? My pa came from Poland, from a place called Sos-no-wee-etz or something like that.'

'I suspect this to be so because I also am a Pole.' Kowalsky looked puzzled.

'But I thought you were an Austrian . . .?'

'Sometimes I am, sometimes not. But, my dear Lieutenant, we Poles must talk seriously: while I myself completely understand and sympathise with you and your Captain about the regrettable error of identity that has just taken place, I fear that my government may not take such a benign view of the matter. In fact I would go so far as to say that this has all the makings of a most serious diplomatic incident. My ship has been much damaged and men have been injured. We can hardly brush the dust off our clothes and go on our way as if we were two cyclists who have just collided on a street corner.'

A cloud had fallen across Kowalsky's rosy, blond features. He was evidently a more intellectually acute man than his Captain and was no doubt seeing in his mind's eye a succession of far from agreeable images: official reprimands, blocked promotions, perhaps even court martials. He called Commander Dahlgren over. Dahlgren fumed and spluttered, but in the end Zaleski managed to convey to him as well that just because the Austro-Hungarian naval ensign happened to bear a passing resemblance to that of Peru – if one was mentally retarded, that is – this did not mean that the Dual Monarchy could be treated in as offhand a fashion as a bankrupt and anarchic Latin American republic. By the time Zaleski had finished even that peppery and obtuse man had become noticeably less self-confident than at the outset of the interview, as it dawned upon him that ship's captains who involve their governments in exchanges of diplomatic notes are rarely viewed with much favour at the next promotion round. When he judged that this realisation had finally sunk in, Zaleski broke suddenly into a radiant smile; quite different from his normal rather sombre expression and, for someone like me who knew him well, deeply disquieting.

'But there: we must not worry about this.'

'How so?'

'Captain, we are both sailors, not diplomats. And as sailors we know that life aboard ship demands a good deal of – how do you say? – giving and taking. I am quite sure that with a little good sense on both sides, this regrettable matter can be quietly forgotten. Now, permit me to explain . . .'

The outcome of Linienschiffsleutnant Zaleski's explanation was that, an hour later, the two vessels were lying alongside one another. A damage party of a hundred or so sailors from the *Tappahannock* was helping our men to clear away the wreckage of the fore topmast while the remainder of the gunboat's crew – the Captain and First Officer among them – were in coaling fatigues, working like maniacs to transfer three hundred tonnes of coal from their bunkers into ours. Zaleski watched them from the poop, so as to avoid getting coal-dust on his whites. His features bore that look of quiet satisfaction that one sees on the face of a cat which has just succeeded in making off with a large sausage from the meat safe – and then getting the blame laid on the dog. It must be said though that the Americans were very smart about their work: even swabbed the decks down for us afterwards. And just before they left, in order to demonstrate that we Austrians were men of honour, we invited the blackened, sweat-soaked Commander Dahlgren down to the chartroom to see an entry made in the log: '6 March, 10.23 a.m., 21° 13′ N. by 76° 04′ W., fell in with US gunboat *Tappahannock*. Exchanged newspapers and checked chronometer. Were asked for news of Peruvian frigate *Arequipa* but unable to be of assistance.'

We all felt afterwards that we had done the Americans a considerable kindness by merely relieving them of their entire stock of bunker coal in exchange for not mentioning certain matters in our log. After all, the *Tappahannock* had masts and sails, albeit of a rudimentary kind, and would doubtless make port – eventually. When we lost sight of them towards sundown Linienschiffsleutnant Zaleski and I were at the head of the mainmast with a telescope. The last we saw of them they had the boats out and were towing their ship across the calm evening sea. As for us though, we were proceeding under steam once more, bowling along towards Callao at a brisk twelve knots.

But this was only a temporary respite from our troubles, for once we had docked at Callao on 8 March we soon discovered that our visit to that port was going to be anything but a pleasant run ashore. When we first dropped anchor in Callao Roads it looked as if our stay was going to be an agreeable if rather prolonged spell in an exotic foreign port with plenty for us to see and do. As soon as we were moored the Captain and the GDO went ashore to contact the local shipyards and get estimates for the repairs to the foremast and the necessary work on the ship's hull below the waterline. Neither task looked like being much concern of ours: the repairs to the buckled, shot-damaged mast would mean docking the ship and lifting the mast out with a heavy crane, while attending to the leaks in the hull would require at least a week in drydock. Both jobs were work for professional shipwrights, so there seemed to be no reason why the crew should not spend most of the three weeks or so on shore-leave, sampling such delights of the Peruvian coast as fandango halls, pisco and aquardiente at twenty cents the bottle and unlimited opportunities for brawling and debauchery among a waterfront milieu drawn from every seafaring nation on earth.

The main concern of the officers was in fact that we should have any crew left when the time came for us to sail. Crimping was a major industry in those West Coast ports in the last days of sail. Boarding-house landlords ashore would seduce entire crews to desert with promises of free lodging and cheap liquor, then wait until their victims were paralysed with drink and sell them as a job lot to the skipper of some outward-bound ship in return for a handsome commission. There were certain restrictions in theory on crimping naval men – the local magistrates were supposed to help the naval police capture deserters. But looking at the local magistrates in Callao we decided that little help was to be expected from that quarter. It was not only competition from merchantmen that we had to fear; there were also the local navies. Both the Chilean and the Peruvian fleets in those days had many foreign sailors – chiefly English and Scandinavians but also a good few Germans and Dalmatians. Pay was good – at least, when it arrived – and there would no doubt be many in the waterfront dives who would try to talk our men into changing their cap-ribbons.

For us cadets however there could be no thought of desertion: we were not ill-paid and feckless conscripts but embryo officers of the Noble House of Austria. So the usual round of official receptions and culturally improving visits was laid on for us. Callao was after all the seaport for Lima, and Lima was the capital of Peru: in fact the first national capital we had visited on this voyage. We travelled up to Lima and tramped dutifully around the monuments. We saw the sights, such as the conquistador Pizarro's bowels preserved in a glass jar in the cathedral. We attended receptions given by the local Austrian and German communities, and we went by train up into the Andes to be entertained for a few days on the estancia of one Herr Schnabel, an Austrian Jew who had done well as a quinine planter and who dressed his Indian servants in the green-and-grey Steierischer tracht, complete with lederhosen and braces embroidered with edelweiss. There was a minor earthquake, and also a revolution which we somehow failed to notice until it was over and we read about it in the newspapers.

We arrived back at the ship after an absence of five days to find the whole vessel in the condition of a recently overturned ant-heap. The ship repairers had given the Captain their quotations, the quotations had been cabled to Vienna for approval – and the Ministry of Finances had refused to sanction them on the grounds that the 1903 naval budget had been greatly reduced, and that the Hungarians were now blocking supplementary estimates in the hope of extorting concessions from Vienna over the new internal customs tariff. Festetics cabled Vienna once more: the *Windischgrätz* was lying at Callao in a damaged state, certainly unfit to put to sea and sail half-way around the world unless major repairs were carried out first. Was he to abandon the vessel and repatriate us all by steamer, or would the Ärar kindly forward us some money? What were we to do? The reply, when it came, was the most depressing that one could receive from a government department in Old Austria: 'Matter receiving our most earnest consideration.' Well, that was that: we had all heard about the civil servant whose request for a week's leave while his wife was having a baby had received such earnest consideration that it had finally been granted when the child was forty-two years old. In the end there was only one thing for it if we wanted to see Pola again before we reached pensionable age: we would have to do the repairs ourselves.

The extracting, repair and restepping of the foremast was one thing: in theory at least we could perform that task with our own resources. The drydocking though was much more of a problem. How could we hire a drydock if Vienna would not pay for it? The only money aboard was the gold coin in the paymaster's safe, and we could not part with that unless the men were to remain unpaid for the rest of the voyage, which was utterly illegal. In the end it was Linienschiffsleutnant Zaleski who resolved the problem for us, after consultation with Herr Schnabel at his estancia. Half the crew would remain at Callao to work on the mast under the supervision of Linienschiffsleutnants Mikulić and Svoboda. Meanwhile the other half of the crew would accompany Zaleski himself on a two-week cruise up the Peruvian coast in an old and very shabby brigantine, the *Huasco*, hired for us by Herr Schnabel. Zaleski assured our doubtful Captain that when he returned the ship would be able to go into drydock; just wait and see.

I was with the half of the crew who stayed behind to work on the foremast, which was badly buckled about two metres above the upper deck from being taken aback when we had nearly hit the iceberg, and further damaged just below the cross-trees by the shell from the American gunboat. The lower mast was a giant, slightly tapering tube of iron some thirty-five metres long by a metre and a half in diameter at its widest and weighing around twenty tonnes. Removing it for repair and then replacing it without the aid of a large dockyard crane was going to be a daunting task. And while I have to say that none of us had much time for Linienschiffsleutnant Mikulić as a human being, we all had to acknowledge his abilities as an engineer for the way in which he set about this problem over the next ten days.

Our one resource aboard the *Windischgrätz* was abundant muscle power: a hundred and twenty men all told to be set to work. First we struck what was left of the fore topmast, then sent down the spars and removed the standing rigging until the lower mast was left standing on its own as a bare pole. Then we cleared everything from the ship's hold in the way of the mast step so that the Carpenter and his assistants could go down with sledgehammers and crowbars to extract the massive bolts which held the heel of the mast to the keel. While they were doing that – about two days' work just by itself – the rest of us were put to work setting up the lower fore- and main-yards – each around thirty metres long – into a sheerleg crane, stepping the ends on either side of the deck to make a towering two-legged derrick over the damaged mast. Then a stupendous arrangement of the heaviest blocks and tackles aboard was bent to a strop of anchor-chain wrapped around the mast just above what Mikulić had calculated to be its point of balance.

After five days of incessant labour, working from well before dawn to late at night, all was ready: the mast was free and waiting to be lifted out of its socket, ten metres deep and extending down through four decks into the hold. At first light on 17 March we were mustered and put behind the capstan bars. At the order we began to walk around, heaving at the bars to click the pawls over the capstan ratchet. Blocks creaked and chains clanked as the hawsers took the strain. Slowly, ever so slowly, the chain strop around the mast began to tauten. The spars of the sheerleg started to bend slightly under the strain. Had Mikulić calculated the loads correctly? By the looks of it we would soon find out. We walked around, heaving harder at the bars now, stepping at each turn over the ominously humming steel hawser, stretched taut as a giant guitar string just above the deck. Suppose that it parted under such a strain? Torpedomeister Kaindel said that he had once seen a wire hawser part – and whip back to flick off a bystander's head so deftly that no executioner's sword could have made a neater job of it. We tried not to think about it, and kept pushing at the capstan bars; resting and pushing, resting and pushing. There was a sudden grinding rumble from forward, and the deck shuddered beneath our feet. The mast was free.

Hour after hour we tramped around the capstan, raising the mast perhaps a couple of centimetres at each circuit. By now a crowd had gathered on the quayside to watch. Three metres, four metres: suppose the tackles parted or the sheerlegs collapsed under the strain? The mast would certainly drop clean through the ship's bottom and sink us at the dockside. If nothing else, that should give the onlookers something to remember. But the gear held, and about 3.00 in the afternoon there came a shout from Bo'sun Njegosić up forward:

'Mast heel clear of the deck, Herr Leutnant!'

Now came the delicate part of the operation. Tackles had already been rigged from the masthead down to the fo'c'sle and back to a windlass. Now a tackle was attached to the heel of the mast as well and led up to the main top. The idea was to swing the mast until it was horizontal and lower it gradually on to the baulks of timber waiting along the deck. It might all go badly wrong: the tackles might break under the strain or the mast might swing out of control. But Linienschiffsleutnant Mikulić had planned the operation well: the mast was swung forward without mishap, the lowering proceeded under control, and by nightfall the great iron tube was lying safely along the deck, waiting for the blacksmiths to punch out the rivets and rebuild the damaged sections. Once they had done that, all – all! – that we had to do was to sway the thing aloft once more and lower it back down through the decks to restep it, then rerig the entire foremast.

This took us another eight days, working late into the nights by the light of hurricane lamps while a makeshift forge glowed on the deck below. Meanwhile there was no news whatever of Linienschiffsleutnant Zaleski and his hundred or so companions aboard the *Huasco*. What had become of them? What were they doing? The mystery was not resolved until the last week of March, just as we were swaying aloft a new topgallant mast, when the *Huasco* suddenly reappeared in Callao Roads, laden deep in the water. She docked alongside us and the men came aboard: weary, filthy with greyish-yellow dust and inexpressibly fed up.

'What were you doing?'

'Scraping birdshit, that's what: six hundred tonnes of the bastard stuff. I hope I never see another pelican as long as I live!'

It appeared that Herr Schnabel had used his extensive business contacts to lease a guano island and about two hundred miles up the coast, and that our men had been used as hired labour to dig the filthy stuff and load it aboard the *Huasco* so that it could be sold in Callao. The money thereby obtained – once Herr Schnabel's commission and the cost of hiring the ship had been deducted – would be used to pay for the ship's drydocking. There was talk of sending Zaleski back to Europe under arrest to face court martial: using enlisted men for private profit had been forbidden in the Habsburg armed forces at least since the late eighteenth century. But success is a powerful argument for the defence. The world price of guano was high at that time, so when it was sold it fetched a price which not only paid the drydock charges but also left a reasonable sum over to be used for buying much-needed provisions. So the matter was overlooked for the time being – except by the men, who got nothing out of it but their bare wages and their skin burnt to blisters by the ammonia in the bird droppings – so concentrated (we were told) that it turned people's hair ginger and stripped the paint off exposed woodwork.

The work in drydock took five days in all. We completed our labours and prepared to sail on 4 April, tired out but justifiably pleased with ourselves for having effected major dockyard repairs without a dockyard. The last telegram received from Vienna before we sailed read REPAIR MONEYS NOW AUTHORISED STOP PROCEED AS PER QUOTATION STOP.

14

STILLE OZEAN

If some compensation were due to us for the past four months – for our various batterings off Tierra del Fuego, then our miserable tedious crawl up the Chilean coast, then our exertions at Callao and on the guano island – we could scarcely have asked for anything better than our twenty-six-day crossing of the eastern Pacific, from the coast of Peru to our first landfall in the Marquesas Islands: four thousand nautical miles at a steady seven knots with an unvarying south-easterly breeze on our port quarter. There was scarcely even the need to handle sail, with that wind blowing us along as evenly and as benevolently as an electric fan. Instead we sailed on day after day, with our noonday positions marked on the chart along the 10th parallel of latitude as regularly as if we had spaced them out with dividers. This was the Pacific Ocean just south of the Equator, the great enchanted sea which we had all read about as children, with its atolls of palm-fringed coral, its perpetual summer and its nubile brown girls in grass skirts and garlands of flowers ready to offer coconuts and all manner of solace to weary seafarers. Yet all that we saw of it on this passage was the same unchanging ultramarine sea, the same sun rising in the east and passing almost overhead to dip below the western horizon, the same black-velvet nights and the same train of three or four Pacific albatrosses – smaller than the Cape Horn version – languidly soaring and swooping astern of us for days at a time without ever seeming to pause for food or sleep. It was rather as I imagine it must be to travel through space.

There was however no lack of work aboard the ship in those

weeks: all the never-ending care and maintenance necessary aboard a wooden sailing vessel. We took advantage of the peaceful seas and settled weather to spend much of each day hanging over the side in bo'sun's chairs busy with pots and brushes upon the ship's paintwork, which we had not had time to attend to while we were lying at Calleo. We had been in the tropics now for nearly three months, after as many months in the cold and wet of the Southern Ocean, and the hull planking had shrunk considerably, with the result that the ship was now spitting oakum on a grand scale as the caulking fell out.

There was also the ship's bottom to attend to, foul with weed and marine growth after nearly ten months at sea. The drydocking at Callao had allowed time for the copper sheathing to be removed only over the larger and more persistent leaks. Elsewhere the bottom had been untouched, and the accumulation of weed and barnacles was slowing us down quite markedly. As usual, it was Linienschiffsleutnant Zaleski who came up with an ingenious if non-regulation answer.

'Very well,' he explained to us, 'I've had these mats made up...' We looked doubtfully at the mats: great coarse wads, about two metres long by a metre across and made of old hawser interwoven with lengths of half-unravelled wire cable so that strands stuck out everywhere. '... What we'll do, then, is bend lines on to each end of them, then run them beneath the ship. Two parties of cadets will then stand at opposite sides of the deck. One party will haul up the mat while the other keeps the line just taut enough to hold the thing against the hull. The second party will then haul the mat back beneath the keel to its side of the ship. In this way we will scrub the ship's bottom clean of marine growth. Is that clear?'

It was clear, and we set to work. The results after the first half-hour were certainly encouraging, to judge by the quantities of weed that floated to the surface. Zaleski joked with us about patenting his invention when we got back to Pola and leaving the Navy to go into business. But then there was a shout from the forward companionway. It was the Bo'sun.

'Herr Leutnant – the Carpenter says to come below at once, if you please. The ship's making water!'

After that no more was heard of the scouring mats. If weed and barnacles were now all that was holding S.M.S. *Windischgrätz* together, two thousand miles from the nearest land, then we all felt that it would be prudent to leave well enough alone.

Since there was not a great deal to be done in the way of sailing the ship, we cadets could at least fill in the time by catching up on our theoretical studies and general education, which had taken second place to practical seamanship while we were in South American waters. We were now into such navigational arcana as lunar observations, which were still being used in 1903 – albeit rarely – to determine longitude and correct dubious chronometer times. We must have been the last year of Marine Academy cadets to study such matters. Lunar sights could only be worked up by long and complex calculations, and even then the results were uncertain, since the moon moves fast and is very near to the earth, which means that tiny errors in observation can lead to very large ones in fixing the ship's position. Most naval officers had long since given up lunar observation in favour of the chronometer, which was anyway now much more reliable than it had been a century earlier. But there were still a few diehard moon worshippers about in the early years of the century. Linienschiffsleutnant Svoboda was once such. Although regarded as a rather easygoing officer, he was unquestionably a superb mathematician and became a professor of mathematics at Prague University in the 1920s. He held that a properly trained navigator had no need whatever of a chronometer, only a set of lunar tables and an ordinary pocket watch to give the time to the nearest hour. With these means he invariably fixed the ship's position as accurately as we could with sextant and chronometer. But there were still few of us who wished to follow him. Three foolscap pages of closely written calculations is one thing on a balmy day in the central Pacific, with perfect visibility and the nearest land hundreds of miles away. It might look very different, we felt, in a gale after a month at sea, with a lee shore somewhere in the offing, the heavens obscured by cloud and the chart-table bucking and rearing like a panic-stricken horse.

It was now that our scientists came into their own aboard the *Windischgrätz*. Up until now they had taken no great part in the life of the ship, confined to their cabins and laboratories for most of the day or busy pottering about on deck or ashore with collecting jars and wind-measuring apparatus. While we were lying at Callao we had at least been spared the company of Professor Skowronek. He had gone off for three weeks up into the Andes and had returned to the ship just before we sailed, laden down with skulls and artefacts ransacked from Inca tombs. He had even brought back two complete mummies, shrivelled and crouched like two ancient, eyeless babies. But now we were at sea he was back on form, striding about the decks in his loden plus-fours and interfering in everybody's work. In the end he became such a nuisance that the Captain invited him to give a series of daily lectures to the cadets; more out of a desire to keep him occupied each afternoon than in the hope that he would impart anything likely to be of much use to us in our chosen profession. The course would be entitled 'Racial Hygiene'.

We soon found that the afternoon lectures on the poop deck comprised a good deal more than an exposition of the Professor's system of cranial measurement – though naturally we went into that in some depth, accompanied by a series of blackboard calculations so recondite that even Linienschiffsleutnant Svoboda declared himself baffled by them. It seemed that as a result of his skull-collecting activities the Professor was now a great deal nearer than he had been when we left Pola to producing a set of tables which would allow the whole of mankind to be measured and graded according to race, using a set of complicated formulae based upon index of width to length, parietal frontal and occipital breadth, cubic capacity, foramino-basal depths, lobal formation, facial angle and a host of other such factors.

'What I am endeavouring to do,' he informed us, 'is to isolate those cranial features that make a Swede a Swede and a Kalahari Bushman a Kalahari Bushman. By careful study and measurement of skulls originating from various races and historical epochs I am gradually identifying those constant factors that lead some racial types to produce great civilisations while others remain permanently mired in the crassest barbarism: what it is, for example, in the formation of the typical Chinese skull that has allowed that race to build one of the world's most inventive and ingenious cultures – then allow it to sink back into the hopeless morass of sloth and complacent ignorance in which we see it today. Why is it that the Japanese race has suddenly emerged from centuries of slumber to create within a few decades a nation justly described as the Prussia of the Orient? Why did the Spanish race degenerate so utterly once it gave itself over to miscegnation with the Indian peoples of South America? Why is the Jew everywhere and in all epochs an anti-cultural element: a parasitic growth upon other civilisations, incapable of creating anything of his own? Why is the Dane sober, brave and loyal, the Italian excitable and treacherous, and the Negro stupid, slow and credulous? What became of the Ancient Greeks? All these, I say, are questions that will be of the utmost relevance in this new century, and ones that science will surely answer now that the work of the immortal Darwin has finally rid us of the pernicious Judaeo-Christian doctrine that all men are equal. My own modest researches, far from demonstrating that all men are equal, have led me to doubt whether all men are in fact even men, and whether a revision of the crude category "homo sapiens" may not be long overdue. Let me give you an example of what I mean. Cadet Gauss: step forward if you please – and try not to walk flat-footed even if you can't help it.' The Professor grinned, and a half-hearted, rather embarrassed titter went up from the audience: Max Gauss might be Jewish but he was not flat-footed. He got up and made his way forward, his face like thunder.

'Remove your cap, boy.' Gauss took off his cap. 'Now, pray stand still a moment: this won't hurt.' The Professor produced his combined boxwood scale and calipers, now elaborated by an arm projecting forward so that facial angle could be read. Gauss stood there like Regulus in the hands of the Carthaginians as the scale was clamped across his head and the Professor adjusted screws and slides, scribbling figures down on a notepad as he did so. When he had finished he removed the device and sent Gauss back to his place while he busied himself with a slide-rule and a pencil.

'Index seventy-eight; facial angle eighty degrees – hmm, rather on the high side so let's correct that downwards by making allowance for spheno-ethmoidal angle; cranial capacity estimated at 970 cc, corrected to take account of age and body weight; basi-occipital depth thirteen centimetres – yes, we'd better correct that by a factor for petrous-temporal depth I think ... There, an over-all racial index of 1.89, absolutely median for a Jew: powerfully developed calculating abilities as shown by the formation of the occipital area of the brain – a sort of cash register on legs – but stunted moral development as shown by the abnormally small frontal lobes, and atrophy of the spheno-temporal area leading to a near-total absence of the manly virtues such as courage, fidelity and endurance. Now ...' His eyes scanned the rows of cadets seated cross-legged on the deck. At last he lit upon a suitable candidate. He pointed. 'Come forward if you please.'

The cadet stepped forward, a Greek god of a boy: blond, blue-eyed and with the sort of arrogantly handsome features which, a generation later, might have been seen on posters in occupied Europe, glowering out from under the brim of a steel helmet and inviting suitably qualified persons to volunteer for the Waffen SS. The gauge caliper was produced and clamped on to his head, the same measurements were taken and noted down, and the calculations were made as he stood there watching with interest.

'Splendid; perfect Nordic stock: well-developed reasoning and creative powers combined with strongly formed faculties of courage and loyalty and accompanied by modest development of the basal area, indicating restraint in the bodily appetites and a correspondingly high degree of moral sensibility. What's your name, boy?'

'Fischbein, Herr Professor.'

A roar of laughter went up from the audience. For once the Professor had been caught off balance. Perhaps a joke was being played upon him . . . 'Is that your real name, boy, because I warn you . . .'

'I most obediently report that yes, Herr Professor: Moritz Fischbein, third-year cadet.'

'I see. Where do you come from?'

'From Czernowitz, Herr Professor.'

Skowronek licked his lips. 'What are your parents' names, if I might ask?'

'Lucjan Fischbein and Rachel Abramowicz, Herr Professor: my father is kantor in the synagogue.'

'I didn't ask you what he is, I asked what his name was. Are you their biological child – I mean, not adopted or anything like that?'

'With respect, yes, Herr Professor.'

'Were any of your family converts perhaps?'

'One of my aunts became a Catholic, Herr Professor.'

'That's not what I meant,' he snapped. 'Are you a Jew, then?'

'Why of course, Herr Professor.'

'Are you quite sure of that?'

'With respect, quite sure, Herr Professor. If you would care to look . . .' He started to unbutton his trousers.

'No, no – that's quite enough. Thank you. You may return to your place now, Fischbein. Of course, my system is still at an early stage of development, and there are anomalies in all schemes of classification. Nothing is ever one hundred per cent perfect. Racial throwbacks occur from time to time . . . Very well, the class may dismiss. That will be all for today.'

Other shipboard relations were not as cordial as those between the cadets and the scientists. Linienschiffsleutnant Mikulić's skilful management of the foremast repairs at Callao had earned him the grudging respect of all those involved and had done something to restore his professional standing after the incident with Matrose Houska and the rope scourge. But this meant that he was able to strut about the ship once more making everyone's life a misery, now that he had worked off the threat of an official enquiry. In the GDO's opinion, 'flying-fish sailing' of the kind we were now engaged in was very destructive of discipline aboard a warship since it allowed the men to get slack from having too little to do. Thus the entire watch on deck – and the watch below too during the hours of daylight – were to be kept busy at all times with some task or other, whether necessary or not. And the more exhausting and pointless the task was, it seemed, the better Mikulić liked it: men standing around the deck picking oakum for four hours at a stretch under the full glare of the tropical sun, spaced too far apart for them to break the monotony by talking; shot-drill, in which the men had to stand in a circle and pass cannon balls from one man to the next, round and round for hours on end; sandpapering the anchors with powdered glass and old canvas; simply standing men on the fo'c'sle to 'keep watch for whales'. A silent but none the less powerful mood of rebellion was growing against the GDO. Sometimes Mikulić would relieve his own boredom by trying to provoke this resentment into open revolt, by manhandling a sailor until he resisted, beating the daylights out of him and then challenging him to lodge a complaint with the Captain – which he dare not do for fear of being court-martialled for assaulting an officer. But for the time being the resentment bubbled beneath the surface. Whatever his undoubted skills as a seaman, Mikulić was a remarkably poor judge of human nature and probably believed that he had indeed cowed the lower deck into submission. Time would show that he was dreadfully mistaken on that point.

Tempers aboard were wearing thin anyway. In those days long sea voyages under sail tended to produce after a couple of months a mild state of melancholic insanity which I believe the French in the Sahara used to call 'le cafard'. The cramped quarters, the daily routine of watch-on, watch-off and the same faces – we had long since heard all one another's yarns many times over – all worked together to make people moody and irritable. But above all now, on this interminable Pacific crossing, it was the unchanging disc of sea beneath the relentless sun; and the night varied only by the phases of the moon; the feeling that the ocean had been exactly like this for the past five hundred million years, would be exactly like it for another five hundred million, and that we microbes drifting across it on our speck of dust counted for less than nothing. As day followed identical day we began to suffer from strange fancies: that time had stopped; that our efforts to chop it into manageable segments by means of chronometer, hourglass and ship's bell were nothing but feeble attempts to hold back the infinite, all enveloping vastness of eternity like striking a match at the bottom of a coal mine; that we were not in fact moving at all, despite the appearance of doing so; that in the middle of this blue immensity our ship had become the geometrically defined point which has a position but no substance. Gunroom conversations over supper were taking on a disquietingly philosophical tinge: earnest debates over questions like: Is time an illusion? or Can one know nothing?

This growing mood of oddness was certainly affecting the Captain to a greater degree than any of the other officers. It was true that he had not asked for the job. Korvettenkapitän Count Festetics had had greatness unexpectedly thrust upon him at Pernambuco and might reasonably have expected to be Captain only for as long as it took the War Ministry to send out a replacement. But that had not happened, and this amiable, well-intentioned, considerate, impeccably korrekt officer had quite patently failed to grow into the job over the intervening months. Perhaps this would have been expecting a great deal of him; for, if one stereotype of life aboard sailing ships is true, it is that their captains did tend to be rough, tough, loud-voiced, hard-bitten men endowed with bullet-proof self-confidence and unshakable faith in their own judgement. Or perhaps it was rather that captains like that were the ones that tended to survive, for of all the modes of conveyance ever devised by man the fully-rigged deep-water sailing ship must have been about the most dangerous. I read somewhere years later that even in the decade before 1914, when charting and coastal marks had improved beyond recognition from what they had been fifty years before, a merchant sailing ship registered at Lloyd's was on average rather more likely to end her days at the bottom of the sea than in the breaker's yard.

Commanding such vessels was a trade that demanded instant

judgement, unhesitating action and iron nerves; also the ability (if need be) to force reluctant, exhausted or frightened crews into obeying orders. True, things were slightly less raw aboard naval vessels, with their large crews and all the sanctions of naval discipline to back up a captain's orders. Likewise, even aboard merchant ships, there were some very effective captains who were mild-mannered, quiet and physically unimposing. It was just that in general, someone like Slawetz von Löwenhausen, endowed with the voice of a bull and the appearance of a Bayreuth Heldentenor, was at an advantage before he even set his foot on the deck planks. Everyone agreed that Korvettenkapitän Count von Festetics was a fair-minded, scrupulously decent man. It was just that he was indecisive, rather timid and unable to impose his will upon his subordinates. We all despised Linienschiffsleutnant Mikulić as a human being. But we all respected his professional judgement and, given the choice between sailing under him and under Festetics, most of us would have gritted our teeth and chosen Mikulić. After all, what is the use of being a nice man if you end up putting your ship on to a lee shore in a gale?

Festetics was certainly well aware of the popular verdict on him after our ignominious failure to round Cape Horn. Likewise his professional stock-market quotation had not been much improved by the incident with the U.S.S. *Tappahannock*, where it was only Zaleski's quick-wittedness that had saved us from being blown to matchwood. Ever since Callao he had retired to his staterooms for most of the time and left the running of the ship to his officers: never a happy policy, and all the more so when Mikulić was known to detest Zaleski – 'that slippery polak' as he called him – and to despise Linienschiffsleutnant Svoboda as a weakling. We saw the Captain at Sunday divisions, but very little during the rest of the week. Even invitations to supper in the saloon were now infrequent. The galley telegraph reported that 'der Alte' was now a helpless alcoholic, lashed to his bunk for most of the time and gagged to stop him from biting his tongue out in terror at the armies of blue hedgehogs swarming in through the cabin windows and crawling over the deckheads. But reports that the Captain has the DTs have been a stock-in-trade of the galley newsvendors ever since men first put to sea, so these yarns were generally discounted by public opinion on the lower deck.

It was not until the third week of April that we realised at last that something was seriously amiss. It was the usual warm midafternoon on the poop deck, beneath the downdraught of sails that were drawing as steadily as they had been drawing for the past three weeks. The ship was rustling through the waves at her usual seven knots, with only the stern-wave to tell us that we were moving at all across this flat, unvarying disc of deep cobalt blue. The cadets not on watch had been convened at four bells for the afternoon navigation class, dealing this time with certain theoretical aspects of Greenwich hour angle: correction for slight variations in day length during the earth's annual orbit about the sun, the sidereal year and other such items which, although of little practical significance in getting a ship from A to B, may be of use in front of examination boards in navigating a young officer from the rank of Seefähnrich to that of Fregattenleutnant. Zaleski was otherwise engaged for the afternoon, so the class was being taken by the Captain. We got out our notebooks and pencils. The globe, chronometer and sextant were laid out on a blanket-covered table, the blackboard was set up, and we began.

It was only when we got on to the question of observing a fixed object from a moving position that we began to realise that something was amiss.

'Of course, since light takes seven minutes to travel from the sun to the earth, what we are observing when we take a sextant sight is not the sun's position in the heavens, but its apparent position: the place where it was seven minutes ago. Also we must bear in mind that we are observing it from a platform which is itself moving, which introduces a slight distortion into our calculation. Of course, aboard this ship moving westward at seven knots the error is so infinitesimally small that we may safely disregard it. But suppose for the sake of argument that we were travelling around the world at 10 degrees south latitude in one of Count Zeppelin's airships. If we were able to travel at one thousand nautical miles per hour – an absurd proposition, but let us take it as given for the purposes of this exercise – then we would be able to keep up with the sun, so to speak, as the earth rotates, with the result that even though a chronometer aboard our airship would keep ticking and record the progression of the hours, we would carry local noon around the world with us. In fact, if we were able to fly faster than one thousand knots we would be leaving the sun behind and apparently making time run backwards, or speed up its progress if we flew eastwards against the sun. In fact . . .' Festetics spun the globe so that the seas and continents merged into a greyish-green blur, '. . . in fact, if I could make my airship travel faster than the speed of light I would be able to orbit the earth so as to arrive before I set out, and if I did this a sufficient number of times I would be able to make the chronometer run backwards in reality and travel back into my own youth when I too was a spotty-faced cadet like you and took up this rotten profession and condemned myself to a life of drifting across the oceans in a wooden crate full of smelly Croats and a lot of deluded young idiots like yourselves who think that they've signed up for a life of adventure like I did but who'll soon find themselves stuck behind a desk filling in forms all day and serve the stupid bastards RIGHT!' He snapped the blackboard pointer across his knee and flung the pieces over the side, then sat down on the deck planks weeping uncontrollably.

There was an uneasy silence for a while, broken only by the Captain's muffled sobs and the embarrassed shuffling of forty-odd pairs of adolescent feet. Ought someone to comfort the poor man? But he was the Captain after all, next only to God . . . In the end it was Max Gauss who slipped below to call Dr Luchieni and the Chaplain, saying that the Captain appeared to be suffering from sunstroke. They led Festetics below to his cabin, and that was the last we saw of him for quite some time, apart from occasional glimpses of him seated in a deckchair on the poop deck with a blanket over his knees, staring at the horizon and muttering to himself while two burly seamen kept a discreet watch on him from the mizzen shrouds in case he tried to jump overboard. An announcement was made at divisions next morning that the Captain was unwell and that Linienschiffsleutnant Mikulić would assume his functions until further notice, with Zaleski as acting GDO. Yet another officer down, then: the fourth since we had left Pola. What was wrong with this ship? The lower-deck oracles like the Cook and the Sailmaker began to prophesy that it stood to reason that with a cabin full of dead men's skulls down below the ship was going to be unlucky: in fact as things stood we would be lucky to reach the Indian Ocean before we sank.

We made our landfall on the morning of 1 May. The evening before, the look-outs had reported an unusual cloud formation over the western horizon. Also seaweed had been sighted, and frigate birds, which (Herr Lenart assured us) rarely travelled more than a day's journey from land. All that evening our Kroomen had stood by the fo'c'sle rail, nostrils dilated, sniffing the air and telling everyone nearby to 'Halten yo' maul,' as if noise nearby would disturb the olfactory sense. I had asked Union Jack what he was doing.

'Mass' Ottokar, Ah smell shore. Ah smell all kinda bush, all kinda beef belong shore.'

He was right: next morning the dawn revealed the dark, cloud-capped peaks of mountains over the western horizon. The entire watch on deck crowded to the fo'c'sle to look, staring the ship forward through the water. According to our charts this was the island of Hiva Oa, one of the most northerly of the Marquesas group and now a French colony.

This news caused considerable excitement among the better-read cadets. The ship's library contained a copy of Melville's *Typee*, and most of us whose English was good enough had lain in our hammocks or on some secluded patch of deck, steaming slightly as we read how the delightful Polynesian girl Fayaway had slipped off her flimsy pareo and held it up for a sail when she and the hero Tommo were out canoeing on the lake. This was to be our first South Sea Island. Surely they would allow us shore-leave after a month at sea? If they did, then we hoped that

Fayaway's granddaughters would not hurl themselves upon us all at once but form an orderly queue.

They did allow us shore-leave. But it was not a bit as we had expected. The bay at Atuona, the island's village-capital, looked quite unlike the South Seas as we had always pictured them. There were a few palm trees, but the island behind them was jagged and threatening, with dense, gloomy dark green forests climbing the slopes of the sugar-loaf mountain above the bay. The ocean waves crashed not on coral beaches but on menacing rocks of black basalt. No maidens in grass skirts with hibiscus flowers in their hair came out to welcome us; in fact when we got ashore Atuona reminded us of nowhere quite so much as Port Stanley with sunshine. The few houses were of white-painted clapboard and corrugated iron, not palm thatch. There were two Catholic churches, a Chinese-run general store, a bar (closed) and a gendarmery post with the tricouleur flapping above it in the breeze. As for the inhabitants, they seemed to be largely half-caste Polynesian-Europeans, were mostly middle-aged, were all encased up to the neck in black and all wore on their faces that expression of buttoned-up severity which I would recognise in later years as the characteristic look of provincial France. The picture was completed by a pith-helmeted gendarme on a bicycle and large numbers of grim-looking French missionary priests in white soutanes. We wandered about aimlessly for a while, then ventured inland to explore the wooded side-valleys of the mountain and view the remains of one of the mysterious island temples: a massive overgrown mound of stone blocks now being forced apart by tree roots. A fallen stone idol lay amongst the undergrowth, covered with moss. It was all immensely depressing. The oceanographer Dr Szalai, who knew the Pacific well, told us that when Admiral Dupetit-Thouars annexed the place in 1842 there had been something like forty thousand Marquesan islanders. Fifty years later the population had fallen to less than a tenth of that number. Syphilis, measles, religion, drink and despair had done for the Marquesans what they were now doing for the Indians of Tierra del Fuego. It was as if the ghosts of that snuffed-out world still haunted the place and poisoned the lives of the survivors. We went back on board that evening in a state of considerable depression, not just on behalf of the poor dead Marquesans but for ourselves as well. Adventure? In the year 1903 even the remotest islands of the furthest Pacific had gendarmes patrolling them and little blue-and-white-enamelled notices announcing that *Il est formellement interdit* . . . So much for the bare-breasted girls and the cannibal warriors braining one another with war clubs.

Our departure from Hiva Oa was delayed a few hours next morning because our surgeon Dr Luchieni had been called ashore unexpectedly. The island had no resident doctor and the local curé had sent a message asking him in the name of Christian charity to come and attend to a European who resided above the village, living in sin with a native girl. The man was a notorious drunkard, brawler and mocker of religion, the priest said, and a thorough nuisance to the whole island. But he had been ill for some time and was suffering in particular from a persistent ulcer on his leg. Dr Luchieni had treated the ulcer and left ointment and instructions. Payment had been mentioned: after all, the k.u.k. Kriegsmarine was a navy and not a travelling charity clinic for the entire world. But since the patient had no money in the house Luchieni, who never liked to push matters, had finally been persuaded to accept by way of payment one of the paintings with which the man was trying – evidently with no great success – to earn a living. Luchieni had been doubtful; but since he hated offending anyone he had finally accepted the canvas and brought it back aboard, still slightly sticky and smelling of linseed oil. He hurried it down to his cabin without showing it to anyone; for fear of being made a laughing stock, it seemed, since the boat's crew reported that the painting was absurdly bad – couldn't make head nor tail of it, and since when have trees been blue and grass pink? At supper that evening the surgeon was quizzed about his recent visit, particularly since there was absolutely nothing else to report from our stay at Hiva Oa.

'Yes, he was a very awkward patient indeed; the curé was quite right about that: a half-caste of some sort, but not Polynesian that's for sure. More like an Aztec if you ask me.'

'What was wrong with him, Luchieni?'

'Oh, the usual. Maladie d'amour I'm afraid: tertiary syphilis, partially cured years ago and now breaking out again. I went to treat him for an ulcer on his ankle, but the fellow's in terrible shape every other way as well – which doesn't surprise me one bit after twenty years of absinthe and fornicating with native women.'

'What's the painting like? You must show us. There's not been much else to laugh at of late.'

'Awful; absolutely indescribable. No wonder the fellow's had to come out here if that's how he paints. Even the cannibals would go into fits at the sight of it. I don't know much about art, but if you ask me a donkey with a brush tied to its tail could do better. The only reason I accepted the wretched thing was that the poor devil was broke and ill and I felt sorry for him.'

In the end though Dr Luchieni's painting did have one brief public showing, on the poop deck next afternoon as we sailed towards Samoa. It was used to illustrate the latest in Professor Skowronek's lectures in the series 'Racial Hygiene'. This one looked like being well worth attending. It was entitled simply 'Degeneracy'.

The lecture certainly lived up to its promise: in fact was spoken of in later years by the cadets of the 1899 Jahrgang as being quite the high point of the voyage as far as entertainment was concerned, fit even to stand comparison with the Captain's recent disquisition on time travel.

'Degeneration of races,' the Professor told us, 'may take place from a number of causes, but chief among these are disease, racial admixture and erosion of the masculine principle of authority. All of these evils are present in our own society as we enter the twentieth century; and if left unchecked they will work as surely towards its downfall as they did towards that of ancient Rome. And in our case as in that of the Romans the chief agent of decline, the plague rat carrying the deadly bacilli . . .' he fixed his eye upon Gauss, '. . . is the Jew, the eternal nomad of the world, the parasitic fungus spreading his spores into every corner of civilisation; in the case of the Romans by means of Christianity and racial dilution, in our own epoch by means of socialism and syphilis...'

We all started shoving Gauss and pointing at him. 'Please, Herr Professor, it's him. He's undermining the service by trying to sell us his sister and sign us up for the Social Democrats. Some of us have picked up a dose already and our noses are dropping off...'

'Be silent and spare me your puerilities. This is a serious scientific lecture and you are future officers of a Germanic empire. Be quiet or I'll call the Bo'sun.' We shut up at that and sat still.

'As I was saying, one of the principal causes of degeneracy is racial admixture. In the case of the Danubian Monarchy, I regret to say that we need scarcely dwell for long upon this topic. Suffice it only to say that if continued miscegnation among Teuton, Latin, Slav and Jew ever produces a common Austrian racial type then as a eugenist I shudder to think what it will look like. The only future that I can see for the Habsburg Monarchy, speaking as a racial scientist, is the early fusion of the Germanic parts of the Empire with the German Reich, cession of Hungary and protectorates over the Slav lands, and then a rigorous legal ban on intermarriage within these areas, reinforced by a programme for gradual elimination of dysgenic elements by means of population exchanges and compulsory sterilisation. It will be rather like trying to unscramble an omelette, but if it is not done then I can see no hope for the survival of German civilisation and culture in Central Europe. The Jew is working away beneath it all, and in many of our cities syphilis has already reached epidemic proportions, poisoning future generations by producing enfeebled offspring even among those who survive to propagate. But throughout the world one now sees the same dismal picture of the white race under threat from its inferiors. A hundred years ago the problem was nowhere near as great. Travel was difficult, so populations stayed relatively fixed and the preservation of racial purity largely took care of itself. The flaxen-haired German peasant sitting at the door of his cottage playing with his blue-eyed children was in no danger from the teeming Israelite swarms of the Polish ghettoes. The Negro remained sunk in immemorial savagery in the fever-ridden swamps and jungles of his benighted continent, and the swarming yellow mass of the Chinese river plains stayed exactly where it had been for six millennia. But then came the steamship and the railway, and half a century later we are beginning to see the consequences: the once-German city of Vienna which now contains more Jews than Palestine and more Czechs than Prague; Chinese coolies invading the west coast of America; the black stain seeping up the Mississippi to colour the formerly white cities of New York and Chicago; the Hebrew mass pouring across the Atlantic to infect the United States. The white race, I say, the world's redeemer, is now everywhere under threat from inferior stock. Science created the problem, and science must solve it.' He paused to sip from a glass of water. 'But how has this state of affairs come about, that the Caucasian, once the master of the world, should now find himself challenged by peoples without one ounce of his virility or creative energy? One reason, as I have pointed out, is the physical sapping of the race by syphilis. But the other, just as deleterious in the long run, is the systematic erosion of the male principle of leadership in favour of the feminine. Any unbiased observer will tell you that female skulls are in many respects similar to those of the typical Jew or Negro: the over-development of the instinctive and emotional portions of the brain and the corresponding atrophy of the moral and ratiocinative areas. Woman is the Jew on a world-wide scale: creatively barren; a mass of instinct and sensuality; selfish; blind to any principle higher than self-interest; and incapable of any objective moral appraisal or nobility of sentiment. This is not woman's fault of course, merely the work of aeons of evolution through natural selection. But to deny the fact is to deny science itself, while to ignore it and allow the female principle to become elevated in the counsels of a nation is nothing short of racial suicide: to replace manly courage, loyalty, bravery and obedience – the virtues of the ancient Romans and the Nordic tribes – with their opposites: deviousness, cupidity, deceitfulness, sensuality and artfulness. Future officers of the Austro-German Navy, I say to you now that Sparta must be your model: the woman confined to her proper functions as domestic helpmate and breeder of warriors. Otherwise we are doomed to be engulfed by the triple tides of brown, black and yellow.'

He turned to one of the two veiled easels behind him. 'And now, cadets, I shall give you a graphic illustration of degeneracy, kindly donated to us by Korvettenarzt Luchieni, who found the thing too awful to keep in his cabin even when turned to the wall. It was given to him yesterday by a Frenchman on Hiva Oa as a payment for medical treatment.' He twitched the cloth aside with a flourish.

I see it still in my mind's eye: the canvas glowing in the freshness of its colours; the deep indigo blues and the rich wine-reds; the vibrant green of the tropical foliage and the flaring white of the hibiscus flowers; and the three female figures, two standing and one seated; the tawny earth-colour of their skin and the sad, flat, vacant Polynesian faces staring into nowhere, eternal and unreachable as that toppled idol we had seen in the forest grove. We all gasped and held our breath, some in horror and others in a sort of wonder. It was so utterly unlike any painting we had ever seen in that world before colour magazines, where popular art was limited to vapid mass-produced lithographs of 'Dawn in the Salzkammergutt' or 'The Fiacre Drivers' Ball'.

'There, utterly unspeakable, isn't it? Amazing to think that at the beginning of the twentieth century, four hundred years after Dürer and the Flemish masters, such a loathsome daub should be seriously offered for sale as art outside the walls of a lunatic asylum. Without form, without likeness, without subtlety of expression, without story or moral, without the faintest hint of that grandeur of spirit that art should seek to capture or the nobility of action that it should seek to inspire. But I will tell you young men how this obscenity came to see the light of day. It is not a pretty story, but wonderfully illustrative of my thesis that racial degeneration is accompanied by cultural decay. The "artist" – for want of a better word – seems from Dr Luchieni's report to be himself the product of race-mixing: a Frenchman, but with a strong infusion of non-white blood. It also appears that some twenty years ago this degenerate gave up a stable job in a bank and abandoned his wife and children to come out to the South Seas, here to drink, daub and fornicate away his remaining substance while infecting himself with syphilis from a succession of squalid ménages with native women. The disgusting blot that you see before you now is the end result of this process: a visible testimony to the combined effects of miscegenation, syphilis and surrender to the ensnaring wiles of the female sex. Observe the savage, crude colours resulting from erosion of the optic nerves. Observe the total lack of any attempt at realism in the treatment of the trees and foliage. Observe if you will the three Kanaka damsels themselves, our three dusky Graces...' He laughed. 'Here at least I am prepared to admit that perhaps our artist has rendered nature truthfully and done his sitters justice, if in a ham-fisted fashion. At least, I am ready to believe from what I have seen of them that most Polynesian women are as stupid and as brutally ugly as these charmers of ours. But as for the rest, it is a vile, pitiable thing; a running sore; a smear of pus and excrement. If you wish to understand how utterly foul it is, what an abomination, what a denial of everything that the white race has achieved in pictorial art over the past thousand years, then I can hardly do better than offer you a standard for comparison...'

He tugged at the cloth over the second easel. It slipped aside – and another gasp went up from the assembled audience. We all knew from the sailors who cleaned the Professor's cabin that he was a keen art collector, with special reference to the female nude. But since he kept his cabin locked most of the time this interest had remained a matter for hearsay. Now though we had ocular proof, simpering before us in all her dimpling coyness. It was a sizeable lithograph entitled (if I remember rightly) 'A Roman Bride Disrobing', by the Viennese classical-historical painter Teofil Scheibenreither. Actually the title was rather misleading: it should have been 'Disrobed' not 'Disrobing', while as for the 'Roman' part, I cannot say how many women in ancient Rome had fair hair and blue eyes, or the sort of physical charms which Viennese male society used to describe as 'molliert'. But that was by the by: there were a few marble columns and vases in the background to show that this was a serious historical painting and not a pin-up, and anyway she was certainly a fine figure of a girl; depicted with all the photographic hyper-realism of which painters had become capable by the early 1900s; every goose pimple faithfully depicted, but with the bodily proportions (I suspect) slightly altered to make her splendid hips even more curvaceous and her bosom even fuller than the model's had been. There was even – since this was 1903 and artists were becoming daring – a discrete hint of pubic hair and other such things that would have been tactfully omitted a decade earlier, or covered with conveniently falling wisps of drapery.

The poleaxing effect of this sudden display on forty sex-starved adolescent boys after ten months at sea may perhaps be imagined. There was stunned silence for a while, then faint groaning noises from the back of the audience. The Professor disregarded them.

'Now this, by contrast, may justly be termed great art: a woman of the Caucasian race in all her unabashed glory, fit to be the companion of a white man and the bearer of his children. Observe the high Nordic forehead, the open honesty of the blue eyes, the solid child-bearing hips...' The groans grew more audible. '... the robust yet graceful thighs, the firmness of the breasts...'

Gauss sat next to me moaning softly and panting, 'Stop him someone. For God's sake stop him...' he murmured, 'I can't bear it...'

'... Such a creature, I say, is fit to be the mother of German children, and the man who immortalised her splendour is fit to be called an artist.' He flicked the cloth back over the painting; in many cases just in time too, I should think, to judge by the noises from the back. 'However,' he turned back to Dr Luchieni's recent acquisition, 'what shall we say to this beastly thing? I will tell you, cadets: we shall say nothing further to it. One does not debate with degeneracy; one identifies it, like a louse or a plague rat...' He reached behind the table, and brought out his heavy double-barrelled shotgun. '... and one takes appropriate measures to deal with it.'

He laid the gun on the table, picked up the painting from its easel, then walked over and propped it up in the mizzen shrouds. He returned to the table and picked up the gun, cocking it as he did so. 'One does not reason with degeneracy, I say, one eradicates it; extirpates it; cauterises it like a festering ulcer...' He raised the gun to his shoulder, took aim and fired both barrels.

Professor Skowronek was a capable shot, as he had demonstrated on the unfortunate Strandlopers on the coast of the Kaokoveld some months before. The painting exploded in a shower of brightly coloured shreds of canvas. When the smoke cleared we saw that the frame was still intact, though twisted, but that the entire centre of the picture had vanished. The Professor put down the smoking shotgun and pointed at me.

'You, boy – Prohaska, isn't it? – go and throw that wretched thing overboard will you? Very well, cadets, that concludes my lecture for today.'

As he packed up his things and the class dispersed to its duties I took the remains of the painting down from the shrouds. A corner of the canvas was still intact: a glossy-leaved breadfruit tree and part of one of the women's heads. One sad, slanting eye looked at me reproachfully as I walked towards the poopdeck rail, as if to say, 'How could you do this to me as well, after everything else?' I hesitated for a moment, looking at it – then flung it overboard. It was caught and lifted for a moment by the draught in the ship's wake, then fell into the sea. One of our attendant albatrosses swooped down from his everlasting station astern of us and hovered over it for a few moments to see if it was worth eating. He quickly decided that it was not, and adjusted his great wings to soar up without any apparent effort and resume his position. I went back to my duties and the painting was soon forgotten. Scheibenreither's 'Roman Bride' however remained in our collective mind's eye for quite some time afterwards, often referred to and discussed by the gunroom's resident art critics. We cadets might not have known much about painting, but we certainly knew what we liked.

15

THE ISLES OF THE BLESSED

Our first major port of call in the Pacific was Apia, on the island of Samoa, which we reached on 16 May. We had deviated somewhat from our previous course along the 10th parallel of south latitude, but there was no help for that: Samoa was now a German colony, and since Austria-Hungary was Germany's principal ally it would be unthinkable for an Austrian warship to sail in the central Pacific without stopping by for a few days to pay her courtesies.

After our dispiriting taste of French Polynesia as exemplified by Hiva Oa, we confidently expected the worst from Samoa. The Germans had been there since the 1880s, so by now the islanders would certainly all be in field-grey pareos, marching up and down palm-fringed parade grounds to the bellowing of drill sergeants and the sound of conch-shell bands playing 'Preussens Gloria'. Thus it came as a pleasant surprise to us when we landed at Apia to find that although the colonisers and missionaries had made some changes – like stopping cannibalism and putting the islanders into more decorous clothing – most of the Samoan way of life seemed to have been left intact. I suppose that really there were too few Germans there to do much else. The place had been acquired almost by accident – Kaiser Wilhelm always referred to it as 'that preposterous island' – and since it had no strategic importance whatever no one in Berlin seemed very interested in it. There was a German governor and some colonial police in Apia, a German corvette at anchor in the harbour and a few copra planters inland; but otherwise life went on much as it had always done, except that the local King (with whom we had an audience) had bought himself a splendidly Bismarckian cuirassier's uniform, complete with spiked helmet, to wear at court functions, and now spoke passably good German. Also there was a convent in Apia, containing fifty or so Ursuline nuns from Mecklenburg. They conducted a well-equipped and highly efficient hospital, and also ran a boarding school for the daughters of the local nobility where the girls were taught German, scripture, needlework and all the rest of the 'Kinder-Kirche-Küche-Kranke' syllabus prescribed for girls in Wilhelmine Germany.

We went ashore to pay the usual courtesy visits: tea with the Governor, visits to copra groves and breadfruit plantations and so forth. We were invited to the homes of the local German and native notables, and we went up the hill one hot afternoon to visit Robert Louis Stevenson's house at Vailima. We visited the novelist's grave – he had died only a few years before – and I actually placed my hand on the desk at which (the present owner of the house claimed) *Treasure Island* had been written.

There was not a great deal else to see in Apia during our week-long stay. The Captain had been landed to stay with the Governor, on the grounds that a change of scenery might help him recover his spirits. The scientists were ashore on various missions, and most of the crew were on shore leave, so the ship was very quiet as she rocked gently at anchor in the bay. On the afternoon of the third day Gauss, Tarabochia and I were ordered to man the gig to row Fregattenleutnant Bertalotti ashore to visit the dentist in town. And as we pulled across the sparkling water we saw a most extraordinary spectacle coming the other way. It was the Headmistress of the convent school, Sister Roswitha, coming out to the ship to pay us a visit. She was sitting beneath a parasol in a cane armchair in the middle of an outrigger canoe, and the canoe was being paddled by six of her senior pupils, all dressed in high-necked white muslin gowns, with long white gloves and with veiled hats on top of their thick-coiled black hair, but plying their paddles as though they had been born to it – which of course they had. They all smiled at us most charmingly as they passed by, and Sister Roswitha raised a hand in greeting, beaming at us from behind her steel-framed spectacles and bidding us 'Grüss Gott' in her strangulated North German accent. They paddled on to the ship, and we deposited the lieutenant at the jetty. He told us that he would be about two hours, since it was an extraction and gas would be required, but he instructed us to wait for him further down the shore, in a small bay just beyond the town. The day was calm, but bad weather had been predicted and Apia harbour could get very nasty in a high wind. Back in 1889 an entire British-German-American squadron had been smashed up here by a hurricane, the only survivor being the British sloop *Calliope*, which had managed to claw her way out to sea by a feat of seamanship that was still spoken of with awe in naval circles.

We dropped the boat's anchor into the limpid water and settled down to a long, boring afternoon of watching the fish flit across the coral sand below us. But after a few minutes we heard voices coming to us across the water: young female voices. We looked round. It was the convent girls in their canoe, paddling towards us. Evidently Sister Roswitha, now being shown around the *Windischgrätz*, had not wished to leave her young and very pretty crew moored alongside, exposed to ogling and moral danger from lustful sailors, and had told them to paddle to the shore and wait for a signal to come and pick her up. The girls – about the same age as ourselves I should think – were now anxious to impress us with their German, which was quite good except that they had a rather sing-song intonation and tended to pronounce the consonants F and V as P.

'Guten Tag Jungen, sprechen Sie Deutsch pielleicht?'

'Of course we do. Do you go to school over in town?'

'Why yes: we are all good German Catholic girls now – say the rosary, wear dresses and not eat people any more.' They all nodded their agreement to this. 'But what are you poor boys doing out here all alone? This must be ve-e-ry sad.' The girls all murmured and agreed that it must be very sad for us. 'Why do you not perhaps swim to pass the time?'

'Maybe it is because they cannot swim,' another girl added helpfully.

'Yes, yes, it is because the poor lonely white boys cannot swim: they are afraid of the water. They do not want to get their nice white uniforms wet, or expose their poor pale German skins to the sunshine.' One of the girls splashed us with her paddle. Gauss flicked water back.

'We're not Germans, we're Austrians. And we can swim as well as any of you. I bet you've forgotten how to anyway, wearing those silly long dresses and being cooped up all day in a convent with a lot of dried-up old nuns. I mean, whoever heard of South Sea islanders wearing gloves and hats for paddling canoes?'

'Ooooh you beast! How dare you say such things!' The others all cooed in agreement, rejecting these calumnies. 'I'll show you who can swim and who can't . . .' She took her hat off, pulled off her gloves – then in front of our astonished gaze, started to unbutton her dress. 'Come on! We'll show them, won't we?'

They did. We stared in goggle-eyed disbelief as they slipped out of their hats and gloves and dresses. They were wearing nothing underneath. There was simply a flurry of white, then a glimpse of six lithe, cinnamon-brown shapes with their long black hair tumbling across their shoulders. Then splash, splash-splash: they had dived into the water like so many seals, leaving a rocking canoe full of discarded clothing. We looked around us in astonishment. Where were they? A minute passed by, then two. A ghastly thought suddenly struck us: had we offended their honour in some way with our banter and compelled them to restore it by committing mass-suicide, much as the Japanese were said to kill themselves at the smallest affront? Suddenly a head broke surface behind us, then two, three more. They were laughing and seemed hardly to be out of breath at all after their long spell underwater.

'There, Austrian boys – can you swim like that? I bet you can't.' She turned to the other streaming wet heads. 'I do not think it is clothes that they are wearing: I think that those are really their skins. The Europeans have been wearing them for so long the two have grown together.' They all laughed, and began splashing us again, then flicked over and dived, waggling their bottoms at us in derision as they submerged.

'Is that what you think?' Gauss called after them. 'We'll show you. Come on Prohaska, Tarabochia – the honour of the Imperial and Royal Fleet is at stake!' He was struggling out of his jersey. We did likewise, and a few seconds later we were plunging into the sea after him.

I was a moderately good swimmer for a Czech I suppose, and Gauss and Tarabochia were excellent. But compared with these Samoan girls we were scarcely past the paddling-pool stage. They seemed to be somewhere between human beings and dolphins, such was their speed in the water and their ability to stay submerged. They were well-built girls certainly, but none of them was exactly barrel-chested, so I can only suppose that constant swimming since infancy had altered their physiology to allow them to stay underwater for minutes at a stretch. Time and time again I would take breath and dive, then open my eyes to the stinging saltwater and see ahead of me in the blue a shimmering brown shape, and try to grasp it and fail. Sometimes they would taunt us by allowing us to touch an ankle before they flipped their feet and shot away. But more usually we would break surface, gasping and spluttering for breath, only to see a laughing girl bob up a few metres away from us, apparently quite unaffected by ninety seconds or so of underwater swimming, and stick her tongue out at us and challenge us to catch her.

This must have gone on a good ten minutes or so, by which time I was beginning to feel uncomfortably waterlogged around the sinal passages. I broke surface again, and saw through streaming eyes one of them perched on the bow of their canoe, mocking me. I blew out the water and wiped my eyes clear, laughing.

'There, you little minx, got tired at last didn't . . . Oh God . . .'

It was not their canoe; it was one of our eight-metre rowing cutters. And it was not a Samoan girl in the bows but Linienschiffsleutnant Svoboda, his face purple with rage.

'Prohaska you stupid bastard – what in the ten thousand names of Satan do you think you're up to?'

'I obediently report, Herr Leutnant, that these girls challenged us to a swimming competition . . . They said that we couldn't catch them because Austrians don't know how to swim... The honour of the service...'

'Shut up, you imbecile! Honour of the service? Do you realise that all the time you've been disporting yourself bare-arsed with these hussies out here Sister Roswitha's been watching you through a telescope? She's down in the wardroom now, with the Surgeon waving a bottle of smelling salts under her nose. The GDO's going to have your tripes for this. Get your clothes on quick and get back aboard. You're all under arrest.'

So we got dressed, and the convent girls waved us a sad goodbye, treading water and peering over the edge of their canoe. They knew that, if they were in trouble when Sister Roswitha got them back to the convent, we were going to be in trouble to the power of three when Svoboda got us back aboard our ship.

They were right: we got a most ferocious going-over from the acting GDO. The only good thing about it was that since Mikulić was ashore, staying with a copra planter, that office was temporarily filled by Linienschiffsleutnant Zaleski.

'You're extremely fortunate to find me in charge this afternoon, you young idiots. If it had been Linienschiffsleutnant Mikulić he'd certainly have had you triced up to a grating and flogged to ribbons and never mind what the *Dienstreglement* says. Now, let me see: you abandoned the boat placed under your charge – I know that she was at anchor but it's the same thing – and you comported yourselves in such a manner as to bring discredit upon the House of Habsburg, the Imperial and Royal officer corps and the good name of your ship. So what do you have to say for yourselves?'

'With respect, Herr Schiffsleutnant,' I said, 'we were in fact trying to defend the honour of the Navy and the officer corps from a calumny levelled against them by members of a non-European race. If they hadn't been girls and this had been Fiume, not Samoa, we'd have been obliged to challenge them to a duel, or at least horsewhip them.'

He sucked his teeth. 'Fair point, Prohaska, fair point. But there you are: neither of us was born yesterday. Austria is Europe's premier Catholic power and the House of Habsburg is the world's leading Catholic dynasty, principal earthly guardian of the True Faith for five centuries past. So as future Austrian officers you can't expect to go cavorting around bollock-naked with a lot of convent girls under the eyes of their Headmistress and expect to get away with it, even if the little vixens did lead you on. Sister Roswitha was snorting fire and sulphur when they took her ashore, threatening to lodge a formal complaint with the Governor that you'd been trying to debauch her girls.' He paused and regarded the three of us with his half-closed black eyes as we stood to attention before him. 'Is that it? Did you intend . . . doing anything with them?'

'Obediently report, Herr Schiffsleutnant,' said Gauss, 'that of course we did. They were all very nice-looking girls, and even out here they don't take their clothes off in front of young men unless they expect something to come of it.'

'And did you?'

'Obediently report that no, Herr Schiffsleutnant. They were too fast for us in the water. Honestly, these Samoans swim like fish. We were trying to corner them towards the beach, then drive them out of the water and towards the bushes; but that was when Linienschiffsleutnant Svoboda came on the scene.'

'I see.' Zaleski stroked his moustache reflectively. 'Very well, in view of what you have told me I hereby declare you guilty of serious misconduct and sentence you all to five days' dark-arrest, in irons, on bread and water. I also sentence you each to an additional two days' dark-arrest for un-seaman like lack of initiative. Swam too fast for you, indeed: I'm twice your age but I tell you if it had been me I'd have had each of them in turn even if they'd had to carry me back aboard on a stretcher afterwards. Really, six of them and three of you: that's two each. I don't know what the younger generation's coming to. Abtreten sofort!'

The Spaniards have a saying, I believe: 'Take what you want – and pay for it.' We paid for it with seven stuffy, dark, purgatorial days on stagnant water and ship's biscuit down in the bowels of the ship, with fetters chafing our wrists and ankles as we tried to sleep on the rough planks and with only the cockroaches and the smell of the sanitary pail for company. But it was worth it, every last bit of it. Youth is tough, and the fusty pitch darkness of the cells was lit up for each of us by a memory of sun and blue sea, of young laughter and the flash of sleek brown bodies in the water. For me those few minutes that afternoon long ago have always been a kind of film projection inside the dark cinema of the head, still as luminous now as it was then. In the years since, the memory of it has sustained me in many hours far darker than I ever knew in that cell.

On the eighth day the fetters were unlocked and we emerged blinking and stiff into the sunlight. The ship had already been three days at sea, we knew that from her motion. But there had been another change: we had sailed without Linienschiffsleutnant Zaleski. He had gone ashore on the fifth day of our stay at Apia with Dr Pürkler the geologist and a working party of sailors. Dr Pürkler was after crystalline samples from a rockface some way inland, and in order to secure them blasting had been necessary. One charge had failed to explode. Zaleski had gone forward to see what was the matter – and had been blown fifteen metres as the dynamite exploded, ending up unconscious, with a depressed fracture of the skull, several cracked ribs and a broken collarbone. They had brought him back to Apia in a litter. The surgeon at the convent hospital said that he was in no danger, but that recovery would take several weeks. Our shipboard nursing facilities were very limited compared with those of the hospital, so it had been arranged that Zaleski would stay there to convalesce and then return to Europe as a passenger of the German Imperial Navy, aboard the corvette that would shortly be sailing home to pay off at the end of her commission. So Mikulić was now acting Captain, Svoboda acting GDO and three of the junior lieutenants acting watch officers. What was wrong with this ship? We had now lost five officers. At this rate they would be promoting ordinary seamen to the wardroom long before we reached Suez. Captain Festetics was still suffering from his occlusion of the brain, despite his stay ashore in Apia, so we were now effectively at the mercy of Linienschiffsleutnant Demeter Mikulić. It was not an enticing prospect.

It appeared also that S.M.S. *Windischgrätz* had sailed from Apia amid a certain bad odour. Not only had there been the business with Sister Roswitha's convent girls, there had also been trouble over the scientific side of the visit. Professor Skowronek had been brought back aboard, we learnt, virtually under armed escort on the fourth day of our stay, charged with public-order offences by a local magistrate and bound over to keep the peace. It seemed that in his efforts to obtain some skulls of pre-colonial Samoans he and his assistants had gone a few kilometres inland from Apia and started to dig their way through an old tribal burial ground, in broad daylight and apparently treating the presence of a native village a few hundred metres away as being of no consequence whatever. The villagers had gathered, and Skowronek had only been rescued from summary lynching by the arrival of a native police detachment led by a German sergeant. Skowronek had demanded that the reputation of the white race should be upheld by firing a few volleys into the crowd, and then perhaps burning their village for good measure. The sergeant had demurred, and instead arrested the Professor for causing a breach of the peace and desecrating burial grounds, before leading him away to spend the night in the cells at Apia police barracks. Skowronek's disgust knew no limits.

'Me, Herr Leutnant: one of Europe's most highly regarded men of learning, being taken away in handcuffs by a gang of barefoot policemen in skirts led by some officious popinjay of a Feldwebel. It's monstrous; outrageous; an insult to the very spirit of rational enquiry and scientific endeavour. I demand that you lodge a protest with the Governor straight away. There's an Austrian consul in Apia: what on earth is he for if not for cases like this?'

'I will ask the Captain to write a note to the Governor, Herr Professor,' Svoboda had said; 'but, with respect, I think that the local police may have a point. The islanders are very attached to the memory of their dead ancestors, I understand, and could hardly have been expected to look kindly upon foreigners disturbing their spirits by digging up a burial ground.'

'Stuff and nonsense: the spirit is a totally discredited piece of medieval mumbo-jumbo. Science has proved that man is matter and nothing more – and if a lot of cannibals want to dispute the point then as a man of science I'm more than ready to convince them of their error with the aid of a Maxim gun. You won't find a much more convincing argument for the primacy of matter than four hundred rounds per minute! Try standing the spirit up against *that*!'

We picked up the south-east trades again, west of Samoa, and ambled along on the next leg of our circumnavigation: back up to 10 degrees south again and along that parallel towards the Solomon Islands and New Guinea. We had hoped that we might be heading for Australia, since we all wanted to see that continent's marvels before we went home and be able to say when we got back – with only minor exaggeration – that our voyage had taken us to each one of the continents (there was some argument with gunroom purists as to whether North America constituted a separate continent, and whether a near miss with an iceberg was really a visit to Antarctica, but youthful enthusiasm tends to discount such pedantry). It was not to be, though: we were heading north of Australia, and the most reliable galley rumour was that we were to spend a fortnight or so on surveying work in the western Solomons, then make our way back to Pola by way of the Dutch East Indies and Suez.

The islands were smaller now, but more thickly sprinkled across the sea: authentic atolls many of them, with palm trees and reefs of coral. The green hills of Fiji passed by on the southern horizon, then came more islets as we skirted the Gilbert and Ellice group. But we sailed on without visiting them, and only dropped anchor on 5 June in the harbour at Tulaghi, the 'capital' – for want of a better word – of the British Solomon Isles Protectorate. There were no more sunlit atolls now, but jungle-clad mountains protruding from the sea, sombre and rather menacing since more than one of them was in fact a dormant volcano. There was so little at Tulaghi that no one bothered going ashore except for provisions. But the British Commissioner Mr Woodford came out to us for supper that evening, in the saloon since the Captain was now judged well enough to receive visitors.

'You're heading for New Silesia I hear, Captain?'

'Yes Mr Woodford, that is correct. The Institute for Geological Science in Vienna has requested us to carry out a survey of the Tetuba Berg mountain on that island.'

'Well, rather you than me is all I can say. New Silesia's the last unclaimed island in the group, now that the French and the Germans have sorted out their dispute over Choiseul Island. They say the reason for nobody claiming it is that the geographers can't decide whether it's part of the Solomon chain or an offshore island of German New Guinea. But the real reason is the natives, everyone knows that.'

'Why is that? Do they believe themselves to be natives of New Guinea or Solomon Islanders?'

Woodford laughed heartily. 'I'd like to see the man brave enough to ask them. The European powers can't decide which one gets the island because the charts are very poor, that's certainly true. But that's largely because up until about 1880 any ship that tried surveying the place tended to disappear. Even the blackbirding schooners always avoided New Silesia. But tell me, why are your people so interested in the island?'

'I understand from Dr Pürkler here that it may contain large deposits of very high-grade chromium ore vital to modern steel-making processes, like those perfected by our own Skoda works at Pilsen. My government has asked us to investigate with a view to Austrian companies exploiting the deposits at some future date. In particular I gather that the Tetuba Berg which we are to investigate is effectively a solid block of chromium oxide.'

'I see. Well, if I were going to New Silesia I can tell you that keeping my head on my shoulders would be a far more pressing concern to me than looking for chromium.'

'Are the natives hostile then?'

'You could put it like that. Myself, I think that the savagery of the Solomon Islanders has been greatly exaggerated, particularly by the missionaries back in England when they're about to pass the collection plate around. Missionaries and cannibals seem to need one another. Myself, I go around these islands unarmed and I've never come to any harm, though I'll admit I've had one or two nasty moments. But there are two islands where I wouldn't lightly go ashore. One's Malaita and the other's New Silesia.'

'How far inland would you advise us to venture then, Mr Woodford?'

'That depends how far can you run in thirty seconds, Captain. Never go further inland than that if you don't want to leave your head behind, and always take good care to keep your boat's stern to the beach so that you can take a flying leap into it if necessary.'

'Do the natives attack all white men on sight?'

'Not all: there's a few missionaries on the coast at Pontypridd. One of them's a Catholic, one of your people: a Father Adametz who works for a Belgian religious order. He's been there for years and although I hold no brief for the RCs – I'm Church of England myself – he seems a decent enough sort of chap. He comes into Tulaghi about once a year and we talk sometimes. He knows all the native languages and the tribespeople seem to trust him, but even he daren't go too far inland. As for the other two missionaries, they're Englishmen the pair of them, and they set up on New Silesia as part of the same mission. But now they're at loggerheads and stirring up the natives against one another. I think there may well be trouble soon, and when that happens one or other European power – probably us – will have to take the place over.'

Festetics's ears had pricked up at the remark over the Catholic missionary.

'You said, Mr Woodford, that the Catholic missionary is "one of our people". Did you mean by that that he is a Catholic and Austria is a Catholic power?'

'No, no. Excuse me if I didn't make my meaning plain. He's an Austrian subject I understand – or at least was: from Bohemia or somewhere like that.'

'Thank you: that is *very* interesting information. But in general you would advise us to be careful when we visit New Silesia?'

'My advice to you, Captain, would be not to visit the place at all. But if you really want to risk your lives then make sure that even when you're anchored offshore, you keep a strong deck-watch at night – and by strong I mean men with rifles in their hands and cutlasses at their belts. The natives are experts at cutting out ships in the dark. There was a French sloop a few years back was overrun one night and burnt out. Half the men went to feed the sharks and the other half got made into long pig to feed the islanders. One of the chiefs told me afterwards that Frenchmen don't taste as sweet as the English: probably on account of all that coffee and red wine. Oh, and keep a good stock of pig-iron and rocks about the deck: they're useful for dropping through the bottoms of their canoes when they try boarding you.'

'Are the natives armed with guns?'

'Oh indeed yes: mostly old Snider rifles. But don't worry; they hardly ever hit anyone except at close quarters. They always set the sights to six hundred yards to make the guns shoot harder. It's axes and war clubs that you have to watch out for; also sticks of dynamite nowadays, thanks to the traders.'

'You make these islands sound a very dangerous place, Mr Woodford.'

'So they are; and I freely admit that some of the natives are every bit as bad as the white ruffians who come here kidnapping slaves for the plantations in Queensland. The Solomons are no place for ladies' maids or teachers of deportment. But I think that by the sound of it you're soon going to find that out for yourselves.'

It was perhaps fortunate that there was so little to visit in Tulaghi, because our acting Captain Mikulić had forbidden us shore-leave on the grounds merely that it was his good pleasure to do so. Now in effective command of the ship, the GDO had made plain his intention of tightening up the discipline which he believed had grown lax during a year at sea. We might soon be in action against real enemies, so (he announced) he would set about turning us from a floating hotel back into a warship. So that day and the days that followed it, as we sailed along the passage between the islands, were passed in a haze of gun drills, endless scouring of objects already scoured almost to disappearance, painting of fittings painted the day before, tarring down the standing rigging until it gleamed like ebony, shot drills for everyone not engaged on anything else, and punishment rowing for those who were judged not to be entering into the spirit of the thing. The latter punishment was particularly hated since it consisted of dropping a cutter astern with a couple of buckets trailing in the water behind it and forcing the rowers to keep up with the ship – preferably under the full glare of the midday sun. One of the cutters was nearly lost in this manner north of Guadalcanal Island, when from sheer exhaustion its crew let the ship sail on out of sight. They were not recovered until next morning, when Mikulić promptly gave them two days' dark-arrest for straggling. The punishment cutters were encouraged to keep up with the ship in future by having their sails and water barricoes taken away, so that if they fell astern the crew would almost certainly die of thirst or be eaten by the islanders. Meanwhile, aboard the ship, the rope's end came back into use, wielded by Mikulić himself and a few of his trusted aides. Before long many a man had a line of red weals across his shoulders to prove it.

Yet we knuckled under and obeyed. Naval discipline is ferocious, and while at sea in those days even an acting captain was effectively God. If the Bo'sun or the Provost or any of the junior officers had demurred and refused to obey a lawful command then they would be guilty of insubordination at least, and have ended up in the cells with a few teeth missing. If we had supported their disobedience, insubordination would have become mass refusal of duty as defined in the *K.u.K. Dienstreglement*; and, if persisted in, mass refusal of duty would have become outright mutiny, rendering us liable to be hunted down by the authorities of all the civilised powers and, if captured, to be returned to Austria in chains to face court martial and a probable twenty-five years' hard labour in a prison-fortress. Military discipline is potentially one of the most dangerous of human inventions. How often in my life have I seen hundreds of grown men terrorised out of their wits and driven like automatons to their deaths by some miserable little creature whom they could have crushed like a flea between their finger- and thumbnails had they so wished – but who has been set above them in the military hierarchy and is therefore never to be questioned. In the old empires of Europe military discipline was the undisputed queen of the arts and sciences: let a Feldwebel bellow, 'Marschieren, Marsch!' and the most profound of philosophers, the most learned of professors, the most sublime of composers would swing his arms and march with the rest.

What else could we do? Mass refusal of duty can sometimes succeed, but not while a ship is at sea – where it automatically becomes mutiny – and not without absolute solidarity on the part of the refusers. The problem with the latter condition was that Mikulić had the true bully's instinct for spotting the likely resisters and isolating them from the rest. A favourite trick of his at divisions was to saunter along the rows of men, pick one of them out at random and summarily sentence him to five days' dark-arrest in chains on bread and water. The man would be led below by the corporals, and Mikulić would address us from the bridge, legs astride like some petty colossus.

'There, you herd of swine. I've just given a man five days' dark-arrest for nothing at all. So just think what you'd get if I thought you were guilty of anything. Very good – Bo'sun, turn out the watch below for some weapons drill. Too much sleep is bad for you.' And the men who had just come off watch and turned in would be rousted out of their hammocks once more and chased up on deck to stand in the sun and shoulder arms, present arms, order arms, shoulder arms, present arms for the rest of their watch below.

The worst of Mikulić's offences though was committed one morning when we were anchored in a bay on the north side of Guadalcanal, the day after we sailed from Tulaghi. This was not going to be more than a few hours' stay – Dr Lenart wished to go ashore to collect some plant specimens. However, there was enough time for the men to take their regulation daily bathe, which they had missed at Tulaghi because of bad weather. The bay in which we were anchored was deep and full of strong currents, so a sail had been suspended in the water between two spars to form a makeshift swimming pool. As junior cadets of the watch, Gauss and I were given the job of standing by with the dinghy, as required by regulations. It was boring work, sitting there in the glare of the sun as the men splashed and larked around in the water and were then called back on deck after ten minutes to allow the next party to bathe. The last lot were bathing now. One of them was a young rating called Crocetti, a Zara Italian. Since the GDO was otherwise engaged Crocetti decided to take a swim outside the sail. He struck out into the bay and swam around the boat.

'Crocetti,' I called, 'get back in that pool at once.'

'Are you going to make me, then, little dumpling-eater of a cadet? Who takes any notice of you?'

'Get back in, I say, or I'll report you to the officer of the watch for insubordination.'

'Insubordination to whom? You're not officers . . .' He stopped suddenly and stood in the water with his mouth open, face frozen and the colour of paraffin wax.

'There you silly sod, you've got cramp now, haven't you? That'll teach you to cheek officer cadets.'

Gauss elbowed me.

'Prohaska, let's row over to him. There's something wrong.'

There was indeed something wrong; as we pulled Crocetti over the gunwale we found that he seemed curiously light – which was scarcely surprising since about a third of his body was missing: his entire right leg and hip sheared off obliquely from just below the waist. Entrails spilled out like glistening pink and orange spaghetti as we dragged him over the gunwale and laid him out on the bottom boards, gushing and trickling blood like a burst water tank. We were too shocked to feel any revulsion. Gauss tried to apply tourniquets, but it was quite hopeless: he just faded and died from loss of blood as I knelt beside him trying to take down a last message to his parents. We were being watched all the while by a line of silent spectators along the rail. Among them was Linienschiffsleutnant Mikulić. He was not pleased as we came alongside with the body.

'What do you mean, coming alongside with a boat in that state? You look like a floating butcher's shop.'

'I obediently report, Herr Leutnant, that Matrose Crocetti is dead.'

'Serves the stupid bastard right for disobeying orders. Now you can just dump him over the side.'

'But Herr Leutnant...'

'Shut up and do as you're told. I'm not keeping the ship here for burial services and all that nonsense. The shark's eaten half of him so it might as well have the rest. Over the side with him now and look sharp about it, because if I come down there to you you'll wish the sharks had got you as well.'

So we tumbled what was left of poor Crocetti into the water. As he sank towards the bottom we saw dark shapes nosing towards him. A murmur of anger went up from the men on deck – until Mikulić turned to them and ordered them back to their duties. Perhaps only a dozen men had seen the incident, and it was recorded in the log as 'Matrose Dominico Crocetti lost while swimming; believed to have been attacked by sharks.' All the same, it was widely discussed on the lower deck that evening. Sailors in those days were religious people for all their noisy profanity, and by ordering the disposal of a dead comrade without a proper burial service Linienschiffsleutnant Mikulić had declared himself the enemy of God as well as of men. Trouble would take time to come, but come it surely would.

The village of Pontypridd was marked on the chart of New Silesia as its only settlement. Doubtless there were others inland, but since the interior of the roughly oval island was marked 'Still unexplored', Pontypridd was effectively its metropolis and port of entry from the outside world. It certainly looked peaceful enough as we sailed on the morning of 19 June into the wide, coral-bordered gulf called Pontypridd Bay. Jungle-covered hills rose almost directly from the shoreline. In the distance, about ten kilometres away, was the cloud-covered peak of the Tetuba Berg (2,235 metres) and beyond that the summit of Mount Trumpington (2,453 metres). Pontypridd Bay was at the south-western tip of the island. Opposite the bay, fifty-odd miles away, a far-off bank of blue just visible across the Scharnhorst Strait, was the mountainous coast of New Ireland, part of German New Guinea.

Pontypridd itself – heaven alone knows what its real name was

– lay at the head of the bay, a collection of huts along the shore. On each side of it, at opposite ends of the bay, were two smaller settlements, which Mr Woodford had told us were the encampments of the two rival English missionaries Mr Tribe and Mr Musgrove. The larger of the two – we did not as yet know which one it belonged to – seemed to have a copra plantation attached to it, and a sizeable wooden jetty. But Pontypridd proper, where we were to land, was a Solomons native village pretty well unaffected by European civilisation, apart from a small church that we distinguished from the surrounding palm-thatch huts only by the crucifix above it. There were forty or so native huts raised on bamboo stilts – much less neat dwellings to look at than those of the Samoans – a long canoe-house which was also used as a burial ground for chiefs (hence the rather odd smell inside it) and a canoe slipway made of sand and lumps of coral. Apart from that there was not a great deal worthy of note; only a single muddy street, dirt, flies, naked children, a few mangy dogs and a great many long-nosed pigs rootling in the mud: something like a European wild boar to look at but less bristly. All refuse here was thrown on to the beach to be carried away by the tide – including dead bodies, we were told, since only chiefs were considered worthy of a special grave. I have sometimes read in the years since that the seas around the Solomons became infested with sharks only during the Second World War, when the great naval battles that raged here between the American and Japanese fleets left the waters full of drifting corpses. All I can say is that when I was there forty years earlier the local sharks were already abundant and clearly possessed a well-developed taste for human flesh.

The New Silesians themselves were not a particularly prepossessing lot: certainly nothing to compare in looks with the tall and powerfully built Samoans. They were mostly short, dark-brown to near-black in colour, and resembled no one quite so much as Abyssinians with their disturbing pointed-tooth grins and their incredible, extravagant masses of fuzzy hair – which to my surprise was often reddish in colour and sometimes almost blond, though whether from bleaching or not I cannot say. They were cordial enough to us when we were ashore, but not as affable as the Samoans. They left us with a strong impression that they regarded this island as their country and were not willingly going to hand it over to anyone else: in other words the sort of natives described in the gazetters of the day as 'savage, mistrustful, surly and intractable'.

As might have been expected from one of the world's leading racial scientists, Professor Skowronek found a genetic interpretation of the islanders' cultural inferiority. 'The natives of these islands,' he told a group of us assembled on the quarterdeck, 'are among the lowest and most degenerate racial types known to science.' He turned to a group of three or four island menfolk who had come aboard on some errand or other. 'Observe, if you will: they are even of inferior and weakly physique.' We looked at the smiling men, naked except for lap-laps. They were slightly shorter than us, it was true, but they looked far from inferior in physique; in fact seemed very sturdy and well-muscled indeed.

'Here, my good fellow,' the professor beckoned one of the natives over; 'take this good German beer and drink it: it may help to build you up.' He proffered the man a bottle of Pilsner lager beer taken from the wardroom's much-depleted stock of such comforts. Then he turned back to us. 'Let us see now how our savage friend here deals with the problem of opening the bottle. This should be a good illustration of the inferior reasoning powers possessed by such poorly developed specimens of subhumanity.'

The man looked at the bottle for a moment or two. It had a crown-cap and he had no bottle opener. So he simply took the bottle between his betel-stained teeth and crunched the neck off, spitting the fragments of broken glass over the side before draining the contents at a single gulp. It was certainly an impressive enough demonstration, but not quite one of physical degeneracy.

The Catholic missionary priest at Pontypridd was indeed an Austrian as Mr Woodford had told us: we ascertained that much on our first visit ashore when Gauss and I delivered an invitation for him to come aboard to supper that evening. He was Father Adamec – or Adametz as he now spelt it: a Czech from the town of Iglau in southern Bohemia. Not that he regarded himself now as an Austrian – or perhaps ever had. A large, benign, bespectacled man in his late fifties, he had last seen Bohemia nearly forty years before.

'I'm here with the Redemptorists,' he told us in the captain's saloon that evening over supper, speaking a German creaking and rusty from decades of disuse but still marked by a strong Czech accent, 'so really the Order's the only country I have now. I trained in Belgium, at Louvain, then came out here in – when was it now? – 1876 I think. I've only been back to Europe once in all that time, and that was just to Marseille. I believe that Franz Joseph is still Emperor, but that's the sum total of my knowledge about Austria. We don't get newspapers here very often, and when we do they're from Sydney and months out of date. Language? Well, as you can hear, my German's pretty moth-eaten these days and my Czech's not much better. My Superior visits about once every eighteen months and we talk in French, and the rest of the time I work in the local languages or Bêche-de-Mer English, which is a sort of local argot right through these islands.'

'If you will forgive me for saying so, it seems rather strange for an Austrian priest to be carrying on the work of mission in French and corrupt English, not in German.'

'Why should that be, for goodness' sake? Our Lord preached in Aramaic and St Paul in bad Greek. A language is just a tool. It always amused me when I was on Réunion for a while to hear the French administrators telling off the natives for speaking Creole – "a mere patois of French" – as if French weren't a mere patois of Latin. As for being an Austrian, I can't say that I've given the matter much thought in recent years. I was born and grew up in Bohemia, a subject of the House of Habsburg, but that's all there is to say about it.'

'But do you not feel uncomfortably exposed here, alone among these cannibals and headhunters without the protection of a European power?'

'Not in the least. In fact I'd feel a lot more uncomfortable *with* it. Christ preached to the crowds from a fishing boat, I always understood, not from a cruiser with its guns trained on the shore.'

'Do you get anywhere with you preaching among these people? Mr Woodford at Tulaghi told us that they are among the most savage of all the Solomon Islanders.'

Father Adametz laughed. 'That reminds me rather of a notice that I once saw on a cage in Brussels Zoo: "Attention: Cet animal est méchant: si on l'attaque, il se défend." No, I've been here for most of a lifetime now and I have to say that I'm a good deal less convinced of the value of preaching than I was when I first arrived. You see, these are simple people by our standards, but in many ways their societies are much more complex than ours. Frankly I doubt just how much of the Christian Gospel they can take in at a sitting, their mental world is so utterly different from our own. Take forgiving your enemies, for instance: their whole society is based on scrupulous repayment, both for good and for bad. To them, forgiving someone an injury is as ludicrous an idea as it would be to us if, say, a court declared a man innocent and sent him to jail, or if a political party was elected because it had got fewer votes than its rivals. Take away one leg of the stool and the whole thing falls over. No, our work here is the work of decades, not of years.'

'But what about the abominable practices of these tribes: cannibalism and head-hunting and slave-raiding? Do you condone those as well?'

'As for cannibalism and head hunting, you certainly have a point there. But if you kill people in wars what are you supposed to do with them afterwards? I remember that a couple of years ago I translated a newspaper article about the siege of Plevna for the benefit of a local chief: five thousand men killed in an afternoon, or something like that. He just grinned and said, "Then they must have had a memorable feast that evening." Where their other customs are concerned my instinct is to leave them alone if they don't get in anyone's way. I was on Tahiti for a while before I came here and I saw what the missionaries did there, tearing up a whole way of life by the roots and giving the people nothing but Sunday schools in return. No wonder the poor wretches just curled up and died of despair. They tried some of that in these islands of course, the Protestant missionaries. There was one on Choiseul Island a few years ago, I believe, who persuaded the local chief to give up polygamy. So the chief held a great feast, at the end of which he set his favourite wife and her children aside – then killed all the others with his war club. And there was the Anglican missionary up on Bougainville who taught his converts to play cricket. They thought it was a splendid idea: particularly if one set a row of shark's teeth down each edge of the bat. There were several hundred killed and eaten at one match I understand. It lasted three days and only ended when the Germans sent a gunboat from Rabaul to shell the place.'

'But surely, Father, does that mean that you have no interest in spreading Christianity and European civilisation to these heathen?'

'I'd have to think about that; particularly about the implication that Christianity and European civilisation amount to the same thing. Our Lord was born and died in Asia, I believe, not in Lower Austria. As for spreading the Catholic faith, yes of course that's what I want to do, otherwise I would hardly have lived here for the past quarter-century; but in terms that these people can understand. My wish is to baptise their way of life, not to uproot it or superimpose a poor copy of Europe on to it. But as I have said, that's work for more than one lifetime.'

'But these islanders are savages, sunk in the grossest barbarity and ignorance. Do the other missionaries here take as tolerant a view of this as you appear to do?'

'Who? Mr Tribe and Mr Musgrove? I doubt whether they are capable of taking a tolerant view of anything; particularly of one another. And they certainly have a very poor opinion of the Catholic Church – in fact keep denouncing the Holy Father as the Antichrist. I understand that Mr Tribe was working on a translation of the Bible into Tetuba in which "the Evil One" was translated as "The Pope". But now he's changed that I believe and cast poor Mr Musgrove in that role instead.'

'Are these two Englishmen rivals?'

'You could put it like that, though when they came here five years ago they were fellow-missionaries working for the same organisation. They fell out with one another about two years ago. I try to be affable to them both and to make up their quarrels in so far as I can – particularly since they're now having an effect on the tribes inland. But I can't say that I've managed to get very far in either respect. Do I understand that you propose paying them a visit?'

'Not exactly, Father; we're inviting them aboard tomorrow evening.'

'I see. Well, be prepared. If you want to see the Cannibal Isles at their most savage then you could scarcely do better than meet those two.'

16

SAVING GRACE

I found next day that if anything Father Adametz had understated the case regarding the two English residents of New Silesia. I was sent off in the gig at eight bells next morning to present the Captain's compliments to each of the two missionaries and invite them aboard S.M.S. *Windischgrätz* for drinks the next evening. My first port of call was Mr Tribe's mission, called 'Spurgeonsville', on the far side of Pontypridd Bay. As we rowed up to the large and well-constructed landing stage I saw that the settlement consisted of some twenty palm-thatched huts, arranged like barracks, a wooden church – a sort of garden-shed construction with a spire on top – and a prefabricated wooden bungalow with a verandah. I also saw that behind the mission was quite a substantial copra plantation. Smoke was rising from the copra boilers and large heaps of the rancid-smelling brownish substance lay alongside the wharf awaiting collection. Above the beach to one side of the landing stage, facing across the bay, stood a large red hoarding painted in metre-high letters with the words SERVANTS, LOVE THY MASTERS AND CHEERFULLY OBEY THEM THAT ARE SET IN AUTHORITY OVER YOU. Quite apart from the grim nature of the text, it struck me as a curious thing to have placed in that particular spot, since the natives who passed by from time to time in their canoes must have been quite illiterate in English or in any other language.

We moored at the landing stage and I left my crew – four sailors armed with rifles and cutlasses, just in case – to make my way up to the bungalow, which I assumed to be Mr Tribe's house. As I walked through the settlement I saw several native women, dressed not Pontypridd-fashion in a lap-lap and nothing else but in singularly hideous dresses which I later learnt were called 'hubbards' and manufactured to clothe the poor naked heathen by church ladies' sewing guilds in the English cities. They seemed to have been made to a standard size and consisted of a tube of material, put together on the same lines as a ship's funnel, surmounted by a sort of flounce like that of a curtain pelmet or the fringe around a lampshade. Even the wearers seemed ashamed of them: at any rate, as soon as they saw me they scurried away in apparent terror. I saw one of these creatures dozing on the steps of the bungalow, so I went up to her and asked, 'Please, where Missa Tribe?', hoping (as proved to be the case) that Bêche-de-Mer English would operate on the same principles as Krio in West Africa. She stirred and gazed at me stupidly. She was of indeterminate age and certainly looked far less healthy than the natives over in Pontypridd: had a skin rash on her face and seemed to be suffering from rickets. She got up and limped on to the verandah, pointing me towards a side door. I knocked. No answer. I knocked again. The door was opened at last by a thin, exasperated-looking man in shirtsleeves with no collar and with a knotted handkerchief on his head.

'What do you want?'

'Good-morning. Do I have the pleasure of speaking with Mr Tribe?'

'The Reverend Mr Tribe to you,' he snapped. 'And who might you be anyway?'

'Cadet Otto Prohaska, from the Austrian steam corvette *Windischgrätz* currently lying in Pontypridd Bay. My Captain sends his compliments and hopes that we may have the pleasure of your company at a reception aboard the ship at seven-thirty tomorrow evening.' I handed him the invitation. He ripped open the envelope and pulled out the invitation card, then began to read it, tracing the words with his fingertip and forming them silently with his mouth, eyebrows knotted in growing puzzlement. At last he looked up at me.

'What d'you mean, invitation, you cheeky young pup? This

'ere don't make no sense at all. If you're trying to guy me then I warn you . . .'

I took the card from him. 'Ah yes, excuse me: that is because it is written in French. Permit me to translate it for you: "Captain of Corvette Count Eugen Festetics von Szentkatolna requests the pleasure of the company of Mr and Mrs Samuel Tribe . . ." '

'The *Reverend* Mr Samuel Tribe if you please . . .'

'My apologies – "the Reverend Mr Samuel Tribe . . . at a reception aboard the Imperial and Royal Austro-Hungarian Steam Corvette *Windischgrätz* at seven-thirty p.m. on 20 June 1903. RSVP." ' He eyed me suspiciously.

'What's all this "RSVP" then? It's the Jesuits isn't it? Admit it.' It was my turn to stare bewildered. Then a light dawned.

'With respect, Reverend sir, I think that you may perhaps have in mind the Society of St Vincent de Paul. No, it stands for "repondez s'il vous plaît" – "please reply".'

'You're French, aren't you? I heard that there's a ship in at Pontypridd. Now let me warn you that we're a British evangelical reformed Protestant mission here and we're not going to stand no nonsense from your sort . . .'

'No, no, I assure you we are not French. We are in an Austro-Hungarian warship engaged on a scientific voyage. We have put in here at New Silesia for a week or two so that our geologists can carry out a survey inland.'

He snorted. 'A likely story and all: you're Papists aren't you? That apostate blackguard Adametz asked you here didn't he? Well, let me tell you here and now, I'm not going to stand for it, I'm not. Anyway, where's Austro-Hungaria when it's at home?'

'Near Germany, though more to the south and east.'

'Are you Romanists?'

'Excuse me . . . ?'

'Do you worship the Pope and the Virgin Mary and cardinals and all that carry-on?'

'The Austro-Hungarian Empire is a Catholic power, certainly; but that has nothing whatever to do with our being here.'

'Poppycock: you've come here to convert the niggers, haven't you? Own up: you've got dozens of your Jesuit priests below decks just waiting to land. I've read all about your sort: the perfidious whore of Babylon, drunk with fornication and the blood of the saints. You want to come here and burn us all at the stake, like as not, and then bring out your monks and nuns and set up monasteries all over the place. Well, I know your game, don't you worry. You just tell your Captain from me: the Penge Reformed Evangelical Baptist Missionary Society has its eye on the Roman harlot and her nefarious doings!' I was rather taken aback by this cascade of bile: whatever its many other faults, the Danubian Monarchy's innate laziness and reluctance to wake sleeping dogs at least made it very tolerant in matters of religion.

'Please, please, Reverend Mr Tribe, I assure you that your suspicions are entirely without foundation. We have only one Catholic priest aboard, the ship's Chaplain, and to be quite honest with you I doubt whether he could convert anyone to anything. He is a nice man, but Lieutenant Zaleski says that if the conversion of the Germanic peoples had been left to Father Semmelweiss then we would still be worshipping rocks and oak trees.'

He was staring at me, puzzled. And, young as I was, I suddenly realised that in this world there are certain people before whom it is not a good idea to perform such pirouettes upon the ice, their minds being quite unable to grasp figures of speech. I could already sense that in the Reverend Mr Tribe of the Penge Reformed Evangelical Baptist Missionary Society I was dealing with a very obtuse person indeed: not just ill-educated but positively dim. He grunted.

'Hmmmph! That's as may be. Well, young fellow, you just go and tell your Captain we're having no truck with the Catholic' (I noticed that he pronounced it 'cafflick') 'powers here. The RCs are up to mischief, I know that; stirring up the blacks against those whom the Lord has set in authority over them. Well, I for one ain't going to stand none of it, see? Martha!'

There was a timid voice from within the bungalow. 'Yes, Reverend?'

'Bring out me boots and me going-out hat. I'm going to get to the bottom of this. That reprobate scoundrel Musgrove's behind all this I'll wager.' A domestic appeared carrying a pair of long brown boots and a pith helmet. She was white, but slight of build and meagre of appearance, wearing a long dress and a mob-cap of the kind that one sees sometimes in children's picture-books. To describe her as 'mousy' would be a calumny against mice.

'Here they are, Reverend.' She placed the boots and helmet by a wicker armchair, casting a furtive sideways glance at me, then stood by with her eyes cast down and her hands folded, awaiting further orders. Mr Tribe put on his boots and the helmet, then dismissed her with a curt nod. As he strode down the steps of the verandah he turned and wagged an admonitory finger at me.

'You haven't heard the last of this, I can tell you. Ten years I've laboured here in the vineyard of the Lord among the heathen, getting the niggers to cover up their nakedness and learn the value of honest toil, and I don't intend letting your lot come here and spoil it all. That priest Adametz of yours lets the women in Pontypridd go around with their bosoms bared to all the world without saying anything, or so I've heard. What sort of religion do you call that?'

He left me standing on the verandah. I thought that before I left, courtesy demanded that I should present the Captain's compliments to Mrs Tribe as well, who had not appeared during this interview. I leant through the open window to ask the servant who had brought out the boots and pith helmet.

'Excuse me, but could you please tell me where I might find Mrs Tribe?'

She sniffed, and wiped an eye on her pinafore. 'I am Mrs Tribe.'

While I was making my way back towards the jetty and the waiting gig I saw a party of plantation labourers coming in from the groves with hoes over their shoulders. As they shuffled through the dust I noticed that they were chained ankle to ankle.

After my reception at Spurgeonville I feared the worst as we approached the landing stage at Mr Musgrove's missionary outpost, 'Rehoboth', on the other side of Pontypridd Bay about two miles distant from our last port of call. As we neared the shore I saw that it too had its red-painted hoarding pointed out to sea. This one proclaimed IT IS IN THE LAKE THAT BURNETH WITH EVERLASTING FIRE THAT ALL UNBELIEVERS SHALL HAVE THEIR PART. With a welcome mat like that I had every reason to suppose that I might be in for an even more churlish reception than that which I had experienced from the Reverend Mr Tribe. My fears on this score only increased as we came up to the landing stage to find ourselves facing a number of islanders, naked except for lap-laps, but well armed with rifles and spears. As they led me towards the mission I saw that it was surrounded with barbed wire and emplacements of sandbags. One of these contained a Nordenfeldt machine gun on a pedestal. The Nordenfeldt was a museum piece even in 1903, but somehow I still doubted whether it had been placed there purely for its decorative value.

The reception at the landing stage was rather chilly, even though the natives had been perfectly courteous. But Mr Musgrove was quite cordial to me in the living room of his hut, cooled by a fan in the ceiling operated by a native pulling a string outside. He was a florid, tubby man with a shapeless face and the disturbing, soft-boiled eyes that one sees sometimes in people who are mildly sub-normal. His head was conical in shape and topped with a bush of curly hair that stood up at the front in a quiff of permanent surprise. He had been here five years, I understood, but still seemed not to have got used to the heat. At any rate, whereas Mr Tribe had received me in shirt sleeves order, Mr Musgrove was wearing a sweaty vest with dangling braces.

'Sit down, sit down, young man, and let us enjoy together a time of warm fellowship in the Lord, now that His all-seeing Providence has brought you to this far-flung community of God's chosen people.'

Tea and biscuits were brought in by a native servant and placed on the table. The tea was poured out and I waited for the biscuits to be handed around. But Mr Musgrove sat still and silent for several minutes, eyes rolled up and apparently trying to remember something important. Ought I to do something? English domestic manners were not familiar to me and perhaps the etiquette of the tea ceremony demanded that I should pass the biscuits or something of that kind. I coughed politely. This seemed to release a switch inside his head: he launched into a long, rambling mumble which began, 'We just thank you O Lord for your abundant goodness and mercy which has brought us together to share this time of communion and the bountiful fruits of thy saving love towards sinners . . .' and so on and so on for the next ten minutes or so, by which time the tea was cold and covered with an unappetising brown crust. It was tea with milk – from a tin, naturally – and although this was not the first time that I had been offered this curious beverage (we had been liberally plied with it in Cape Town) I still found it rather disagreeable even when hot. But I was a guest, so I pretended to enjoy it.

'Now my young lad, in what may I perhaps be of service to you?'

'Ah, yes; you must excuse me, Mr Musgrove. I am here to present my Captain's compliments and to invite you to a reception aboard my ship at seven-thirty tomorrow evening.' I handed him the envelope. He took it and stared at it vacantly.

'To what ship do you allude, young man?' (He pronounced it 'hallude'.) I sensed at once that I was dealing with someone who had to have things spelt out to him. Surely every native on the island must know of our arrival by now: the only other ship to call here was a copra schooner which came every six months or so to load the produce of the Spurgeonsville plantation.

'The Austrian steam corvette *Windischgrätz*, currently at anchor further down the bay. We are here for a week or so to carry out a scientific survey inland.'

He stared at me round-eyed for a few moments – then fell down upon his knees and clasped his hands, mumbling faintly to himself. He remained like that for a good fifteen minutes, until once again I began to wonder whether some action was required on my part. Quite apart from anything else I was rather thrown off balance by these ostentatious displays of piety. Austria was a Christian country to be sure, but in all practical respects Christianity had as little influence on people's lives as astronomy, and considerably less than astrology. One attended mass on Sundays and on holy days of obligation, went to confession once a quarter, abstained from visiting houses of ill-repute in Lent – if one was particularly devout, that is – and that was about the extent of it. If asked, most Austrians would have numbered the Emperor's birthday on 18 August among the festivals of the Church. At last he got up.

'Well, young fellow, you can go and tell your agents of Satan in Australia that the people of God on the island of New Silesia stand ready. Is it not written in the Book of Revelation that the Great Beast, the Man of Sin, shall come from a far southern country?' I was unable to answer him on this point, although I was fairly sure that I remembered from somewhere that the Antichrist would come from the north. But I felt that I must correct him.

'By your leave, Mr Musgrove, I said "Austrian", not "Australian".'

He stared at me with those disturbing blank eyes of his: Austria? Australia? I could almost hear his brain wrestling with these two concepts. Then he smiled ingratiatingly. 'Of course, of course: Austria, not Australia; I see now. You must excuse me. I've been out here five years now and the quinine plays up the auricular faculties something chronic after a while. Not that I'm complaining of course – don't think that for one moment: "Thy will be done, O Lord." What sort of reception is this though? Is it a religious assemblage or what?'

'Not in the least, Mr Musgrove. It is a small party which our Captain is holding for the Europeans on New Silesia – although of course there are only three of you.'

He looked at me through half-closed eyes. 'Is the serpent Tribe going to be there?' I wondered for a moment what the Serpent tribe might be – perhaps some local clan – then realised that he meant his one-time partner the Reverend Mr Samuel Tribe of Spurgeonville mission.

'Mr Tribe has been invited, along with Mrs Tribe. The Paymaster was unable to write her full name on the invitation because he was not entirely sure that there was a Mrs Tribe.'

Musgrove laughed slyly at this. 'Yes, and she's unaware of it as well, if you get my meaning. Nothing but a common harlot before he took up with her. No young man; if Tribe and that Romanish apostate Adametz are going to be there as well then I shall not confabulate the assembly with my presence. "Be ye not yoked with unbelievers", sayeth the Apostle. Anyway, do I take it that beverages of a spiritual character will be served at this here "reception" of yours?' He pronounced the word 'reception' to make it sound like 'orgy' or 'cannibal feast'.

'Why of course: hospitality will be offered and there will be musical entertainment. Our ship's band is highly regarded and has played to appreciative audiences wherever we have landed.' He pursed his lips.

'No drop of alcoholic beverage shall pass my lips, neither shall I frequent music halls nor listen to profane merriment: those were the vows I took when I was admitted to the congregation of the Lord's Elect in Penge.'

'Am I to understand then, Mr Musgrove, that you will be unable to attend?'

He suddenly looked thoughtful – and fell on his knees once more in prayer. This time it went on for a good half-hour, myself shuffling awkwardly from one foot to the other as he groaned and mumbled softly to himself. A fly buzzed around the room and settled on his nose. I wondered whether I should brush it off, but it seemed not to bother him so I left it where it was. At last he got up.

'The Holy Spirit has spoken unto me. I must visit your ship to preach to your crew and baptise them. What time is this reception?'

'Seven-thirty tomorrow, Mr Musgrove. But as for baptising our crew, I think that you will find that they have all been baptised already, apart from a few Jews. We have a Catholic chaplain aboard and we all have to go to mass on Sunday mornings. Surely your task here is to baptise the islanders, not Europeans.' He had stuck his fingers into his ears.

'Worldly wisdom, worldly wisdom: have ye nothing to do with the wisdom of this world.' He unblocked his ears and stared at me in that disturbing, high-grade-mental-defective way of his. 'He who is not with the Lord is against Him. None shall be saved on that great and terrible day of the Lord but those whom the Lamb has sealed with his blood. Baptise the islanders? You'd get more sense talking to lampposts than to these naked blackguards. No, those on this island whose names have been written in the Lamb's Book of Life have joined me already and forsaken their evil ways.'

'Do you mean, they have given up cannibalism and head-hunting?'

He stared at me as if I were not quite right in the head. 'No, boy; given up the Penge Reformed Evangelical Baptist Mission Society I mean: that scoundrel whoremonger Tribe and all his works of darkness. I came out here five years back to be his partner in the saving of lost souls, but when I got here I found I was nothing but manager of his confounded copra plantation. So the spirit of the Lord came unto me one night as I lay sleeping, an angel holding a fiery sword and an open book. And the Spirit said unto me, "Arise, George Musgrove, forsake those who love not the Lamb and take thee across the waters of the bay to a place that I shall show thee, and thou shalt call it Rehoboth, and I will gather there unto me an holy people, an elect nation, and I shall make of them a mighty army to smite mine enemies and strike fear into the hearts of all the peoples that dwell on the earth." So I arose as the Holy Spirit commanded and came here. And lo, a letter did arrive for me the following day to tell me that the Holy Spirit had also moved the hearts of those whose abode was in Penge, and they had come out from among the unbelievers and separated themselves from them to become the Penge Reformed Free Evangelical Baptists. And since that day, both on this island and back in Penge, many that were in darkness have come to see the light and cleave unto us.'

'I see. So does this mean that the mission that you represent is a different religion from Mr Tribe's?' This was all deeply puzzling to me: in the Dual Monarchy most people were Catholics, and the rest were Orthodox or Jews with a sprinkling of Protestants in Hungary and a few patches of Muslims in the Balkans. Within those blocs though – which were as much national as religious – there was hardly any disagreement whatever about what was believed. The idea of religious sects constantly splitting like amoebae and anathematising each other with such ferocity was one that I found very strange. But as soon as the question had passed my lips I saw that I ought not to have asked it: Mr Musgrove would now take it upon himself to correct my ignorance.

It was not until late afternoon that I managed to get away and stagger back to the gig waiting at the landing stage, its crew slumped on the benches half prostrate with sun and boredom. The previous five hours had been one seamless garment; a single interminable monologue during which Mr Musgrove had explained to me the reasons for the schism between the Penge Reformed Evangelical Baptists and the Penge Reformed Free Evangelical Baptists. Most of it passed over my head, I have to admit, as I sat there glassy-eyed, exposed to the fury of Mr Musgrove in full theological spate. Not that the man ranted and raved: that at least would have been a diverting spectacle. Instead he droned on and on and on in an even monotone, scarcely pausing to draw breath as he flicked endlessly through the pages of his Bible to draw my attention to various proof-texts underlined in red pencil. His discourse was punctuated throughout by 'amen's and 'praise the Lord's, while the rest of it was conducted in a curious stilted language which I would recognise years later issuing from the mouths of dogmatic Marxists: the characteristic discourse of people who think not in words and images but by bolting together prefabricated ideas like the sections of a corrugated-iron hut. But even if the language was flat and artificial-sounding the ideas it contained – or such of them as I could grasp as the flood swept them past me – were luminously crazy. So far as I could make out the centre of it was that the three frogs which issue from the mouth of the Evil One in the Book of Revelation were the three persons of the Holy Trinity, and that Mr Musgrove and his followers had been appointed by a vengeful God to chastise the world and purge it of this doctrine, converting it in the process to something called 'conditional immortality', which I understood not at all. It was all quite splendidly confused; but I could divine at least that, if Musgrove knew anything about it, when the day of wrath dawned it would go very badly indeed with anyone who was not a follower of the Penge Reformed Free Evangelical Baptist Missionary Society. All in all it looked as if the Captain and the officers were in for a long evening of it tomorrow. I hoped that I would not be called upon to serve in the saloon.

Next morning I went across to Pontypridd to run a message to Father Adametz. He received me in the modest single room of his hut beside the church. It was a native hut except for a mahogany prie-dieu, a book-case – fronted with zinc gauze to protect the books from insects – and an old-fashioned French oleograph of the Sacré-Coeur with a little red oil lamp before it. Father Adametz cut the top off a fresh coconut and poured out the milk into a glass for me. We spoke in Czech, which he was delighted to be able to practise after so many years of disuse.

'So, young man, you have already met Mr Tribe and Mr Musgrove I believe?'

'Yes, Reverend Father, I had to deliver invitations to them yesterday.'

'Were they civil to you?'

'Quite civil. But Mr Tribe was rather brusque and seemed to think that we were part of a Catholic plot to annex the island, while Mr Musgrove, although he was more courteous, just went on and on about theology, which I'm afraid I hardly understand at all.'

'Then you got off lightly. They are both very unpredictable I fear. Sometimes they greet me as a friend and sometimes they shout abuse at me and threaten to call down lightning to blast me and my church. I often think that it must have something to do with the phases of the moon.'

'I suspect, Father, that they are cordial towards you when they are particularly hostile towards one another.'

'That may well be so. Of course, they were working together at one time, about three years ago, and then they were very unpleasant indeed towards me and the Holy Father. But then they fell out and Mr Musgrove set up his own mission, and since that time they seem to have reserved most of their bile for each other, always trying to steal one another's converts.'

'Do they have many?'

'Mr Musgrove, yes. But not Mr Tribe any longer. It's a sad story. He came out from England to start a mission here about ten years ago, sent by some little conventicle of Protestant heretics in a suburb of London I believe. But they were short of money, so he started a copra plantation to try and support the mission, working it with slaves who had escaped from the inland tribes or from other islands. The copra plantation did well, he entered into an arrangement with a factor in Sydney and – well – things progressed from there: he came out here as a missionary, became a missionary-planter, then a planter-missionary, and is now just a planter, although he still calls his settlement a mission.'

'What does he do for labourers? It was quite a large plantation by the looks of it, so surely he must need lots of workers.'

'Ah yes, indeed. The supply of runaway slaves soon became inadequate, so he took to using what is known locally as "indentured labour" – that is to say, slaves in everything but name, supplied him by the Tetuba tribe up in the mountains. They're a ferocious lot, always at war with their neighbours, and they can't eat all the people they capture so they sell them to the blackbirders for the Australian sugar plantations or to Mr Tribe. His labourers live in barracks, I understand, and get nearly enough to eat, and have to listen to his sermons every Sunday. I believe that Church discipline is very strict – which is scarcely surprising since Mr Tribe's converts have rifles and the plantation workers haven't. I've never visited the place, but I hear that they have a row of underground cells, and have just erected a very handsome whipping post in front of the church. All they need now is a gallows of their own and Spurgeonsville will be complete.'

'And what does Mr Musgrove do about all this?'

'Mr Musgrove refused to go on being Mr Tribe's plantation manager, which is at least to his credit. But when he set up his own mission he took up with the Tetuba tribe's chief enemies, the

Wakere. Most of his converts are from there or people who escaped from Spurgeonville.'

'So at least they have somewhere to go. Is that not a good thing? The missionaries can spend their energies snarling at one another across the bay and leave everyone else alone.'

'I wish the world were that simple. The trouble is that both missions are now interfering inland. Tribal warfare was always a way of passing the time on these islands. But at least while they were fighting with stone axes it was never too dangerous. Now that rifles and dynamite are getting into their hands in quantity however the whole business is getting out of hand and becoming very destructive. The Tetuba were always the stronger of the two, and I suspect – though I have no firm evidence for it – that Mr Tribe has been providing them with rifles so as to keep up the supply of labourers for his plantations. But now Mr Musgrove is at that game as well, shipping weapons to the Wakere. It hasn't come to serious fighting yet, but I think that it may soon do so. I have tried to use my good offices to make peace, but what can I do when I have two other white men on the island doing their best to provoke a war?'

'They sound very wicked men, Father, this Tribe and Musgrove.'

He thought a while. 'Not wicked in themselves, I think; just two rather stupid, very little men with set ideas and no imagination whatever, sent out here to a place where they can make people do as they tell them. I get the impression that in their own country neither of them would have been much more than a shop assistant or a junior office clerk; but here in New Silesia they are emperors and popes. When men as small-minded as that pair are given power over others then there's bound to be trouble.'

I returned to the ship to face a blast of wrath from Linienschiffsleutnant Mikulić for having taken so long delivering the message. Shore-leave had now been forbidden. This caused a great deal of resentment. It was not that there was much to go ashore for, or that there was much risk of desertion – that is, unless the deserters wanted to end up being baked in a pit-oven and have their heads smoke-dried for posterity over a slow fire. It was rather the thought of being cooped up for the rest of the stay aboard a cramped and stuffy warship in a hot climate while the shore was only a few hundred metres away. But Mikulić had his own remedy for brooding discontent on the lower deck, which was to keep the crew so busy that they would scarcely be able to remember their own names, let alone the delights of shore-leave.

And anyway, he said, why were they complaining about being unable to walk on dry land? Before the day was out he would see to it that the crew got enough terra firma under their feet to last them the rest of their lives. A rough parade ground had been cleared on a patch of waste ground some way along the shore from the canoe slipway. For the rest of the day the entire lower deck would exercise at small arms in preparation for sending survey parties inland the next day. Half the crew would perform arms drill under the supervision of their NCOs on the main deck while the other half would row ashore to tramp up and down the parade ground. Then they would change places so that the lot who had just worn themselves out for the past four hours handling their Mannlicher rifles would now be able to shoulder them and march around for a change – and vice versa. Once they had spent a total of eight hours drilling, the lower deck would be divided up into their landing parties and would set to work getting their weapons and accoutrements ready for their march upcountry. One party of sixty men would accompany Dr Pürkler about twenty kilometres inland to climb the Tetuba Berg and carry out a geological survey – as well as trying to parley with the local chieftains about a possible sale of mining rights. The other party of thirty men would accompany Professor Skowronek and Herr Lenart on a specimen-collecting trip towards Mount Trumpington.

The reason for the sudden frenzy of weapons drill was that fighting was more than likely than not. As Mr Woodford had warned us at Tulaghi, the inland parts of New Silesia were extremely dangerous. Several survey parties had attempted to climb the Tetuba Berg in earlier years but all had failed – or perhaps, if they had succeeded, had never regained the coast to tell anyone about it. Father Adametz had warned us already that the Tetuba tribe regarded their mountain as taboo and believed that the end of the world would come about if anyone ever disturbed the spirits who were supposed to dwell on the summit. If we were wise we would have left the place well alone. But it seemed that the discovery of an Austrian priest living on New Silesia had set Mikulić's mind working, from what I could gather while I was serving at dinner that day. Vienna was already interested in New Silesia because of its mineral wealth, he said, and the island had still not been claimed by any other European power. What could be simpler than to annex the place on the grounds that Austrian subjects were menaced by unrest among the natives?

'But so far as I can see, Mikulić, the priest-fellow isn't menaced by anyone. He seems to live quite amicably with the islanders.'

Mikulić grinned. 'Not when I've finished with them he won't.' I sensed that he could already see himself signing his name 'Baron Mikulić von Neu Schlesien'.

The cadets were to stay with the ship and not form part of either landing party, so we were spared most of the arms drill that was being inflicted on the lower deck that sultry afternoon. Instead we were to carry on with our instruction aboard the ship, which would consist today of the last in Professor Skowronek's series of lectures on Racial Hygiene. It would keep us on the poop deck, out of everyone else's way, and it would also allow the Professor to finish the lectures before he went ashore on another skull-collecting expedition. It appeared as he unveiled to us a blackboard covered in columns of closely written figures that most of his system of cranial classification was already in place: a complex and exceedingly obscure set of indices, which, when multiplied together and divided by the number one first thought of, so to speak, would give a single coefficient by which any human being's degree of intellectual and moral evolution could be assessed. I have to say that most of this passed over our heads: it was a sticky, airless afternoon with thunder grumbling in the distance, and anyway the incessant bellowing, crashing and banging of arms drill made it difficult to concentrate. Only Max Gauss seemed to be interested, jotting down notes as the Professor held forth. Surely not, I thought: that Gauss of all people should be taking this stuff seriously. It would be over soon anyway – the Professor was just launching into his summing-up.

'So, cadets, as a result of my lengthy researches over the years, supplemented by the ethnological material which I have been able to collect during this voyage, I have been able to demonstrate to you this afternoon for the first time the Skowronek system of craniometric indices which, I trust, will soon supplant the earlier models developed by Retzius, Welcker, Huxley, Török and others. By means of my system it should be entirely possible to grade the human population of Europe according to its racial origins and genetic potential. It will unlock the door to history. We shall know at last from the formation of their skulls why the German is brave and diligent, why the Latin is excitable and fickle and why the Slav is lumpen and slow. It is not climate or history or religion that determine these things but the configuration of the skull, and now that we know how skulls are configured we have an absolute, infallible system for . . .'

'. . . For telling you what you know already.' It was Max Gauss who had spoken. There was dead silence for what seemed like several minutes. The Professor stared in disbelief, as if a cat had just asked him the time.

'What did you just say, young man?'

'With respect, Herr Professor, I said that your system is one for telling you what you know already – or for confirming your own prejudices, if you want me to put it that bluntly.'

'Gauss.' I hissed in desperation, 'for God's sake shut up!'

'What on earth do you mean, you insolent young pup? How dare you . . .'

There was a disturbed shuffling and murmuring among the class. Had Gauss taken leave of his senses? He would be flayed alive for this . . . But he went on. 'Your "scientific system" for determining character and mental aptitude from the formation of people's skulls is, so far as I can see, a rigmarole of nonsense. What you have done, Herr Professor, is start out from the assumption that Swedes are loyal, intelligent et cetera and Negroes maladroit and stupid, and have then fiddled around with all your various indices to prove these assumptions.'

'How dare you question science . . .!'

'With respect, Herr Professor, what you have just explained to us is no more science than palm-reading. What you have here on the blackboard is a set of assertions – some of them very dubious as mathematics, by the way – based on premises that are every bit as open to question as those which you are trying to prove.'

'Your sheer impertinence amazes me, young man. What qualifictions do you possess, a mere naval cadet, that allow you to offer such insolence to one of Europe's most respected men of science?'

'Nothing, Herr Professor, except a little common sense.'

Skowronek smiled maliciously. 'Ah, of course, I remember now. You're the Jew-boy, aren't you? There, cadets, you have before you a perfect example of the carping, criticising, know-it-all attitude of the Eternal Jew: the product of a brain formation perfectly adapted to denigrating the work of others, but essentially sterile and incapable of creating anything of its own . . .'

'Excuse me, Herr Professor, but I had always thought that the task of science was to explain, not to create . . .'

Skowronek fairly exploded at this. 'Explain, you mongrel-degenerate? Jew-science may explain; German science creates! The purpose of *our* science, my young Hebrew friend, is not to sit observing reality but to shape reality! German science does not explain what we see with our eyes. It confirms what we know already with our blood!' The diatribe was interrupted by the arrival of the Provost and two ship's corporals, who dragged poor Gauss off to the lock-up while Professor Skowronek went to the Captain to complain in the very strongest terms that he had just been publicly insulted by a junior cadet. Gauss was in for it now and no mistake: probably locked up below in irons for the rest of the voyage and dismissed from the Marine Academy in disgrace when we arrived home. What on earth had possessed him to do it, the mad fool? Austrian learning in the year 1903 was not quite as militarised as that in Germany, where university professors would commonly lecture in uniform. But what it lacked in parade-ground rigour it more than made up for by its high opinion of itself. Ours was a society that ran on deference and reverence for age. No one below the age of thirty was regarded as having anything remotely worthwhile to say, and men of forty would commonly try their best to look sixty. A seventeen-year-old cadet who dared to question a university professor was simply asking for trouble.

Mr Musgrove's visit to us that evening did nothing to ease the already tense and peevish atmosphere aboard the *Windischgrätz*. As it happened he was the sole guest at the reception, Mr Tribe having already (we assumed) turned down the invitation and Father Adametz having been called away to minister to a sick parishioner. This meant that the Prophet of Penge had the wardroom all to himself and the undivided attention of the assembled officers; a situation which he clearly regarded as having been arranged for him by Divine Providence so that he could preach to them. Most of the wardroom spoke English, but even so very few of them seemed able to make anything of the confused, rambling sermon which Mr Musgrove delivered to us from a chair. Politeness and the liberty to be accorded to a guest prevented anyone from saying anything. But even so the mood was one of intense embarrassment. In the end all that we could make of it, apart from the stuff about the three frogs and the doctrine of conditional immortality, was that Mr Musgrove regarded the ship as having been expressly sent by God so that it could bombard Mr Tribe's mission outpost and inaugurate the Kingdom of God on New Silesia. In conclusion, Mr Musgrove invited us all to kneel in prayer. There was some murmuring about this, but in the end the laws of hospitality prevailed and Linienschiffsleutnant Svoboda motioned us to kneel. So, with glasses still in their hands, looking indescribably awkward, the twelve or so officers knelt down for Mr Musgrove to conduct a prayer and blessing. Then, before anyone had realised what was happening, Musgrove had produced from his pocket a medicine bottle with a sort of brass sprinkler on the neck and had started shaking it over the assembled company. Cries of protest went up as red drops spattered on immaculate white uniforms.

'Mr Musgrove, if you please – what is the meaning of this . . .?'

'Bathed in the Blood of the Lamb – John came baptising you with water but I shall baptise my people with blood . . . Sealing those whose names are written in the Lamb's Book of Life . . .' He was still ranting about blood and juvenile sheep as Mikulić and Fregattenleutnant O'Callaghan laid hold of him, one on each side, and propelled him towards the companionway to be placed on a boat leaving for the shore. Meanwhile in the wardroom I and the other orderlies were scurrying about fetching wet napkins as the officers tried to dab the red liquid off their clothes. The surgeon was of the opinion that it was some kind of red plant dye, since real blood would have coagulated in the bottle. But all the same, behaving like that at a reception was simply too much. Everyone knew that the English were not quite right in the head and that allowances must be made, but even so . . .

Next morning at dawn the two landing parties were mustered on deck to be inspected before going ashore. The big surprise was that there had been a change of plan regarding leadership of the main party. Dr Pürkler's survey expedition heading for the Tetuba Berg would be led not by Linienschiffsleutnant Svoboda as originally intended but by the Captain himself – though in a purely representational role since Svoboda would still be organising the trip. Festetics had announced the day before that he felt better, and Dr Luchieni had taken the view when consulted that so long as he himself went along to accompany him – with a straitjacket discreetly packed away just in case – he could see no reason why the Captain should not go ashore. The change of air and scenery in the mountains would do him no harm and might even do him some good. And anyway, he would undeniably be useful as a sort of walking figurehead for the expedition. It might be necessary to negotiate with the Tetuba chieftains about certain matters like sale of mineral rights, and this ex-courtier's aristocratic bearing and unquestionable grace of manner would certainly impress the natives rather more than Linienschiffsleutnant Svoboda, who was a capable officer but otherwise a squarish, plebeian Czech with about as much charm and elegance as an upturned bucket.

The other party, the one escorting Professor Skowronek and Dr Lenart towards Mount Trumpington, would be led by Fregattenleutnant Bertalotti as planned. The Professor, still in a bilious mood after his argument with Max Gauss the previous afternoon, was already announcing how he wished the party to proceed even before it had clambered down into the boats.

'The formation of the negroid brain renders it incapable of appreciating abstract reasoning or of making any moral evaluation. The only argument that it understands is force and physical chastisement. We must therefore make it plain to these headhunters from the very outset that we will not allow anything or anyone to oppose the onward march of the white race and scientific progress. Any attempt to oppose the progress of European civilisation must be met with immediate and crushing force.'

They were certainly quite impressive-looking formations, those two parties as they formed up into columns on the patch of flat ground beside the canoe slipway. Each was headed by a standard-bearer and buglers, the larger expedition was going to pull the Uchatius landing gun along behind it, and in addition to the ranks of sailors in full marching order there were considerable numbers of native porters engaged to carry their supplies; and further porters to carry supplies for the porters who were carrying supplies for the porters, etc., etc. In all, the larger expedition must have numbered about two hundred men and the smaller around 120. A wondering crowd of natives looked on as the buglers sounded the 'Generalmarsch' and the columns began to move up the trackway leading inland. The ribbons of white and brown snaked along for a while, just visible through the trees. Then the dense green foliage of the New Silesian jungle swallowed them up.

We who were left aboard knew that we would be in for it as soon as the last man of the last column had disappeared into the forest. The cadets were unhappy at not being allowed to go along with the expeditions: but our unhappiness was as nothing compared to that of Linienschiffsleutnant Mikulić, who had hoped to lead the Skowronek party. That expedition was heading for the Wakere country around Mount Trumpington, and the lieutenant clearly felt that this particular tribe was long overdue for a dose of civilisation since they were reported to be inveterate cannibals and headhunters; fewer in number than their Tetuba rivals but far more ferocious. According to Father Adametz, few white men except for Mr Musgrove had ever tried making contact with the Wakeres, and the few survivors among those who had attempted it had usually arrived back at the coast in full flight with poisoned arrows whizzing about their ears and Snider rifle bullets kicking up the dust about their heels. Mikulić though would have none of this:

'Parley with the nigger chieftains? No white man sits down to talk with a lot of bare-arsed black savages if he wants to keep a shred of self-respect. Just shoot our way through, that's the thing: twenty rounds rapid fire and burn their huts down afterwards. That'd soon show them: start as we mean to go on.'

But having been left to mind the ship, instead of being able to extend Europe's civilising mission to the lower races of the world, Mikulić was still going to make someone's life a misery. He decided anyway that the ship's standard of smartness was not to his liking and that we would therefore be employed on conducting a general overhaul in preparation for our voyage home.

Exactly why the GDO should have been dissatisfied with the ship's smartness would have been a complete mystery to anyone unfamiliar with naval discipline. S.M.S. *Windischgrätz* might be a sorry mess below the waterline, a mass of leaks, decaying timbers and rusting bolts; but as regards those portions of her that were exposed to the public gaze, there could be no faulting her appearance. The ravages of Cape Horn had long since been made good and her paintwork was once more an immaculate splendour of white and buff; her brightwork an insolent blaze of brass and gilding; her standing rigging as perfectly blacked-down as a kitchen grate. The Wahrendorf guns on the battery deck might have barrels so worn that there was scarcely any rifling left inside them to engage the lugs on the shells; but on the outside they had been brought to a hallucinatory black gloss like that of a patent-leather dancing pump. For Linienschiffsleutnant Mikulić, however, all this was still not enough, and no sooner had the expeditions marched out of earshot than he drove us all to work overhauling items of gear which we had previously been unaware that we so much as possessed. Even the cast-iron ballast pigs had to be lugged up from the hold, scaled of their rust, sanded smooth and painted with red lead. We were well used to hard work aboard sailing ships, which required endless maintenance merely to keep them seaworthy. But this was getting beyond a joke. Even the toil of repairing the foremast now seemed to emerge from the mists as a pleasant memory. At least there had been some point to that back-breaking labour. And there was the presence of Mikulić himself to add to the drudgery, unrestrained now by any higher authority than himself aboard, able to stride around finding fault with everything, making people do everything again, knocking over pots of paint as he passed by, handing out summary punishments and encouraging everyone with a rope's end and kicks in the backside. There was just something about the man: Zaleski had the trick of easing the severest labour by turning it into a jolly, setting teams to work against one another with a prize at the end and encouraging everyone with praise and jokes. But Mikulić would have made a corvée out of any job; made folding paper napkins seem like pulling an oar in a slave-galley. There was no help for it, we all agreed: some people are just born that way.

17

MAROONED

Next morning it was up at first light and on with the scraping and painting. All morning we toiled, below decks or on deck in the full blaze of the sun with no awnings spread. About 10.00 a.m. the duty cook appeared in front of Mikulić, saluted and obediently begged to inform him that the cask of salt beef allocated for the next few days' lower-deck dinners had something wrong with it: smelt funny even before the lid had been opened. Mikulić strolled across, hands behind his back, to where the oaken barrel was standing by the galley door.

'Well, what's wrong?'

'I obediently report, Herr Leutnant, that this meat's gone off.'

'Nonsense; open the cask.'

The cook's assistant obediently took his crowbar and levered out the lid of the cask. The tropical sun itself seemed to dim and grow faint from the appalling stench that arose from the barrel. Everyone within range stood back to a safe distance. But Mikulić just sauntered up to the barrel and peered in, then sniffed deeply.

'Nothing wrong with this, just well matured, that's all. What are you complaining about?'

Meanwhile Steuermatrose Mayer had been summoned. He was the crew's Proviant Kommission delegate for the month: the rating elected every four weeks by regulation to oversee the quality and quantity of the rations served out and thus to discourage pilfering and corruption among the ship's provisioning officers. He blenched visibly as he smelt the contents of the cask.

'Obediently report, Herr Leutnant, that this meat's rotten. The men won't touch it.'

Mikulić shoved his face into Mayer's. 'Are you telling me, sea-lawyer, that you wish to disobey me? The men will eat it or hang.'

'I most obediently report, Herr Leutnant, that the men will not eat it. If there is any disagreement regulations require me to report...'

Mayer never finished the sentence: he was knocked flat, then dragged to his feet and knocked flat again, then kicked around the deck once or twice, then finally picked up and stuffed head-first into the cask of decaying beef, where he was held bubbling and struggling until he was almost drowned. At last Mikulić let him go, so that the Bo'sun could haul him out and set to work reviving him. Mikulić was slightly out of breath, but otherwise completely unruffled. He dusted his hands and announced to the onlookers that any of them could expect similar treatment if they chose to disobey orders. He then sent us back to our work. At dinner he strode up and down the lines of mess tables on the battery deck making sure that the men were not eating their stew – which under regulations they were perfectly entitled to do, provided that they got nothing else at that meal. After dinner all hands were ordered back to work at once, without the hour's after-dinner rest prescribed by the *Dienstreglement* since (Mikulić said) there had been no dinner for the rest to be after. They complied in sullen silence, but an ugly mood was spreading even during the uneaten meal below decks. It started to come to the boil when the men came up the forward companionway after the mess tables had been squared away – to be greeted by the sight of the carcass of Francis the ship's pig, hanging lifeless by his hind trotters as the blood dripped from his throat on to a sawdust-covered tarpaulin. Mikulić had taken advantage of the men being below to order the Cook and his assistants to slaughter the animal, thus providing fresh meat for the wardroom as well as putting a stop at last to the creature fouling the decks. There was a sudden buzz of anger. For a moment it looked as if mutiny was about to break out – but the moment passed in hesitation, and the crowd dispersed to their duties as bidden by the Provost and the Bo'sun, muttering darkly. For all his unclean habits Francis the pig had been held in real affection by the lower deck, endlessly spoilt with titbits and allowed the run of the ship. Given the circumstances in which he had come aboard the *Windischgrätz* his sudden slaughter was something worse than murder, it was blasphemy – nothing less than making mock of the gods who ruled the sea and ordained the fates of those who sailed upon it.

It happened about five bells on the afternoon watch. A party of men were working aloft on the mizzen-mast rigging: the Krooman Union Jack, the young Czech sailor Houska who had been given a cut of the whip by Mikulić off the coast of Chile, and an Italian sailor called Pattiera. Mikulić was standing by the foot of the mast watching a party of men at work in the waist. Suddenly, *dunk!*, a steel marlinspike came whistling down from above: one of the No. 6 kind used for splicing wire hawsers; the very largest, about the size and shape of a cucumber. It embedded itself a good four centimetres in the deck planks just by the lieutenant's left foot. There was no warning shout from above, so I imagine that it had fallen by accident; at any rate, anyone who decided to try assassinating Mikulić by that means would have been pushing his luck to extremes. As for Mikulić, though, he moved not a centimetre, merely looked down at the spike embedded in the deck, then up into the rigging. Then he strolled across to the rail and gazed over the side towards Pontypridd as if nothing had happened. After a minute or so the owner of the spike, Pattiera, came down the ratlines and scurried furtively across to the foot of the mast to pick up the tool, evidently hoping that no one had noticed. He had pulled it out of the deck and was on his way back to the shrouds when Mikulić stopped him, a pleasant smile on his face.

'Lost something, Pattiera?'

'Er . . . no . . . I mean, obediently report that . . .'

Mikulić's first punch threw him against the rail. He tried to get up, but before he could stagger to his feet the lieutenant was upon him, pummelling the wretched man until he was sprawling upon the deck, then kicking him as he tried to roll aside, then picking him up by the collar to lean him against the mast and use him as a punch-bag. Pattiera was soon unconscious, lying on the deck in a pool of blood and vomit. At least, I hope he was unconscious, because when he had ceased to move Mikulić picked him up by his collar and the seat of his trousers, carried him to the rail and dumped him overboard to the sharks, who had been hanging around under the stern ever since the uneaten dinner had been thrown over the side. Pattiera never broke surface again. Instead, after a while, the water under the taffrail became tinged with blood. They found some of him washed up on the beach opposite next day, I believe, but hardly enough to be worth burying.

Tarabochia and I had been horrified witnesses to this scene, along with a couple of ratings. Mikulić turned to us.

'There, fell from aloft into the sea, didn't he? Now, you men up there, come down and let's deal with you. Attempted murder of your commanding officer? That would be a death-penalty offence normally. But I think we'll just let the two of you off with a good flogging.'

By this time the Bo'sun and the Provost had arrived on the scene. 'By your leave, Herr Leutnant,' said Njegosić, 'but flogging was abolished in the Navy in 1868. And you'd need a court martial to sentence someone to it even if you still could. If you are accusing these two men of attempted murder, then with respect Herr Leutnant they ought to be arrested and taken back for court martial in Pola.'

Mikulić smiled. 'Folklore, Bo'sun, mere lower-deck folklore. Flogging was suspended by the Archduke Albrecht's reforms, not abolished, and it can still be used in extreme circumstances at the discretion of a commanding officer on active service when a court martial cannot be convened without unreasonable delay. Well, I'm commanding officer, we're ten thousand miles from Pola and since we've put armed parties ashore this morning on a war footing then I deem us to be on active service. Is anyone going to argue the point with me?' He looked around; clearly no one was. 'Very wise too. Now, my friends, we shall lock you up for the night, while the Sailmaker knots me a cat-o'-nine-tails, and in the morning at eight bells we shall give each of you thirty-six lashes, which is unfortunately the maximum permitted under regulations. But never fear, I'll see to it that they are good ones. As for you, my nigger-man...' he turned to Union Jack, 'I've often wondered whether you fellows are the same colour all the way through. Well, tomorrow we'll find out, won't we? In fact I think that I'll get your friend Starboard to do the flogging in your case. You people have such strong arms it would be a pity to let it go to waste. If he refuses to do it then I'll have him flogged as well.'

There was nothing that we could do, short of outright mutiny. Such a course of action was discussed in muted voices on the lower deck that evening, but in the end the balance of opinion was against it. Half the crew were now ashore with the exploring parties. If the remainder took over the ship and stayed at Pontypridd then the landing parties, when they returned, would certainly put down the mutiny – particularly since most of the ship's armoury had gone ashore with them. But if the crew mutinied and put to sea they would scarcely be in better case: the cadets would almost certainly side with the officers – in which case there would be too few hands to manage the ship – and they would also be abandoning their comrades presently ashore in the landing parties on an island full of particularly ferocious cannibals, without succour perhaps for months until a copra schooner or a passing gunboat came to their aid. And in any case, there was the question of what to do after the mutiny even if it was successful. By the year 1903 a warship taken over by its crew had little chance of hiding even in the remotest corners of the Pacific, now that most of its islands were colonial possessions and the telegraph cables reached to the most out-of-the-way places. The only hope of refuge would be in some of the more insalubrious republics of Central America. The younger and more volatile portion of S.M.S. *Windischgrätz*'s crew had already evaporated, so to speak, at Cape Town and at Callao, where a further seventeen men had jumped ship. Those that remained were mostly long-service professional seamen with families back home, not some rootless gang of wastrels from the fo'c'sle of a merchant ship. The Austrian government had all their particulars and would certainly have them posted as wanted men throughout the civilised world. No seaman with a wife and children back in Pola was really much attracted by the prospect of spending the rest of his life shipping aboard merchantmen under assumed names or working as a miner somewhere in the Amazon jungle. In the end the matter was left unresolved, beyond a vague agreement to send a collective telegram of protest to the War Ministry and the Emperor when we reached the East Indies.

About 3.00 a.m. there were shots and a great rushing about of boots on deck. The entire crew had been ordered below at sundown and forbidden to come on deck until Auspurren at 5.30, so we just lay in our hammocks and listened. Had a mutiny broken out after all? There was an anxious mood in the gunroom. We all heartily detested Mikulić, but we knew that if it came to it, our status as cadets would compel us to side with him against the lower deck. Then about 4.00 Tarabochia came below from his watch.

'It's Houska and the black man: they've escaped!'

'How?'

'No one knows for sure. A sentry saw them clambering over the side about an hour ago. It's raining so that you can hardly see your hand in front of your face. They jumped overboard and swam for it. They were fired at and maybe one of them was hit, or perhaps the sharks got them like Pattiera. Anyway, in either event they got away from der Mikula, so good luck to them.'

While collecting the breakfast coffee from the galley a couple of hours later I learnt what had happened. Somehow – nobody could explain how – Houska and Union Jack had managed to get hold of a saw blade, which they had used to cut through the timber bulkhead of their cell into a boiler-room ventilator trunk. They had then wormed their way up inside the narrow shaft until they reached the deck, and there hopped down barefoot from a ventilator cowl to steal to the side and jump overboard before anyone saw them. A search of the shore at first light had revealed footprints leading up the beach towards the bush – but only one set of footprints.

Father Adametz came aboard at eight bells to pay us a visit.

Shooting could be heard inland, up in the mountains, but he said that by the sound of it it was routine tribal warfare and probably did not involve our landing parties – at least, not yet. Then Mikulić emerged from his cabin and gave the astonished priest a public dressing-down, demanding that he should give all possible assistant in tracking down the two escapees. Father Adametz refused, saying that he was a missionary priest and not a naval policeman. Mikulić blustered and threatened. The priest stood firm and refused to go ashore to organise a search party.

'Very well, Reverend Father,' said Mikulić at last, 'have it your own way then: you are an Austrian subject as far as I am aware – at least, you don't appear to have ever become anything else – so using the powers vested in me as acting Captain of this vessel I hereby place you under arrest for failing to assist the Imperial and Royal naval authorities in apprehending deserters. Provost – take this person down to the cells.'

'But this is monstrous . . .'

'Oh, Father, just one thing before you go below.'

'And what might that be, Herr Leutnant?'

'This paper which I have just had typed out: I wondered if you might care to cast your eye over it and sign it.'

'I have left my reading spectacles in the presbytery. Might you be so good as to tell me what it says?'

'Certainly. The gist of it is that since your mission here on New Silesia is now threatened by unrest among the native population, you are appealing to the Austro-Hungarian government for protection.'

'But that's simply outrageous. Neither I nor my mission have ever been threatened by the local people. And anyway, the Austrian government as represented by scoundrels like yourself is just about the last power on earth I would ever ask for protection against anything . . .'

'Tut, tut, Father: "scoundrel" is a most un-priestly word. Anyway please yourself. A couple of days in the lock-up may make you change your mind. But remember that as soon as you sign this document you can go ashore a free man and we'll forget the charge of aiding deserters.'

Father Adametz having proved uncooperative, Mikulić announced that he himself would lead a party ashore in search of the two fugitives. Here at last was his longed-for opportunity to go inland and put Europe's civilising mission into practice. He was fairly licking his lips in anticipation as the landing party got ready.

'They can't have got far barefoot and not knowing the country. Perhaps the two of them have been eaten by cannibals already. All I can say is that if I manage to lay hold of them they'll wish they had.'

The landing party, though well armed, consisted of a bare twenty men, far too few for the task in hand. That was perfectly all right by us: nobody would much care if Linienschiffsleutnant Mikulić got eaten so long as the others made it back to the ship. From my point of view there was only one snag; I had been selected to be the party's standard-bearer.

My task was to carry the red-white-red ensign on its heavy staff, rolled up while we were marching and encased in a long oilskin cover to protect it from the rain. This mean that I could not carry a rifle, so I was armed with a cutlass and a heavy, clumsy old navy-pattern revolver. It looked like being a thoroughly doleful outing in the steamy heat after the previous night's rain. Rifle fire was popping away at intervals in the hills as we set off from the beach at Pontypridd, marching in the tracks left by Landungsdetachement Bertalotti the previous day. Quite what we were supposed to be doing though was far from clear. We had beaten the scrub by the beach to no effect, so the fugitives must be far away by now, hiding among the jungle-covered valleys and foothills around Mount Trumpington. Even from what we could see of the landscape from the bay it was clear that the entire k.u.k. Armee might spend the next year searching the forests and still not find them.

About eight kilometres inland, at the mouth of a mountain valley, we came upon our first native settlement, a collection of palm-thatch huts. We were clearly among different people now from the coast dwellers. These huts were far more unkempt even than those at Pontypridd, like a collection of epileptic haystacks scattered among the banana groves. Two young men watched our approach from several hundred metres away. Mikulić shouted to them. They turned and ran. Mikulić snatched a rifle from the sailor behind him, rattled the bolt, brought it to his shoulder and fired. One of the men flung his arms in the air with a yell and fell over. When we reached him he was already dead, shot through the neck. Mikulić stirred the man's lifeless head with his boot and remarked that that would teach him not to resist arrest.

The other inhabitants of the village had evidently fled into the bush at our approach. Cooking fires still burnt beneath pots, but the only human being left in the place was an old, blind man rocking on his haunches by the fire inside a hut. Neither his age nor his condition saved him from interrogation by Linienschiffsleutnant Mikulić; nor the fact that he quite patently understood not a word of Bêche-de-Mer English – not even after tourniquets had been twisted around his withered legs and his arms had been bent up behind his back until the sinews cracked. All he did was howl incoherently in some language unknown to us. He was still trussed up howling inside the hut as a torch was applied to the thatch. We marched on, leaving the village ablaze behind us as pigs ran about squealing in panic and fowl flapped along the muddy trackway with their wing feathers on fire. The results of our enquiries had been negative.

We got some way further with our investigations at the next village up the valley. Here as well the natives had fled into the forest at our approach. But we came upon a young man, crippled in both legs, trying to escape by swinging himself along above the ground on his hands. He spoke some Bêche-de-Mer; in fact spoke a surprising amount of it once his feet had been roasted in the fire for a while. He told us that a strange black man wearing a sailor's striped vest and nothing else had passed through the village a few hours before. There had been no white man with him. Mikulić thanked the young man for his assistance by shooting him through the head before the huts were set ablaze.

I had to trudge along miserably behind Mikulić throughout

this nightmare procession of murder and arson, sweating profusely and with the flagpole wearing a groove in my shoulder.

'Well,' he announced to me as we left the third village in flames behind us, 'so much for our ferocious cannibal tribesmen with their Snider pop-guns. Show the bare-arsed monkeys a little resolution and they scatter like mice. If we take this island as a colony all Vienna needs to do is send me out here with a hundred well-armed men and I'll clear the place for settlement inside a month.'

By evening we were in the wooded valleys between the Tetuba Berg and Mount Trumpington. There had been quite a lot of confused firing during the afternoon, and once or twice a distant report that sounded like something heavier than a rifle: perhaps our ship's Uchatius gun, people said, but more probably the sticks of dynamite which were such a popular weapon in these parts. But the noise of firing was kilometres away and seemed to have nothing to do with us. During the whole of the day we had met with no resistance whatever, the local people merely running away at our approach. It was not until the sun was sinking on to the horizon that we saw our first armed natives: two parties of them running across the mountain trackway a few hundred metres ahead of us, the one gang apparently in pursuit of the other. Both war parties forgot their own quarrel for a moment or two as they stopped to stare at us – then resumed their skirmish until a volley from our party scattered them all and left eight or nine dead bodies lying on the track and among the trees. Mikulić grinned as we passed them and said that it would be quite inappropriate for white men to show any partiality in a dispute between natives.

The inevitable happened just as dusk was falling. Mikulić was looking about as we marched for somewhere for us to bivouac for the night. We were well up among the mountains now and the evening air was falling chill upon our sweat-soaked clothing. The trackway wound up among trees and boulders covered in ferns and mosses. It was splendid cover for an ambush. We had two men scouting ahead of us to guard against such a possibility, as recommended in the *K.u.K. Handbuch des Infanterie Gefechts*.

But the natives had evidently not read that excellent publication, and I suppose that the two scouts had been quietly dealt with long before our party came into view. At any rate, when they fell upon us it was quite without warning: seventy or eighty yelling warriors hurling themselves at us from all sides at a point where we were too strung out to get into formation and where the track was too narrow for us to use our rifles to any effect. A few seconds later Landungsdetachement Mikulić had dissolved into knots of men desperately trying to defend themselves with rifle-butts and cutlasses against black bodies rushing at them from all sides.

Mikulić was beside me near the head of the column. He drew his sword and revolver, running one assailant through and firing at another as I tried to disencumber myself of the standard and draw my own pistol and cutlass. I fended off one man who came at me by hitting him in the stomach with the butt of the flagstaff – more by accident than by design – and tried to swing at another with the cutlass as he passed me, losing the cutlass in the process. I knew that these were the last moments of my life – and after what I had taken part in that day my main concern was that I should indeed be killed and not taken prisoner. Mikulić was hit in the arm by a throwing spear as I managed at last to pull the heavy old revolver out of its canvas holster and draw back the hammer. A man was standing by a tree above the trackway, taking aim at us with a rifle. Without thinking I raised the revolver in both hands – it was far too heavy for a seventeen-year-old – took aim and pulled the trigger. The recoil sent me staggering backwards. When the smoke cleared I saw that the native had dropped his rifle and fallen to his knees, examining his stomach with both hands. Then he toppled over. I realised in a curious, detached sort of way that I had just killed a man.

I turned to Mikulić – and saw that he was lying with his mouth open and his head in a spreading puddle of blood. A gaping hole marked where his left eye had been. One of our men, a senior rating called Strohschneider, stood behind him with a smoking rifle.

'Sorry, Herr Schiffsleutnant,' he said as he bent over the dying

Mikulić, 'it went off in my hand so to speak. Funny how they do that sometimes, isn't it? Compliments from Pattiera and Houska anyway.' Then someone rushed past us and seized my shoulder as he ran. His voice was hoarse with fear.

'Quick! Run for your lives!'

We did as he said, and ran away downhill through the trees with the rest of the fleeing remnants of our party. I had stopped only to pick up the standard: I cannot say why, except perhaps that years of 'Approved Reading Texts for Use in Junior Schools' had drummed it into me that abandoning flags to the enemy was something that aspirant Habsburg officers simply did not do. It was certainly a great encumbrance to me as I ran, tumbling over boulders and falling among tree roots. But I kept going, and suddenly realised that the tribesmen were not pursuing us, other than with a few wildly aimed parting shots; presumably because they were too busy plundering the dead up on the trackway. Soon I found myself slowed down by breathlessness to a walk, wandering along a pathway with only Strohschneider for company. We could hear the rest of our party among the trees nearby, but it was nearly dark now and we dared not call out for fear of running into more natives. Neither of us had the remotest idea where we were now that we had lost the trackway which had brought us here, but after a whispered conference we both reasoned that, since the island was really nothing but a twin-peaked mountain protruding from the sea, if we kept on heading downhill we were bound to reach the coast sooner or later. Provided of course that we encountered no more hostile natives: an eventuality about as likely on New Silesia as not encountering any Catholics in the Vatican. We paused only long enough for me to detach the red-white-red naval ensign from its staff and roll it up inside the oilskin cover to make a bandolier of it. Then we set off again downhill.

As things stood I was far from comfortable at being in the company of Strohschneider, who had just shot his commanding officer and who knew that I was the only witness to the deed. I had every reason to suspect that once we reached the coast he might well be far more dangerous to my long-term health than any number of cannibals. But Fate decreed that we were not to reach the coast that night, because we had barely gone a hundred metres when we found ourselves suddenly in a forest clearing – already occupied by twenty or so armed natives resting after some earlier affray. They leapt to their feet and took after us as we tried to run for it. One threw an axe, which felled Strohschneider, then I tripped and four or five of them tumbled on top of me. Oh merciful God, I thought, please let it be over quickly. Then I realised that I was being dragged to my feet by the yelling mob with my arms pinioned behind my back. They were not going to kill me after all – at least, not just yet.

As my chattering captors propelled me along the trackway I was almost fainting with fear. Did these people torture their captives before they ate them? I suddenly remembered *Coral Island* (was it?) and the cannibal feast: the one where the shrieking victim lay trussed up while the revellers sliced particularly choice cuts from his living body and grilled them at the fire. I saw as they dragged me along that they were also dragging Strohschneider – by his feet, with his head trailing blood along the ground behind him.

After what seemed hours of being half led, half pushed along by the warrior band I found myself entering a village of some sort. I opened my eyes – and found myself looking at Mr Musgrove, dressed in a grubby, bloodstained singlet and braces with a bandolier of ammunition over his shoulder and a rifle in his hand. He was flushed and wild-eyed in the torchlight, his face grimy with powder smoke. In the square in the middle of the village, fires were burning and groups of warriors were seated round them, laughing and singing. It looked as if they had had a good day, whatever it was that they had been up to.

'Right-ho,' he said cheerfully, 'another of them that work iniquity, delivered into the hands of the righteous . . . here, don't I remember you, young man?'

'Mr Musgrove, please save me from these people. I am only seventeen. I had nothing to do with the crimes we committed earlier today. It was my commanding officer, who was a maniac and is now dead.'

'What crimes are you talkin' about?'

'Burning villages and torturing people for information.'

'Which villages?'

'Down the valley there, leading up from Pontypridd.'

'Oh, them. That's all right then: they were only Tetuba unbelievers. Your lot just saved us the trouble.'

'Why? What on earth is going on?'

The great and terrible day of the Lord, young fellow: the Day of Wrath, when the meek shall arise and smite them that do wickedness; when the workers of evil whose names are not written in the Lamb's Book of Life shall cry for the rocks to fall upon them and the hills to hide them, but help there shall come none. Yea, the fowls of the air shall feast upon their carcasses and serpents make their nests where once they had their abode.' He turned to the warriors who had captured me and said something to them. They bound my hands behind my back and I found myself being shoved into a low hut with an earthen floor and a wooden grille for a door. I lay there face-down in the dirt. Noises of revelry came to me from outside: a wailing chant accompanied on war drums which I gradually recognised as the hymn 'What a Friend we Have in Jesus', which I had heard until I was sick of it the year before in Freetown.

Well, whatever was going on I was certainly for it. Was it to be tonight or tomorrow? Mr Musgrove and the Christian Gospel seemed not to have weaned these people away from tribal warfare – in fact appeared merely to have whetted their appetite for it – so what hope was there that they would have persuaded them to give up head-hunting? Weary now and drained by fear, I hoped only that they would kill me soon and get it over with.

After an hour or so the grille was pushed aside and Mr Musgrove came in. He brought food for me: some steaming taro in a calabash and some slices of roast meat. He fed me, since my hands were tied behind my back, and it was not until I had bitten a piece of the meat and swallowed it that a suspicion came into my mind. It was not quite pork, and not quite veal either. I spat the rest out – unobtrusively, I hoped, since my sole slender hope of survival lay with this man, who was a fellow-European even if he was patently insane.

'What will they do with me, Mr Musgrove?'

He gazed at me in the flickering light with those odd, half-wit's eyes of his. 'Oh, they'll do away with you in due course I suppose: knock you on the head like the rest. They usually do. The Chief of the Wakere is a mighty man of valour in the sight of the Lord and he likes me to read him the Old Testament, particularly the Book of Joshua and the bits about the Children of Israel and the Canaanites. He doesn't take prisoners usually.'

'Mr Musgrove, you say that these people kill their prisoners. But I thought that you had converted them to Christianity?'

'Oh, so I have, young man, so I have: the spirit of the Lord has come upon them most fruitfully and made them a mighty nation in His sight and a terror to all those that love Him not.'

A sudden, unspeakable thought struck me. 'Mr Musgrove, did these warriors come across a party of sailors from my ship earlier today?'

He looked at me in surprise. 'Why? Of course they did. I thought you knew that. The Tetuba infidels were fighting them about midday and getting the worst of it like the Midianites of old when the host of the Lord God came upon them both and smote them alike with the edge of the sword. Most of your people ran away back towards the coast I believe, but the followers of the Lamb took some of them alive. Here, wait a minute...' He got up and went out. When he came back he was carrying something wrapped in a roll of bark-cloth. 'I know this one already. I wondered if perhaps you recognised the other...' He unwrapped the two severed heads. One was Korvettenkapitän Count Eugen Festetics von Szentkatolna, managing to preserve even in death a certain look of aristocratic disdain, as if it were too tiresome and vulgar for words to be done to death by a tribe of headhunters. The other, staring blankly with his mouth open in a permanent, silent scream, was our geologist Dr Pürkler.

'You brought them here alive. So does that mean...?'

'Yes; they're saying the tall man was a bit too much on the stringy side for their liking, but the other was just about right.'

'But Mr Musgrove, these followers of yours eat their enemies...'

'Oh yes, of course they do. But is it not written in the Book of Numbers, "He shall eat up the nations his enemies?" And again in the 21st Psalm, "The Lord shall swallow them up in his wrath"?' He took a piece of the roasted meat and chewed it reflectively. 'Yes, this one tastes better, they're quite right.'

I made no reply since I was too busy being sick in the corner. It was a curious thing, I thought later, for me to have found one of my captains dead outside a Brazilian bordello and then to have eaten a roasted slice of his successor. These were both eventualities quite unprovided for even in the *K.u.K. Dienstreglement*.

Mr Musgrove left, and I lay for some time as the firelight flickered outside and the noises and hymn-singing continued. They would come for me soon, I knew. Curious, I thought: so many cannibals had been converted by missionaries in recent years; it was just my luck to have run into the only known case of a missionary who had been converted by cannibals.

After a while the grating slid aside and someone came into the hut. I looked up. It was a black, near-naked figure with a great fuzz of hair. Well, this was it: this was the duty butcher come to kill and dress me for the pit-oven. I said the Act of Contrition to myself and shut my eyes tight as his hand grasped my shoulder to turn me over. I hoped that he knew his job and would perform the task neatly.

'Mass' Ottokar, you hear me dere?' I opened my eyes – and found myself looking into the face of Union Jack. He put his finger to his lips. 'Mass' Ottokar, you come now along o' me – no make plenty too much talka-palaver shit.' He got to work with his knife on the cord that bound my wrists, then started to dismantle the flimsy back wall of the hut. Five minutes later we were stealing away into the darkness.

For someone totally unfamiliar with the geography of New

Silesia, Union Jack was a remarkably good guide. I suppose that the forest was similar to that of his native land, and I also imagine that his sense of smell helped guide us back to the coast as it had done when we were approaching the Marquesas. At any rate, he motioned me to stop on several occasions so that he could dilate his nostrils and sniff the air. It was a dangerous journey to be sure: the whole island was now alive with war parties of one side or another. A full-scale guerre à l'outrance had broken out between the Tetuba and the Wakere – and by the look of it the once-mighty Tetuba had been getting the worst of it, judging by the numbers of dead bodies and burnt villages we came across as we descended from the mountains. But we got through. Union Jack was sufficiently like the New Silesians in appearance to pass for one of them in the moonlight, and whenever we came across a band of warriors he got around the problem of having me with him by the simple expedient of getting me to hold my hands behind my back and slipping a halter over my neck to make it look as if he was leading a captive Austrian sailor.

There might be quite a few of those, we concluded as we stumbled time after time over items of equipment, apparently thrown away by men in flight, and sometimes over dead bodies. I would have identified them if I could, so that next-of-kin could be informed when – and if – I got home, but nearly always the head had been cut off already as a trophy. It may sound callous of me, but I was greatly disappointed not to find a body in a Norfolk jacket and loden plus-fours among the dead. I still remembered the incident of the two Strandlopers, and it would have been gratifying to know that Professor Skowronek had at last fallen among people whose enthusiasm for skull-collecting equalled his own.

Early next morning Union Jack and I arrived back at the coast on the far side of Pontypridd Bay. The first thing we saw as we emerged from the trees on to the shore was that a column of smoke was rising from Mr Tribe's mission settlement at Spurgeonsville. By the look of it the converts of the Penge Reformed Free Evangelical Baptist Missionary Society were already settling accounts with those of the Penge Reformed Evangelical Baptist Missionary Society, presumably converting Mr and Mrs Tribe and their disciples into long pig in the process. But a far greater and more disturbing surprise was in store for us as we walked out to the edge of the water so that we could look down the bay towards Pontypridd. I stared, then stared again. Something was wrong, but it took a few moments for it to dawn upon my fatigue-numbed brain. I could see the huts of Pontypridd, tranquil as ever among the palm groves in the early morning light. But where was the ship? I rubbed my eyes. Perhaps it was a trick of the light, the white hull masked by the reflection of the water and the masts lost against the dark background of forested hills. I looked desperately around Pontypridd Bay. Perhaps the ship had merely moved to a safer mooring. But no, there could be no doubt about it: S.M.S. *Windischgrätz* had weighed anchor and departed. Union Jack and I had been left behind, marooned on an island of cannibal tribesmen currently engaged in a war of extermination. In all probability we had escaped being eaten last night only to find ourselves on the menu for next week.

After I had seen what became of Mr Tribe's mission, I had good reason to fear for the safety of Father Adametz's flock at Pontypridd. With their priest a captive aboard the *Windischgrätz*, they would be helpless against Mr Musgrove and his Wakere fanatics. But I need not have worried: the coast-dwellers had already closed ranks and had sent emissaries to tell the Prophet Musgrove's war parties, politely but firmly, that the people of Pontypridd were well armed and were not taking sides in the war between the Tetuba and the Wakere. In any case, as we found when we reached Pontypridd, Father Adametz was already back among his parishioners.

It was he and Union Jack who paddled me out that evening in the priest's dugout canoe to a small offshore island a few kilometres down the southern side of Pontypridd Bay.

'You should be safe enough here,' he told me. 'This island is taboo to both tribes, so they wouldn't dare set foot on it. But if you show your face back in Pontypridd they'll make long pig of you for sure, neutral ground or no neutral ground. The story going about is that the Wakeres caught that ethnologist professor fellow of yours pillaging one of their skull-houses for specimens. An insult like that can only be wiped out in blood. And as far as the Tetubas go, your landing party's activities yesterday haven't won you many friends in that quarter either. Both tribes are after the head of every Austrian sailor they can find. I think that I can hide your black man here back at the mission for the time being. In a lap-lap he'd pass for a Solomon Islander; I can tell them that he's a Catholic from Santa Cruz or somewhere come to work as my house-boy. But as for you, you'll just have to stay here until the next copra schooner arrives. Set one foot on shore and I guarantee you'll be dead before the other one's out of the canoe.'

'What happened to the ship, Father?'

'I can't really say: it was all very confused and I missed most of it anyway through being down in the cells. Your lieutenant's landing party set off in the morning, and everything seemed quiet until about midday. But then there was a great to-do all of a sudden. Your ship's band was practising, and it suddenly struck up the "Marseillaise". There was a lot of shouting and running about on the decks above me and some shots as well. After an hour or so they came down and released me, along with your young friend who was in the next cell. They were very apologetic and were going to row me ashore, but they soon forgot about that because what was left of your Captain's expedition started arriving back at the beach.'

'Were there many of them left? The Captain and Dr Pürkler were killed and eaten because Mr Musgrove showed me their heads. And we counted five or six dead bodies when we were on our way back here.'

'I think that most of them escaped, but only because they ran for their lives and left everything behind them. Quite a number of them were wounded, and they all seemed very anxious to get back aboard the ship. A few of them even waded out into the water and tried to swim – until the sharks noticed them. In the end your men sent boats across to pick them up, taking me ashore in the process. They got everyone aboard, then they just raised the anchor and left as fast as they could.'

'Do you have any idea where they've gone, Father?'

'None at all: they said nothing to me. But I rather got the impression that they were anxious not to stay in these parts.'

'When is the copra schooner due here, Father?'

'Oh, quite soon: no more than six months I should think...' He saw my sudden look of dismay. 'Oh come on; you're a sturdy young lad and the time will pass quickly. Just look on it as an adventure – like poor Benn Gunn the castaway in *Ostrov Pokládů*.'

Father Adametz was correct in thinking that I would be safe on the islet. It was a tiny, low-lying, roughly circular hump of coral about three hundred metres across, covered in palms and bamboo thicket. It had once been a burial ground for Tetuba chiefs and was believed by both tribes to be crawling with ghosts and evil spirits. I need have no fear that they would attempt to cross the two hundred metres of water that separated it from New Silesia proper. But it was still a dismal enough patch of ground to be confined upon for the next half-year or so. It was gloomy beneath the shade of the trees. The place smelt of fever. And everywhere among the groves the ground was dotted with little rectangular hummocks made from lumps of coral. There was no need for headstones to tell me that I was condemned to spend the next six months living alone in a cemetery. Father Adametz said that he would be able to visit me once a month, on the nights when there would be no moon. The natives were intensely superstitious, he said, and huddled together in their huts on moonless nights in the belief that a star might fall on their heads if they ventured outside. He would keep me supplied with quinine from his own stock and also provide me with a few tools and other necessaries to keep me going, but otherwise I would be on my own.

I began my stay next morning by inventorising my worldly goods as specified in *Coral Island, The Swiss Family Robinson* and other such grossly misleading manuals for castaways on South Sea islands. I had on me my white duck trousers and jacket (both much torn); a vest, stockings and a pair of underpants; a pair of boots and one gaiter (left). My pockets contained a clasp knife, a stub of pencil, the key to my sea-chest and a ten-haller coin. I had a fishing line, a tinderbox and thirty days' supply of quinine left with me by Father Adametz; but apart from that my only other possessions were the Austrian naval ensign and its oilskin cover, which had remained tied about my chest throughout my capture and escape the night before last. All in all it was a pretty dispiriting collection of objects: only the knife, the tinderbox and the fishing line of the slightest use to me in my present plight. Food and water at least would be no particular problem: coconuts were abundant, there was taro growing wild on the island, there was a small spring of fresh water on the seaward side, and fish could be caught for little more trouble than that of wading out into the channel between the island and the coast – fortunately too shallow for sharks – and reaching down into the water to seize them. I was soon evaporating salt from seawater to season this otherwise rather insipid diet.

Shelter was more of a problem. The rainy season would soon set in and I needed to make myself somewhere to live. But there was plentiful bamboo on the island, and Father Adametz brought me an old saw on his next visit, so once I had mastered the trick of weaving palm fronds I was able to build myself a reasonably rainproof hut. As for clothing, I was anxious to spare my already much-damaged uniform from wear and tear. I wished to look presentable when the copra schooner arrived; an exile rather than some half-deranged hermit, and also it had sentimental – almost religious – value for me as the last tangible link with the service of which I was still a member and the distant homeland which I had now not seen for over a year. I could have gone around stark naked if I had wished, since there was no one to see me. But somehow this seemed to be inconsistent with the dignity of the Habsburg officer corps, so I compromised by going about my daily round – fishing, collecting coconuts and so forth – wearing the red-white-red naval ensign as a sort of sarong knotted about my waist. My uniform I wore only on Sundays and for important dates like the Kaisersgeburtstag on 18 August, which I celebrated by lighting a beacon fire and hoisting the ensign to flutter bravely from the top of the tallest palm tree on the island as I sang the 'Gott Erhalte'. There was no one to see or hear, but somehow it made me feel better to know that even here, marooned on a coral island ten thousand miles from home, I was still a loyal subject of the Noble House of Austria celebrating my Emperor's birthday along with fifty-four million other of his loyal subjects.

18

CIVILISATION AGAIN

Boredom and isolation were my great enemies during the nine weary months that I spent imprisoned on that graveyard island. Those of you who have not lived near the Equator can perhaps never quite grasp just how monotonous life can be in those regions: only two seasons; climate rather than weather; the trees always green; the sun coming up in a glorious but short-lived dawn to pass always more or less overhead before sinking below the horizon in a few minutes of twilight; each day almost exactly like the ones before it and the ones that will follow. For those born in that part of the world it must all seem perfectly natural, but for me after a while it was all intensely melancholic. Used to a crowded, communal life aboard a warship always sailing from one place to another, the sudden transition to the life of an anchorite on an island stuck firmly in the same place was bound to be rather disturbing – as was the sudden realisation that I was now entirely responsible for myself, thrown absolutely on my own resources after a life ordered to the second by the ship's bell, the bugle and the watch-bill.

I suppose that I coped with it reasonably well: at least I was a youth of some education, a trainee officer, with inner reserves of character and training to fall back upon. But it was still a great problem filling in the empty days. I have always been quite good with my hands, and bamboo was abundant on the island, so I had soon manufactured myself a bed, and also a chair and table. But once these rather basic needs had been satisfied I went on working with knife and saw, so that by the time I left I had constructed enough cane furniture to stock a moderate-sized department store; so much of it in fact that I was obliged to build another hut in which to keep it. I also set about using the vertebrae of a large species of fish that I used to catch to make a necklace as a present for my sweetheart back home in Austria. It was not until I had laboriously strung together a row of these makeshift beads that I realised that I did not in fact have a sweetheart back home in Austria. Never mind, I thought, it will do as a present for some future sweetheart. But after I had drilled and threaded another two complete rows the thought suddenly struck me, Would I want to be associated with the sort of girl who would go around wearing jewellery made from fishbones? I decided that on balance I would not, and threw the thing away.

Yet still there was time to be occupied, unless I wanted to go mad with boredom and loneliness. I set up a wooden post, as described in *Robinson Crusoe*, and cut notches on it to mark the days – quite unnecessary since Father Adametz had left me a church calendar, but never mind, since it gave me something to do. I also ordained a strict daily routine based as closely as possible on the life of a warship: Auspurren at 5.30 a.m., Schaffen at 12.00 and Retraite at 9.30 p.m., with all the rest in between. But with only me as the crew it was somehow rather unconvincing. In the end Father Adametz saved my sanity by bringing me a copy of a book which a visiting ship's captain had left with him: *Navigation Simplified* by Captain P. Thompson FRAS, 'Younger Brother of the Trinity House and for the last thirty-one years Senior Examiner of Masters and Mates' as the flyleaf proudly announced. It was a textbook of marine navigation for British merchant service officers swotting for their mates' examinations. I think that I never saw a book quite so misleadingly entitled, because Captain Thompson seemed to have gone out of his way to make marine navigation as dauntingly complicated as possible; but the book had mathematical tables and an 1899 almanac in the back, and I had a stretch of flat sand at low tide each day on which to draw figures with strings and pegs stuck into the beach, so by means of diligent study I was soon pretty well up on the more recondite aspects of celestial navigation, able to intimidate even Marine Academy lecturers in later years with my knowledge of spherical trigonometry and double altitude of stars by the direct method.

As for constructing boats in order to escape, that was out of the question from the very start. The coast of German New Guinea was a good fifty miles away across the Scharnhorst Strait – and reputedly as infested with savage tribesmen as New Silesia. Bougainville Island was two hundred miles in the other direction – same remarks apply concerning natives – while Tulaghi was five hundred miles away. Quite apart from the distances involved, the memory of hauling aboard what was left of Matrose Crocetti after the shark had finished with him that morning off Guadalcanal was a powerful deterrent to any such boating ventures. All I had to do, after all, was to sit tight and await the arrival of the copra schooner from Sydney. I could not venture across the strip of water to the mainland, that was for sure. Father Adametz was quite right about the natives not defying the taboo to come across and attack me. I never saw anyone in the scrub across on the mainland, but just because I could not see them did not mean that they were not there, keeping watch in the undergrowth. The only way to put the matter to the test was to cross over and see what happened.

Father Adametz came to visit me each month, on the nights when there was no moon and the islanders were cowering in their huts for fear that bits of the heavens might fall on them if they went outside. He would spend the evening chatting with me by the light of a hurricane lamp, and would bring me reading matter from his own collection. Most of it was achingly dull devotional literature in old-fashioned Czech – still printed in Gothic type – or in French: *Les Mille Petits Fleurs de Jésus* (Liège, 1861) and stuff of that sort. I was an indifferent Catholic, but Father Adametz was a kindly, tactful sort of man and never pressed religion on me; in fact seemed rather apologetic that such books were all that he could lend me. When we talked it was entirely about secular matters: where I lived, my family, my schooldays, life aboard ship and things of that sort. I think in fact that the visits gave him as much pleasure as they did me. He was a good listener, and although he had been far too long away from Europe for us to have much in common except language, I sensed that he valued me as a last link with the distant homeland which he would now most probably never see again. He would often smile at some remark of mine, and nod sagely and say, 'Ah yes; I remember that I thought that once myself. I too wanted to be a chimney sweep or a circus acrobat when I was your age – which is why I ended up out here as a missionary priest.'

As for my other visitor, I have to say that I could well have done without his company. I had only been on the island a few weeks when Mr Musgrove came paddling up in his canoe to pay me a call. For the time being, at any rate, the cannibal evangelist was absolute ruler of the entire island of New Silesia, except for the Catholic enclave of Pontypridd. Mr Tribe's mission at Spurgeonsville had been laid waste with fire and sword, whilst Mr Tribe himself and his wife seemed – although Mr Musgrove was very oblique about this – to have gone the way of all white people who fell foul of the Wakere tribe. The Penge Reformed Free Evangelical Baptist Mission and its adherents now ruled the roost in New Silesia. The Tetuba tribe had been driven to the far western extremity of the island – 'like the Canaanites before Joshua and the Host of the Lord' according to Mr Musgrove – and were now dying of starvation in the bush. Mr Musgrove hoped that they would soon be enslaved, eaten or driven into the sea and that the righteous would rule the entire island – which they would then use as a base for evangelisation of neighbouring islands, once Mr Musgrove had procured them the necessary rifles and dynamite with which to carry out the Lord's work. He told me that hundreds of Tetuba had already undergone baptism by being herded into a nearby bay where the sharks had devoured those who had not drowned immediately. 'The water was quite pink at the end of it,' he said, 'but they died saved for Jesus.'

In view of all this, you may well imagine that I always felt a certain indefinable sense of unease when I was in the man's presence – which, sad to say, was quite often. He would sit there sighing and rolling up his eyes and muttering at intervals so that I was never quite sure whether it was God or me whom he was addressing. And he talked such impenetrable nonsense. So far as I could make out, he regarded my recent narrow escape from being eaten – which he had done nothing whatever to assist – as a sign from above that I might be a potential convert after all: my name perhaps written in pencil rather than ink in the Lamb's Book of Life. At any rate, each visit tended to become a three- or four-hour sermon in which he expounded the tenets of the Penge Reformed Free Evangelical Baptist sect, flicking interminably through the pages of the Bible which he would always bring with him and marking texts for me in red crayon. All that I could do during these sessions was sit and look interested, trying desperately not to fall asleep or even to yawn. I sensed that, pending the arrival of the copra schooner, Mr Musgrove might well be the arbiter of my fate. Thus far it had only been the taboo which had kept the islanders on the other side of the narrow strait that separated my islet from the mainland. Mr Musgrove evidently had great influence with them, and if he managed to talk them into throwing away this particular superstition along with the rest then it would soon be all up with me: Roti de Bohème au Sauvage that very same evening. The man might quite well achieve that end by accident – he seemed to proceed through life like a sleepwalker. But he might also accomplish it by design if he decided that I was not suitable material for conversion, or perhaps not sufficiently respectful towards him. So I had to nod and agree with him, and ask intelligent questions – but not too intelligent – from time to time.

I also had to keep the sheaves of pamphlets and religious tracts which he used to bring me, instead of using them to light the fire when the rain put it out. Mr Musgrove had a small printing press over at the Rehoboth mission, boundless enthusiasm for writing and an apparently unlimited stock of blank paper. He also had some knowledge of typesetting – but, on the whole, rather less than he had of spelling, punctuation and grammar, which is to say very little indeed. Every couple of weeks he would bring me another sheaf of smudgy, densely printed tracts (he always printed right up to the edges of the paper) full of the roth of Gob and the spirrit of the Lard. I tried reading some of them when boredom became too oppressive, particularly as the rainy season drew on and kept me indoors most of the time. But really they were extremely heavy-going: formless, structureless, rambling on and on without any sort of logical or grammatical framework and thickly scattered with underlinings and CAPITAL LETTERS. The only question was, who on earth read such stuff out here in New Silesia, where everyone except Mr Musgrove, Father Adametz and myself was illiterate? In the end I came to the conclusion – confirmed in later years by all the rest of the propaganda I read, whether Communist, Fascist or religious – that it spoke only to itself: not so much a means of getting ideas from one head into another as a kind of ritual activity designed to keep thought at bay and stifle doubt in the mind of the author.

So the days dragged by, weeks turning into months as the notches crept inexorably up the edges of the post: nothing day after day but the sun, the sea and the gloomy shade beneath the trees. As the sixth month passed by without any sign of the copra schooner a nagging anxiety began to take hold of me. Perhaps the vessel would never arrive? Perhaps word had reached the factors in Australia that Spurgeonville had been destroyed by the natives and they were frightened to send a ship here? Perhaps the ship would refuse to take me even if it did arrive? After all, I had no means of payment for my passage other than an Austrian ten-haller piece, which I suspected would not get me very far even in the Pacific. Perhaps I would be marooned for ever on this beastly islet, among the graves of the dead. Had the *Windischgrätz* reported me missing? Had I perhaps been numbered among the mutineers, so that even if I were rescued I would only be exchanging my tiny islet for a cell in the Pola Naval Prison? Would Mr Musgrove persuade his followers to cast aside their taboo about the island – but not their taste for human flesh – so that they would come swarming across the channel one day to kill and devour me? I began to be prey to strange fancies, took to sleeping in a different place each night, and became obsessed with keeping watch on the shore opposite.

All Souls' Day passed; and Christmas, and New Year 1904. Before long Ash Wednesday was upon me, as marked by Father Adametz's church calendar. I asked him what I should do for a Lenten penance, and he told me to stop taking sugar in my coffee.

'But Father,' I said, 'I have tasted neither sugar nor coffee for eight months past.'

'In that case,' he replied, 'it'll be an easy penance, won't it?'

The rainy season came in earnest: rain pouring down for whole days at a time and the waters of Pontypridd Bay grey and flecked with foam as the palm trees thrashed and writhed in the wind. The nights in mid-March were particularly rough. I lay on my bamboo bed with the hut twisting and creaking about me as thunder boomed and the wind howled sea-spray across the tiny islet. At times it seemed to be even money whether the hut would blow away first, taking me with it, or whether the waves would sweep the island bare. But after a couple of days of this it was calm and still once more and the sun shone. I went out to relight my fire and bake some taro. It began to rain again about midday, so I returned to the hut and sat down to work on yet another bamboo stool. Somehow the work went badly. A joint split, and I flung the stool aside in a fit of petulance. I tried to read something from a yellowed Catholic tract, *L'Humilité du vrai croyant*, which Father Adametz had brought me on his last visit just before the bad weather began. The words seemed not to make any sense even though I could read French quite well by now. I tried one of Mr Musgrove's tracts, then a passage from *Navigation Simplified*. I ate some cold baked taro, but it stuck in my throat. I lay down, but could find no rest for my aching limbs. I began to shiver, and pulled the naval ensign over me as a coverlet. By nightfall I was in the grip of a raging fever.

I might have lain like that for hours, days or even weeks; I cannot say. Time ceased. The wind was up again now, making the hut flex and groan about me as I raved in delirium. But I saw little of it as the storm roared above. The lightning that flashed in the trees above was the glimmering of an Apollo candle compared with the firework display inside my head, while the thunder that rent the heavens could barely make itself heard above the din that filled my ears. My aching skull was crowded as the Via Sergia in Fasching week with a thousand frightful and ludicrous phantoms: the Lamb of God with its fangs dripping red as it devoured men's bodies; the Samoan convent girls at Apia, and Mikulić flogging them until their backs ran with blood; Professor Skowronek lecturing on racial degeneration until his face turned into a grinning white skull. Milli Stübel's tooth-drilling soprano warbled 'Frölich Pfalz, Gott erhalt's' in my ears until I screamed for mercy. Blue flames of sulphur burnt behind my eyes; demons riding on whirlwinds dragged my tortured body from Spitzbergen to Senegal and back again as successive waves of deathly chill and burning fever swept over me. I lapped rainwater that dripped through the roof, but still my throat was cracked with thirst like the bottom of a cattle-pond in a drought. I vomited, sweated, shivered, longed for death to end my sufferings.

I managed to drag myself off the bed to pass water – and saw in a sudden, brief moment of lucidity – rather like the eye of the passing hurricane – that my urine was now the colour of blackberry juice. Well, I thought to myself, that's it then: blackwater fever. It was usually fatal, so how much longer would it keep me hanging around like this? What a pity that I had dropped the revolver when I fled from the skirmish with the tribesmen. Just one bullet now would bring me peace. It scarcely mattered though: I would soon be dead anyway. Father Adametz would come to visit in three weeks and find my blackened, putrefying corpse lying on the bed. It pained me deeply to think that I would cause that good man the distress of finding me in that condition, not to speak of giving him the trouble of digging a hole to bury me. But I supposed that it could have been worse: at least word of what had happened would eventually get back to Austria and my relatives would be spared the distress of never knowing what had become of me – at the end of my short-lived and inglorious career as a seafarer.

The fever abated for a few hours – then rose to a new crescendo of delirium which had me howling and gripping the edge of the bed to keep myself from becoming airborne. It was grey daylight now, and although there was no lightning any more, the thunder had become more violent and insistent than it had been during the night: a steady drum-roll of booming. Or was it all inside my head? I had not the faintest idea as I lay there convulsing like a prisoner being stretched on the rack. A great spasm shook my body. I knew that I was dying, the end not far off now. The tremor passed, and a curious feeling of peace flooded through me: a sense of rest after labour. I noted with curiosity that the hut was filled with radiant light, and that my body had become weightless; that I was floating aloft, borne up by dimly perceived beings around me, shimmering with white and gold. I managed to croak a few words through fever-cracked lips.

'Tell me, are you angels?'

There was a roar of laughter as Father Adametz translated my words into English.

'Angels be buggered, son: we're the Royal Australian Navy.'

It was three weeks before the cruiser H.M.A.S. *Parramatta* could land me at Sydney. They had come to New Silesia to do a job, and the job could not be interrupted just to get a sick naval cadet to hospital. The task which they had been sent to carry out was to put down unrest on the island of New Silesia and annex it to the British Solomon Islands Protectorate; partly in order to prevent further tribal warfare and partly to keep it out of the hands of certain unspecified European powers. They did the job in a firm but essentially fair manner, chasing the Wakere back into the mountains after an impressive hour-long bombardment of the Rehoboth mission-encampment: the tremendous booming noise which I had heard that morning and taken to be a symptom of my fever. They had now landed a resident district officer and a force of native police. The only disappointment had been their failure to capture the Prophet Musgrove, who had run away with his followers into the mountains at the first salvo and who was probably killed and eaten by them shortly afterwards as a charlatan, since nothing was ever heard of him again.

As for myself, I was in a very bad way for my first few days aboard the *Parramatta*. People very rarely survived black-water fever, I was told later by the Surgeon. But youth is resilient, and I was up and about in a dressing gown by the time we weighed anchor and left Pontypridd Bay. The Australian Navy were very kind to me. The captain, Commander Robinson, came to visit me in the sick-bay every day. It was thus largely from him that I learnt what had become of the *Windischgrätz* after her hurried departure from New Silesia, and of the fate of the two landing parties. The ship had indeed suffered a mild sort of mutiny – though he spared my feelings by not quite calling it that – and had shambled her way to Rabaul in German New Guinea, where she had gone aground on a reef and the crew had surrendered to the authorities, demanding an amnesty from Vienna and repatriation by steamer. He was not quite sure what had happened thereafter, but he believed that in the end the whole sorry business had been sorted out somehow; that the *Windischgrätz* had been refloated and patched up, and that she had then sailed for home. As for the landing parties, a total of fifteen men had been lost from Landungsdetachement Festetics – including Festetics himself – and three from Landungsdetachement Bertalotti. The Mikulić party had suffered worst, losing sixteen men out of twenty.

As for the egregious Professor Skowronek, he and the rest of the Bertalotti detachment had barely escaped with their lives after his attempt to ransack a Wakere skull-house. They had reached the coast with half the tribe on their heels, and had only been saved by Providence in the unlikely shape of a blackbirding schooner lying in a secluded bay. All in all the New Silesian adventure had coast the k.u.k. Kriegsmarine thirty-four lives for precisely nil return. Questions were asked in the Imperial Reichsrat. The Hungarians became difficult and the War Ministry took alarm. It was the end of the short-lived Austro-Hungarian drive for colonies.

I was landed and sent to hospital in Sydney on 6 April 1904, my eighteenth birthday. I was pretty well cured by then, though in a very run-down state, so after a fortnight's rest in Australia I was put aboard a steamer for Yokohama, where I boarded the light cruiser *Temesvár* returning to Europe after a cruise in Far

Eastern waters. Aboard her were Alessandro Ubaldini and the rest of my classmates from the 1900 year, who were now on their ocean voyage. They were the first Marine Academy year to do so aboard a modern steam-driven warship. If nothing else the disastrous, broken-backed world cruise of S.M.S. *Windischgrätz* had convinced even the parsimonious Imperial and Royal Ministry of Finances that the day of wooden warships driven by sail was long past.

It was aboard S.M.S. *Temesvár* on the voyage home that I heard the full story of what had happened to the *Windischgrätz* after her arrival in Rabaul, under the command of Linienschiffsleutnant Svoboda – on the edge of a nervous breakdown – and a committee elected by the crew. She had indeed run aground at the entrance to Rabaul harbour – but deliberately, in order to stop herself from sinking as a result of damage suffered in a cyclone on the way. The crew had been interned in barracks on shore while the German Governor-General desperately cabled Berlin for instructions as to what to do with two hundred mutinous sailors of an allied navy. It looked in the end as if the *Windischgrätz* might be broken up in situ while a prison ship was sent from Pola to bring everyone back to face court martial. But the situation was saved, as so often before on that ill-fated voyage, by the genius of one man: by a man in civilian clothes who happened to walk one morning down the gangplank of a passenger steamer in Rabaul harbour, followed by a rather nice-looking young woman whom he had married a few weeks before in American Samoa. The man was Linienschiffsleutnant Florian Zaleski of the Imperial and Royal Austro-Hungarian Navy, and the young woman had until recently been Sister Ulrike, a nurse in the Ursuline convent hospital at Apia. Zaleski was still officially convalescent – even if this had not stopped him from seducing nuns. But for all his often rather creative approach to service regulations the lieutenant was a man who recognised his duty when he saw it. Frau Zaleski was booked into a hotel, the steamer tickets back to Europe were cancelled, Zaleski's civilian clothes were packed away, and that very same afternoon he set to work putting S.M.S. *Windischgrätz* into a fit state to return to Pola.

It had been several weeks' work to pump her out and repair the worst of the storm damage, but the men worked with a will, and at the end of August 1903 the battered steam corvette left Rabaul cut down to her topsails, with a windmill rigged on deck to work the pump and with the leaking, racked hull strapped together with cables to prevent it from falling apart. By rights this floating abortion ought to have vanished without trace somewhere in the Indian Ocean. For once though the sea and the elements were kind, and on 29 October His Imperial Royal and Apostolic Majesty's steam corvette *Windischgrätz* was towed into Pola harbour after an absence of sixteen and a half months. She was promptly condemned as unseaworthy and hulked for use as a mine storage depot. The old ship was still there in 1918, moored at Valle Vergarola, and was not finally broken up (I was told) until 1923, having survived the k.u.k. Kriegsmarine and the Dual Monarchy by five years.

I anticipated the worst when I finally stepped ashore at Pola in July 1904: at the very least a detailed interrogation about the activities of Landungsdetachement Mikulić in New Silesia and the circumstances that had led to its near-annihilation by a tribe of headhunters. In the event, however, I found myself treated not as a defaulter but as a national hero – 'the Castaway of the Cannibal Isles', whose fealty to the Noble House of Austria was such (the official citation said) 'that even as he lay racked with fever on that lonely isle he wore the red-white-red ensign wrapped around his body to protect it from injury and insult'. I was singled out for special mention in despatches, and received an Ausdruck der allerhöchsten Zufriedenheit from the Emperor, which secured me the Silver Bravery Medal – the youngest person ever to receive it I believe. I was interviewed by the press and generally cossetted by a naval officialdom who were doing their utmost to make the *Windischgrätz*'s disastrous cruise look like some sort of triumph. I thought that at the very least, having spent nine months stuck on a desert island, they would make me drop back a year at the Marine Academy. But instead I was given special permission to remain with the 1900 Jahrgang and make up my studies in the summer vacation. The result was that I passed out as a Seekadett by special warrant in September 1904, three months after the rest of my year but with three months' seniority to make up the difference.

This was pleasing – but not half so pleasing as finding that my friend Max Gauss had suffered no permanent damage from disagreement with Professor Skowronek on the subject of craniometry. He had been released from the lock-up by the mutineers, and when Linienschiffsleutnant Zaleski took over command of the ship at Rabaul two months later he had quietly lost all charge-sheets still outstanding against members of the crew. As for Professor Skowronek himself, I am glad to say that I never saw him again. On his return to Austria he wrote a luridly coloured book about his experiences and generally made a great name for himself as a fearless explorer among savage peoples. The Skowronek system of skull measurement was formulated in 1908 in the book *On the Cranial Classification of Races*, which ran into eleven editions and became the standard work on the subject in the German-speaking countries and Scandinavia. The Professor himself died in 1924, but his work lived on long after his death. One of his most admiring readers in those years was a failed chicken farmer called Himmler. He later wrote a dedication and preface to the eighth edition, and had a special pocket version printed in 1941 for the use of racial hygienists in the field. Always remember, dear listeners, that just because an idea is demonstrably absurd that does not mean that it might not end up by killing you.

So what came in the end of the world-cruise of S.M.S. *Windischgrätz*? Not a great deal really, I suppose. The oceanographic survey work was certainly of lasting scientific value, and I am proud to have been associated with it. But as for the rest the wind soon carried it away. The Imperial and Royal Colony of Austro-Hungarian West Africa rapidly went the way of all previous Austrian colonial enterprises. The Foreign Ministry registered our claim to the coast west of Frederiksborg as soon as

Count Minatello returned to Vienna. But then things started to go wrong. The British Ambassador, then the French Ambassador, arrived at the Ballhausplatz to deliver strongly worded protest notes complaining about Austrian interference in West Africa. Germany turned out to be a good deal less supportive than had been hoped, and the United States a good deal more solicitous for the territory of its Liberian protégé than had been expected, immediately despatching a cruiser to West African waters to underline its concern. In the end the Emperor refused to sign the annexation decree and the whole thing collapsed in an ignominious heap. Of his Kroo subjects signed up in the k.u.k. Kriegsmarine, Jimmy Starboard, Honesty Ironbar and the rest were paid off when the *Windischgrätz* reached Pola and sent back home by steamer. As for Union Jack, my rescuer that night at the cannibal feast, he accompanied me to Sydney aboard the *Parramatta* and was put aboard a liner sailing for West Africa via the Cape. I saw him to the gangway that morning and we shook hands and embraced, then waved goodbye as the ship steamed out towards the harbour mouth. When I got back to Pola I wrote out a report on his gallant conduct, and made sure that his back pay was awarded for the nine months he had spent hiding with Father Adametz. This was duly forwarded to him along with the Bronze Service Medal, addressed simply to 'Mr Union Jack Esq., Bunceville, Kroo Coast, West Africa'. I hope that he received it.

The whole story of the cruise of S.M.S. *Windischgrätz* was not finally related to me until one evening in the year 1930, in the dining-room of the Grand Hotel in the Polish seaside resort of Sopot, on a stretch of Baltic sand dunes just south of the new port of Gdynia. I was in my late forties, a Polish citizen for the past three weeks and a Commander in the Polish Navy for two, recently returned from South America to organise that service's infant submarine arm. Commodore (Retd) Florian Zaleski had left the Polish Navy the year before and was now at Gdynia as a consultant on mine warfare. He had prospered greatly after the return of the *Windischgrätz*, elevated to the rank of Baron and promoted two ranks to Fregattenkapitän, which was a thing almost unheard-of in the Austrian service. He had also served with distinction in the First World War, until he was invalided out of the Navy in 1917 as a result of wounds received while leading a cruiser squadron in an action with the British off Valona. We had sometimes passed in corridors and nodded to one another in those years – the k.u.k. Kriegsmarine was a small force and everyone knew everyone else – but somehow our service paths had never crossed sufficiently long for us to be able to sit together and talk. This meeting over dinner was our first encounter in nearly twenty years.

We sat until the small hours in that dining-room, long after the waiters had cleared the other tables and gone to bed. We talked of old times, and the world that was gone, and reminisced about our voyage around the globe aboard that decrepit old wooden sailing ship in the sunlit opening years of the century. The early-morning light was gleaming on the little grey pretend-waves of the Baltic before Zaleski fell silent for a while, puffing reflectively at a cigar and gazing out to sea. I sensed that a certain matter would soon be broached. He spoke at last.

'Yes, Prohaska, and there was that business with the Lost Archduke, do you remember all that?'

'How did it finish? I didn't get back to Pola until the middle of '04, so I never did hear how it all ended. The last I knew of it was when we were ashore that morning with Mikulić on the Brecknock Peninsula, digging up a dead sailor's bones and loading them into a box. What on earth was all that in aid of?'

He gazed out across the water beyond the hotel windows, and sighed. 'Yes, I did intend to make a clean breast of it all when we got back to Pola. With Festetics and Mikulić both dead there was no reason why I shouldn't of course. But I soon discovered that the whole affair had gone too far for it to be turned around. They'd told the Emperor, and too many people's careers were at stake.'

'So where did the bones fit in, and what became of them?'

'It happened like this. I got back aboard with the landing party that morning after we'd come across Herr Orth in his hut up in the mountains. I went straight to Festetics in his cabin and told him what we'd found – and showed him the communion medal in case he didn't believe me. He stared at it for a while after I'd told him. His face had gone the colour of a lettuce and I had to pour him a brandy to steady him. You remember old Festetics as well as I do: the ex-courtier, the loyal servant of the Noble House of Austria and all that. He just stood there saying, "But Zaleski, this is terrible... terrible... Whatever shall we do?... The Monarchy will be the laughing-stock of Europe..." You see, we'd been looking for a dead man; and now here he was at last, alive and well, barking mad and intent on coming back to Vienna with a simply dreadful light opera in his pocket – and with the police ready to arrest him and his floozy for insurance fraud as soon as they set foot on Austrian soil. Remember, Festetics had been an ADC at court during the Mayerling affair: he kept telling me that the Dynasty could never survive another scandal like that. And of course, in this particular case a certain Korvettenkapitän Count Eugen Festetics von Szentkatolna would be the bringer of the bad tidings... So you see, we had to find a dead archduke before the insurance investigators found the live one. Your people went ashore to dig up a skeleton, the communion medal was dropped in with the bones, and Festetics concocted the rest: the wreck of the *St Margaret* discovered in a lonely cove down at the end of the world, the archduke's remains lying half-buried in the shingle, the communion medal discovered with them: all rather romantic really in a melancholy sort of way – "a Habsburg to the last" and so forth. I saw the cable he sent from Punta Arenas: so beautifully written that you'd weep reading it.'

'Wasn't there an autopsy?'

'Oh, Festetics saw to that as well, don't you worry: it was carried out on board by poor Luchieni, who had no doubt been extensively leant upon beforehand to reach the right conclusions. Luchieni would have said that it was his own grandmother if you'd threatened his next promotion. He showed me his report, you know? "European male, about forty years of age; strongly protruding lower jaw and evidence of syphilitic infection in the shinbones." "But, Herr Kovettenarzt, I said, I've had syphilis twice but that still doesn't make me an archduke: it's what the philosophers call a necessary condition but not a sufficient one." But he stuck by what he'd written. "Quite so," he said, "but there: if I am a physician I am also a naval officer like yourself, and subject to service discipline. The prestige of the Dynasty is at stake, so science must give way." '

'What happened after that?'

'It all got forgotten, what with one thing and another. I parted company with the ship at Apia, as you know, and then there was the trouble in New Silesia. When the mutineers took over the ship they broke into Professor Skowronek's workroom and tipped his collection of skulls overboard, saying they'd brought the ship bad luck. But our bones were packed away in a box down in the hold and they missed them. I sent a report from Rabaul explaining the whole business, but they'd told the Emperor by then so I suppose that it was tactfully lost somewhere along the way. At any rate, when we arrived at Pola what should we see but flags at half-mast and a black-draped lighter waiting to receive the box – though nobody had been told whose bones they were supposed to be. I was still worried that we might all end up in front of a court martial, so I could hardly call out, "Wait a minute – the whole thing's a hoax, I can explain!" Of course it never got into the papers – Johann Salvator had renounced his titles in 1889 and was not officially a member of the Imperial House any longer. But they still gave him a private funeral in the Capuchin Crypt: just a plain slab in the floor marked J.S. They invited me as well.'

'How did you feel about it all?'

'Pretty dreadful. I wanted to shout, "You've been tricked: this man you're burying is just a common English seaman. The real one is alive in Tierra del Fuego living with an ex-soubrette and as mad as a hatter!" But somehow I couldn't bring myself to do it; not now that I was Baron Zaleski with two broad rings of shiny new gold braid on my cuffs and the Order of Leopold on my chest. And especially not when the Old Gentleman came up to me afterwards and took me by the arm and said, "Zaleski, we are truly grateful to you. This was a dreadful business, but now you have set our heart at rest." I mean, how could I say anything after that?'

'What about Johann Salvator, or Johann Orth or whatever he called himself?'

'Can't say for sure. I did hear stories in Trieste years later that about the end of 1903 a man and a woman claiming to be Orth and his doxy had turned up off a boat from Buenos Aires and tried to draw cheques on a family bank account. They got six months for attempting to obtain money by deception, then the police deported them back to Argentina when they came out.'

'And after that?'

'I've no idea: but when I was at Montevideo with the old *Kaiser Karl* in – when was it – 1912 or thereabouts, I was talking with the Austrian Consul and he told me that someone claiming to be an ex-archduke had been going around the sheep stations in Patagonia years before with an Austrian woman and a troupe of yodelling Indians putting on a really awful operetta; until one night a gaucho in the audience climbed up on stage half-way through Act II and stuck a knife into Herr Orth, who was playing the piano accordion at the time.'

'If he was as bad as when we heard him then I'm surprised it didn't happen during Act I.'

'Quite so. I gather though from what the Consul told me that the assassination was not on artistic grounds. The gaucho was a Welshman called Pablo Hopkins. He objected to them performing on the Sabbath.'

'I see; end of story; sic transit and all that. But didn't it all trouble you afterwards?'

'Sometimes. I'm no saint, but I've always felt awkward with lies. You know how it is though: it didn't really bother me until it was almost too late – until the day when I was lying on a stretcher in my cabin with half the nosecap of a Royal Navy shell embedded in my liver. They'd brought me up from the sick-bay because the Surgeon thought I was a goner, and anyway we'd taken a notable pasting from the Britishers and there were wounded coming in from all over the ship. They just sent the Chaplain to give me the last rites; he'd been wounded as well and had his head in a bandage. I made my confession – and told him about the Johann Salvator business and asked if I needed absolution for that as well? He thought a bit, then said, "No: there is nothing to absolve. The Church has always held that a fiction that conduces towards a state of grace may sometimes be the moral equivalent of the truth." '

So that, if you please, is the story of my first ocean voyage: how the boy from a small town in the heart of Europe came to be aboard a sailing warship on a world cruise and ended up marooned on a desert island in a sort of bourgeois parody of the adventure stories which had led him there in the first place. I hope that it may have been of interest to you, not only as a record of the last days of sailing warships but also of that long-vanished world into which I was born: the old multi-national Monarchy of the House of Habsburg, with its few large vices and its many small virtues; most of the latter quite unappreciated until it was no more. You will probably find it hard to believe that I was young once: that the creature you find here, half-way between the animal and the mineral state, should once have climbed masts in a gale, once had its ears boxed by senior officers and once have swum with Samoan girls in the waters of Apia Bay. Why should you believe it, after all, when I can hardly believe it myself? But it all happened, as surely as the timbers of the copper barque *Angharad Pritchard* lie half-buried in the shingle at the far end of the bay.

We all know where our voyage begins, but who of us can say where it will end? Could that unknown English sailor who stumbled out of a waterfront bar in Montevideo one night in the year 1890 have foreseen that he was embarking on a voyage which would one day bring his bones to rest among the remains of emperors and archdukes in the Capuchin Crypt? Soon I too shall be dead, and they will bury me there in the graveyard just above the beach, not a hundred metres from the remains of the ship which I once boarded that day at Taltal eighty-five years ago. The salt spray from the winter storms will soak our graves as we both moulder away to nothing: the remains of the sailing ship, and the bones of the old man who was one of the last to have served aboard such vessels. Short of a shroud of canvas with a ballast weight tied to my feet, I could not have asked for a fitter burial.

There, they are ringing the bell for supper now. I missed the exposition of the blessed sacrament this afternoon, which should earn me two days' dark-arrest on bread and water if Sister Felicja gets to hear about it. I do not really care now though: these recordings have taken a great deal out of me and I have felt faint sometimes over the past few days, which may mean that I am about to slip my cable at last. But if this is so then I shall die happy at least in the knowledge that I have committed to posterity what I saw of the old Danubian Monarchy and that splendid, rather improbable fleet in which I once had the honour to serve. I lived other lives in the years that followed, but none of them really adds up to very much. I was only thirty-two when the old Monarchy collapsed, yet I realise now – though I never thought that I would live to say it – that the only real country I ever had was Old Austria. It was a unique civilisation, that dowdy, chaotic, paper-obsessed empire that I once served. There never was anything even remotely like it before, and there will certainly never be anything like it again as long as the world turns on its axis – which is probably just as well. So that is why I have spent these months telling you what I remember of it all. There is nothing now that remains to be said – at least, nothing worth the telling – so I shall leave you with these memoirs of mine in the hope that someone may listen to them one day. After all, it would have been the worst joke of all, would it not, for me to have lived so long, to have seen so much, and still to have left no record of it behind me? A life written upon water.